LOVE and ORDER

LOVE and ORDER

JENNIFER UHLARIK

BARBOUR
PUBLISHING

Love and Order ©2025 by Jennifer Uhlarik

Print ISBN 979-8-89151-070-8
Adobe Digital Edition (.epub) 979-8-89151-071-5

All scripture quotations are taken from the King James Version of the Bible.

This book is a work of fiction. Names, characters, places, and incidents are either products of the author's imagination or used fictitiously. Any similarity to actual people, organizations, and/or events is purely coincidental.

Cover image © Kirk DouPonce, DogEared Design

Published by Barbour Publishing, Inc., 1810 Barbour Drive, Uhrichsville, Ohio 44683, www.barbourbooks.com

Our mission is to inspire the world with the life-changing message of the Bible.

 Member of the
Evangelical Christian
Publishers Association

Printed in the United States of America.

DEDICATION:

To my grandmother, Mabel, who lived many of her first eighteen years in an orphanage, and who acted as mother to her younger siblings in that environment. It wasn't an easy life, but God saw you through it all.

List of Characters

Andromeda "Andie" McGovern—attorney

Annalee Ralston—bearded lady

Annie Tunstall—friend of Hattie Ingram

Bess Ingram—boardinghouse owner

Calliope "Callie" Wilson/Kezia Jarrett—Pinkerton agent
(real and undercover name)

Cooper Downing—Cambria Springs sheriff

Cyril Pennock—strongman

Daniel Littrick—attorney

Dr. Darby Chellingworth—medicine show owner

Dutch Uttley—café owner and adopted brother of Rion Braddock

Elisabeth Gates—sharpshooter/trick rider

Ellwood Garvin—foster father to Rion, Dutch, and Seth

Ethan Vost—judge

Hattie Ingram—disabled daughter of Bess Ingram

Hector "Heck" Darden—Cambria Springs telegrapher

Joe Trenamen/Stephen Nesbitt—Pinkerton agent
(real and undercover name)

Josiah Tunstall—young son of Annie Tunstall

Lena Kealey—wife of Seth Kealey and sister-in-law of Rion Braddock

Lucinda "Lu" Peters—dime novelist and aspiring reporter

Marshal Epps—United States Marshal

Maya Fellows—friend/former romantic interest of Rion Braddock

Ollie Sapey—cantakerous older woman

Orion "Rion" Braddock—bounty hunter

Pearl Johnson—brothel owner

Seth Kealey—adopted brother of Rion Braddock

Zebulun Oakwell—judge

Part 1

ON THE TRAIL

CHAPTER 1

Cambria Springs, Colorado Territory
Thursday, June 19, 1873

Cradled in the strange woman's arms as the wagon rumbled through the crowded Chicago streets, six-year-old Calliope wailed. The primal, guttural sound rose in body-racking sobs, and she clawed and wrestled to free herself.

She had to get back to the train platform.

"Stop, child. Please!" The woman's tight grasp faltered, and Calliope squirmed free. Her feet found purchase, and she launched herself—straight from the wagon into the mire. She landed but tumbled forward, mud engulfing her. Inches away, an oncoming team shied violently, the nearest horse rearing then driving its mate toward the nearest storefront. Another driver, heading in the same direction she'd been going, drew back hard on the reins.

She tried to pull free of the cold, sucking mud and—

Callie jerked awake as a scream lodged in her throat.

"Miss Jarrett?" A startling staccato of knuckles on wood punctuated the silence.

Miss Jarrett. . . ? No. She was Callie Wilson—formerly Calliope Braddock.

Her heart pounded, and she fought to free herself from the

mud of her dream.

"Are you all right, miss?"

She stared at her surroundings. A room. . .bathed in the bluish hue of moonlight.

Not a busy Chicago street in broad daylight.

"Miss Jarrett, answer me now, or I'll break down this door!" The knob rattled, and a fist pounded.

As she lurched upright, the bed linens loosened, making her suddenly aware of where—and who—she was.

"Miss Jarrett?" Joe Trenamen rattled the door on its hinges.

Only she mustn't call him Mr. Trenamen—just as he shouldn't call her Callie Wilson. Those weren't the names they were known by in Cambria Springs.

"I'm fine, Mr. Nesbitt," she hollered as she fought to untangle herself from her clammy bedclothes. *Lord, help me, please!* The prayer bubbled in her thoughts as other voices—both male and female—joined his outside her door.

"No disrespect intended, miss, but I'd feel a whole heap better if I could see that for myself."

She froze.

He wanted to *see* her. . .in her sweat-drenched nightclothes, and probably with her hair disheveled after her dream?

Callie fought free. "I think not, sir."

"Then show yourself to me, Miss Jarrett," sweet Mrs. Ingram, the aged boardinghouse owner and widow of the town's previous pastor, called, "so I might assure everyone you're fine and we can all try to sleep."

"All right." Callie rose, untwisted her nightgown from around her, and lit a lamp. "Give me a moment."

She retrieved the petite derringer pistol from her bedside table and stashed it in its drawer. Turning, she caught her reflection in the vanity mirror, and her eyes rounded. Her damp hair barely held to its braid…and her fair skin was paler than normal. She wrapped herself in a shawl and unlocked the door.

"Enter, Mrs. Ingram."

The older woman slipped inside, looking to be certain they were alone.

"My goodness, with all that's happened of late, you gave us a fright. It sounded as if someone was murdering you."

"I'm so sorry." She cleared her achy throat—dry and scratchy from crying out in her sleep. "It was a nightmare, ma'am." But so much more than *just* a nightmare. The recurring images from her childhood had been coming more often of late—several times a month. "I'll be fine."

The white-haired woman motioned to the rumpled bedsheets. "Those will need a change."

Her cheeks warmed. "Please don't go to any trouble. I'm fine."

Mrs. Ingram looked less than convinced. "All right, then. Good night." Before leaving, she checked the pitcher beside the door. "You haven't any water to wash up. Shall I ask Mr. Nesbitt to fetch some?"

"I heard my name," he called from outside the door. "Can I be of service?"

Before Callie could protest, Mrs. Ingram shoved the pitcher out the door. "Would you fill this for Miss Jarrett?"

"Happy to."

As he received the pitcher, Callie caught sight of him over Mrs. Ingram's head. Her heart gave a thrill. His dark locks, mussed from sleep, fell across his forehead and gave him a wild, boyish look that drew the eye.

He ducked out of sight. "Are you well, Miss Jarrett?" he called.

Her cheeks heated even more. "I am. Sorry to have bothered everyone. I was dreaming."

"Glad that's all it was," one of the other female boarders called.

Someone yawned. "I'm going back to bed."

"I'll return shortly with your water, Miss Jarrett."

"Thank you, Mr. Nesbitt." She pushed the door closed. "And thank you, Mrs. Ingram, but I'm plenty capable of drawing my own water."

"Yes, you are, young lady—but as we all know, there's a killer loose 'round these parts. Until he's caught, it's not safe for a woman to traipse outside alone after dark—even to draw water or use the privy."

She hung her head. "Of course. I must still be addled after my dream."

"Are you sure you don't want to change those damp sheets, dear? I fear you'll be uncomfortable."

"Go back to bed. I'll fend for myself."

With a soft farewell, Mrs. Ingram exited. Callie dug a clean nightgown from her trunk and changed, then undid her braid. As she picked up her hairbrush, a soft knock came at the door.

"Miss Jarrett?" Mrs. Ingram's spinster daughter, Hattie, called. "I brought you fresh sheets, in case, Miss."

She hurried to the door. "Thank you, Hattie. You and your mother are very thoughtful."

The woman leaned heavily against the wall, a pained smile gracing her lips. "Do you need help remaking the bed?"

"No. Please—try to sleep."

"All right. Good night, Miss." She hobbled away on unsteady legs, her slow gait stilted and difficult.

"Good night. Thank you." Callie shut the door again, set the folded sheets on the trunk lid, and brushed her hair. Once she'd rebraided it, she dimmed the lamp and peeked into the yard below.

Somewhere out there, a killer walked free. One who'd murdered more than once—in more than one locale.

And she planned to catch him.

With Callie Wilson's panicked cries still ringing in his ears, Joe Trenamen's skin crawled as he stepped from the boardinghouse's back door. In the eerie silence, an unexpected scuffing sounded and sent his heart and senses into a panic. Loosening the Colt Peacemaker he'd strapped to his hip in its holster, he eyed the shadows. Where had the sound come from? It was close. . .yet nothing moved on the porch or in the yard. Inhaling, he eased left—and again, the scuffing sounded.

From under his own feet.

His breath whooshed out in a groan, and with it, all his tension. He wilted against the doorjamb. It was his own boot soles rubbing on the porch planks.

"Breathe, you numbskull. . ."

He set the pitcher down and inhaled the cool, damp air. That did nothing to remove the lingering memories her terrified cries had dredged up. He'd heard such on the battlefield years ago—or in the hospital tent after he'd been shot. He recognized the fright right away. Knowing the sounds he'd heard tonight came from Callie Wilson unsettled him.

A wispy fog wrapped the moonlit yard like smoke on the battlefields where he'd once stood. He shook his head. This wasn't the war.

He'd followed his older brother—his only living relative—into that conflict at the tender age of twelve because Jesse itched to give it back to those who'd murdered their parents. Too young to be a soldier, Joe had served as a drummer—and he'd stayed on after Jesse died at Wilson's Creek. But more than once, he'd picked up a gun and proved himself a better-than-average shot. By the end of those four years, he'd rushed into battle alongside men twice his age and held his own. That was long ago—eight years since Lee surrendered and he'd limped home. Alone...

Lord God Almighty, these thoughts'll lead nowhere good. Please take 'em. He blew out another breath and tried to dislodge the dark images.

What could make the innocent Callie Wilson cry out like she was in mortal danger? She was no more than twenty or twenty-one. What had she seen in her young life? Hopefully nothing so traumatic as he had.

The facts that Allan Pinkerton had hired her and that the woman who headed the Female Detective Bureau had given the young woman her approval said a lot. In his experience, both chose skilled and capable people. And based on a simple case of robbery they'd worked together three years ago just after she'd been hired, she did seem to be an accomplished detective. One he'd enjoyed working with—maybe too much. There'd been a palpable spark and attraction between them from the start, and her open, teachable heart had made him happy to take her under his wing and show her small tricks of the trade. Coupled with the natural interest she showed in his war stories, it had led to a strong attraction.

But that case was easily solved in a few weeks, and they'd each moved on—him back to this ongoing murder case he'd worked for five years and her to other robberies. He hadn't expected to see her again. However, when the female operative he'd been working with had been called away for a family emergency, Mr. Pinkerton sent Callie, who was already out west working on another case—something of a personal nature. Could she handle tracking a murderer?

Someone who'd killed *seven times.*

Seven women. Pretty ones.

Durn it all. Her small stature, porcelain features, and infectious laugh made him want to protect her, when he needed to be focused on putting away the murderer.

"Stop viewing her as a woman to be protected. She's a Pinkerton."

But. . .why was that so hard?

Joe locked the door from the outside. With two young women killed in this community already—one three months back and one found only two days ago—he wouldn't take a chance in leaving the boardinghouse vulnerable, even if he was only stepping away to pump water and return.

Before completing his task, he circled the house's wide, wraparound porch, studying the shadows for anything out of order. At the front, he paced to the fence bordering the street and looked up and down the lightly fogged thoroughfare. Far down the street, a ghostlike figure on horseback moved through the mist but disappeared into what he knew to be the livery stable. No other movement marred the stillness. Pacing back, he completed his circuit, filled the pitcher, and let himself back inside. With the door locked again, he replaced the key and climbed to the third floor.

"Miss Jarrett?" He knocked more calmly than before. "I have your water."

"Just a moment."

Eventually, she opened the door, her brown eyes meeting his. Clad in a nightgown with a heavy shawl clutched around her shoulders, she had her golden-brown hair in a tight braid against one shoulder.

"Thank you, Mr. Nesbitt. Sorry I troubled you." She waved toward the washstand. "Please, put it there."

He set it down then backed into the hall. "You're sure you're well?"

"Yes. Just a nightmare. The images don't linger once I wake up."

"You're fortunate." His nightmares lived for hours, sometimes days, after. "Do you need anything else, Miss?"

"Nothing that can't wait until morning. Thank you. See you at breakfast, Mr. Nesbitt."

They had plans to ride out to the most recent murder scene the following day, but such a young, impressionable woman hardly needed to see that place. Could he deter her?

Should he?

A question to ponder as he tried to get back to sleep.

"See you in a few hours."

CHAPTER 2

Friday, June 20, 1873

"I'm sorry. I know today hasn't gone the way you planned." Joe glanced sideways, his voice resonating with repentant sincerity.

Exasperation still roiled in Callie's belly as she squinted against the slanting rays of sunlight. She'd wanted to reach the most recent murder site in the morning to have as much of the day to look around as she needed. To capture the clearing and the cabin's interior with her pencils and paper. To search for those fine details that could help them home in on the murderer—before time and weather might fade the clues. After all, three days had passed since the victim was found, and even longer since the woman went missing.

"I appreciate you waiting on me—and the way you stepped in and helped Mrs. Ingram and Miss Hattie. I've come to care about them since I've boarded there."

It was Joe's job to haul water for the laundry, and he wouldn't leave Mrs. Ingram and Hattie to do so by themselves. Poor Mrs. Ingram looked as fragile as a twig, and the old burns marring Hattie's legs, though healed, must make the task an insufferable endeavor. So long as they were hauling water, she might as well help with the washing. Which is why they hadn't reached the mountain clearing until midafternoon.

"I haven't spent the time there that you have, but I can see what wonderful women they are. I was glad to help."

Although with her hands raw and sore from the scrubbing, would she be able to sketch with any accuracy? Would there be any clues left to sketch?

The clearing was silent as. . .a grave. She gulped at the thought. The sun-dappled grass made an inviting picture, despite the run-down cabin in the center. If she had time, she'd sketch it out, as much for her own pleasure as to capture the scene of the crime and any clues it may hold. It was more important to sketch the cabin's interior, where the murderer's seventh victim was found, and, if time permitted, the clearing afterward.

She dismounted and walked her gray mare, Lady, into the clearing, eyeing the ground as she moved. At the sight of various hoofprints, she quickly led Lady wide of that area, hoping to preserve them for sketching later. Perhaps she'd still have time before heading back to town.

Near the rickety cabin, she retrieved her rifle from its scabbard and slung her leather pouch across her body. Leaving Lady to crop the lush grass, she headed toward the entrance, Joe on her heels.

The door, hanging cockeyed on its hinges, protested loudly as she opened it, and the musty smell of decay assaulted her nose. Surely they hadn't left the victim's body here, had they? She gripped the rifle tighter.

Sunlight streamed through various holes in the roof. A good thing, since a thick film of dust blocked the sunlight from penetrating the windows. A once-sturdy table lay overturned at the room's center, one leg broken. The tabletop blocked her view of the floor beyond. One ladder-backed chair stood several feet from the table. A second lay overturned beside it. Against the back wall sat a threadbare settee, a fair-sized hole in its seat where some animal had probably burrowed. Above it was a small, filthy window, and beside it, a door leading to the yard. Along the right wall, another doorway led into the next room, where a potbellied stove sat. Doubtless, the kitchen. To the left, another doorway, and beyond it, a rusted bed frame devoid of its mattress.

Callie inched into the cabin but gave an involuntary shiver as an unnatural heaviness settled over her. She backed out again.

"Everything all right?" Joe laid a gentle hand on her shoulder.

Her hair stood on end. Whatever had happened in there left a palpable feeling in the air. Pressing her eyes closed, she straightened her spine and tried to calm herself.

"It's fine. Simply preparing myself."

"Good, because this could be very ugly."

She nodded. *Lord, no matter how stupid my brothers made me feel—how often they said I couldn't do this—I've known I wanted to work for Mr. Pinkerton since I first arrived in Chicago. I didn't let anything keep me from my dream, and here I am. But this place is more than a little frightening. This is what I was meant to do, so please protect me as I look for clues.*

Extracting paper and pencil from her leather pouch, she stepped into the room again. Another whole-body shiver claimed her, but she held herself in check. She needed to do this. She'd *asked* to do this. And if she didn't, she'd let Mr. Pinkerton down.

Leaning the rifle against the doorjamb, Callie eyed the room then set pencil to paper and roughed out the basic shapes. The overturned table, ladder-back chairs, settee, doorways. She'd been told this was the room where the victim was found, although nothing in sight from the doorway indicated a murder had occurred there. Perhaps a scuffle, with the overturned table and chair, but that could be explained by some animal rummaging in the shoddy building—a bear or a wolf, perhaps.

She filled in the sketch's details, capturing enough features to trigger her memory, she hoped. If only she'd had more time... But she didn't, so she readied another paper and paced toward the toppled furniture. There...there was the evidence. She drew a big breath, and Joe came alongside her, her rifle in his hand.

The dirt floor was stained with the victim's blood, the large pool having flowed toward the back door. Also marring the floor were various boot, bird, and animal prints.

In this very spot, a seventh young woman's life had expired. Callie tried to breathe deeply, but all she managed were some shallow gasps as an oppressive heaviness pulled at her.

"Callie."

At his whispered call, she faced Joe.

"I know this is hard. Are you all right?"

"It's an unbearable thought. A woman died here." An almost convulsive shiver gripped her.

Lord, help.

"If this is too much, we can go. I'll take care of it."

When the shivers passed, she forced a deeper breath. "No. This is why I'm here."

She squatted to study the tracks—particularly the boot prints. There were many—and most were probably from when the victim was found and removed, but the heel of one print stood out, for it had a telltale crescent-moon-shaped notch gouged from it. Was it from the time the victim was killed or— No, it had to be from the murder. Few of those prints remained, having been wiped out by others that came later. Callie nodded and sketched the track.

"What do you see?"

"A distinctive boot track. I'll show you when I'm done."

Careful not to disturb anything, she maneuvered to the table's far side and squatted for a closer look from that angle. Her stomach churned at the expected sight—a mixture of excitement and dread. Drawing another paper from her bag, she folded it into a makeshift pouch and plucked something from the floor. She stretched about ten strands of long, light-colored hair taut, then wrapped them around three fingers before slipping them inside the envelope. She folded the top twice, scrawled *Victim Seven* on the outside, and tucked it into her bag.

Every victim had been found with her hair completely shorn and removed from the scene. That detail had alerted Mr. Pinkerton and his other operatives that the seven murders were related—whether murdered in Chicago, St. Louis, or farther west. Why did the killer have such a penchant? Chilling...She fought off another shiver and forced her attention back to the gruesome scene.

"Are you all—"

"Stop." She glared, stalling his words.

"What?"

"Did you treat Mrs. Cantor this way—asking her every time she moved if she was all right?"

A sheepish look overtook him, and he shook his head. "No."

"Then don't do it to me. Please." She rose, took her rifle from him, and slung it over her shoulder. "Thank you for your concern, but I've been a Pinkerton for three years. I'm not the absolute novice I was when we worked together before. Yes, it's a difficult scene, but I'm doing all right."

She circled the room, scanning for any other clues. After minutes of silent inspection, she paused at the front window. There, about even with the height of Joe's elbow, the miry glass had been wiped—no, *smudged*. It was far from clean. She peered closely at it. A reddish haze tinged the smear.

"Her blood, maybe?" She indicated the smear, and Joe came to look.

"Could be. Or someone else's?"

She pursed her lips and tilted her head. A small reddish-brown stain marred the dusty windowsill. Two steps toward the doorway, a droplet-sized stain had landed on the dirt floor, and above it, partway up the wall, a mottled shred of fabric hung from an exposed nail.

As she tucked it away in her pouch, the sound of an approaching horse filtered into her awareness. Her senses clanged a warning. Shoving her papers and pencil into her satchel, she let the rifle slip from her shoulder and tipped the barrel up.

⌒

"Now hold on just a minute." With an open palm, Joe shoved the muzzle of the gun toward the floor. "That's likely to be Cooper Downing." Since Callie's true identity was a closely guarded secret, he'd intended to bring her out this morning unbeknownst to the sheriff. His identity was also a secret, though he'd let the lawman know of his presence and purpose as a courtesy. He'd arranged the previous day to ride up here with the sheriff this afternoon, alone—but his and Callie's late departure had thrown the timing off.

"Please let me handle this. Just play along."

"Play along?"

"You know—improvise but follow my lead." He strode out of the abandoned cabin.

The sheriff rode toward the solitary structure, his expression fierce. "What in blue blazes, Nesbitt?" He urged his horse forward. "I was waitin' for ya in town. Then Bess Ingram told me you already left."

As he stepped farther into the yard, Callie Wilson stepped out of the derelict structure.

"Oh, thank goodness! Sheriff—" She heaved a breath and hurried out.

"Who're you?" Downing gaped. "And what're you doin' in that cabin?"

"It's all right, Sheriff. This is Kezia Jarrett." Joe glanced her way, then back to the lawman. "An artist. One of Mrs. Ingram's other boarders."

Downing slid from his saddle. "I want an answer. What're you doin' here, Miss?"

"Kezia—"

"I came up here to draw and found this beautiful meadow." She fanned her face and panted. "It seemed a perfect spot. However, I was warm after my ride, so I sought shade in the abandoned house." Her expression twisted with a disturbed look. "Something terrible must have happened inside."

The sheriff shot her a stern look. "Ain't you heard? There's a killer loose in these mountains. Someone died in there. What lies beyond that door ain't fit for a lady's eyes."

"I wish I would've known before—" Tears spilled down her porcelain cheeks, now rosy. She drew a handkerchief from her sleeve and patted her cheeks.

Downing huffed. "Come away from that house, Miss. You're muckin' things up good."

"I beg your pardon, sir! How could I have known?" She started toward Lady. "I'll just ride back to town and—"

Joe put himself between her and the horse. "That's not wise."

Her brown eyes turned stormy. The woman was putting on quite a show. "Why? I'd like to go home now!"

"I don't want the tongue-lashin' that awaits me if Mrs. Ingram discovers I failed to escort you safely back to the boardinghouse. Please wait. Let me assist the sheriff with his business, and we'll all head back together."

She shifted an uncomfortable glance between them. "How long will that take? It'll be growing dark—"

"We'll be done long before dusk, Miss," Sheriff Downing said. "Especially if you disturbed the scene in there."

Miss Wilson huffed. "Again, how was I to know?"

"Reckon you weren't, but with the danger in these parts, you shouldn't be out ridin' round by yourself. Now stay outside and try not to get yourself in any fixes."

The woman's features turned stony, and she drew herself to her full height—which wasn't much. . .she was a petite thing— then planted one hand on her hip.

"I appreciate your concern for what you perceive to be my delicate sensibilities, Sheriff, but I'm no weak-kneed woman. I'll be fine by my lonesome."

"Both of you, stop." Downing's blustery irritation mixed with her flinty defiance was a recipe for trouble. "We'll be out in a few minutes. Please wait." He gave her a discreet wink then followed Downing inside.

As Joe entered again, the stale air and rottenness hit him anew. The sheriff cursed under his breath.

"Sorry. Weren't s'posed to be no one here. I'll have me a talk with Mrs. Ingram—ask her to warn the little gal to stay in town."

"Don't worry about her, Sheriff. I'll speak to both her and Mrs. Ingram on your behalf." If the lawman warned Mrs. Ingram, she might become even more protective, limiting Miss Wilson's ability to do her job, even in town. "Now show me what we came to see."

Downing moved past the overturned table and motioned to the stained dirt floor.

"The victim was stabbed?"

The lawman's Adam's apple bobbed, and his voice went hoarse. "Thirteen times."

Joe squatted. "And her hair was cut off?"

Sheriff Downing cleared his throat. "Shaved clean off. Whoever killed her must've taken it. We didn't find any hair."

"Did you know the woman, Sheriff?" Joe glanced his way.

"She was a...soiled dove from a brothel in town." The lawman ground out the words as if they pained him.

Another soiled dove. Was it wrong to thank the Lord that it wasn't a young wife or mother like some of the previous victims? A lady of the night should matter no less than a more upstanding citizen, yet the idea of two children growing up without their mother haunted him. Perhaps it hit too close to home.

He'd worked this case since the first report five years ago. Miss Nancy Carlin—niece of a former United States senator— had been murdered while traveling to Chicago on the Illinois Central Railroad, one of the rail lines that had contracted the Pinkertons to protect the goods transported by them. Finding the young woman murdered in a boxcar, with her raven hair shorn completely, made the case more than personal to Mr. Pinkerton.

A second young woman, mother of two, Tilda Wadwell, had also been a passenger on the same rail line almost a year to the day later and was found murdered at the St. Louis depot after exiting the train. The fact that her reddish-blond hair had also been shaved alerted Mr. Pinkerton the two murders were probably linked. But they'd had nothing to go on. No suspects. Operatives had found nothing linking the women, other than they'd ridden the same rail line and their hair had been shaved.

In the three and a half years since Mrs. Wadwell's death, five more women had died in similar circumstances. A couple of prostitutes, another young mother, and two single women.

None of them had been anywhere near a train, but in each case, the woman's hair had been removed.

What sort of man would murder so many women—and why take their hair? It made no sense.

What depraved mind ever did?

Bracing a hand against the overturned chair, Joe studied the dirt floor more closely.

The sheriff craned his neck. "What're you finding?"

As an operative, he'd learned not to give away all his secrets. Plenty of western lawmen were trustworthy, but the West had its share of shady characters who wore badges. Until he was sure about Cooper Downing, he'd keep this close to the vest.

"There are animal prints in the dirt."

"That's what led to Serafina bein' found. Couple kids saw buzzards circlin' above this place. They found the door wide open." He paced toward the settee and stared out the window, his voice thick. "Critters had open access..."

"Serafina?"

"That's what folks in town called her: Sweet Serafina." The sheriff's face as red as the setting sun, he jammed his hands in his pockets. "Her real name was Sarah Jacobs."

He logged the name in his mind. "Thanks, Sheriff."

Concerned for Miss Wilson standing in the heat, he rose and looked toward the obscured window just as the hazy shape of a horse and rider bolted into view. A wild yell split the quiet, and both he and Sheriff Downing lunged for the doorway as a black horse, its rider hunched low, raced through the clearing, scattering their mounts. In an instant, all three horses were gone—his and the sheriff's in one direction, Callie's in another.

Downing slapped his hat against his thigh and Joe gawped. But when a groan sounded from his left, he spun to find Callie Wilson sprawled on the ground, seemingly right in the path the horse and rider had just taken.

CHAPTER 3

"Miss Jarrett!"

Joe Trenamen's voice sliced through Callie's pounding skull, and a large shadow blocked the sunlight.

"Can you hear me? Kezia?"

She groaned again. Not good. Not good at all. Everything hurt. . .

"Say something. . .please."

She blinked at Mr. Trenamen and, over his shoulder, the sheriff. "Stop yelling. I hear you." Despite the ringing in her ears.

"What happened?" The sheriff's voice was gentler than before.

"A black horse. . .with three white stockings." She pressed her eyes closed, hoping to clear her head.

"We saw it." Mr. Trenamen took her hand, his voice and touch both soothing. "Did it charge you?"

She cleared her throat. "Lady spooked and drove her shoulder into me. Knocked me flat."

"Did she trample you?"

"No."

"Anything broken?"

Callie tested her limbs. "Nothing feels broken." Just tender. Probably bruised. And her throat was so dry. She'd been reaching for her canteen when the rider appeared.

"Can you stand, Miss?"

"I—I think so."

Both men helped her, first to a sitting position, then to her feet. Once standing, she leaned heavily into Joe's side.

"I know you said not to ask, but. . .are you all right?" he whispered.

Realizing the inappropriateness of their proximity, she separated herself. "I'm fine, thank you." But that had been quite a wallop. "Would either of you have a canteen?"

"Mine's on my saddle. And who knows where that is now. . ." The sheriff huffed.

"Same as mine." Joe shook his head.

She swallowed hard, attempting to work moisture to her parched throat. "I'm thirsty."

"Ain't no well on the property." Sheriff Downing waved up the mountain. "The former owner hauled water from a nearby crick, and it's bone-dry right now."

Eyes on the ground, Joe bent to retrieve something. "Here." He rose. "Settle this under your tongue." When she didn't immediately take the offering, he pushed it into her palm.

"A pebble?"

"Put it under your tongue. It'll cause you to produce more saliva."

"It's. . .been on the ground."

He arched a brow. "It'll keep you from feeling so dry until we can find fresh water."

Sheriff Downing grinned. "That's right good advice, Nesbitt!" He retrieved his own pebble and, after brushing it against his shirt, deposited it under his tongue.

"Saved me more than once in the war." Joe also placed a pebble under his tongue, staring at her the entire time.

"You're joshin'. You were in the war?" Downing looked skeptical. "You're too young."

"I was twelve when it started. Served as a drummer."

While they dickered over Joe's war service, she rubbed the tiny stone between the folds of her skirt then slipped it under her tongue. To her surprise, it did help.

"Gentlemen?"

Both went silent.

"Could we find our horses, please?"

Sheriff Downing stared. "You feelin' up to traipsin' through these mountains whilst we search, or do you want Nesbitt to walk you back to town whilst I go after 'em?"

They were only a mile or so from Cambria Springs, and the hour was growing late. The last thing they needed was to be stranded on foot on these steep, wooded paths after dark, but she also couldn't leave Lady. The mare had been a gift from her parents. Having her close helped keep the homesickness at bay—a reminder of their love.

If only she could stay and search for more clues while the men tracked the horses, but her companions would never agree. "Let's find them before returning."

Mr. Trenamen loosed an ear-piercing whistle. After several seconds, he turned. "If Rusty's able, he'll return at my call. Hopefully, we'll catch 'em quickly and be back before Mrs. Ingram serves supper."

With a sigh, she retrieved her rifle from the grass, pain lashing her as she straightened.

As he settled his hand on her shoulder, his thumb brushed the crook of her neck, sending something akin to lightning through her. "You sure you're up to this? If not, I'll walk you back to town."

His touch still sparking, she brushed his arm away. "I need

to find Lady. She's special to me."

"All right, but speak up if you need a rest." He stalked away, and the sheriff hurried to catch up.

She rolled her eyes heavenward, pulse racing. What on earth was that? Joe Trenamen was a fellow operative. She must guard against any schoolgirl infatuations and other entanglements.

"Kezia, are you coming?"

Sheriff Downing had already started down the path, so she scrambled to catch up, falling in behind him, and Joe brought up the rear. Despite her aching muscles, Callie stayed primed to throw her rifle to her shoulder. Once more, Joe split the air with his shrill whistle.

"Sheriff, did you recognize that black horse?" she called, grasping a tree trunk for balance.

"Don't reckon so."

Per Allan Pinkerton's instructions, she shouldn't let anyone know she was an operative, so she couldn't be too direct with her questions—but she could play the part of an inquisitive woman.

"Why would anyone want to drive off our horses?"

"Prob'ly just be some young buck havin' him a drunken time."

"But the way he yelled, startling our horses, makes it seem more purposeful." Could it have been the murderer?

If so, was he trying to lead them into a vulnerable position? They made easier targets on foot, especially with the sun sinking in the afternoon sky.

They walked in relative silence, though the rustling underbrush and crunching leaves would easily give their location away. Callie scanned the ground, then craned to see past Sheriff Downing. The rider had certainly disappeared quickly in the dense trees.

The trail narrowed, underbrush pressing in. In places, the scrub snatched at her skirt like grasping hands. The sun dipped lower, and she slung the rifle over her shoulder so she could pull herself up by the nearby tree trunks. Her foot slipped, and she toppled face-first into the dust. Downing spun, and Joe was at her side.

"You hurt?"

Her cheeks warmed. "Only my pride…" She wouldn't mention her stiffening muscles.

Joe helped her up and retrieved her rifle as Callie brushed the front of her dress bodice. He stifled a laugh.

"What?" She glared.

"There's dirt smudged from your nose to your chin, and there's something white slopped all over your dress."

There were, in fact, several whitish streaks marring the dark blue fabric at about knee level. Brushing at them only smeared the thickest line. She'd probably brushed against a bird's droppings.

She dabbed the sticky white substance with her handkerchief and rubbed her face with her sleeve. Unladylike, but she'd known she'd get her hands—and more—dirty as an operative. "Better?"

Joe looked almost pained. "May I?"

Face flaming, she let him rub away whatever smudge marked her face. After an instant, he stopped. "That'll do for now."

Embarrassment complete, she slung her gun over her shoulder and grasped the nearest tree. "Then let's carry on before we lose the light."

⌐

It was well after dark when they'd rounded up the horses, and Callie Wilson was obviously exhausted and in pain. He'd insisted she ride in front of him when they'd found his mount, Rusty, miles from the cabin. She hadn't argued, which told him what bad shape she was in, especially when she'd leaned into him and closed her eyes. From what he remembered of her three years before, she took the Pinkerton motto of "We Never Sleep" to heart...

But she was asleep now. Or was she passed out?

Lord God Almighty, please let her be all right. Please. I should've taken her back to Mrs. Ingram's immediately.

Why hadn't he?

Because she hadn't acted like she was in pain at first. Because she'd already scolded him for coddling her. Because he'd enjoyed watching her work inside the cabin—seeing her sharp eye for details and how quickly she was able to capture the scene with her drawing.

And because, durn it all, he found her attractive, and that made it hard to think straight.

"Cambria Springs ain't got a real doctor." Sheriff Downing twisted in his saddle as they approached town. "Got a barber who serves as undertaker, dentist, and doc as needed. Want I should fetch him?"

He glanced at Callie, so still in his arms. Was she injured—or simply exhausted? "I'll ask Mrs. Ingram to look at her. If he's needed, I'll fetch him."

"Want I should take your horses to the livery?"

"Thanks, but the fewer people who can make connections between us, the better." And he wanted a good reason to escape the boardinghouse if Mrs. Ingram lit into him for his ill-advised decisions.

"Suit yourself. Should we come into town from different directions?"

"Probably best."

"Fine, then. I'll circle 'round." Downing let them pass. "You need me, I've got a small room behind the jail."

"Noted."

"Night, Nesbitt."

"Night, Sheriff."

Once he finally made it back to town, he drew up outside Mrs. Ingram's house.

"Miss Jarrett? Kezia. . ." He used her undercover name to remind her of what role she was to play. "Let's get you inside."

She stirred slightly as he dismounted and pulled her into his arms. Thankfully, as he approached, the boardinghouse door opened.

Hattie gasped. "What happened? Is Miss Jarrett—"

"Alive." He hefted Callie into a better position, and her head lolled to his shoulder. "Though she may be injured. Please call your mother while I take her to her room."

"I'm here." Mrs. Ingram hurried down the hall. "What happened?"

Joe climbed the stairs, relating how their horses had been driven off and Callie knocked down. By the time they reached the third floor, his muscles burned.

Mrs. Ingram hurried inside to light Callie's lamp. "Bring her in, son. Hurry."

He gingerly laid her on the bed, and Mrs. Ingram took over, shooing him out. As he exited, Hattie shuffled in to assist.

"Ma'am, I need to take care of our horses," he called from outside the door. "You want that I should send for anyone before I do?"

"Thank you, Mr. Nesbitt. If that's necessary and you're not back, I'll have the neighbor boy go."

"Yes, ma'am." As he descended, the other boarders asked after Miss Jarrett. He told them Mrs. Ingram was looking after her then slipped into the darkness beyond.

After watering their mounts thoroughly outside the livery,

he found two stalls next to each other and rubbed both horses down. His mind churned between Callie Wilson and the case. Questions about both percolated in his brain—though mostly all the questions he hadn't thought to ask Downing due to his concern for his fellow operative.

"Pull it together, numbskull."

He couldn't afford costly mistakes. Not with a seven-time murderer on the loose.

With the horses settled, he searched the livery for any black horses. He'd not seen the animal well through the cabin's filthy windows, and by the time he and Downing made it outside, the horse was nearly swallowed up by the trees. Callie had said the animal had three white stockings. Which three legs? Had she seen the rider? He'd not asked. . .

His shoulders slumped. There were no black horses—with or without stockings. And even if there had been, that didn't mean they'd found the killer. As Downing said, it was probably a drunken idiot raising Cain. Or. . .it could be their target trying to keep his identity hidden.

Leaving the stable, he scanned the deserted street. Maybe he'd pay Downing a quiet visit to ask the questions he'd not asked earlier. Perhaps by then, Mrs. Ingram would have Miss Wilson settled so he might calm his racing thoughts and sleep.

CHAPTER 4

Saturday, June 21, 1873

Wagon wheels churned. Voices shouted. Horses whinnied.

Calliope froze, trembling, as she searched for a way out of the mayhem.

She screamed, sobbing again.

Pounding hooves rushed up, and someone grabbed her, wrenching her arm as he plucked her from the mud. In a heartbeat, a burly, bearded man hauled her into his saddle. She clung to him, panting. His horse dodged and swerved, finally galloping free of the pandemonium. At the street's edge, the man slowed to a stop.

"Are you all right, child?" His voice was thick with a strange accent.

Shaking, she couldn't answer.

He turned and motioned toward the wagon she'd jumped from—now stopped in the middle of the street.

"Is that your family?" He indicated the couple gawping in horror from the wagon seat, along with the five boys staring her way from the wagon's bed.

She shook her head. "They took me from the train. I belong with Orion and Andromeda Braddock."

"Those are your parents?"

Again, she shook her head, sniffling. "My big brother and sister. Mama and Papa are dead."

Callie roused from the dream as homesickness stole her breath. It had been fifteen years. Would she ever find her brother and sister? She'd tried. But the dozens of letters she'd written to the orphanage that had put them on the train met with only an occasional apologetic response, stating they couldn't help.

However, after Mr. Pinkerton hired her, he'd sent her to New York on a brief job, and once she'd wrapped that business up, he'd encouraged her to track down her brother's and sister's whereabouts. Days of searching through a damp and musty basement had unearthed an adoption agreement for Andromeda. She'd been chosen in St. Louis by a childless couple, Mr. and Mrs. Michael McGovern. She'd found no paperwork on Orion's adoption, but by God's grace, a longtime employee of the orphanage had been on that train and recalled her, Andromeda, and Orion. He'd kept a journal of the trip's happenings and wrote that her brother had been taken in by a farmer, along with a couple of other boys from the train, only a couple of days' travel from Cambria Springs.

That was why Mr. Pinkerton had sent her west a year ago—to search for her brother in between official agency jobs. And when Mrs. Cantor was called away from this multiple-murder case, Mr. Pinkerton had called her in. She was the nearest female operative. After months of seeking her brother, she was no nearer to finding him than the Pinkertons were to finding the murderer of seven women.

A soft knock interrupted her thoughts, and she snapped her eyes open. Sunlight poured through her window as Callie stretched and groaned, body aching. At nearly the same moment, Mrs. Ingram pushed her door open and entered with a tray.

"Thank goodness, you're awake. Good morning, dear girl."

She stifled a yawn. "Good morning."

"That's the second night in a row you've given us a terrible fright. Promise me we won't have a third."

A fright. Yes. . .she supposed it had been, though when she'd briefly awakened and spoken to Mrs. Ingram the previous evening, the frail woman had been rock-steady, ordering Hattie and the other boarders to fetch this or hand her that as they'd checked her for injuries.

"I'm so sorry." She attempted to push herself up.

"Whoa, now." Mrs. Ingram set the tray down, then assisted her. "Go slowly. You're bruised."

Yes—from shoulder to hip, from the feel of it.

With help, Callie leaned into the pillows Mrs. Ingram fluffed behind her.

"There, now. How do you feel?"

The movement pained her, but. . . "I'll live."

Her broad smile warmed Callie. "I brought you a light breakfast. If you manage this well, I'll bring you something more substantial." A dainty, flowered teacup and saucer and two pieces of bread with jam filled the tray.

"It looks delicious. Thank you, Mrs. Ingram."

The woman grinned. "There's a handsome young gentleman asking to see you. Are you up to a visit from Mr. Nesbitt?"

Warmth flooded her cheeks at the idea of Joe Trenamen seeing her still abed, but. . .they needed time alone to talk, and it seemed Mrs. Ingram was willing to allow it.

"Yes, ma'am."

"I'll send him up." She left. Minutes later, heavy footsteps clomped up the steps and down the hall toward her door. When Joe appeared, his features were drawn and eyes rimmed with dark circles.

He scrubbed a hand across his unshaven jaw. "You're a welcome sight." His voice was huskier than normal. "How are you feeling?"

She put the bread down. "Given the circumstances, I should probably feel a whole lot worse." Callie nodded toward the chair. "Please, come in. Sit."

Looking uncomfortable, he dragged the chair nearer, though still some distance away—she assumed for propriety's sake. "You're sure you're well enough?"

"I am." Her room was situated at the end of the hallway, though all she could see of the hall was the wall facing her door. She dropped her voice. "Are we alone?"

"Everyone's downstairs."

Good. "Did you and the sheriff find anything more inside the cabin?"

He shook his head. "That horse and rider interrupted things before I got to look myself."

"You could've looked while I was sketching."

"I should have."

She shrugged, instantly regretting the painful movement. "Why didn't you?"

He rubbed his forehead. "I was watchin' you work—recalling that brand-new, green operative from three years back."

"I'm not near so green now."

"No, you're not."

His words and his appreciative smile warmed her.

"I'll ride out there again today, since I know you're not in a dire circumstance."

"I would've liked more time there. Maybe I can pull myself together and ride with—"

"No." He shot her a stern look. "You need to rest."

She fluttered her eyelashes at him. "I suppose."

He scrubbed his jaw. "You said you'd show me your drawings later."

"Right. Where's my bag?" She motioned across her body,

imitating where the satchel had hung.

At the same moment, they both spotted it lying on the vanity on the far side of the room. He retrieved it while she gently set the tray aside, and once he passed it to her, she removed the contents.

"I drew these of the cabin's interior." She passed him the sketches, then held up another page. "And this is the distinctive boot track I saw around the blood pool."

"There were lots of tracks around there." Skepticism settled in his gaze.

"Yes, but other tracks made from this boot had partially been wiped out by animal tracks and other boot prints, so it had to have been made before animals came on the scene, and before anyone found the victim."

Joe's brows arched. "Who taught you that?"

She narrowed a look at him. "I told you. . .I've learned a lot in three years."

He agreed with a nod.

"But it's sound reason, isn't it? If I step in the mud and you step in the same place right after me"—she held out one hand, then placed her other on top of it, slightly askew — "then your boot will wipe out this part of my track, showing that mine was in place first."

He grinned. "That's right."

"So, because many of these tracks were obscured by others, we can assume they were there before the victim was found." She recalled the other things she'd tucked in her bag. "And—" She leafed through her papers until she found the two paper pouches. "Strands of the victim's hair and fabric that was stuck on an exposed nail not far from the window." She opened the pouch and shook the scrap into her hand, taking a closer look. "The fabric may or may not have anything to do with the murder."

Callie cocked her head. "It looks to me like shirting material."

He rose and looked at the scrap. "I have to say, I'm impressed."

"So you think these are related?"

"The fabric could just as easily be the old hermit's as something connected to this case. But you've a fine eye for detail." He released her hand.

"I am a Pinkerton, you know. . ."

Yes. Yes, she was. And she'd become a good one. When they'd worked together years ago, she'd had a general understanding of investigative work with natural skill. But Kate Warne she wasn't. That was then. The petite young woman had grown confident, stepping right into the improvisation he'd asked of her, even before he'd set the stage with a cover story, which proved her quick mind and ability to think on her feet.

"I am aware. You don't have to keep proving yourself to me." The woman had sand.

He paced back to the chair as she sipped her tea. "After I brought you here last night, I went to the livery to care for our horses, and—"

She set the teacup down a little too quickly. "Is Lady safe?"

"She was when I left her."

Relief washed over her features. "Thank you. I appreciate you caring for her. She was a gift from my parents."

He paused. "So you do have family."

"Oh, yes. Mother, father, and five brothers."

"They must love you to give you such a fine mare."

"Mama and Papa do. My brothers are another story entirely."

"What do you mean?"

She released a sarcastic laugh then sighed. "I was the only adopted child. Papa had all five boys with his first wife, lost her to illness, and married Mama a couple years later. She wanted a girl to dote on. Me. The boys saw me as an interloper, and very spoiled."

Adopted. . . He'd not imagined that. "What happened to your original family?"

She dabbed at her eyes. "I was very young, so I don't recall, exactly. I just know they died."

"I'm real sorry. Should've kept my mouth shut. . ." He'd never have wished such a thing on her, but at least she'd had a second chance at a family. He never had. . .

"Anyway, my brothers would pretend to let me come along on their adventures but would often abandon me, sometimes miles from home. More than once, Papa had to come find me. I once spent two nights in a cornfield until he came."

His gut roiled with anger. "Didn't your pa do anything?"

"Tanned their hides repeatedly, and eventually, he sent the oldest two off to boarding school, with the threat that the others would follow if they didn't act right. I learned not to trust any of them—but I sometimes followed at a distance and learned some tracking, hunting, and fishing. Of course, when I announced my dreams of working as a Pinkerton, they laughed. But I have them partly to thank. I wasn't going to let their nay-saying deter me."

So that's why such a young woman would leave home to become a Pinkerton—she was determined to prove herself to the contemptuous brothers who'd dismissed her dreams.

And she would. Especially if he had anything to do with it.

"Thank you for fillin' me in. As I was telling you, after taking care of Rusty and Lady, I stopped by to talk to Sheriff Downing. If he suspected you were an operative, he didn't let on."

"That's good." She took a dainty bite of the jam-slathered bread.

"Downing told me the victim's name was Sarah Jacobs, and she was. . ." He hung his head. "She was a. . ."

"Prostitute?"

His face turned feverishly hot. "Yeah."

"You needn't choose your words. I'm a Pinkerton first, a lady second."

Oh, Lord God Almighty. . . He blew out a breath.

He'd had more than one direct conversation with Mrs. Cantor before she left the case, and it was only mildly uncomfortable. But Mrs. Cantor had been a married woman and understood the subtleties of men and women. Callie was young, delicate, beautiful, and unmarried. She ought not know anything about such relations yet. It felt like he was the one blushing while speaking so frankly about the lives of soiled doves. It was unsettling.

He rubbed at the ache forming in his head. This would take some getting used to. "I'll try to keep that in mind."

"What else did you learn?"

"She, uh. . .worked. . .two nights before her body was found, and apparently, there was a fella waiting for her. Real shortly before the brothel closed, she took a fella to her room and didn't come out, although someone said they heard her yelling about wasting her time." He cleared his throat. "Come morning, she and the man were nowhere to be found."

"She was abducted, then?"

"Abducted, or she went with him willingly. No one's sure, nor does anyone recall much about the man. It was a busy night."

"Not even a general description?"

"Supposedly, the man kept to himself, waiting on Serafina; but in general. . .big, dark hair, and they think a beard."

A derisive chuckle escaped her lips. "That could be half the men in the territory. Sheriff Downing, for example."

He settled his elbows on his knees. "Yeah. This is exactly

what we've dealt with for the last five years. We've found no connection between the murdered women. Seven women from different walks of life, in different locations. And seldom do we find anyone who can offer anything helpful. Just a general description of a big man with dark hair and a beard. Some say the man is big but of a lean build. Others say he has a thicker, stockier frame."

Miss Wilson stared from over her slice of bread. "Do you have notes on the murders? Witness accounts? Anything?"

"Of course I do." Meticulous notes, on every single murder, just as Mr. Pinkerton asked.

"May I see them? Perhaps I'll see something you've missed."

Had no one given her a thorough explanation of the case before sending her to assist? "You haven't read the copies of my files yet?"

"I assume those are in Chicago. I came directly from my last case—around Denver."

He was a fool. He knew she was coming from somewhere much nearer. Why hadn't he realized she would need to see his documentation? "I apologize. I'll bring everything upstairs before I head to the cabin."

She turned those expressive brown eyes his way and smiled. "Thank you, Joe. Maybe now I can get somewhere."

CHAPTER 5

Joe chafed. How had he not realized?

Callie Wilson was presently looking through his files. He'd prefer to be there with her, calling attention to various details. But she'd encouraged him to return to the cabin before anyone else did. And he knew it wouldn't have been appropriate for him to sit in Callie's room any longer. He'd given Mrs. Ingram the story that they were old acquaintances—which was true—but they needed to keep an appropriate distance. Not spend endless hours together for seemingly no reason. Besides, she'd said she would rather read the files privately and think on them without him inserting his own slant. She promised they'd talk once she'd read it all.

He'd had no time to write up the previous few days' happenings, although she'd been in town for those and wouldn't need his chicken scratch to understand. But he had to get them recorded. He'd rehearsed the details so he wouldn't forget anything. Soiled dove Sarah Jacobs, also known as Sweet Serafina, approximate age thirty, was killed in the secluded cabin a mile from Cambria Springs. Just as the other victims had been, her body had been peppered with multiple stab wounds—in her case, thirteen.

It would have been so helpful to see the body at the scene, but as chance had it, he'd ridden out of town the morning she'd been discovered, and Downing had taken it upon himself to deliver the corpse to the barber-turned-undertaker before he returned. So he'd missed seeing the woman where she was killed. And because Downing didn't know Callie was also a Pinkerton, she hadn't been notified. With the damage wild animals had done to Miss Jacobs' body, the lawman had her buried immediately, so short of exhuming the corpse—which would raise questions they couldn't afford—neither he nor Callie had seen her, at the scene or afterward.

Worse, no one could definitively describe the man Serafina had last been with.

Of all the luck.

His mind drifted to the cabin. He'd take another look at the interior, but especially scout the outside. He and Callie hadn't had time to explore the yard before the sheriff arrived—and then the rider scattered their horses. He forced his mind to that incident. Was that the murderer, and if so, what had he accomplished by scattering their horses? He'd only delayed them. There was no guarantee he was the culprit. More likely, Downing was right—it was some drunken fool sowing his oats.

But was it?

This was the first time they were able to get to the crime scene soon after the murder, at least since the first two in Chicago and St. Louis. All the others had been more remote. Two deaths had occurred in this area in the past three months, so the murderer could still be near. He'd had the distinct feeling, as they traipsed through the woods the previous afternoon, that they were being watched. Nothing specific, just that old heaviness between his shoulder blades. Like during the war.

This case had him on edge unlike any he'd worked—but why?

Because women were being stabbed, and their bodies left to

the elements—and the trail kept going cold until another body turned up. That would serve to remind him there was still a killer victimizing women of all sorts. Those with connections, like the first woman. Those with no connections, like the prostitutes. And those in between—women with families, children who depended on them. He didn't want any chance that Callie Wilson would end up on that list, because. . .durn it all, *he liked her.*

His face heated.

"Rusty. . ."

His horse swiveled an ear toward him.

"I'm a blasted fool."

Joe rode into the clearing. The cabin stood just as they'd left it. He dismounted and, this time, tied Rusty to a tree, not wanting him to run off again. Then, he paced the clearing, looking for the black horse's hoofprints. It took some time to seek out the trail the rider had cut through the cabin's yard, but once he found a track, partially obscured by grass, he bent and studied it. Not the best imprint.

He sighed, scanning for more tracks. The grass was thick enough to prevent leaving a clear print. He found a few other incomplete ones as he meandered back toward the trees. The nearer he got to the foliage, though, the less formed the tracks became until they petered out altogether beyond the tree line.

He looked at the cabin, mentally placing himself inside it when the horse had burst into the clearing. He was looking in the right place, yet there were no tracks. Not wanting to get too far from his horse, he moved down the path into the trees. The only tracks were Rusty's, those he'd just made. He tapped his toe in frustration then stalked across the clearing, headed toward the path they'd taken in pursuit of their scattered horses.

No tracks. None. Not the mystery horse's, nor their mounts'. Not even a boot print. And they'd left plenty last night.

Snatching his hat from his head, he ran his fingers through his hair. Someone had gone to a lot of trouble to be sure there were none to find.

"What am I dealing with. . .a ghost?"

⌒

Moving carefully, Callie washed, dressed in a summery yellow calico, and then arranged her hair. Grabbing her satchel, she headed toward the door but stopped.

Her derringer. . .

When Mr. Pinkerton sent her west, she'd promised she'd carry it wherever she went. Had Mrs. Ingram found it? Turning back, she checked the drawer in the bedside table. Empty. Callie checked the blue dress she'd worn yesterday, and her breath whooshed out when she found it still concealed in the pocket.

After checking the diminutive weapon, she looked at the odd white stains on her blue dress. At the time, she'd thought it was bird droppings, but now she wasn't so sure. It wasn't just one splotch. Instead, white marks crisscrossed the blue material in thin, sweeping lines. Was it sap from some ground plant? Hardly likely it was a bird's leavings. . . She needed to attend to the stains before they set permanently. But after hours of deciphering Joe's notes, copying some and summarizing others, her eyes needed a rest. She'd go through the rest this evening before returning them. So, despite her stiff, sore muscles, she was going out. She ought to wash the dress, but a walk outside sounded more appealing—and easier.

Heading downstairs, Callie called out for Mrs. Ingram, who appeared from the direction of the kitchen.

"Dear girl, you shouldn't be up."

"I can't stay in bed any longer. I'm going to check on Lady at the livery."

"I'd feel better if you had someone with you, but Hattie's the only one here."

"You needn't send an escort. I'm fine. Just stiff. The walk will do me good."

Concern creased her brow. "All right, then, but please be careful."

"Yes, ma'am. Do you need anything while I'm out?"

"No, child. Enjoy your walk. You're going just to the livery and back?"

She would be watching and listening for anything pertaining to her case. "That depends on whether I see anything I'd like to draw." She patted her satchel. "I won't leave town, and I'll be back long before the evening meal."

"That's what I needed to hear." The woman patted her arm. "Enjoy your stroll, dear."

"Thank you." She exited the house and smiled at the lone gentleman who tipped his hat as he drove past in a buggy. The walk to the livery was uneventful, with few people on the street. Odd. Were they so spooked by the recent murder they'd gone into hiding? The same street hadn't seemed sparsely populated the day before when she'd headed out.

Upon reaching the stable's entrance, the hostler met her.

"Can I help you?"

"I'd like to look around."

He shrugged. "You looking for something particular? Maybe I can point you to it."

"I wanted to look in on my gray mare, Lady. And. . .while I was out riding yesterday, I saw an especially beautiful black with three white stockings. Would you happen to know such a horse?"

The hostler thought. "You can look around, if you like, but I don't reckon we got any black horses like you describe. The only gray we got is in that second row on the left. 'Bout halfway down. But she was brought in by a dark-haired fella last night, along with a chestnut."

"Yes. Mr. Nesbitt. He's a friend."

"All right, then. The gray mare's that way." He waved again. "Let me know iffen you need something, Miss."

She turned toward the nearest row. *Lord, please let me find the horse from yesterday.*

She walked up and down the rows, pausing at any stall containing a black horse—and there were few enough of them. Not finding the horse, she sighed. As she reached Lady's stall, disappointment wound through her. She hadn't really expected such a break to come easily, but she could hope.

Lady greeted her with a nicker. Joe had taken good care of her. Lady's coat shone like she'd been brushed well. Her stall was clean and dry, and she was in good spirits. She spent several minutes with the horse before leaving the livery—this time, headed toward the mercantile.

As she turned onto Center Street, she noted the strange sound of a pipe organ playing a lively tune, and near the town square, a larger-than-average crowd. This must be where all the people had gone. Folks on foot had gathered around some central point, and farther back, men on horseback watched while interspersed among the waiting wagons with people standing in the beds, craning to see over the crowd.

A pipe organ. . . What was the attraction? She tried to put on some speed, but the lingering stiffness reminded her to take it easy. It would take time to regain her normal pace and abilities.

As she drew nearer, the lively music ceased and a booming voice, thickly accented with an English lilt, rose above the murmuring crowd. At the center of the melee was a dark-haired gentleman in a suit standing near a line of strange, boxy wagons, each painted red with black-and-gold accents. Though she was too far away to hear the man's words, he obviously beckoned people to come near. The crowd complied. As she approached, the bold words on the wagons' sides, painted in gold, came into focus.

Dr. Chellingworth's Heaven-Sent Miracle Elixir

A medicine show? She'd heard of them, but she'd never seen one. This could be a fortunate turn. With so many people gathered, she could get a feel for the townsfolk—something she'd not been able to do since her arrival.

She meandered toward the swelling crowd, scanning for a spot where she might see some of the goings-on.

CHAPTER 6

Joe dismounted outside the livery and watered Rusty.

The young hostler came to the doorway. "You the one who brought in that handsome gray?"

"Yeah." Concern snaked through him. "What about her?"

"Some woman was just pokin' around, wantin' to see her."

"What woman?"

"Don't know her name. Real pretty. Little—shorter'n me by a couple inches. Brown hair, sparkly brown eyes. Wearin' a yella dress."

An involuntary grunt escaped him. Yes, Callie Wilson's eyes sparkled, especially when she laughed—but what right did this young upstart have noticing that? "That's my friend, Miss Jarrett. She owns that mare."

The kid shrugged. "With all the strange stuff goin' on 'round here, just figured to make sure."

"Thanks, but she's none of your concern." What was she doing traipsing around town after getting so bruised? He motioned in the direction of Lady's stall. "She still here?"

"The horse, or the woman?"

"Both."

"The horse is. The woman walked that way a couple minutes ago." He waved toward the town's center.

Then she couldn't have gone far. "Thanks."

"Want me to take your horse?"

"I'll come back later." He'd check on Callie first.

Once Rusty finished drinking, Joe mounted and walked the big chestnut down the street. As he neared the next intersection, distant music caught his ear, and he turned toward it.

The sight of a small woman in a cheery yellow dress flitting around the edges of a crowd caught his attention. Callie. With her small stature, she'd have little chance to see anything unless she could find her way to the front. He rode up, dismounted, and came to stand slightly behind her.

He leaned near. "Having trouble?"

She whipped around, a hand over her heart, though the sudden movement must have hurt her. Her broad smile faltered, and her eyes flashed with momentary pain. He reached to steady her.

"You startled me, Mr. Nesbitt. And yes, I can't see past the crowd."

"What're you doin' here?" he whispered.

"I needed some fresh air, and I stumbled upon this."

Near the line of medicine show wagons, an Englishman rattled off a loud carnival-barker's spiel.

He hooked a thumb toward the show. "You *want* to see this foolishness? These types of people are charlatans."

Miss Wilson smiled sheepishly. "I have my reasons."

Hopefully, they had nothing to do with spending money on snake oil.

"Can you sit a saddle?"

"I doubt I'd be ready to ride any distance, but if I'm sitting still..."

"All right, then." He shortened the left stirrup to fit her, then helped her onto Rusty's back until she sat with her right leg hooked around the saddle horn and her left foot in the stirrup.

"Thank you, Mr. Nesbitt." Her brown eyes glittered, and his heart pounded. He took the reins and, standing by Rusty's head, turned toward the line of wagons. Over the heads of the crowd, three balls flew into the air in regular succession, and the onlookers gave a collective gasp followed by applause.

Moments later, the tall Englishman returned.

"Good afternoon, one and all. My name is Dr. Darby Chellingworth, and my entourage and I have come to America to both entertain and heal our across-the-pond neighbors."

"Bring back the juggler!" a man hollered, and others around him applauded.

"I certainly will. But first—I must tell you about my Heaven-Sent Miracle Elixir. This special blend of medicinal herbs and ingredients can cure all that ails you. We have seen this remedy help with rheumatism, arthritis, heart issues, neuralgia, hair loss, memory loss. Dr. Chellingworth's Heaven-Sent Miracle Elixir can speed the mending of broken bones, as well as take down swelling from bruises, strains, and sprains. And it will stave off fever, chills, and every respiratory malady."

"All that in one bottle?" another man from the far side of the rowdy bunch shouted. "Sounds too good to be true!"

"Aww, hush up and let him talk!" someone quipped. "The sooner he hawks his magical potion, the sooner he brings back the juggler."

"Now, now." The good doctor raised his hands as if to quiet the protests. "Just as the name indicates"—he waved a hand toward the name emblazoned on the various wagons—"my elixir is a miracle in liquid form, straight from the throne room of heaven."

Some in the crowd guffawed at the grandiose claim, while many others murmured approvingly.

"We want the juggler!"

"Our original Elixir will handle most every malady that might befall man or beast. But for our fairer customers, we have a special, gentler variety of our Heaven-Sent Miracle Elixir to deal with a woman's delicate constitution and needs."

Joe shook his head. "What hogwash. You aren't honestly buying his claims, are you?"

As he glanced back at Callie, her focus was set on some distant point at the far side of the crowd, the way a good hunting dog locked on to its target.

"Miss Jarrett?"

She glanced his way, then back. "Help me down, Mr. Nesbitt. Hurry."

⌒

If the crowd weren't so dense, she would just ride across the square, but with so many packed into the square, she'd never make it on horseback.

"Please, get me down."

Joe lifted her down easily. "What's the all-fired hurry?" He spoke in a tone only she would hear.

"There's a black horse with at least one stocking across the way."

She nodded toward it and immediately headed to see the horse. In her haste, pain gripped her hip, and she nearly tumbled into the dust. But getting her feet under her once more, she tried again to weave through the crush of bodies.

As she did, an ear-piercing whistle split the air, and the people turned in that direction.

"Move!" Sheriff Cooper Downing's familiar voice boomed. "Make way. All of ya!"

The lawman stood on the roof of a nearby building not far

from where she'd left Joe.

"Clear this street!"

"I mean no harm, sir!" Dr. Chellingworth shielded his eyes from the afternoon sun. "We've come to entertain, amaze, and heal the good people of Cambria Springs."

"Aww, go peddle that snake oil somewhere elsewhere, huckster!" someone bellowed again.

She focused once more on the cross street. "Pardon me, please." People allowed her to slip past, though not easily. There just wasn't much room.

Sheriff Downing's voice boomed again. "You can put on your show but not in the street! Set it up in the field west of town."

For an instant, the crowd held its breath.

"All right, my good man," Dr. Chellingworth called. "Thank you! We'll move directly."

The crowd cheered, with some discontented grumbling mixed in. People moved in all directions, catching her in a swirl of bodies until she was bumped and jostled, pain lancing her more than once.

Lord, help! I need to get across this square.

"Move out of the way," a woman growled behind her, and seconds later, someone tapped her shoulder.

A slender woman of medium height, face cloaked by her sage-colored bonnet—a perfect complement to her darker green dress—stood behind her. "Where you tryin' to get to?"

"Straight across the square."

"Follow me." She set off with purpose, plowing her way to the boardwalk where she stepped into the shadows of a building in the mouth of an alley. She turned.

"Thank you so much!" Callie smiled at the taller woman.

"It was painful watching you gettin' trampled in that mess."

"I do appreciate it." She squinted to see the woman's face

through the shadows. "I'm Kezia Jarrett. And you are. . . ?"

"Annalee Ralston." The woman unknotted the wide fabric ties of the bonnet and pushed the fabric back to reveal beautiful green eyes and. . .

A dark beard? Callie gaped.

"I'm with the show," she whispered. "The Bearded Lady."

Miss Ralston had subdued her long beard into two braids and pinned them near her temples.

Finding her composure, Callie looked away. "I don't mean to stare."

The woman guffawed and tugged her bonnet back in place. "Missy, Dr. Chellingworth keeps me around so people *can* stare."

Pain lanced her heart. What an unfortunate life!

After hiding any sign of her unusual appearance with her bonnet, Miss Ralston stepped out of the shadows. "Hope you'll come see the show."

After Miss Ralston's kindness, how could she not, despite feeling so bruised?

As the pipe organ began to play, the woman looked toward the wagons. "Gotta go." She tugged her right sleeve down and rubbed at a light-colored stain at its cuff. "Please come. We'll be here at least until tomorrow."

Callie nodded. "I will." She'd find a way. . ."Thank you again. You were very kind to help me."

The woman departed, and Callie stared.

A bearded woman. . . She'd never seen the like!

Only after Miss Ralston disappeared did Callie carry on toward the intersection where, from across the square, she'd seen the tail end of a black horse near two arguing men. By the time she reached the corner, the street was much more crowded, and the men and the horse had vanished.

She needed to find that horse. Was it the one that had

stampeded their mounts? If she could find horse and rider, she might find a connection to her case. Maybe…Callie scanned the square. An older, white-haired, white-bearded man had angrily stabbed a finger in the chest of a much younger, dark-haired fellow. Did the horse belong to one of them? She couldn't be sure, but it was a start…if she could just find them.

Ignoring her pain and fatigue, she crossed toward the dry goods store and peered in the windows. It was empty except for the bald clerk and one blond customer. By the time she reached the building's corner, the mountainous incline had left her winded. Passing the alley's opening, she slumped onto the nearest bench. If she could catch her breath, perhaps she'd have the gumption to tackle the hill.

Meanwhile, the horse was probably getting farther away.

Lord, am I on the right path, or am I chasing jackrabbits? Callie breathed deeply, trying not to wince as her corset pinched her tender side.

Defeated, she eyed the incline, rested a moment more, then rose. As she did, something clattered in the alley, and a low groan sounded. Heart pounding, she squinted into the twilight between buildings.

"Hello?"

Another groan.

Definitely human.

Callie inched toward the shadowy opening. "Hello?" This time, she reached into her dress pocket, feeling for her derringer. "Is someone there?"

A man's hazy form rose unsteadily from behind some discarded crates and leaned against the wall.

The white-bearded man—only now, his beard was streaked with blood.

"Sir, are you injured?" Gripping the hidden pistol, she took a tentative step into the alley's mouth just as a hand clamped her shoulder.

⁓

Callie whipped around, brown eyes huge, and sank her tiny peashooter into his gut.

"Whoa, now." Joe shook his head. "Put that away."

She gulped and obeyed.

"Stay here."

That alley was the last place she needed to be, particularly with a fella acting hurt. For all she knew, that was the murderer trying to tug at her sympathies. As small as she was, even a strong boy might subdue her and drag her off to some secluded spot. The thought gave him an involuntary shudder.

She stepped back.

Joe loosened his pistol in its holster and stepped into the alley. "You okay, mister?"

The strong stench of whiskey wafted toward him as the glassy-eyed man tried to push away from the wall.

"Let me help you." Joe looped his left arm behind the unsteady man's back, keeping his right free to grab for his pistol, if needed. "There's a bench out here where you can sit."

He guided the man to it, and he collapsed onto the seat.

Joe squatted, looking up at him. "What happened?"

He was bleeding from the nose, though he seemed uninjured otherwise. He produced his handkerchief and pressed it into the old man's hand, then guided the hand toward his face. "Why don't you hold this under your nose?"

The fella stared at the cloth, then complied.

"What's your name?" He tried unsuccessfully to catch the man's eye.

"Did someone hit you?" Again, he fought to gain the man's focus.

After a few more dazed blinks, the old man finally did make eye contact before glancing around the street. "Yeah. . ."

"Who?"

Callie shuffled closer, her voice quiet. "He was talking to a dark-haired young man, also with a beard. About your age, Mr. Nesbitt, but—"

"Murderous—" Fortunately, the handkerchief muted his final word—one unfit for mixed company.

He arched a brow. "Hope you're not calling *me* that."

"Not you." He sneered. "Don't even know you." He stood on wobbly legs, nearly knocking Joe backward.

"Whoa." He rocked to his feet as the old man tottered.

"Meant that good-for-nothin' Rion Braddock."

He plowed into Miss Wilson as he stumbled past.

Her jaw slack, she stared like a lost little girl, then came to her senses. "Wait!" As he stepped off the boardwalk, she caught his arm. "Who did you say?"

The man tried to shake free. "Let go."

"What name did you just say? Please. . ."

He glared at her hand, then grabbed her hair and jerked her head back. Callie shrieked.

Joe sprang toward them, but the man sent her reeling toward a nearby water trough. Feet tangling in her dress hem, she fell against the trough, one hand bracing its rim while the other sank to the shoulder in the water. The trough's contents sloshed first over the back, then the front—straight down her dress.

"I said let go, you nosy little—" Again, he finished with a slurred word unfit for a woman's hearing.

Wanting to pummel the man, Joe went instead to her side. "Are you hurt?"

Her face had turned a frightening shade of white. Eyes brimming, she pushed away from the trough and stared at her sodden, muddied dress.

"Did he hurt you?" He squeezed her shoulder gently. "Callie?"

She jerked her gaze up, dashing away tears. "*Kezia*. And I'm fine. Just. . .wet!"

Callie shrugged free of his grasp and, with a flourish of muddied yellow calico, darted a glance toward where Whitey had stood. He was gone, but a half circle of onlookers took his place, far too interested in the pretty, half-drowned woman.

"Y'all go on." Joe shrugged out of his lightweight coat and wrapped it around her. "There's nothing to see."

CHAPTER 7

Sunday, June 22, 1873

After the mishap with Lady two days ago, then the rough handling by that cantankerous old fool yesterday, Callie ached. Yet she'd dressed for Sunday services and ridden in the wagon with Hattie, despite the church being only a short walk from the boardinghouse. To her irritation, once they arrived, they discovered the itinerate pastor had moved that week's meeting—and the picnic afterward—to the field where the medicine show had been told to set up. She loved Sunday services, but tolerating the hard wooden pews for the length of the sermon held little appeal. The hard ground held even less. Yet here she sat as people spread quilts and blankets under shade trees, facing the arched line of the medicine show wagons.

People milled, talking with others. Young children darted and chased. Near the edge of the crowd, the older boys made eyes at the pretty girls nearby, who giggled and blushed in response. A petite woman with a head of shiny raven hair stood near the end of the street, a book balanced on one forearm as she worked a pencil over the page with her other. The gal glanced up toward the medicine wagons, then back to the page, scratching with the pencil repeatedly.

Another artist? Callie's interest piqued, though before she could rise to investigate, the medicine show's pipe organ began to play her first mother's favorite hymn, "Come, Thou Fount of Every Blessing," and her mind shot back more than a decade to the many times she recalled Mama humming or singing the tune. The traveling pastor invited everyone to join, and around them, people began to sing. Homesickness swept her until she almost couldn't breathe.

Lord, help me. I don't want to fall to pieces now over something I can't change.

From the medicine show wagons, a beautiful woman with long red ringlets in a buckskin dress, a muscle-bound man a head taller than any in the field, and three others she couldn't make out stepped out and found places at the edge of the crowd. She watched them, trying to keep her mind from the memories attached to the song.

Several hymns later, the music ceased, and the pastor quieted the crowd. "Thank y'all for your willingness to worship outdoors on this beautiful day. Did everyone enjoy the pipe organ?"

Some applauded politely while others were more raucous in their agreement.

"Our illustrious visitors, Dr. Chellingworth and his company, offered to provide music for our service." He motioned to an odd man of moderate height and build, thinning chestnut hair combed to one side, and facial hair that covered only his jawline and chin. "And it seemed a shame to miss the opportunity to worship with some real accompaniment."

Callie stared at the odd Dr. Chellingworth. To add to his strange appearance, he wore spectacles with dark lenses. Catching Joe's eye, she leaned close. "I've never seen darkened spectacles like those."

He glanced up, searching, then nodded. "I have. In the war.

A few soldiers wore 'em on long marches. One day when I had a fearsome headache, a fella let me borrow his." His blue eyes sparkled as he grinned. "They were unexpectedly soothing."

Why did she find the idea that he'd served in the war so intriguing? Plenty of men had, probably even ones in this very crowd. Only he hadn't been a man. Joe was just a boy at the time. Every time he mentioned it, pride and admiration swelled in her heart. How fearless he must be to have served at such a tender age.

She leaned nearer, dropping her voice low. "In case I haven't said so, I admire that you served. Especially when you were so young."

His cheeks reddened, and a wry grin tugged at his lips. "Thank you. I was just following my brother. I didn't understand the horrors I was getting into."

"But you served the whole time, even after your brother passed. It was very brave, and I respect you for it."

He seemed to stand a little taller. "Thank you. That means a lot, coming from you."

If she thought it appropriate in such a setting, she'd have hugged him, but she focused on the pastor. He'd asked some question, and many within the crowd had raised their hands. Dr. Chellingworth, standing next to him, pointed to one of the nearest families with their hands up.

"Where has your family come from, sir?"

"Denver."

He welcomed them and asked their names, then moved on to greet several others and ask their names and locations. Shading his eyes, he looked toward the back of the crowd.

"You, sir. Standing at the back. What is your name, and how far have you come?"

Many in the field turned, including Callie.

"Ask somebody else," a man grumbled, though she couldn't tell which spoke. None of them had their hands raised.

"Oh, come now. We're all friends. Please. Share your name."

As she scanned faces, her eye snagged, and her breath caught loudly. The same dark-haired man she'd seen arguing yesterday—now with a gun belt slung low, like a gunfighter—glowered at Dr. Chellingworth, then pulled his hat lower and stalked away.

Her jaw slack, Callie pushed to her feet and went after him, hurrying despite her aches and pains.

"Sir, stay, please!" Chellingworth called. "Forgive me for putting you on the spot."

Clearing the crowd, Callie looked one way, then the other, and spotted the man heading back toward town. She followed, fighting to catch up.

"Pardon me!" she panted as she closed the gap.

He seemed not to hear.

"Sir! In the blue!"

He turned, his features hard. "What do you want?"

She stopped short, and for an instant, she could only stare.

"Well?"

"Forgive me." A thickness settled in her throat, making it difficult to ask the question burning on her tongue.

He arched his brows in scorn. "Speak up, or I'm leavin'."

When she still couldn't force out a sound, he gritted his teeth and stalked away.

Panic lanced her. "Are you Orion Braddock?"

The man's steps faltered. Hand resting on the butt of his pistol, he turned slowly. "Who's askin'?"

"Call—" She caught herself. "You may call me Kezia Jarrett."

His eyes narrowed. "And how d'you know my name?"

Lord, it is him! Decades-old emotion roiled, and the urge

to weep lodged in her throat. Or to break her cover and run to him, bury herself in his embrace.

If he *would* embrace her...

What if he didn't want to be found? That thought had never crossed her mind, so deep was her desire to reunite with her brother and sister. It nearly knocked the air from her lungs.

Oh, Lord God...please let him have yearned for me like I have him!

"Were you the man..." She fought tears. "Were you arguing with a white-haired gentleman yesterday in town?"

Confusion clouded his gaze before he stalked up. Towering over her, he glared. "Ellwood Garvin ain't no gentleman, and you'd do well to cut him a wide—" His eyes narrowed more, and he leaned in before giving a tiny shake of his head. "Cut that one a wide path, Miss. Now, name your business with me. Otherwise, I'm gone."

⌒

The loud gasp Callie released unfurled a huge warning flag in Joe's mind, and the wind of his thoughts snapped it to sharp attention when she'd darted up and hurried away. As soon as she departed, Mrs. Ingram gave him *the look*, and he took off in pursuit. His heart thundered as petite Callie Wilson charged after the big gunman. Durn it all, it was Sunday, and they were attending services, so he'd left his own guns locked in his room at the boardinghouse.

How stupid of him!

Lord God Almighty, what is she doing?

Ahead, she hurried after the man, obviously winded, and finally got him to turn. But when he did, his hand was on his pistol...

Sweet Jesus, protect her. Please!

"Were you arguing with a white-haired gentleman yesterday

in town?" she asked as Joe neared.

Ahh. This fella must be the other half of that pair Whitey was arguing with yesterday. But Whitey had mumbled a name—one she'd seemed quite interested in. Was this about finding the black horse that had stampeded their mounts, or was it about finding the man who bore the name Whitey muttered?

The gunman glared at her in a way that set Joe's teeth on edge. "Ellwood Garvin ain't no gentleman, and you'd do well to cut him a wide—" The fella paused, a look of befuddlement flashing in his gaze. With a shake of his head, he continued. "Cut that one a wide path, Miss. Now, name your business with me. Otherwise, I'm gone."

"Kezia?" What was her interest in this gent? He strode up.

"Who's this?" The fella jutted his chin in Joe's direction.

With a perturbed look, Callie turned, then faced the man again. "Stephen Nesbitt, another resident in the boardinghouse where I rent a room."

Joe extended his hand. "Yes, sir. And you are?"

"My name's nobody's b—"

"Orion Braddock." Her voice shook.

Braddock's bearded jaw firmed. "What d'you want with me?"

"I, um—" She froze.

He had no idea her business with Braddock, but she'd gone to lengths to chase him down. He should help her keep him close.

"Well, sir. Mrs. Ingram, who owns our boardinghouse—her husband used to pastor the local church before his passing. The dear woman doesn't like seein' anyone turned away from Sunday meetings, so we're asking you to stay. . ."

What he'd said about Mrs. Ingram was true—to a point. Had Callie not gotten up, the woman might have sent him after Braddock, especially given Braddock looked like he lived on the fringes of polite society. Who better to invite to hear the Lord's Word than a man on the edge?

Callie's confusion dissolved. "Yes. Please. Come sit with us—or listen from our wagon—but stay. I can't imagine anyone else will ask your name so publicly, and I won't blurt it again."

"That'd be helpful."

"So you'll come back?" Hopefulness seasoned Callie's voice. Who was this Braddock fella to her?

"Y'all are invitin' me to church. . ." Braddock eyed them skeptically.

Her boldness returning, Callie shot him a pointed look. "Have you ever attended services, sir?"

"Men like me don't frequent such places." A hardness edged his voice.

"Please, try it today." Her voice was gentle.

As he looked first at Joe, then Callie, a muscle in Braddock's jaw twitched. "I heard the singin'." He heaved a breath, shrugged, and shook his head. "Some of my dearest memories contain one of those hymns." He shot Callie another strange look, and her eyes brimmed.

"The music brought back some powerful memories for me as well." She nodded.

Braddock stared at her. "What'd you say your name was again?"

She lifted her chin. "Kezia Jarrett."

Finally, the man gave a grudging nod. "Fine, Miss Jarrett. But only because I ain't had a pretty gal talk sweet to me in a mighty long time."

CHAPTER 8

Once the service ended, Orion was quick to scramble to his feet, and Callie bolted up after him.

"Thank you for sitting with us." How could she innocently ask him to stay?

He stepped off the quilt, looking uncomfortable. "Ain't been to a Sunday meetin' since I was a wee thing. Brought back some memories. Thank you, Miss."

Mrs. Ingram rose as well. "I'm pleased you chose to join us, Mr. . . ?"

Callie held her breath. How would he introduce himself?

Orion squirmed before meeting her eyes. "Rion's fine, ma'am."

"Mr. Rion. Pleasure to meet you, sir." Mrs. Ingram nodded. "Even before the medicine show rolled into town, the church had planned a picnic for after the service today. You're welcome to stay, if you'd like. I believe Dr. Chellingworth and his bunch will be entertaining us in a short while."

Rion shook his head. "I appreciate the offer, but—"

"Please?" The word slipped from Callie's lips unbidden, and the boarders turned questioning glances her way. "You'd delight us all if you'd stay." She darted a glance at Mrs. Ingram and Joe, who'd wandered over. "Wouldn't he?"

They chorused their agreements.

Rion squirmed again. "Why're y'all bein' so kind?" He scratched at his beard. "Y'all are good, upstandin' folk. You ain't the type that usually gives me no never mind."

Callie cocked her head. "Why do you say that?"

He squinted. "Ain't nobody thrown much softness or care my way. Unlike you, in your fancy clothes and finery."

Oh dear. What experiences had he lived through since they were separated? Her own had been a mixed bag of hardship and love—adored by her adoptive parents. . .but hated by her adoptive brothers.

Had Rion wanted for even that much goodness? Or had his life gone off track in adulthood?

Mrs. Ingram offered a placid smile. "We all need kindness, Mr. Rion. Please accept ours."

He gawped, looking like he might crawl out of his skin. "Y'all didn't plan for me. There won't be enough food. Just enjoy the show, and I'll be about my business."

Lord, this is my brother! She almost couldn't breathe. *How do I convince him to stay?*

From her stool near the edge of the quilt, Hattie cleared her throat. "What are you afraid of, Mr. Rion?"

Every eye swung her way.

Joe's discreet, warning headshake was surely meant to stall Hattie's question, though she couldn't possibly reel it in once it was dangled out there.

Appearing befuddled, Rion's jaw cracked open. "Ain't afraid of nothin', Miss."

"Then stay. You said we seem like kind, upstanding people, and we've more than enough food to accommodate you. I made much of it myself, and I'm told I'm a fine cook."

"She is," several of the others confirmed.

He squirmed, but finally nodded grudgingly. "All right. I'll stay."

"Thank you, Mr. Rion." Emotion knotted Callie's throat. "We're happy to have you."

⌒

What happened here? Every one of Mrs. Ingram's boarders seemed pleased as punch that they'd convinced Rion Braddock to stay. In the months Joe had lived at Mrs. Ingram's boarding-house, he knew her to be a faith-filled woman who often made newcomers and outsiders feel at home—but they were usually women. And Callie had been the one to follow this gunman and convince him to stay—not Mrs. Ingram. Now the others had joined her cause. Even he had, without fully understanding why.

Her interest in Braddock seemed more than a question of whether he knew about the black horse, particularly when, at moments, she seemed nearly overcome with emotion. It was uncharacteristic.

"Mr. Nesbitt?" Mrs. Ingram's gentle call pulled him from his spinning thoughts. "Why don't you and Mr. Rion bring the picnic basket and the jugs of water from the wagon."

"Yes, ma'am." He motioned for Braddock to follow.

Walking shoulder to shoulder, they were well away from the others before either man spoke.

"So what's Miss Jarrett's story?" Braddock asked in a hush.

"What do you mean?"

"Pretty little gal like that, in her fancy clothes, chases down a man like me? What's she after?"

A chill raced down his spine. "Lay a hand on her, and you'll deal with me. She's nothing, if not a lady."

"You her beau, or somethin'?"

That was a shot across the bow. "Shouldn't matter. There are proper ways to treat ladies, and—"

"I know how to treat a gal right, Nesbitt. Just readin' the table, so to speak. Is she spoken for?"

Joe's hackles rose. "I've more than a passing interest, so back off."

Braddock smirked.

Reaching over the wagon's gate and dragging the picnic basket and two earthen jugs of water nearer, Joe turned on Braddock. "And since you've called it to our attention more than once, exactly what type of man are you, *Mr. Rion*? What's *your* story?"

With a discreet glance, the gunman lifted one jug, then the other, keeping his voice low. "As you already know, the name's Orion Braddock. What I said to Miss Jarrett is the truth. I ain't had much softness in my life. Not many I call friends. No place to live. I roam. It suits me."

"What do you do for money?"

"This and that. Sometimes lawman. Done some cattle work. Right now, I'm huntin' a few bounties."

The information rolled off Braddock's tongue with practiced precision—which meant either it was a well-told lie or it was the truth.

"Who're you hunting?"

Braddock eyed him. "You tryin' to steal my bounties?"

Lifting the basket from the wagon box, Joe laughed. "I'll steer clear of your bounties so long as you steer clear of Kezia Jarrett."

"I'd shake on it, but my hands are full." He hefted the jugs. "Your word'll do."

CHAPTER 9

As they indulged on Hattie's delicious fried chicken and pota-
toes, Callie's eye kept straying her brother's way. If he noticed,
he didn't let on.

"Miss?" Rion grinned at Hattie as he gleaned the last bit of
meat from a bone. "How'd you learn to cook so good? This is
about the best chicken I ever did taste."

Hattie blushed as she nodded in Mrs. Ingram's direction.
"Mama taught me."

His eyes widened under his hat's brim. "You're mother and
daughter. Guess I missed the family resemblance."

Mrs. Ingram laughed. "You'll find little likeness between us,
Mr. Rion. My husband Owen and I adopted Hattie after she
lost her family."

Hattie nodded. "I was small when it happened, so I don't
remember it."

"Thank God!" Mrs. Ingram patted her arm.

"Yes, thank God. Before my third birthday, my family's
home caught fire. By some miracle, I survived, though my legs
were badly burned. My parents and infant brother perished."
Swallowing hard, she nodded toward her adoptive mother. "The
Ingrams heard of the fire, and when they learned of my survival,
they traveled for weeks—all the way to Fort Laramie—to lay

hands on and pray for me. I was in the care of an army doctor, with no real prospects of who would take me in. Once they saw me, they took charge of my care. It's by the grace of God and their prayers that I didn't succumb to my injuries."

Mrs. Ingram grasped Hattie's hand. "Owen and I never did have children, though we wanted many. In our older age, God brought us a beautiful daughter."

Already on the edge of emotion, Callie fought tears. "I hadn't heard that story."

"I thought we'd told you, child."

Only that Hattie had been burned—but not how.

Before she could put her thought into words, Dr. Chellingworth—now dressed in black trousers, a red coat, a white shirt with some kind of a flecked pattern, a string tie, and his dark-eyed spectacles—stepped from one of the wagons and, in a booming voice, called the field to order.

"Thank you, one and all, for staying for our show. As many of you already know, my name is Dr. Darby Chellingworth, and many of my entourage have come to America both to entertain and to heal our across-the-pond neighbors." He spouted some of the same lines he'd said from the previous afternoon's introduction in town, and after only a moment, he stepped back. In his place, a slim man, taller than Joe, stepped out in black trousers and a crisp, white shirt, his mop of medium-brown curls falling across his forehead. Without a word, he produced three red balls from his trouser pockets, promptly dropped two, and made a frantic show of chasing both down. The crowd chuckled. As he stood again, curls flopped into his eyes, and with an exaggerated puff, he blew the hair so it cleared his eyes—but fell back again. Pocketing the balls, he overdramatically parted his curls, tucked them behind his ears and, licking each palm, smoothed the hair. Again, the crowd laughed, and he began to juggle.

Eyes pinned on the display ahead, Rion cleared his throat. "Count yourself lucky you were taken in by good people. Plenty of orphans ain't so fortunate."

Callie's breath caught, and she focused on the last bites of her chicken to keep from looking his way. If only she weren't undercover. If she were between assignments or wasn't working for the Pinkertons at all, she could reveal who she was.

But it was because she was an operative that she'd been able to come west and look for Rion. She couldn't risk their investigation by revealing her true identity, yet balancing the two objectives was proving harder than she'd imagined.

"Were you an orphan?" Joe's direct question jarred her from her thoughts.

For a moment, Rion didn't move. . .then he nodded slowly, his voice gruff. "Lost my folks when I was ten. They went out late one night—somethin' to do with my father losin' his professor job at Columbia College real sudden. They never came back. Found out later, they were in a carriage accident."

She tried to draw a breath as a wave of homesickness crashed over her. She'd been young—just days shy of her sixth birthday. Two loving parents had kissed her good night, and she'd awakened the next morning as an orphan.

One of the other women turned a compassionate gaze his way. "Were you an only child?"

"I was the oldest. I was s'posed to take care of my sisters, but—"

Callie's stomach roiled. "But what?" She couldn't recall all the details of how they'd been separated—only that they were.

He glanced at her, then back to the juggling act, which consisted of the original man and now a buxom, dark-haired woman in a pale blue dress. The two pitched brightly colored batons back and forth, each moving farther apart, to the delight of the crowd.

"After I got caught stealin' food to feed my sisters, we were taken to an orphanage then put on an orphan train. They promised they'd keep the three of us together, but my littlest sister got placed out near Chicago, and the middle one in St. Louis. I got dumped out here with an ornery old cuss."

Head swimming, Callie dug her hand against her tender ribs. The jolt shocked her enough to clear her thoughts some, but when she probed a particularly painful spot, her breath whooshed out louder than she'd intended.

All eyes turned her way, and Rion squinted. "You all right, Miss?"

She covered her mouth, gave a cough, and cleared her throat. "Forgive me."

What a fool she was making of herself.

He eyed her a moment more, and she took a long gulp of water.

"Have you ever tried to find your sisters?" another women asked.

"Yes, Miss." Rion looked her way. "Gone back to both cities at least half a dozen times."

Her heart pounded. Rion *had* wanted to find them. Feeling suddenly faint, Callie laced her fingers and squeezed her palms together in her lap. How could she sit, feet from her brother, listening to his account of their separation and *not* react?

Lord Jesus, help me.

"Kezia?" Joe's voice dripped concern.

"Are you all right, dear?" Mrs. Ingram swooped in, cradling her face in both hands. "Can you hear me?"

"Yes, ma'am." She focused on the older woman's face.

"What's wrong, child?"

"I—" She gulped a breath. "Nothing. Just a moment of dizziness."

Mrs. Ingram shifted a hand to her forehead. "You look pale.

Perhaps, after the last few days, we should get you h—"

"No, ma'am. I don't want to trouble anyone." Callie straightened and pulled free of Mrs. Ingram's grasp. "The feeling is already starting to pass."

"Child, have some sense." Mrs. Ingram locked an ironclad stare on her. "You were nearly trampled by a horse, then handled roughly by that awful man. You need to rest."

"Beggin' your pardon, but..." Rion looked their way. "What happened?"

Joe spoke first. "Miss Jarrett and I were in a clearing up in the mountains, and some durn fool stampeded our horses. Kezia's mare knocked her down as it ran off."

"It left her bruised." Mrs. Ingram caught her eye, as if reminding her.

Rion's glance narrowed. "You know who did it, Miss?"

"Some hothead on a black horse," Joe blurted.

"That could be a fair number of people. You got anything more to go on? What'd the rider look like?"

This time, she cut him off. "It all happened so fast, we didn't see many details."

"Understood. What's this about rough handlin'?"

"Yesterday. We found the man you were arguing with in an alley, disoriented, with a bloody nose."

"Yeah, I bloodied it. What about him?"

"I asked him a question, and..." They'd not told anyone how the man had grabbed her hair. "I got jostled and fell."

"He almost pitched her into the watering trough."

"I fell against it, and water slopped down the front of my dress."

Rion's eyes went cold. "I told ya earlier. Steer wide of Ellwood Garvin. He's the ornery cuss what took me from the orphan train. He murdered two girls years ago. Other orphans, like me."

No one, including Joe, spoke, too stunned by Braddock's admission. Then Mrs. Ingram stood.

"We should get you home."

"No, ma'am." As Callie shook her head, her hand strayed to her forehead, and she forced herself to stillness. Joe's heart lurched. "I don't want to ruin everyone's day."

"I'll take her." At the same moment Joe spoke the words, Hattie echoed the sentiment.

Mrs. Ingram looked at them. "Thank you both, but I'll drive her home. Hattie, if I know you, you're already uncomfortable. Come along, if you don't mind. You can stay with Miss Jarrett, and once I get the horses put up, I'll return. In the meantime, Mr. Nesbitt, you stay with the others."

With a killer on the loose and newcomer Rion Braddock right here, how could he disagree? Besides, he and Braddock needed to talk about what he'd just said. "Yes, ma'am. I'll help Kezia to the wagon."

While the other women repacked the basket and carried it toward the wagon, Joe rose and helped Callie up. Behind him, Rion Braddock offered his assistance to Hattie.

In minutes, Mrs. Ingram, Hattie, and Callie sat on the wagon bench as Mrs. Ingram backed the team away. He and Braddock watched until they were headed into town.

"Reckon I'll get on myself." Braddock nodded in the same direction.

"Why don't you stay? Tell me more about this. . .what'd you say his name was? Garland?"

"Ellwood Garvin."

"What'd you mean—he murdered two girls?"

"Exactly what it sounds like." Braddock nodded. "The man

collected orphans. Mostly, he wanted the boys for cheap labor around his homestead. He worked us hard—and gave us little enough to eat. But twice in the four years I lived at his place, he took in a girl—supposedly to cook and keep house. When they first came, they smiled at us boys, shot us some enticing glances. But before long, they started pullin' inside themselves. No more smilin' or meetin' your eyes. A couple times, I saw bruises on their arms or faces." For an instant, he simply shook his head, a hard look in his eye. "We all figured he was. . .usin' them hard too."

To Joe's understanding, the town leaders usually worked with the orphan trains to ensure the children were placed into decent, upstanding homes. How had Garvin been given multiple orphans— especially girls? "Why do you think he murdered 'em?"

"He said the first ran off in the night. She came to stay soon after I arrived, and then she wasn't there no more. The second one? She came two years later. I was older. I understood more. Not long before she disappeared, I noticed her belly was roundin'—and not because she was eatin' good, if you understand my meanin'."

His own belly churning, Joe nodded.

"Then, one night, we heard awful screams from the house. The oldest boys tried to get inside, but Garvin had the doors barred. The next day, he told us she'd run off too."

"But the doors remained barred. . ."

"All the way till morning. We watched. Those doors never opened, and we never saw her again."

If Braddock was telling the truth, could Garvin be their murderer? He didn't fit the description of tall with dark hair and beard, but. . . "You lived there, and who else?"

"In the years I was there, he had a handful of us boys. Seth, Pete, Bobby, Dutch, and me."

"Dutch—as in the café owner here in town?"

"One and the same."

He eyed Braddock. "What happened?"

The man shrugged. "We all figured it was only a matter of time before he came for us. So we ran off. Pete headed to California, Bobby went to Texas. Me, Seth, and Dutch hid out in the caves here in these parts. None of us ever went back. Garvin's place is a week's travel from here, but on occasion, he shows up around here. Always a sorry time when he does."

"Does Garvin have any sons of his own—not adopted?"

"None I know of." Braddock's brow furrowed. "Why?"

"Curious. I like to keep my eye out for danger, and often, traits like those can run in families."

"To my knowledge, the man never married. And I ain't aware he's got kin."

As Braddock spoke, a gunshot rang out. Heart hammering, Joe hunched low and spun to face the noise, pawing his thigh for his missing pistol. Braddock also spun, jerking his Colt free, though he stopped short of taking aim.

In the distance, a woman with a head of red curls, wearing a buckskin dress and a Stetson hat, stood atop one of the wagons, rifle to her shoulder, as she fired at someone on the farthest wagon. The man held something up for the crowd to see. Gasps and applause ensued.

Both he and Braddock breathed deep and let the tension drain from their muscles. His cheeks hot with embarrassment, Joe glanced at the other man, who looked just as uncomfortable. Braddock holstered the pistol.

A wagon rumbled into view and turned their way. Driven by a man, it was full of women of all ages and sizes. Beside him, Braddock grunted.

"What?"

He jutted his chin toward the oncoming wagon. "Soiled doves."

"How do you know—" He shook his head. "Never mind.

What do you figure they're doing?"

"Town ordinance says they can't open saloons and brothels on Sundays. Since they can't *be* the entertainment, they're probably comin' *for* the entertainment." Braddock motioned toward the ongoing show.

He'd never been one to seek such company—but he'd seen plenty of prostitutes who congregated and followed the troops during the war. They were a bawdy bunch with language to match. None of Mrs. Ingram's boarders needed to be exposed to such behavior.

"You really figure they're coming here?"

"Guarantee it. None of the businesses in town are open, and they're headin' this way. Ain't much beyond but mountains."

Joe glanced to where his housemates watched the woman sharpshooter line up for another shot.

"You want to help—"

The roar of the gun interrupted, and his nerves fired, sending his mind back to a smoky battlefield. He shook off the feeling, cleared his throat, and tried again.

"Would you mind helping me gather the other women and get 'em headed toward Mrs. Ingram's place?"

"Reckon I wouldn't."

Together, they hurried back to the remaining four women and urged them to gather Mrs. Ingram's quilts, the earthen water jugs, and any other belongings and come along. Desiring to see the show, two of the gals resisted until the doves pulled up and spilled out. It only took a couple of mouthy comments before all of Mrs. Ingram's gals hurried to comply. With Rion Braddock leading and Joe bringing up the rear, they walked the ladies out of the field, almost without issue.

Almost.

As they neared the edge of the crowd, one of the doves

watched Braddock file past. She sneered at Mrs. Ingram's boarders, but her gaze drifted back to Rion, and the sneer dissolved into surprise.

She rushed up and grabbed his shirt. "You're the one."

Joe urged his charges past Braddock with an admonition to *keep walking*, then hurried to Rion's aid. "Let him go, Miss."

"You were with—"

Braddock grabbed both her hands, entwined in the fabric of his shirt, and must have squeezed them. Her face contorted as she released him with a whimper.

Once free, he shoved past her, and Joe followed. They caught up to the women and ushered them through the parked wagons and back toward town.

"What was that about?" Joe eyed Braddock.

"Durned if I know," Braddock growled. "I'm convinced half those doves are loco."

"Do you know her?"

"Do I look like a man who frequents such places?"

"How am I s'posed to answer that? All sorts of men do."

"Well, I ain't one of 'em." He uttered the words between clenched teeth, his gaze stony.

Then what had the woman been thinking?

"You got them?" Braddock nodded toward the women. "Or do you still need me?"

"I figure I can get 'em home safe from here."

"All right, then. Good talkin' to ya." He cleared his throat. "Ladies, thank you for the enjoyable mornin'."

He tipped his hat, and as they neared one of many full hitching posts along the street, Braddock veered off and untied two fine mounts—a smaller brown, and a big black with three white stockings.

CHAPTER 10

Once Mrs. Ingram unlocked the door, both Callie and Hattie entered.

"Do you need help up the stairs, Miss Jarrett?" Mrs. Ingram called.

Callie shook her head and started upstairs without a word.

At the top of the steps, she paced down the hall to the second flight, her ear snagging on the whispers of the other women.

"Let her rest, but be sure to check on her, please."

"Yes, Mama."

"I'll be back as soon as the medicine show is over."

"We'll be fine."

Callie climbed the second flight, headed to her room, and locked herself inside. There, she fell across her bed, buried her face in a pillow, and let several convulsive sobs grab her.

She'd found and talked to her brother, but she was no closer to rekindling a relationship than before. In fact, for all she knew, he might disappear, and she'd never see him again.

Lord, what was I to do? Once they were undercover, they weren't to break cover for any reason.

In some of her Pinkerton training, she'd learned how the first female Pinkerton, Kate Warne, had lived so deeply undercover on one case that, even after solving the robbery and convincing the thief's wife to reveal where the money was hidden, she had carried on a friendship with the woman for months until they'd naturally drifted apart. The woman never suspected Mrs. Warne was anyone other than a dear friend with her best interest in mind.

Such a life had sounded so opulent and exciting, and she'd loved it. Until today. Today, she'd seen no way to reveal her identity to the brother she'd longed for these last fifteen years.

Would she ever see Rion again?

She sobbed into the pillow, heart shattered. She had no way to find him. Doing so would take more pure, dumb luck—just like this time.

⌒

"You want to explain yourself?" Joe glared Rion Braddock's way.

"Explain what?"

He stabbed a finger toward the black horse. "That's the animal that scattered our mounts. Kezia coulda been trampled."

Braddock shook his head fiercely. "I don't know what you saw, but I was nowhere near these parts the past few days."

"Where were you?"

"What—you plannin' to check up on me?" Braddock turned that same smirk on him as he had earlier.

"Gentlemen!" one of the women snapped. "Do you both mind?" She turned to him. "Mr. Nesbitt, we'd like to go home, please."

Joe scowled Braddock's way before he finally turned. "All right."

That sneer tinged Braddock's voice. "Y'all have a nice day— and please, tell that pretty Miss Jarrett I hope she's feelin' better real soon."

Irritated, he shoved past Braddock. "Let's go."

No one spoke as they carried on. Once they made the turn

to head toward the boardinghouse, Joe allowed a discreet glance behind them and found Braddock watching their retreat. A chill swept him. The big man eyed them with that smug look. Was it just that Callie had seen him arguing with Garvin near a black horse that made her follow him—or was there more?

As they neared the livery a few blocks from home, Mrs. Ingram exited the boardinghouse's fenced yard but stopped as the ladies hurried her way.

"What happened?" she asked as they turned into the gate.

"We left when some of the doves from one of the bawdy houses came to partake of the entertainment."

The old woman's jaw firmed. "Thank you, Mr. Nesbitt. That was a wise decision."

Like a mother hen, Mrs. Ingram gathered her chicks inside. Before he followed, Joe took one final glance back and found Braddock on his big black horse, watching from far down the street.

Lord God Almighty, that man's makin' me uneasy.

CHAPTER 11

When a soft knock sounded at her door, Callie jerked her face out of her pillow and dabbed her eyes and nose with her handkerchief. She cleared her throat softly to hide the tears that surely marred her voice.

"You don't need to check on me, Hattie. I'm well enough. Just resting."

"It's not Hattie."

Joe's deep voice jolted her, and she wrestled herself up to sit on the edge of the bed. "I, um. . ." She fought to swallow her tears. "You didn't stay to see the show?"

"Plans changed." He paused. "May I speak to you?" Another hesitation. "Without a door between us? I have some news."

News. . . About Rion?

She rose and, handkerchief in hand, looked in the vanity mirror across the room. Her hair was mussed; her eyes were puffy; her dress was rumpled. Oh, she was a sight.

"Just a moment, please."

Callie tucked the stray wisps of hair into place, tried to smooth her dress, then splashed a little water on her face. It would do nothing to resolve her swollen eyes, but at least she might feel more refreshed. Once she'd patted her face dry, she opened the door and, despite her best effort, turned a pitiful attempt at a smile on him.

"What news?"

He stared—then glanced down the hall. Finding no one, Joe pushed his way into her room and closed the door.

"What's the matter?" His voice rumbled, concern once again dripping from his words. When she couldn't bring herself to answer, he ducked to meet her eyes. "Callie, please. Talk to me. What happened out there?"

She couldn't force herself to tell him. Not when she'd nearly broken her cover. Nearly failed... He might tell Mr. Pinkerton, and she'd be removed from the case—or worse, from the agency.

"Why'd you follow Braddock in the first place? Was it just that you'd seen him arguing, or...?"

Callie gave a single, hesitant nod. "He's the only lead we had." And not even a lead on the murders, specifically. Simply a lead on who'd run off their horses.

"So why are you crying?"

How could she explain without risking her job...or giving away too much? She had to divert attention from the truth.

"I... It started with Mrs. Ingram explaining how she and her husband adopted Hattie. I hadn't heard that story, and my heart broke for Hattie."

"It's a hard story, but it was more than that." Again, he ducked to meet her gaze. "Was hearing a story about another orphan too difficult?"

She nodded.

He rubbed his palms down his pant legs. "I understand. Seeing my parents murdered in Kansas before the war because of their staunch support of abolition has made me feel the pain of others who've been orphaned."

Her throat growing thick with emotion, she lunged into his arms, and words tumbled free.

"I was adopted from an orphan train." A hiccuping sob slipped out. "The same train Rion Braddock was on."

⌒

Overcoming his shock, Joe circled her in a reassuring embrace. "So you recognized Braddock?"

She nodded against his chest. "I recognized his name when Garvin said it—and his likeness today. I—I knew his sisters a little bit—especially Andromeda." She sobbed again, and he pulled her tighter.

Orion. Andromeda. What names. . .

Joe shook his head. "What are the odds?" No wonder she'd been on the verge of tears. This hit close to home. And what strength of will. She'd held herself together despite this shock.

"Hard to believe." She barely breathed the words.

He rubbed her back, liking her small frame tucked against him. "So where were you adopted?"

"In Chicago."

"How old were you?"

"Six. I was terrified. Terrified when they put me on the train and terrified when they took me from it. I was so scared, I. . ."

He stroked her back, enjoying her nearness and the fact that she was sharing a vulnerable piece of herself. "You what?"

"I jumped from Papa's wagon into the middle of the busy Chicago street. I could've been killed, but Mr. Pinkerton rode up on a horse and plucked me out of the mud. Carried me to safety."

"Allan Pinkerton saved your life?"

She drew back to look up at him, eyes still teary. "It's why I've always wanted to work for him."

Joe chuckled. "That's amazing."

"I owe him so much. I don't want to disappoint him. We

have to solve this case, Joe."

Even through her tears, she was beautiful. He smoothed the stray hairs back from her eyes and, without thinking, bent nearer. "We will," he whispered.

He pressed his lips to hers, and she gasped under the gentle pressure. Startled, he pulled back, inches away. "I'm sorry. I—I shouldn't have—" His face burned, and he tried to pull back altogether, but she grasped his shoulders and pressed her lips to his.

Joe's mind reeled. For the barest second, they simply stood, lips touching, until he gently let his mouth wander over hers. This time, her lips parted without the gasp, and she melted against him, returning the affection. He wrapped her in his arms once more, deepening the kiss. She slid her hands to his neck, and her touch sent lightning coursing through him. Breaking the kiss suddenly, he looked around.

"I should go."

"But—"

He opened the door and peeked into the hall before he backed out.

Her eyes brimmed again. "Joe."

His given name sounded good on her tongue, even with her hurt and disappointment coiled around it.

Lord Almighty, help me! I really shouldn't be thinkin' such thoughts. Not about a fellow operative, especially one as pretty as Callie Wilson.

Before he turned, she caught his elbow. Even through his shirtsleeve, her touch was like fire.

Tears spilled down her flaming cheeks. "At least tell me the news you mentioned."

News? "Right. Your Mr. Braddock? He rides a black horse with three white stockings."

CHAPTER 12

Monday, June 23, 1873

The fact that the soiled doves had come to see the medicine show the previous afternoon had caused many of the churchgoing folks to leave, which meant that for a second day, Dr. Chellingworth hadn't sold much of his Heaven-Sent Miracle Elixir. Thus, he and his entertainers stayed on in Cambria Springs.

The medicine show provided just the diversion Callie needed to keep from overthinking the embarrassment of the previous day's kiss. She'd never been kissed before, so the unexpectedness startled her. But she'd *thought* she covered her inexperience well enough. She'd kissed Joe right back. Her heart had pounded, and her head spun in the best ways. It was breathtaking and delightful, and she hadn't wanted it to end.

Yet he'd run off with nothing more than the news that her brother rode a black horse with white stockings.

Was she so repulsive he'd wanted to avoid her at the evening meal and breakfast as well?

"Stop it." She frowned. "Keep your wits, Kezia." She forced her mind back to her drawings.

Callie's pencil flew over the paper, capturing the medicine show's singers, a short, heavyset woman with brown hair and an average-height man with dark locks, liberally streaked with white. Voices as clear as crystal, the pair sang several songs—both hymns and popular tunes. As they finished, they waved and disappeared into one of the wagons. In their place, a woman in a long buckskin hunting shirt, belted at the waist, and an ankle-length skirt made her way to the center, a rifle cradled in the crook of her arm.

Shuffling to a fresh page, Callie began to capture the image of the woman, from her bright-red curls falling over her shoulders to her intricately beaded attire and western-styled hat shading her eyes.

"Good afternoon." The beautiful woman's British lilt was surprising. "What a nice crowd for a Monday afternoon." The woman smiled at the audience. "My name is Elisabeth Gates. Elisabeth with an s."

Callie scribbled her name on the page's corner and quickly returned to her sketching. Miss Gates spoke about her act of trick shooting and riding and what they could expect from her. As she droned on, Callie squinted and sketched, over and over, capturing the woman's likeness.

"Could I have a volunteer from the audience?" She squinted at the audience.

"What kinda help?" a man off to Callie's right hollered.

"Thank you for volunteering, kind sir! What is your name?"

"Now, wait just a minute! I didn't say—"

The crowd guffawed as she laid aside her rifle and marched toward him. "Come, now. Be a gentleman and help a lady in need."

"Aww, really?" The hatless man, about thirty, looked uncomfortable when she extended both hands to him.

"Yes, my good man. Really. What is your name?"

"Me and my big mouth." He stood, stoop-shouldered. "The name's Charlie."

The woman's smile turned teasing, and she patted his cheek. "I promise, you won't mind it a bit, Charlie."

Callie shifted to roughing out the pair's faces and bodies, capturing the moment Miss Gates cupped the stranger's cheek. She drank in the details of the man's features—his long, thin face, auburn hair, and jaw darkening with stubble. It was lovely just to draw, trying to capture enough detail to be a guide for adding more features later.

Miss Gates coaxed him forward and explained his job: to stand atop one of their wagons and throw glass balls into the air for her to shoot.

"You ain't plannin' to hit me, are ya?" The man shot her an anxious look.

"I wouldn't dream of it."

With assistance from some of the other showmen, they both climbed onto two different wagons, and at her call, the man began throwing the balls into the air.

Gunfire split the air, and no matter how fast or how far apart Charlie threw them, Miss Gates never missed, to the delight of her onlookers. After she'd thanked him, the fella headed back to his place, and one of the other showmen replaced him as Miss Gates shot playing cards from his hands and performed other risky feats.

At the end of her shooting sequence, Miss Gates excused herself and disappeared into one of the wagons with her rifle— and emerged again only a moment later, empty-handed. She wore no hat, and her flaming red curls had been tied back with a ribbon. Now, she wore a short-sleeved tunic and a pair of loose-fitting pants, with heavy leather gloves that reached partway up her forearms. As quickly as she stepped out, a beautiful white horse galloped past, and Miss Gates grabbed the saddle horn and vaulted over the horse's back in a fluid movement. Her feet touched down on the opposite side of the horse, and she vaulted again, returning to where she began, then vaulted a third time, landing astride in the saddle. The crowd hooted in excitement.

Callie gaped and leafed to a fresh page to capture the scene. For several minutes, the woman rode back and forth, standing atop the horse's back or dangling from the saddle by one leg or other fantastical deeds until finally, she brought her white horse to a sliding stop, leapt down, and took an extravagant bow. As the crowd applauded with catcalls and hooting, the woman motioned to her horse, gave a two-handed wave, and swatted the horse on the rump. As it trotted off to a waiting handler, she disappeared into her wagon.

Following her, the overly tall man she'd seen before the church service yesterday appeared and, also in a proper English accent, introduced himself as Cyril Pennock, the show's strong-man. Attired in close-fitting pants and some sort of specialized footwear, he wore no shirt, showing off his heavily muscled upper body. For several minutes, he amazed the audience with his ability to tear an entire deck of faro cards in half, bend heavy metal bars around his neck, and break chains with his bare hands. Asking for another volunteer, he chose a heavyset man from the crowd and lifted him with one hand, straight over his head. His final feat was to get ten strong fellas from the audience to play tug-of-war with him—ten against one. In an epic battle of strength, the ten men tried to pull Mister Pennock off balance, but after a short while, he gave one strong pull on the rope and brought them all down.

As the strongman waved to the crowd, Dr. Chellingworth reappeared and thanked the audience for their time. Yet again, he made a pitch for his Heaven-Sent Miracle Elixir, able to cure many common diseases, maladies, and conditions, and directed all who were interested to come to the tent behind the line of wagons to see his collection of oddities: an albino man, a dwarf, a giant, a bearded lady, and much more. Ten cents to view them all.

Along with many others, Callie rose and tucked her drawing into her satchel, then folded the quilt she'd brought to sit on. Discreetly, she felt in her pocket for the coins she'd tucked there. Ten cents to see all the oddities Dr. Chellingworth had assembled—and avoid Joe and the embarrassment of yesterday a little while longer.

⌒

A pail in one hand and a brush in the other, Joe finished cutting in with the white paint beneath the mercantile's roofline and dragged the sizable bead of paint downward, careful not to slop any on the tarpaulin-covered boardwalk beneath. Even in the shade of the new store's wide, covered walkway, it was hot—probably because of the hundred trips up and down the ladder he'd made in painting the exterior walls. He'd made good progress since morning, though his mind wasn't fully on his work. Instead, it was on the pretty little gal he'd kissed.

Almighty Father, why didn't You stop me?

He never should've gone up to see if she was well.

But he should have. He was her fellow operative, after all.

Where he'd gone awry was closing himself in the room with her.

"It all would've been fine, except she threw herself into your arms." He shook his head at his own whispered words.

How could a woman he should have *no* feelings for, except for the concern and admiration of a fellow Pinkerton, entice him so? She'd felt good in his arms. Small and dainty, vulnerable. Her form had melded against his so perfectly it had been hard not to enjoy the moment. Holding her, comforting her, had just felt *right*. But their jobs were such that they both needed to keep level heads, and he already found himself drawn to her. Her skill as a detective. Her determination to prove her brothers wrong. The fact that she was an orphan like him. Not to mention how pretty and defenseless she seemed. His heart and mind had already crossed lines they shouldn't have. So he'd left the boardinghouse immediately after kissing her and busied himself drumming up some kind of odd job to do this week. He'd not returned in time for the evening meal, nor did he stick around for breakfast.

"You're an idiot, Joe Trenamen." He mumbled the words under his breath. "Callie deserves better." He slapped another brush full of paint onto the wood slats of the wall. "Better than you."

"Mr. Nesbitt."

Startled, Joe jerked, sloshing the paint inside the can. Wrapping an arm around the ladder, he turned to find Hattie in her small horse-drawn cart on the street.

"Howdy, Miss Hattie. Hang on a minute." He smoothed out the dollop of paint he'd slapped up, descended, set the paint and brush aside, and strode out to speak to her. "Everything all right?"

"Everything's fine. I'm running errands, then going to visit a friend. Will you be there for tonight's meal?"

"I'd planned on it." Although it would be uncomfortable around Callie, durn it.

"Would you please do me a favor?"

"Hunt up some food?" He'd been asked often enough, and it was always a welcome diversion.

"No, someone else is handling that task. I'll be staying overnight with my friend. I stopped by the post office, and there was a letter for Miss Jarrett. Would you see she gets it?" She held up the thick envelope, addressed in a neat hand.

"Yes, Miss." Wiping his hands on a rag, he reached for the mail. "I'll be heading that way once I finish painting this wall." He indicated the half-painted wall. It would likely be another hour before he'd be finished, cleaned up for the day, and able to get back to Mrs. Ingram's place. "I'd be happy to pass it along."

"Much appreciated."

His thoughts darted in a different direction. "You won't be returning to the boardinghouse tonight?"

"I may not be home for a day or two. My friend, Annie Tunstall, is with child and having a difficult time. Her husband's been called away for a few days and asked me to stay with her until he returns."

His skin crawled at the thought. "Given the. . .difficulties we've seen around these parts lately, please be careful."

She nodded. "I promise."

"Your mother knows where you'll be?"

"Yes. And Annie's nine-year-old son will be with us. She's got decent neighbors on either side. We'll be watched over, I assure you."

"Mind if I check in on you myself—that is, if you're planning to stay more than just overnight?"

"I'd welcome it, Mr. Nesbitt. Thank you."

"All right, then. Count on it." Tucking the envelope into his back pocket, he stepped back, and Hattie waved as she drove off.

When he turned toward the storefront again, two young boys hovered over his paint pail, backs to him. Joe hurried in their direction.

"Hey! Get out of that!" he groused, and both boys bolted up and spun, eyes as big as whiskey barrel lids. Frightened, they ran, something long and narrow trailing from one of their pudgy little fists. As the kid raced past, the string—or whatever it was—caught on Joe's pant leg, trailing a white slash across the blue twill before the kid dropped it in his haste to escape.

Joe watched their retreat, then looked at the paint pail. They'd seemingly not disturbed the pail or brush—both were exactly as he'd left them. But starting from the paint that had dripped from the brush onto the tarpaulin, there were a number of little paint drawings on the canvas—as well as some snaking paint lines. He crossed to the long ropelike thing the one boy dropped and, picking it up carefully, found it was the viny growth of some kind of plant that the boys must have dragged through the paint droplets.

With a sigh, he tossed the vine into the street and set back to work, thankful the boys hadn't caused any further damage.

CHAPTER 13

Callie glanced at the sky, noting the lateness of the hour. She shouldn't have spent so much time perusing Dr. Chellingworth's Collection of Oddities tent as she had. She'd stayed because she'd hoped to meet the talented Miss Gates, as well as to view the unusual men and women found inside. However, when she'd asked her new friend, the bearded lady, whether the sharpshooter would come out to meet with the audience, Miss Ralston had cut that idea down quickly, explaining in her charming southern drawl that Miss Gates usually required rest after all the physically taxing riding tricks.

Disappointed, Callie hurried to the livery to collect Lady and the fishing supplies she'd stashed there before going to the medicine show. She'd promised Mrs. Ingram she would catch their dinner before returning. But where was the best spot? Perhaps the hostler could give her some direction. After she'd saddled Lady and led her to the front, she asked, and he directed her to his favorite fishing hole with a plea to keep the location quiet.

Thanking him, she mounted and set off, grateful the spot was just a little way up the mountain. As she headed to Adams Street, where the young man said she'd find the trail to the stream, a familiar voice called out. As she turned, Joe hurried across the road, a pail and paintbrush in hand. Maybe she should pretend she didn't see him. But no. He was still her partner. She headed over to speak with him.

"Afternoon. Where are you heading, Miss?"

Miss. . . The courteous distance in that word struck like a slap across the cheek.

"I suppose that's my business, isn't it, Mr. Nesbitt?"

He drew back, brow furrowed. "Forgive me. I suppose it is."

Swallowing her hurt, she shot him a half-hearted smile. "Did you need something?"

He transferred the wet paintbrush into his left hand and wiped his hand on the rag trailing from his hip pocket. Then, pulling something from his back pocket, he handed it over.

"Hattie asked me to deliver this to you this evening."

Mama's stationery. . .and her beautiful script. Homesickness flooded her. She cleared her throat, pressing her lips together until she was certain she had her emotions under control.

"Thank you. I appreciate it."

"You all right?"

"Fine, Mr. Nesbitt. Thank you for asking. Anything else?"

"Just curious." He paused. "Did you ever get those white marks out of your dress from that day our horses got scattered?"

"No, why?"

"I didn't think you had. I recall you scrubbing it." He waved at a white slash across his pant leg above the knee. "A couple of young boys were playing in the paint drops while I spoke to Miss Hattie, and one of 'em slashed paint across my pants with a vine or something he'd gotten in the paint. The marks reminded me some of your dress, so I was wondering if you'd found a way to get those stains out."

She shot him a smoldering look. "I'm not doing your laundry, if that's what you're asking."

Joe's cheeks turned a deep red. "I wasn't suggesting that. Just asking."

"Thank you, Mr. Nesbitt, but I can't imagine there being fresh paint on the mountainside that night our horses were run off, so whatever it was had to be from nature. So even if I had gotten the stains out, my methods may not work for your pants. Now if you haven't any more business with me, I need to be off."

"To. . . ?"

"I promised the young man I wouldn't tell."

His eyes rounded then went stormy, and he shifted the pail and brush to his right hand and braced his left against Lady's shoulder. "You're going to meet a young man?" His words leaked from between his clenched teeth.

She met his gaze with a fierce look of her own. "I'm going fishing—for our dinner tonight. But the young man who kindly told me where his best fishin' hole is doesn't want it widely known. Now I'll thank you to move. Mrs. Ingram'll want to eat at a reasonable hour."

Joe's jaw hinged open as he stepped back. Tucking the letter from home underneath her vest, she touched her heel to Lady's side, ready to be away from the discomfiting discussion.

Two blocks down, she found Adams Street and, traversing the steep thoroughfare, found the path her hostler friend had mentioned. Following his directions, Callie found the stream, tied Lady, gathered her rifle and fishing supplies, and settled on the bank. Once she'd dropped her baited hook in the water and coiled the loose end of the string in her hand, she unsealed the letter.

Her mother addressed her by her real name, gave the general news that everyone was well, and promised she would write a proper letter soon—but that the included correspondence had come from St. Louis, and she wanted to forward it quickly.

Hands trembling, Callie turned to the included letter, written in a neat but unfamiliar hand, addressed to Callie Wilson, with a postmark from St. Louis, Missouri.

Where Andromeda had been adopted years ago.

Information Rion confirmed. He'd said he'd gone back, trying to find both of them on multiple occasions without success.

She tucked a finger under the wax-sealed flap and opened it, though before she could unfold the pages, something tugged on her fishing line.

She dropped the letter and gave a sharp pull to set the hook. The line sliced the surface of the water as the fish zigzagged, attempting to flee. She let it go a short way before she began pulling it in. As she drew the line in, hand over hand, she saw that the fish appeared to be a sizable specimen.

A gunshot rang out as she reached to pull the fish from the water. Heart pounding, she lurched sideways for her rifle and jerked it to her shoulder. A moment later, a deer burst through the brush on the far side of the stream, raced past, and careened into the trees beyond.

Leaves rustled and heavy footsteps sounded, then Rion Braddock stalked up the same path, his own gun cradled in the crook of his arm. He stopped short at the sight of her.

"Well, howdy, Miss Jarrett. You see my dinner come runnin' this way?"

She lowered the rifle slowly. "If you mean a frightened deer, it went that way."

"That deer ain't long for this world." He eyed her. "What're you doin'?"

She set the rifle aside and tried to lift her fishing line, though it was no longer in her hand. Perturbed, she found the coil of twine bobbing along the water's surface some distance downstream before it disappeared around a bend. With a sigh, she flung a hand in that direction.

"I promised everyone at Mrs. Ingram's boardinghouse a fish dinner tonight, but your gunshot startled me, and like a ninny, I dropped the line." Both the fish and her hook were long gone by now.

His features turned sheepish. "Real sorry. Ain't used to many folks bein' up 'round here."

"You frequent these parts, do you?"

Rion shrugged. "Like I told your Mr. Nesbitt, I sleep wherever I find to lay my head."

"He's not *my* Mr. Nesbitt." He'd made that plenty clear. . .

Brow furrowing, Rion shot her a strange look. "All right, then. But like I told him, I move around a lot. There's a cave just up that way that makes a good campsite when I need easy access to Cambria Springs." He hooked a thumb in the direction he'd come from.

So he was near enough, maybe she could find him as needed. Not with an address where she could send her correspondence, like with—

Andromeda! The letter. She shot to her feet and spun in a circle, searching for the papers she'd dropped to focus on the fish. The gentle breeze had carried them several feet away and trapped the papers against the brush along the riverbank. Heart pounding, she snatched the pages up, looking to be sure she had both her mother's note and the yet-unread missive, then tucked them deep into her skirt pocket. When she faced him, he watched her with interest.

"Sorry." Her cheeks flamed. "A letter from home. I set it aside when I hooked the fish."

"Where's home, Miss?"

She tugged her vest down and smoothed her skirt. "Illinois."

"Oh?" His attention perked. "What part?"

Careful, Callie. . . She still needed to maintain her cover. "I've spent time in several areas. Barrington, Sycamore. Most recently, Chicago." It wasn't untrue. Extended family had lived in the other places, and she'd spent much time there as a child. "I understand you've made some trips to Chicago yourself?"

"Yes, Miss. Lookin' for my baby sister."

The directness of the statement caught her, and she coughed, her eyes tearing up.

"You all right, miss?"

She coughed again, as if trying to clear something from her throat. "Forgive me. I think I inhaled a gnat." She collected herself, dabbed at her watery eyes, and squared her shoulders. "When would you have been there? I wonder if your visits would've been during the time I might have lived there."

"Been there a few times. The first was. . .I don't know, maybe five or six years ago. Whenever they had that big meetin'—to nominate Ulysses S. Grant for President."

"The Republican National Convention?"

"Don't rightly know what it was called. I just recall thinkin' my timin' couldn't've been worse. Rode the train from Denver to Chicago, not knowin' what was happenin' there that week. There was so many people, just gettin' through town was hard. And tryin' to find one girl in the midst of all that mess? It wasn't likely to happen."

"I was in Chicago at that time." She remembered it well. "You're right. It was incredibly crowded." If he'd not known where to look for her, finding her would've been a miraculous feat. "When did you go back again?"

He waved in the direction the deer had run. "I really need to track down my dinner, Miss, before the meat goes rancid or some predator makes a feast of it."

Disappointment wound through her. "Yes, you do." She

needed to get along herself. "I suppose, since I won't be providing fish for Mrs. Ingram, I should try to hunt something up myself."

She tucked the cloth with the dough balls inside the lidded basket and gathered her things, turning toward Lady as she did.

"Why don't you wait here, Miss Jarrett?"

Callie spun. "Why?"

He shrugged. "Once I track down that deer, I'll have more than enough to feed myself and all y'all."

"You would share your meat with us?"

"Y'all shared Miss Hattie's fried chicken with me, and that was a whole lot less than a deer. Ain't that called bein' neighborly?"

She grinned. "I suppose it is."

"All right, then. Wait while I track down that whitetail, and we'll all eat good tonight." Rion punctuated his statement with a nod.

How long had it been since her brother had provided food for her? "I do appreciate it."

"Least I can do, Miss. My fault you lost your fish." He headed into the trees and brush but paused and turned back. "Is there some reason you painted a handprint on your horse?"

Wide-eyed, she spun to stare at Lady, who did, in fact, have a partial white handprint on her shoulder. She stomped her foot. "Oh, that man!"

Rion laughed. "Nesbitt, I presume?"

"He was painting a building in town and stopped me to talk."

With another laugh, he disappeared into the foliage.

Callie snatched the cloth she'd wrapped the dough balls in, wet it in the stream, and paced to Lady's side to scrub the paint away. As she did, her tears welled. *Lord, thank You! You heard my prayers, and You've let me see Rion again.*

She allowed herself a moment of emotion as she looped the basket's leather strap around Lady's saddle horn, but quickly swallowed her feelings and retrieved the letter from her pocket. This time, without delay, she unfolded the pages.

My dearest sister, Calliope,
> *Yes, you've found the right woman! I can hardly believe it! I never imagined I would speak with either you or Orion again, and yet, you've found me. Your letter was an answer to more than a decade of wondering. Tell me, have you had any success in finding our brother? Oh, I've missed you both.*

Callie's eyes welled again, and she clutched the pages to her chest, a sob wrenching free as she stared at the place where Rion had just disappeared.

"Yes, Andromeda," she whispered. "I've found Rion."

Oh, Lord, how like You to line it all up so that within a day's time, I'd have connected with both my brother and my sister.

"Bad news, Miss?" Rion's voice startled her, and she jerked to see him standing at the spot where he'd disappeared moments before.

She corralled her emotions. "Good news, actually."

He cocked his head. "Reckon I don't understand women much. If it's good news, why're you cryin'?"

Because years of searching were done—and hopefully soon, the three of them would begin rebuilding fifteen years of bonds they'd missed.

She brushed away the wetness on her cheeks. "Happy tears, Mr. Rion."

He shook his head, then motioned. "I found the whitetail. Won't take long to field dress it, and I'll see you home."

⁓

At the sound of Rion Braddock's low laughter coming from the parlor, Joe twisted his neck one way, then the other. The movement did nothing to release the tension in his muscles.

"If it be possible, as much as lieth in you, live peaceably with all men." Joe whispered the words to himself as he stared at Mrs. Ingram's large Bible, open to Romans chapter twelve.

Lord God Almighty, how in blazes did Callie meet up with him again? She'd said she was going to fish, but instead of returning with a basket full of bass, she'd brought Braddock and a freshly killed deer. And Mrs. Ingram, being her kind self, had invited him to stay for supper. Since the meal's end, Callie and Braddock sat in the parlor, talking in hushed tones with occasional laughter.

He looked again at the page. "Dearly beloved, avenge not yourselves, but rather give place unto wrath: for it is written, Vengeance is mine; I will repay, saith the Lord. Therefore if thine enemy hunger, feed him; if he thirst, give him drink: for in so doing thou shalt heap coals of fire on his head."

So why did it feel like the coals were burning him, not Braddock?

"Be not overcome of evil, but overcome evil with good."

With a huff, he placed the heavy Bible back on its wooden stand in the corner, then poked his head into the kitchen where Mrs. Ingram and the other women cleaned up the dinner mess.

"You need anything from me, ma'am?"

Every eye turned his way.

"No, Mr. Nesbitt. You had a full day painting the mercantile. Time to rest. Besides, we're nearly done here." She handed a wet plate to one of the women.

"Yes, ma'am. Think I'll take a walk then. Check on Miss Hattie and her friend." He'd made sure to ask for directions so he could check in at will.

"Thank you. I appreciate that." Her brow quickly furrowed. "Take your gun and be careful. Until that murderous fiend is caught, no one is safe."

"Yes, ma'am." He motioned her nearer. "Do you want me to stay until Rion's gone?"

"That's not necessary. If he doesn't take his leave soon, I'll ask him to go."

"And if he doesn't?"

"Then one of us will run next door for the neighbors," one of the women said as she tucked a dried bowl in its place. "Though I doubt it will come to that."

"Go. Check on Hattie." Mrs. Ingram waved him away. "We'll be fine."

"Yes, ma'am." He climbed the kitchen's spiral staircase to the second floor, retrieved his gun belt, and buckled it around his hips as he headed downstairs again. After pausing near the parlor doorway to tie the holster down against his thigh, he marched out, letting the front door close harder than he should've. Thoughts churning, Joe headed toward Hattie's friend's place.

Braddock appearing when he did yesterday was a surprise, apparently even to Callie. The way he'd watched them all the way back to the boardinghouse had been unsettling at best. Now Callie met him unexpectedly while fishing and brought him home with her. Even more uncomfortable. Was Braddock watching Callie? If so, why? What were his intentions?

The questions kept flowing as he walked, only leaving him more uncomfortable. He shouldn't have left a houseful of women alone with the uncouth bounty hunter. Such men were known to be rough—good with guns, knives, and fists, as needed. He turned onto Annie Tunstall's street and eyed her house—the second one after the last storefront. He should've stayed until Braddock left. But no—like a jealous schoolboy, he'd heard Callie chattering with Braddock, and his occasional laughter, and he'd run away so the green-eyed monster wouldn't possess him.

He cursed himself. "You're an idiot and a fool, Trenamen."

Turning, he hurried back the way he'd come, though before he'd gone more than twenty paces, a shadowy form stepped from between buildings and caught him with a hand to his chest, just under his throat.

Heart rate ratcheting up, Joe slammed the big, scruffy silhouette into the wall and, forearm across the fella's windpipe, leveled his pistol at his gut.

"Whoa, now, Nesbitt! It's just me." The sheriff's voice quavered as he lifted his hands.

"Downing?" He grabbed a fistful of the man's shirt and hauled him out into what little light there was. "What's the wise idea, scaring a man?" He holstered the pistol again. "You just about ate a belly full of lead."

The lawman glanced around, then hauled Joe back into the deep shadows. "You didn't hear me callin' out to you?"

Calling out? If that was true, he *must* be distracted. "I didn't. Why were you calling me?"

"Got a question—and maybe some news."

Already irritated, he huffed. "And?"

"Who was the big fella with the dark hair and beard that sat with Mrs. Ingram's group in the meadow yesterday?"

He squinted, trying to recall whether he'd seen the lawman at the medicine show. "I didn't know you were in the meadow yesterday."

"I wasn't. Had other business."

"So how'd you know about him?"

"Answer my question. Who is he?"

If Braddock was a bounty hunter of any repute, shouldn't Downing know him?

Something didn't feel right, but he couldn't figure if it was because Downing startled him or because he was already on edge. Perhaps it was better to give less information than more.

"We did have a big, dark-haired fella sit with us—invited by one of the ladies. What about him?"

"He have a run-in with a soiled dove there in the meadow?"

"What about it?"

"She came to see me after that tussle. Says he's the fella she last saw with Serafina before she disappeared."

Joe's stomach knotted at the memory of that altercation. She'd grabbed Braddock and said something. *You're the one. You were with—*

And like a fool, he'd cut her off in his haste to get Mrs. Ingram's boarders out of the meadow before things went catawampus.

Ice dripped down his spine, and he stalked off.

"Nesbitt, where you goin'?"

"He's at the boardinghouse now, but he won't be for long!"

CHAPTER 14

Once Callie had locked herself into her dark room, the tears she'd suppressed during Rion's visit burst out, and she flung herself across the bed and wept. Thankfully, this time, she'd held herself together through the entire visit—even laughing despite wanting to throw herself into his arms, sob, and pour out the truth so they could get to know each other again.

But she couldn't allow herself to sink into her emotion, even in private. Not when a couple of things had been niggling at her since those first moments with Rion tonight. After allowing herself a brief cry to release tension, she rose and lit the lamp, keeping the light fairly dim. Pulling Joe's files on the murders from under her bed, she thanked God he'd not yet asked for them back, nor had she offered them. They would allow her to verify details.

Retrieving notes on the first murder, she started skimming for the pertinent details.

Miss Nancy Carlin.

Niece of a United States senator.

Killed in a boxcar at the Chicago train depot.

May 19, 1868.

She skimmed farther. A faint memory of something she'd

read niggled at her. What was it? She read down the next page until. . .there.

Miss Carlin's uncle, Senator Warren Utley of Missouri, stated that his niece had come to Chicago to attend the Republican National Convention with his family, but she'd never arrived at their quarters as planned. Her body was found, cold, in a boxcar from the recently arrived train, lying in a bed of soiled straw. Also found in the boxcar were horse droppings, hay, and oats.

Her breath whooshed out.

Rion had said he and his horse had ridden the train from here in Colorado, arrived in Chicago, and found the city overrun because of the convention to nominate Grant.

Lord Jesus, please. This can't be what it looks like.

Her thoughts spiraled. Rion was in Chicago at the same time the first murder happened. And the body was found in what could have been the very boxcar he rode in.

Oh, Lord God!

No. *No!* Of course it wasn't the same car! Plenty of horses rode on trains. There was no proof that that boxcar had been occupied by Rion and his horse.

Yet as she jotted the details into her own file, her stomach grew queasy. She returned the papers on the first murder and withdrew the bundle detailing the second.

Mrs. Tilda Wadwell.

A wife and mother of two small children.

Found murdered in the St. Louis train yard.

May 12, 1869.

Her body had been found in a hidden area of the yard, her hair shorn, just as Miss Carlin's had been. She'd gone missing two days prior, when impromptu celebrations broke out across St. Louis at the news that the Central Pacific and Union Pacific railroads had finally been joined in Promontory Point, Utah

Territory, marking the completion of the Transcontinental Railroad.

She clamped a hand over her open mouth.

Had Rion not regaled her moments ago with the story of being in a St. Louis restaurant when a horse and rider galloped past, shouting that they'd driven the golden spike? He and others had flowed into the streets to dance and celebrate. But days later, he'd left, dejected, because he'd found no trace of Andromeda—just as he'd found no hint of Calliope a year earlier.

Lord Jesus, no. No, no, no. . .

Joe reached the boardinghouse with Downing close on his heels. Rion Braddock's horses weren't tied at the front where he'd initially left them when he first arrived. But Mrs. Ingram had told him to water his horses at the trough near the barn out back. Were they still there? He hurried to the structure, set far back on the property. The only animals occupying the building were the old horses Mrs. Ingram used to pull her wagon and Callie's gray mare. She must not have wanted to waste time returning Lady to the livery, and with Miss Hattie's little mare gone, there was room in the small barn for her.

"I'll see how long Braddock's been gone." Joe motioned toward the front. "Wait for me beside the gate."

"I'll go saddle my horse instead. Meet me at the livery."

"All right."

Joe tried the back door, found it locked, and hurried around the wraparound porch to the front. It was open. When he burst in, several pairs of eyes met him from the parlor.

"Mr. Nesbitt," one woman called. "Is everything well?"

"How long ago did Mr. Rion leave?"

The women looked between themselves. "Perhaps five

minutes after you left. Is everything all right?"

"Is Cal—Kezia—here?"

"She saw him out and went immediately to her room. She said she was tired."

He didn't wait. Climbing the steps by twos, he nearly bumped into another woman as she descended the steps. He excused himself, raced down the hall to the base of the third-floor staircase, and took those in multiples also. Hurrying to her door, he knocked sharply.

"Kezia?"

Silence reigned.

"Please open the door."

Again, not a sound from inside.

Heart pounding, Joe knocked louder.

"Miss Jarrett?"

This time, shuffling met his ears, and the key turned. Her door opened.

"What in heaven's name...?" Her eyes were puffy and tired.

"Are you all right?" Why didn't she open the door farther so he could see she was unharmed? "He didn't hurt you, did he?"

"Who?"

He ducked nearer. "Braddock."

She gave that frustrated eye roll she did when perturbed with him. "I'm fine, Mr. Nesbitt. Why would he hurt me?"

"Callie, we need to talk."

She shook her head. "Tomorrow would be better, if you don't mind."

"About the case..." He barely breathed the words, glancing down the hall.

Her shoulders slumped, but she stepped into the hall. "What about it?"

"I know Braddock's some kind of. . .friend, or something . . .but how well do you know him?"

She folded her arms. "I was six when I last saw him. How well should I know him?"

"All right. Not well, then." Joe blew out a breath, not liking what he needed to say. "After you left the meadow Sunday, some soiled doves arrived to watch the medicine show, so I got the other gals out of there before things turned sour. But as we were leaving, one of the doves grabbed Braddock and said, 'You're the one.' And in the next breath, 'You were with—' I cut her off before she got the words out, but that same woman went to Downing and accused Braddock of being with Serafina shortly before she went missing."

Callie's cheeks paled. "If he was with her, Mr. Nesbitt, he was probably. . .doing what men do in such places."

"Maybe." Though Braddock had staunchly denied being of such ilk, and Joe had actually believed him.

She reached for the wall, looking suddenly unsteady.

Joe grasped her elbow. "Are you all right?"

"Feeling unwell, I suppose. Perhaps I'm still not myself after Lady knocked me over. I was settling in for the night."

Concern raked down his spine. She'd been through a lot these past few days.

"We should at least question him. Where was he headed?"

Callie's eyes slid shut, and she settled a hand on her stomach. "I wouldn't know."

"You really aren't feeling well, are you?" He tightened his grip. Her eyes fluttered open.

"Go rest. I'll ask one of the ladies to look in on you shortly."

"Please don't. I just want to sleep."

He wasn't sure about that, but he nodded. "All right, but—if you're unwell, call someone for help."

Mute, she backed into the room, shut the door, and locked it.

Almighty God, I'm losing my heart to that little gal. Please take care of her. And help me find Braddock before anyone else is hurt.

CHAPTER 15

Tuesday, June 24, 1873

Was Rion the murderer?

Callie sat up, pressing her hand to her stomach for the hundredth time. The motion hadn't yet settled her roiling stomach.

For most of the night, her mind had churned over what she knew. Rion had been in Chicago at the time of the first murder—and in St. Louis the same week as the second. A soiled dove had come forward to say she'd seen Rion with the seventh victim not long before she disappeared. And he matched the vague description of the murderer: big, dark hair, and dark beard. Was it enough for a conviction? She was no lawyer, but it was enough to make one question.

Even Joe was—

Choking back her emotion, she turned again to the question that had plagued her night. If Rion *was* the murderer, real or suspected, what should she do? She'd spent fifteen years hoping to reunite with her brother and sister—and just when her dream was nearly in hand, fate threatened to snatch it away.

If Rion had killed seven women, she must bring him in. He should hang.

She doubled over with a sob.

It was her job. She'd asked Mr. Pinkerton for this opportunity—and had loved the challenge until that challenge turned impossible.

Shaking her head, Callie rose and dressed. She needed to do something rather than letting her mind spin. Lady was still in Mrs. Ingram's barn. She ought to return her to the livery so there was room for Hattie's mare if she returned today. Maybe the change of scenery would break her repeating thoughts and help her clear her head.

In stockinged feet, Callie carried her boots, hat, and rifle to the kitchen. Only Mrs. Ingram stirred, kneading fresh bread dough.

"You're up early. Is everything all right?"

"Yes, ma'am." She sat in a chair in the corner and slipped into her boots. "I wanted to get Lady moved to the livery this morning so she didn't eat up all your hay and oats or take up Hattie's space. I don't think I'll be long."

"I'd say wait for Mr. Nesbitt to escort you, but he returned so late last night."

Her lips parted. "He did?" Hope sprang up where there'd been none. Perhaps he'd already sorted this out.

"He slept a couple hours, and he's gone again."

Hope died as quickly as it came. If Joe was already out after so little sleep, that didn't bode well. Mrs. Ingram chattered on as, once again, Callie's stomach threatened to rebel.

She forced a smile. "I'll be careful. I've got my rifle, and I'm planning to go only to the livery and back."

"If you must, but there's no rush. I don't expect Hattie before tomorrow—and we've plenty of hay and oats."

Callie nodded, took up her hat and gun, and hurried outside to the barn. When she opened the door, Lady nickered, and Callie slipped the bridle over her nose, then led her out to the hitching post. After an affectionate rub, she returned to the barn but found that Rion had stashed her saddle on the highest row of the saddle rack, out of her reach. Lighting the lantern, she found a wooden crate to stand on, tested its sturdiness, and carried it to the back wall where the saddle waited. As she bent to set the crate in place, a boot track caught her eye, and she paused, squinting in the shadowy light.

Heart pounding, she paced back to grab the lantern and returned. There, a Rion-sized footprint marred the ground, and in its heel, a crescent-shaped scar—just like the one she'd seen inside the abandoned cabin days earlier.

⌒

"Sorry, big fella." Joe patted Rusty's shoulder as he saddled him. "We've been burning the midnight oil, haven't we?"

How in heaven's name had Rion Braddock, a big man with two horses, disappeared like a ghost—there one minute, a vapor the next? From the time he left the boardinghouse the previous night, no one had seen him.

To cover more territory, he and Downing had gone in separate directions. Joe had chosen the far end of town, comprised of the business district at the center and west parts of town, brothels on the south side, and some residences to the north. He chose that direction largely because that was where Callie had headed on her fishing trip. Downing had taken the other end, where a few businesses and many homes were located.

When they'd met back together hours later, neither had found the bounty hunter. And with no moonlight, it hadn't made sense trying to traverse unfamiliar mountain paths, riding over his potential trail, and wiping out clues in the dark. So Joe was up with the first gray streaks of dawn to continue the search.

As he tightened Rusty's cinch, the slow rhythmic sound

of hooves entered the barn and clopped nearer. Movement near the end of the aisle drew his attention, and glancing up, he saw Callie and Lady come into view. He'd have expected Cooper Downing, not her. Seeing him, she stopped short and took off her hat. His heart gave a little skip at the sight of her medium-brown hair hanging in loose waves over her shoulders. Despite the dark circles under her eyes, she was beautiful.

Leaving Rusty, he walked to her, keeping his voice low. "Morning. Are you all right?"

She swallowed hard, straightened, and hooked her hat's string around Lady's saddle horn. "I suppose." She also whispered. "Did you find my—" She stared at a button on his shirt. "—Mr. Rion?"

"Not yet." He ducked to catch her gaze, though she wouldn't meet it. "Callie, I know you consider him your friend, but seven women are dead, and more may be in danger."

She raked a fierce look his way. "Not by his hand!"

Joe's brows arched, and her severe expression dimmed into pain.

"I'm sorry."

Finding no one else nearby, he drew her into the aisle anyway, out of sight of the main entrance, and tugged her into his arms.

"I know this isn't easy for you."

She shook her head against his chest.

"Braddock's not necessarily responsible for anything, but we've got to find him and ask some questions. He's the best lead we've got right now."

A stuttering breath shook her slight frame.

"Do you know where to find him?"

A deafening silence hung between them before she finally squeaked, "No."

"You found him yesterday."

She pulled back to look at him, her expression pitiful. "He found me."

Joe brushed her cheek and smoothed her pretty hair, his heart aching. Especially with the question he must ask next.

"Callie, are you able to be objective?"

She bobbed her head, faintly at first, then more emphatically. "Yes. It's just taken me by surprise. Finding him in the first place—as well as this new turn."

A reasonable answer—but was it truthful? This would bear watching. "Why're you here so early?"

"I was awake, so I thought I'd bring Lady back and get her settled."

"What are your plans today?"

"I'm not sure."

"Will you ride with me? Show me where Braddock found you?"

She bit her lip but eventually nodded. "I suppose."

"All right, then." He paced back to Rusty's side, checked the saddle, and tugged his reins to get him moving toward Callie. When he turned, she had replaced her hat and was turning Lady back toward the livery's entrance.

As they walked their horses out together and paused at the water trough, Downing came trotting down the silent street, aiming his brown horse toward them.

"Nesbitt. Miss." He nodded, then focused on Callie. "Uh, would you give us a minute alone?"

She glanced Joe's way and attempted to hand off Lady's reins, though Joe faced the sheriff. "She can stay."

Downing looked uncomfortable. "You might ought to rethink that, Nesbitt."

Joe stared at the man, handed Callie Rusty's reins instead, and paced to the far side of the livery's entrance. Downing dismounted and joined him.

"We got a problem. Little Josiah Tunstall pounded on my door a bit ago. His mama, Annie, is Hattie's good friend."

Concern wrapped around him like an icy chain. "Hattie's been staying with her while her husband's away."

Downing nodded, staring into the dirt. "The boy heard a scuffle outside near his folks' barn last night. He couldn't see much from his window, but what he did see is a concern. A big fella with dark hair and a beard, leadin' two horses, grabbed Miss Hattie out in the barn. Josiah saw her go limp in his arms, and the big fella wrestled her over one horse and rode off."

Joe's heart stuttered. He should've checked on Hattie. He'd almost reached the Tunstall home when he'd talked himself into returning to the boardinghouse to see that Braddock left. Then Downing scared the bejeebers out of him, and the whole night went cockeyed.

"He said he knocked on my door in the night, tryin' to tell me just after it happened, but obviously. . .I wasn't there."

Joe swore under his breath, but immediately closed his eyes.

Forgive me, Almighty Father. And help. This is all turning sideways.

"I want to talk to the Tunstalls, have a look around."

"Reckon I better tell Bess Ingram. She'll want to know her daughter's missin'."

Joe wiped a hand across his brow. "Kezia?"

She led their horses over and waited.

"Plans have changed. I think it best if you go with Sheriff Downing back to Mrs. Ingram's. Apparently, Hattie's gone missing overnight. It would be good for Mrs. Ingram to have some support when the sheriff breaks the news to her."

"Hattie's. . .missing?" Color drained from her face, and she gulped a breath.

"Don't you worry, Miss." Downing fidgeted with his horse's reins. "We'll find her right quick. I promise."

"Oh my—" Her features contorted, and a sob wrenched free. For the second time that morning, Joe held her in his arms, this time not caring who saw.

CHAPTER 16

Wednesday, June 25, 1873

With the deepest hours of darkness still pressing in outside, Callie awakened with a start from a nightmare—Rion pacing up the steps of a gallows.

Lord, no! This can't be happening. She tried to keep her breathing calm and steady, though the blackness outside seemed to be pushing into her soul, despite the lamp she'd left burning on her nightstand. *How can I have found Rion and Andromeda, only to lose one so quickly? Please don't take him from me—from us. Andromeda deserves to meet him too!*

She quieted to listen for His answer, just as she'd seen Mrs. Ingram do throughout the day. Unlike her aged host, she heard nothing. Instead, oppressive silence pressed in. Maybe one day she'd hear God so clearly, but first, she had to survive this nightmare.

How could so much evidence point to her own brother being the fiend who'd murdered seven—perhaps eight—women?

Oh, Lord, please speak to me! I've watched You do it all day with Mrs. Ingram. Isn't there something you can say to take this heaviness from me?

Mrs. Ingram received the news of Hattie's kidnapping with

as much grace, strength, and faith as one woman could possess. Oh, she'd been horrified, and she'd cried plenty throughout the day. But she'd also gathered her large Bible from the dining room, carried the thick tome to the parlor, and knelt to pray before the Good Book. Callie had never seen such fervor and faith, despite her tears. Then, at moments, she'd pause, quiet herself, and listen. After a moment, she'd grin or laugh, or even release a moan or a sob, but always, she'd answer what she must have heard with a "Yes, Father. Thank you."

She and the other women had stayed close to her through the day, except when Mrs. Ingram had asked Callie to go hitch up Hattie's mare to the cart and bring both home from Annie Tunstall's. It was during that errand that she'd spoken to young Josiah and heard the description of Hattie's abduction firsthand and gotten to look at the scene. Once again, the same boot print with the crescent-shaped notch in its heel marred the dirt all around the barn.

Rion's boot track.

With so much evidence looming, she'd spent much of the day pondering Joe's question. Could she remain objective? She'd already been less than truthful with him. Yes, Rion had found her while he was hunting, but after field dressing the deer, he'd taken her to the cave where he'd made his camp, saddled his big black horse, tied the deer over his other horse, and led her back into town. She could find the cave again, but she'd not shared that fact with Joe then, and she debated whether to now.

Could she turn Rion in if it meant saving Hattie's life, but losing his?

Lord, how do I answer that?

And how could she face Andromeda if she turned Rion in to the authorities and cost her the opportunity to even see him once, much less know him?

What if he was guilty? Hadn't that man, Garvin, called him a murderous. . .something-or-other? Had Rion's life been so harsh that he'd become a monster?

Oh, Lord. . .what do I do?

She sat up, pulling Andromeda's letter from the nightstand drawer, hoping it might bring some clarity.

My dearest sister, Calliope,

Yes, you've found the right woman! I can hardly believe it! I never imagined I would speak with either you or Orion again, and yet, you've found me. Your letter was an answer to more than a decade of wondering. Tell me, have you had any success in finding our brother? Oh, I've missed you both.

Wherever do I begin? I was adopted by Michael and Susan McGovern, which, now that I've written it, you said you already knew. What a job that must have been, to find our records amid so many others in the basement of the orphanage. No wonder Allan Pinkerton hired you as a detective. You always were determined to make a difference, even as a tiny girl.

The words stopped her. Had she been so determined—even before they were separated?

Yes. She'd always desired to leave her mark on the world. And this was one such opportunity. Women were being murdered and communities terrorized. As much as her heart cried to protect the family she'd fought to find, was *that* the mark she wanted to leave? To warn her brother and allow a potential murderer to flee—and maybe kill again? Or could she do what had to be done, no matter the cost?

Oh, Lord, help me!

⁓

The day had been filled with one dead end after another.

Groaning, Joe rolled onto his stomach and buried his face in the mattress. *Dead ends.* Hardly the way to think of it.

He'd prayed for Hattie to *live*—begged God to spare her life. Since they'd not found her body, there was still hope. But with no indication of which direction the man who abducted her—likely Braddock—had gone, there were too many questions...

Like the night before, Joe had taken one direction and Downing another. They'd studied the ground around the Tunstalls' barn, but just like at the abandoned cabin, they found nothing to indicate any unknown horses had been there. In fact, the only tracks that didn't belong were Hattie's—obvious by the small size and her awkward gait—and the large ones with a crescent-shaped chunk cut out of one heel.

A perfect match for the one Callie drew from Serafina's murder.

He rose, lit his lamp, poured water in the basin, and splashed his face. Afterward, he slumped onto the foot of his bed. He'd be wise to sleep while he could. Come dawn, he and Downing would restart their search. But despite how inappropriate it might seem, he felt the urge to see if Callie was awake. If he had his guess, she was probably worrying over Hattie—and her old friend Braddock.

He should look at her sketches again. Perhaps they would shed some fresh insight on his search tomorrow. He tugged a shirt on and, leaving the room, buttoned it as he climbed the stairs on cat feet.

Thankfully, she was the only one who occupied the third floor. That made for less chance of disturbing the other boarders—although everyone in the house was probably awake. He crossed to her doorway, noting the lamplight showing under her door. A good sign.

Joe knocked. Despite the softness of his touch, the sound echoed like thunder between mountain peaks. If she wasn't awake before, she probably was now. Yet, nothing stirred inside.

"Kezia?"

Still no sound. Yet her lamp was burning.

Was she that soundly asleep?

"Kezia." He knocked again.

Still no response.

Concerned, he tried the knob. The door swung open easily, and self-consciously, he peeked inside to find. . .a neat and tidy bed?

Lord God Almighty. . . He stuck his head in.

She was gone.

Please, Almighty Father—don't let her have done something foolish.

Stepping inside, he found her satchel with her drawing supplies atop the trunk at the foot of her bed. In the corner, some of his case files occupied the small desk's surface. He glanced around. Was her rifle gone? Scanning the room twice, his stomach knotted. Yes, gone.

She didn't go anywhere without that gun, so she must've left on purpose—probably to find and warn Rion Braddock.

He turned to leave, but something caught his eye, and he paused. Crossing to the bed, he found a creased paper, lying unfolded atop the quilt. Unable to read it in the dim light, he moved closer to the lamp.

My dearest sister, Calliope,

Yes, you've found the right woman! I can hardly believe it! I never imagined I would speak with either you or Orion again, and yet, you've found me. Your letter was

an answer to more than a decade of wondering. Tell me,
have you had any success in finding our brother? Oh, I've
missed you both.

Calliope? Calliope. . . He leafed through the missive's other
pages and found the signature from Andromeda Braddock
McGovern.

His jaw went slack. "Calliope. . .is Callie."

No wonder she'd acted so odd. She didn't just know him.
They were kin.

CHAPTER 17

Lord, You've brought me this far. Help me the rest of the way. Please let me find Rion...

Callie clutched the dusty lantern she'd borrowed from Mrs. Ingram's barn, holding it out, golden light pooling on the ground while she guided Lady up the steep mountain path to where Rion had found her days ago. The same ride had taken less than an hour coming down from Rion's campsite. But on this, one of the darkest nights of the month, with only a tiny sliver of moon, it had taken her roughly three hours to find her way. It hadn't been easy. Everything looked different bathed in darkness and lamplight. Yet she'd done it—as the sky streaked with hints of dawn, she'd made it back to the stream where Rion first came across her. Now to cross to the other side and take the path to her left. The cave should be ahead.

A shiver raced through her, as much from the cool mountain air as the knowledge she was so close to Rion's camp. What would she find? The evidence, if she could call it such, indicated Rion was probably the murderer. Her own brother. Would she find him with Hattie? Was she alive, or—

She groaned. How could Rion be guilty? He was her kin. And from what she recalled, he was gentle with her and Andromeda. But a *lot* could happen in fifteen years—and his life hadn't been easy.

"Oh, Lord—" She groaned the words, unable to pray more.

For several minutes, she sat in her saddle, letting Lady drink while she searched for the confidence to finish her job. After what seemed an eternity, she urged Lady forward, splashing into the stream before she scrambled onto the far bank and started down the path. However, she stopped feet beyond. Lady's hooves were far too loud in the silence. After another moment, she dismounted, tied Lady, and circled to the horse's right side to draw her rifle. As she stepped out again, a pistol's hammer cocked, chilling her to her core.

"Stop where you are and explain yourself." Rion's voice split the quiet.

Her heart pounded. "Rion Braddock?"

Stunned silence hung there an instant. "Miss Jarrett?"

"It's me."

The hammer uncocked, and a shadowy form moved along the line of trees, well outside the circle of lantern light. "Why're you crashin' around up here at this time of night? You tryin' to get the drop on me?"

"I need to talk to you."

"What in blue blazes is so important you had to interrupt a fella's sleep?"

She trembled. "It is important."

This time, he moved from the darkness, the yellow lantern light casting wicked shadows across his face, even as it glinted on the pistol still in his hand.

"You in some kinda danger?"

That depended on how he took what she had to say. "Could we go to your campsite and talk?"

His brow furrowed, but he nodded and reached to untie Lady's reins. "C'mon. I'll make coffee." He walked ahead of her a couple of feet, then paused and reached for the lantern. Callie didn't resist, happy to not be hefting its weight.

Minutes later, they reached the cave, and he returned his gun to its holster, lying on the cave floor within easy reach of his bedroll. While he stoked the fire, put water on to boil, and loosened Lady's cinch, she peeked into the back of the cave. It was only about ten feet deep, with a low ceiling—and beyond his campfire, the space was empty save for his few belongings. Relief washed through her. Hattie wasn't here. So Rion hadn't abducted her.

Unless. . . Had he hidden her elsewhere? Or already killed her? Dumped her body in some unknown place?

Lord, Rion can't be behind these crimes! Can he?

She stared at the cave's dirt floor—pockmarked with his boot tracks, half of which contained the odd, crescent-shaped mark. Her stomach knotted, and she reached for the cave wall, feeling suddenly sick.

Lord, I don't want to believe he's guilty. . .

He cleared his throat and waved for her to sit on his rumpled bedroll. He sat across from her.

"All right, what's so all-fired important you'd risk your pretty neck to find me in the night?"

Father, give me the words. And give him ears to hear. . .every-thing. Let the truth become evident.

"I haven't been completely honest with you."

Skeptical, he shook his head. "You're worried about a little lie to a stranger?"

"We're not strangers." She plunged in before she had time to think. "My name isn't Kezia Jarrett. It's Calliope Ann Braddock."

He blinked once, then again, and his features hardened. "That ain't funny. Quit your joshin'."

"I'm not joshing. Our parents' names were Richard and

Elise Braddock. You—Orion James—were born on January 4th, 1848. Andromeda Mae was born November 26th, the next year, and I came along on April 5th, 1852. When I was a little girl, I couldn't say your name or Andromeda's, so I called you Owhine and her Dwama."

Rion gaped at her. "I've never told anyone that."

Her throat knotted. "So do you believe me?"

He eventually nodded. "I ain't never told people my middle name, and I'd all but forgot my birthday. Garvin never made no fuss over such things."

A sound somewhere between a sob and a laugh ripped from her throat, and she covered her mouth before more escaped.

"I been searchin' for you and Andromeda for years. Never had any luck. How'd you find me?"

"That's"—she tried to smile, unsure how he'd take the next news— "an interesting story."

"So tell it."

"I'm a Pinkerton."

He looked at her as if a horn had grown from her forehead. "A what?"

"A Pinkerton detective?"

"They let women do that?"

She grinned. "Allan Pinkerton has for most of my life. He hired me, and when he learned that I was searching for my brother and sister, he allowed me a lot of leeway. I went back to New York, found the orphanage, and dug through thousands of papers to find anything I could about where you and Andromeda ended up. I found her adoptive family, and I wrote to her in St. Louis. The day you found me fishing, I was reading a letter from her. She's been wondering about us and wants to see us."

Rion grunted and he hung his head, his eyes unusually watery.

"I couldn't find anything about you, but one of the men who chaperoned us on the train still works at the orphanage.

He'd taken notes on where we all got adopted. He found that you'd made it out here, so several months back, Mr. Pinkerton sent me west on a case and told me I could use my spare time to search for you. So when I saw you at the church service, I—"

"Ran after me and invited me to Sunday meetin'." Hearing the thickness of his voice kicked her own emotion over the edge. As tears spilled down her cheeks, he rose, tugged her to her feet, and wrapped his arms around her.

Safe in her brother's embrace, she wept. And if she wasn't mistaken, so did he.

"I'm sorry I couldn't tell you who I was," she whispered once the storm in her chest subsided.

"Why couldn't you then, but you can now?"

She stepped back, head hanging. "I shouldn't have."

"But. . . ?"

Lord, how do I say this?

"I'm working a case. A series of murders."

"Murders. . . I thought the Pinkertons investigated train robberies, recovered stolen goods, and the like."

"Mostly, we do. But the first two murders were on or near trains we protect, and Mr. Pinkerton took a special interest."

"And how does that weigh on you tellin' me who you really are?"

She slipped her hand into her pocket, grasping her small derringer. "The evidence indicates. . ."

Oh, Lord—help!

"Spit it out."

"Did you take Hattie from town after leaving Mrs. Ingram's?"

"Take Hattie?" His eyes narrowed, and any emotional walls she'd managed to dismantle were erected again in an instant.

"She's missing, Rion. And a witness says a man fitting your description took her."

Joe must not have missed Callie's departure from the boardinghouse by much. Before he could reach the livery to saddle Rusty, she was mounting up outside the building and riding off, lantern in hand. After she departed, he'd paid the livery owner a dollar to watch where she turned, then alert Sheriff Downing to follow. Perhaps it was a mistake, but Joe pursued on foot, figuring she wouldn't be moving fast and he'd be quieter. Plus, Rusty could use a rest.

It had been almost painful watching her lantern bob through the darkness on what amounted to a narrow game trail. Numerous times, she must have made wrong turns because she suddenly backtracked, retracing her steps to pick up where she'd missed the correct trail. Her slow pace allowed him to stay close, despite being on foot, and let him reach the stream as Rion Braddock first called out to her. Now he held his breath outside the cave, straining to hear where Callie would drive the conversation next.

"My description?" Braddock guffawed. "What're you sayin', Calliope? You think I kidnapped her?"

"I don't want to believe it, no. But your boot tracks were all over the floor she was taken from."

"My boot tracks?" His voice turned hard.

"Yes. Like this one."

Joe imagined her pointing to a track in the dirt inside the cave—or maybe the drawing she'd showed him from the abandoned cabin, although she'd left her satchel back at the boardinghouse.

"I'd be plain stupid to wear such boots if I was tryin' to hide my movements, don't you think? If I was on a trail or tryin' to hide my movements, I'd wear moccasins."

"Aside from the tracks, the eyewitness said a big, dark-haired man with a beard and two horses grabbed Hattie."

"You're loco! What reason would I have to take a woman, much less kill one? Y'all told me over dinner that she went to stay with a friend. I didn't know where Miss Hattie was, and I had no reason to seek her out!"

"Then come back to town, and let's sort this out."

From inside the cave, shuffling caught his ear. Joe eased his pistol from his holster.

"You're accusin' me of things because of a boot print?"

"And a description that fits you."

"And a bunch of others too!" Braddock's voice dripped contempt. "I ain't killed no one."

"It's a distinctive boot print. And there's more than just those two things."

"Name 'em."

"Come to town, and I will."

"Durn it all, little girl! You oughta know murder ain't in my character."

Braddock's words grated, and Joe eased the Colt's hammer back, ready to pounce, though Callie was undaunted.

"That's the problem, Rion. We haven't seen each other in fifteen years. We don't know each other."

"That don't change the fact we're kin."

"That's why I came to you alone. We're kin, and the brother I remember always tried to do the right thing."

Relief washed through Joe. How could he have thought she was coming to warn him?

"Please. . .come back to town. Let's sort this out together, because I don't think you did this, but you're the only lead we have."

"Not a very good detective, are ya?"

Joe gritted his teeth at Braddock's taunting words.

"Maybe not, but I'm trying." Callie's voice quavered, and the urge to wrap her in his arms overtook him. Braddock had no right—

"Our jobs are similar, Rion. What would you do if you saw that either Andromeda or I was wrongly accused of murder?"

"I'd give you the benefit of the doubt."

"Would you let us go—even though other bounty hunters and lawmen might shoot us on sight or hang us from the nearest tree?"

"That's what I'm worried about! I certainly ain't killed a woman, but if you take me in, I'm likely to get my neck stretched for it."

"Rion, I can't believe God would allow me to find you just to take you away again. He'll show me how to clear your name. Please come with me."

Joe eased the gun's hammer back in place, though he kept it in hand and stepped into view. "I give my word as well."

They jerked to face him.

"What're you doing here?" they both chorused.

"I went up to ask you about your drawing of that boot print. But you were gone, so I—"

"You a Pinkerton too?" Braddock grunted.

Joe nodded. "I am. Both of us are undercover, so keep it quiet."

"You think I did this as well?"

"Your sister's a fine detective. If she believes you're innocent, then I'm going to hear her out and help her prove it."

Braddock glared. "You both give me your word?"

"Absolutely," she whispered.

Joe nodded. "As a man and a Pinkerton."

His demeanor steely, he blew out a sharp breath. "Fine, then. Take me back to town. But I didn't do what you're accusin' me of."

After sunrise, traveling the narrow game path was much easier, especially since Rion allowed Joe the use of his spare horse, Mischief. He led, with Rion behind him, and Callie at the rear. More than halfway to Cambria Springs, Sheriff Downing met them and listened to Joe's retelling of what had happened. After his summary, Downing recommended he and Callie head to the boardinghouse and check in, so as not to cause Mrs. Ingram any further worry.

"Mr. Nesbitt, a word, please?" Callie called from the back of the narrow path.

He dismounted and pushed past Braddock to reach her.

She leaned down, and her loose hair fell, creating a beautiful brown curtain between them and the other men. He squelched a smile at what felt like an intimate moment, especially as the thought to kiss her took hold.

"Did you mean what you said? You'll help me clear my brother's name?"

"I did. Why?"

"Then don't leave Rion alone with the sheriff. I'm not. . . certain. . .about Downing. He fits the killer's vague description nearly as well as Rion does."

He'd had similar thoughts, especially as he'd pondered the events of the other night. Why had Downing been hiding in the shadows not far from the Tunstall home?

But he *was* a lawman. Surveilling from the shadows wasn't out of line in his business. But why had Downing scared the tar out of him?

She straightened, her hair falling back against her shoulder. Callie cleared her throat. "It's settled. I'll go to the boardinghouse. You help Sheriff Downing get Mr. Rion to the jail."

He nodded, not entirely happy. If Rion Braddock wasn't the murderer, the real culprit was still on the loose. Fortunately, by the time they would separate, they'd be back in town.

At the base of the trail, Callie headed toward Mrs. Ingram's while he and Downing led Rion to jail.

Rion was sullen as they got him down from his horse and walked him inside. Downing took his gun belt and several knives, then searched his saddlebags before locking him in a cell.

Downing swung the door shut and stashed the keys in a desk drawer. "I'm goin' to tend his horses. See if you can't get him to tell ya where he stashed Hattie." The lawman departed.

With him gone, Rion stepped up to the bars.

"Got some questions for you, Nesbitt."

"All right."

"Is Nesbitt your real name?"

He considered before shaking his head. "Joe. Trenamen. But keep that quiet. Folks around here know me by my undercover name."

"What about what you told me at the medicine show? You truly got feelin's for my sister, or is that part of your cover too?"

His brows arched. "That's all true."

"Does she know?"

"I—I need to make my intentions clearer."

Behind him, Callie cleared her throat.

"Now's a good time." She shot him an unsteady smile.

Joe's cheeks burned. "Thought you were at the boardinghouse."

"Mrs. Ingram had a hard night. She's sleeping now, so I came here. Looks like I was right on time."

Braddock nodded. "Listen, Trenamen, I've got no assurances I'm leavin' this cell except to meet the hangman. I need to know Calliope's cared for."

"You're not stayin' here and you're not going to the gallows,

Braddock. We'll find the real killer."

"Promise me anyway."

Joe reached through the bars and offered Braddock a hand. "I won't let anything happen to Callie." He sealed the oath with one firm shake of Rion's ice-cold hand.

Callie came and wrapped her hands around both of theirs. "I just found you. I'm not letting anyone or anything take you away again." She met Joe's eyes. "Now, help me, please. *We* need to save my brother."

Joe glanced Braddock's way before returning his gaze to Callie. "Let's get started."

Part 2

ON THE RUN

CHAPTER 1

Cambria Springs, Colorado Territory
Wednesday, June 25, 1873

It didn't take long for the vultures to circle, waiting to feast on Rion Braddock's carcass. By the time the durn sheriff returned to the jail from putting up his horses then left again to get food for their breakfast, a mob had formed around the door—both men and women—calling for his neck to get stretched. And all the while, Joe Trenamen and Calliope huddled together, talking in circles he couldn't grasp.

"I'm gonna need y'all to slow down and tell me plain, from the beginnin', what you think is goin' on." Rion stared through the bars at Calliope.

His sister!

He was still trying to wrap his head around her standing there. "Because up in the cave, you were talkin' about murdered women, then you said Miss Hattie's been taken. I feel like I'm missin' pieces of this picture you're tryin' to paint."

It was Calliope's. . .partner? beau? both?. . .Trenamen, who answered first. "Five years ago, a woman's body was found in a train car in the Chicago train yard. A train line the Pinkertons work with. The woman had been stabbed multiple times, and her head was shaved bald."

Rion cursed under his breath. "Who would do such a thing?"

Calliope continued. "The woman was a senator's niece, in Chicago for the Republican National Convention, when they chose Ulysses S. Grant to be the Republican presidential nominee."

A chill swept him. He'd been in Chicago looking for Calliope at that time. "All right?"

Trenamen cleared his throat. "A second murder, similar to the first, happened days shy of the first anniversary of that first murder. The second happened in St. Louis. That time, a woman was found in the train yard, near a train the Pinkerton Detective Agency works with. Stabbed viciously a number of times, and her hair shorn. She went missing as people poured into the streets to celebrate the completion of the Transcontinental Railroad."

Calliope's expression dripped sadness. "You just told me about being there during that time."

As the picture they painted took shape, something like dynamite exploded in his chest. "I done a lot of things in my twenty-five years." Including killing three men who were gunning for him. "But I ain't never killed a woman." He rattled the door. "Not in St. Louis. Not in Chicago. And sure as shootin' not here." Why would he shave their hair if he had? "You ain't pinnin' murders on me. Now get me out of this cell, and I'll help you find who did. But it ain't me."

Trenamen held up a hand. "Settle down. We're trying to—"

"You settle down, you—" He loosed a name unfit for his sister's hearing, but just then, he didn't rightly care. He rattled the door harder and longer than the last time. "I'm bein' railroaded—by my own kin!"

"Orion James, stop it!" Despite her eyes brimming with tears, Calliope stared him down. "Believe it or not, I'm trying to save your life!"

Walking to the back of the cell, he smacked the wall with his open palm. Pain jolted through his forearm. "I didn't do this!"

"Did you visit a brothel recently?" Trenamen's voice was quiet.

Rion glared through the bars. "I told you, that ain't my way."

"So you haven't set foot in any such establishment?"

"Set foot in one, yeah. Talked to one of the doves—because the fella I was tryin' to collect the bounty on had roughed her up a while back. Why?"

"What was her name, the one you talked to?"

Rion thought. "Serafina, I reckon. Why is this so all-fired important?"

"When?"

"Tarnation, Trenamen! Answer my question."

Calliope's shoulders slumped. "The soiled dove known as Sweet Serafina was murdered—stabbed with her hair shorn—last week. Her body was found in an abandoned cabin outside of town. Your boot track was in the cabin where her corpse was found."

"The dove that confronted you near the medicine show. . ." Joe Trenamen crammed his hands in his pockets. "She told Sheriff Downing you were one of the last to be seen with Serafina."

Rion's stomach soured. "Whatever you saw, it ain't my boot track. I ain't been to no abandoned cabin 'round these parts anytime recent." Did they even care?

"We need to get to the bottom of why so much of this matches you if you're not responsible."

"Like I said, I'm bein' railroaded." And he'd only discovered that as Calliope unfolded the facts of the case against him. So many facts. . .

How in blue blazes could that be? He had nothing to do with Miss Hattie's disappearance. The afternoon he ate at the boardinghouse, they'd talked for hours. Then he made a beeline right for the cave. By the time he left, few people would've been out, and he hadn't come across anyone. He'd just made his way to the cave.

And yes. He'd gone to talk to the soiled dove at the brothel, but he'd talked to her for maybe ten minutes, probably less. She was very much alive when he left her.

"Since you bring it up, can you think of anyone who would want to railroad you?" Trenamen asked.

He paced to the cot and slumped onto it, his shoulder braced against the thick wall. "Plenty of people. Ellwood Garvin."

"The man who raised you?" Trenamen frowned.

"Don't you dare call what that ol' fool did *raisin' me*."

"Understood. But that's who you mean, yes?"

"Yeah, him."

"You think he'd set you up?"

"He's ornery enough. And he's been accusin' me for years of stealin' from him and killin' those gals he took in. Tryin' to pin what he did on me."

Trenamen nodded. "Who else?"

He grunted. "I'm a bounty hunter. Dependin' on what side of the law you're on, I might be loved or hated."

"True."

Outside the office, the crowd whipped into a frenzy of angry voices, and one rose above them all. Sheriff Downing's.

"Go on! All of ya. We don't know nothin' yet."

Someone shouted something back at him.

"We'll be looking for Hattie again soon. In the meantime, tamp down your anger and go back to wherever ya came from!"

Downing eventually shooed most of them toward their homes or businesses. Once they'd filtered away, he unlocked the door and let himself in, basket in hand. He locked the door behind him.

"Got breakfast, Braddock." He set the basket on the desk, barely in view of where Rion stood. It sounded like he might be unpacking things. "And you two—"

Both Calliope and Trenamen swung his way.

"Bess is awake. She's worried y'all're not there. I told her I'd send ya her way as soon as I could."

The two looked at each other, then faced the cell again.

"I'll be back soon." Calliope's pretty features reflected her concern.

"Don't worry about me." He glanced around. "Got food and a bed. I'm used to makin' do with a lot less."

The little thing looked ready to cry again. To his credit, Trenamen slung an arm around her and tucked her against his side. "We'll be back in a while."

Once they'd left, Downing brought a plate of flapjacks and eggs. Normally, Rion'd put away such a meal in no time. Today, he wasn't hungry—not with how quickly things had turned against him. Downing pushed the plate and a fork through the slot in the bars, and Rion received them. He'd eat some, keep his strength up.

He'd need it. He wasn't staying. . .not one minute beyond what he must.

⌒

Despite the early hour, the town was abuzz with news. Someone had been arrested for Hattie Ingram's disappearance—and possibly for the murders of the other two other women. With such a story to break, Lucinda Peters waited outside the sheriff's office, despite everyone else having left as directed. That would actually make her plan easier to accomplish. As she waited for the door to open again, she jotted in the journal she carried everywhere—notes, questions to ask, or details to recall. But until she spoke to the sheriff and his suspect, she was much too short on the detail aspect.

After some minutes, a key turned, and the door opened. Lu darted onto the boardwalk and caught the knob, waiting for the tall, handsome man and the smaller woman—both of whom she'd seen around the medicine show several days earlier—to exit. That day, she'd seen the woman run after the man now locked inside the jail, and her handsome companion had chased after her. What had all that been about?

Focus, Lu. If she was going to break this story, she had to keep her wits about her.

"Morning." She nodded to them as they exited, and before they could question her, she ducked into the office, much to the sheriff's surprise.

"Who're you?"

"Lucinda Peters. I'm a reporter." Not exactly the truth. She was a writer—of dime novels for now, but no one needed to know that. Especially since she hoped this story would give her the break she needed to get on with a real newspaper and to show her family she had what it took. She waved toward the cell where the big man huddled, eating. "I'd like to speak to you about the prisoner you've brought in this morning."

"Were you just waitin' outside my door? I told everyone to git. That means reporters too."

"If you prefer not to speak, sir, may I at least ask your prisoner some questions?"

The lawman folded his arms across his broad chest. "Are we havin' a misunderstandin' here? I said go away."

She arched her brows, a half smile on her lips. "Please?"

He went to the door and opened it, waiting. When she made no move toward it, he became flustered. "Who do you belong to, woman?"

"Belong to?"

"What man accounts for you? Who's your husband—or your father, as the case may be?"

"I can assure you, Sheriff, I *belong* to no one." Her father and brothers were back east, working their blessed newspaper, much too far away to answer on her behalf. And she had no husband. Didn't want one either—particularly not if it meant going back to her upbringing, where women and girls were expected to be *proper* and look pretty. "I'm my own woman."

He harrumphed. "Then I'll tell ya one more time: Git—or I'll lock ya in one of my cells, missy."

Would he really? She glanced around the sparse office, filled with the sheriff's desk and a few chairs—one on his side and two facing it. And across the way, a wall of wanted posters. In the front corner near the window, a potbellied stove sat cold—the weather far too warm to fire it up in June. And along the back wall, three cells filled the space, each separated by iron bars.

Lu marched to the one adjacent to where the big man balanced a plate of pancakes on his knee. "I'll take this one."

"You little—" He stopped short but stomped into the cell and took her arm. "Let's go. Now."

He tried to guide her through the door.

She dug in, resisting his attempts. "You promised, Sheriff, if I didn't go, you'd lock me in one of your cells. What sort of a lawman would you be if you don't follow through on a promise like that?" She wrestled her arm free. "No one will possibly believe you mean business if you don't carry out your word."

The sheriff's face turned an unflattering shade of red.

The man in the adjoining cell snorted as he eyed them both with an irritated look, then shook his head and forked a bite of food in his mouth.

"You little—" The veins bulged along the sheriff's neck. "Do us all a favor and git, already!"

Lu paced back to the cot and sat, opened her book again, and began to write.

The lawman gaped and, after half a breath, spun and marched out, clanging the door closed, mumbling something about her being deranged.

Lu stifled the self-satisfied grin that leapt to her face. About time...

"Pardon me." She immediately turned to the fellow in the next cell. "Good morning. My name is Lucinda Peters. Might I ask your name?"

He glanced up, then put away another bite of his food, chewing in silence.

Downing stomped out the office door and into the grassy area, carrying a heavy wooden crate.

"What has our friend, the sheriff, arrested you for, sir?"

He forked another bite of the pancakes into his mouth, chewing slowly. She watched for the moment he swallowed to ask another question, but he'd already lined up his next bite and took it before she was able. As he scraped up bits of pancakes and eggs with his fork, he avoided eye contact.

"Does this have something to do with the woman who went missing a couple of nights ago? Miss Hattie Ingram, I believe."

A moment later, the sheriff returned, and the man in the cell crossed to the door, whistling sharply as he did. Holding the plate and fork out through the slot in the door, he waited for the sheriff to collect it and whispered something to him as he did. The sheriff nodded, set the plate in the basket on his desk, and returned to slip a heavy canteen through the bars.

The big man took a swallow, then another, and setting the canteen down near his cot, sprawled on his stomach, head resting on his arms.

"Are you the one who murdered the prostitute known as Sweet Serafina, sir. . .or the previous victim, Mary Redmond?"

He flinched and, after a second, shoved himself up onto his elbows and swung a bewildered glance her way.

"What'd you just say?"

"Did you murder the soiled dove, Sweet Serafina, or the waitress from Dutch's Café, Mary Redmond?"

His face paled. Then suddenly, he lunged up off the cot, whistling sharply again as he went to the bars. "Downing!"

The sheriff sauntered over, his face stern.

The two men huddled at the corner of the cell and, for several minutes, spoke in whispers. If only she could make out half of what they were saying, it could be very useful to her story. However, once they broke their impromptu conversation, the big man—whose name she still hadn't gotten—flopped back on the cot, his expression haunted.

Like a man who hadn't known an acquaintance had been murdered. . .

Lu scribbled in her book.

Suspect was startled by news of either Serafina's or Mary Redmond's murder. Not a feigned shock, either. His face paled as soon as I said their names, and he rose to confer with Sheriff Downing.

"So I take it from your reaction that you weren't aware of Serafina's murder? Or was it Miss Redmond's?"

The big fellow gulped a breath and settled his elbows on his knees, rocking slightly.

Had the news of one or both of those deaths honestly disconcerted him so? A pang of guilt lodged in her chest. How could he not have known? It had been big news, ever since Miss

Redmond went missing on her way home from the restaurant late one night.

The man must be playacting—an accomplished liar who'd kidnapped and murdered several, acting the part of an innocent man.

She pressed on in her questions with one that had plagued her thoughts since she first learned the detail. "Why did you shave the women's hair?" The clippings hadn't been left at the scene, so what in the wide world would someone want with them?

"Stop your yammerin', woman!" Downing growled from around the corner. He clomped across the floor. A door opened, then slammed. When he stepped into view again, he carried a bedroll and a pair of saddlebags.

Downing pulled the large key ring with numerous keys from his desk and paced to his prisoner's cell. "Braddock."

Seeing Downing holding the bedding and saddlebags out to him, the big man rose and pulled them through the bars.

Lu opened her book again and jotted the name. *Braddock.* It was something, anyway.

The loud turning of a lock's tumblers drew her attention, and in a heartbeat, Downing had her cell door open. He crossed to her and, grabbing her by the wrists, pulled her to her feet. Her book and pencil tumbled from her fingers, and as she mentally scrambled to retrieve them, Downing hoisted her onto his shoulder. She screamed, fighting to free herself from his ironclad grasp. He carried her out the front door, down the steps, and to a huge old pine with its lower branches sawn off. Downing dumped her on her backside in the bed of dead pine needles.

"Ow! You brute!" She smoothed her skirt, covering her petticoats so they weren't on display for all to see. Lu glared, though he didn't meet her eyes. Instead, he grabbed an object from the ground and clamped something cold around her left wrist. Her jaw went slack as he locked a shackle in place with a key from that same key ring he'd used inside.

"There, missy." He gathered the now-empty wooden crate he'd carried outside earlier and turned it upside down beside her. "You asked to be locked up. You got yer wish."

"You said you'd lock me in your jail cells."

"You ain't disruptin' my office with all your prattle." He patted the tree trunk. "This ol' girl here *was* the jail before Cambria Springs installed the bars for those cells. This'll be where ya stay until yer ready to follow instructions." He waved to a pile of heavy chain, one end attached to the shackle around her wrist, and the other locked around the tree trunk. "I'll bring you a canteen here shortly, but you got enough chain to move around a bit. Follow the shade of the tree, missy. You'll be more comfortable that way. And I'll leave the crate so's you don't have to sit on the ground."

Downing marched back toward his office, leaving her to gape after him. When the door clattered shut, frustrated tears sprang to her eyes.

This wasn't what she'd intended at all!

CHAPTER 2

Miss Mary was dead.

Rion's mind spun until he nearly expelled the flapjacks he'd downed. Miss Mary was a kind soul who had always greeted him like an old friend when he'd go to Dutch's Café. In fact, the way she smiled at him or paused to talk that extra minute when business was slow had always made him wonder if there wasn't some interest there.

If his life was more conventional, he might just've acted on that wonderment. Miss Mary was sweet enough to make a man want to mend his ways.

In their whispered conversation, Downing had told him Mary had gone missing somewhere between the close of the café the Saturday night of the Founders Day Celebration and its opening the following Monday. That news had sent him reeling all the more. He'd been in Cambria Springs that weekend, and seeing all the extra folks that'd come for the festivities, he worried for Mary's safety since the café was staying open extra long. So he'd promised to walk her the block and a half to her home.

He *did* get her home, durn it all! He'd walked her right to her door, waited whilst she unlocked it, and talked to her for a minute before she offered him her hand with a coy smile. Trying to be anything other than the backwoods simpleton he was, he squeezed her fingers, bid her farewell, and asked her to tuck herself inside. Disappointed, she had. . . And he'd sauntered off into the night, feeling stupid for not kissing her.

But Mary deserved a better man than him.

Only now, she was dead—and he might've been the last to see her alive.

Just like Serafina.

What was happening?

Downing's heavy footsteps drew him from his thoughts.

"You all right, Braddock?"

"Not particularly."

"Need anything for now?"

"Don't reckon so." Except to get free of this cell before they stretched his neck.

"Why don't ya save us all time? Tell me where ya stashed Hattie."

He lunged off the cot, going to the bars. "I ain't seen her since Sunday, down at the medicine show. I ain't killed a soul—not Hattie, Serafina, Mary, or anybody else." So why in blue blazes did it sound like he had—even to his own ears? "I'll thank you to quit accusin' me."

He paced back to the cot and slumped onto it, falling sideways as he pondered the sudden downturn of his life. One minute, his heart was pounding out of his chest as he realized little Kezia Jarrett was really Calliope. The next, she's unfolding a list of demented murders of women—some he knew or had talked to—with all the evidence pointing conveniently at him.

God, You and me ain't been on speakin' terms in a long time— not since You let Calliope, Andromeda, and me get separated years back. . .and since You dumped me with that merciless scoundrel, Garvin. But if You're pullin' the strings, thank You for lettin' my sister find me. Would You please let her be right—that You ain't a God who'd let her find her family only to rip 'em away again right off?

He glanced around, not seeing the question-box of a woman who'd marched in a while ago. "Where'd that little gal go?"

Downing crossed to open the door. There, framed in the opening, was the old pine tree some fifteen feet away and, in front of it, the gal screaming her fool head off in that charming little southern drawl of hers.

"I chained her to the tree."

"Chained her?" Rion pushed himself up, concern swelling in his chest. What was he thinking? It wasn't right to chain any woman to a tree—but that particular gal looked no more than thirteen or fourteen years old.

"That was Cambria Springs' jail before they built those cells there."

He glared at the lawman. "You're a durn fool, Downing! There's a murderer on the loose—killin' women—and you're chainin' one out in public like bait?"

"I won't leave her there forever. Just long enough to prove a point."

Downing closed the door again, though Rion rattled the cell bars. "Hey!"

The lawman faced him.

"Unlock her. Now!"

"Not doin' it, Braddock. For both our sakes. Neither of us needs to listen to that woman's incessant chatter." He turned toward his desk. "Now settle yourself down."

The heavy, plank door opened again, and Downing spun to face it as a form Rion instantly recognized stepped into view.

She stood in her classy blue riding habit, blond hair swept up in a braid she'd coiled at the back of her head, just beneath the top hat trimmed with lace and ruffles.

"Hello, Rion." She stared straight at him.

"Who're you?" The sheriff almost charged her, and she side-stepped with a yelp, straight through the door and to her right, shooting him an insolent look as she did.

"I am Maya Fellows, sir." She began working her hands out of her gloves. "Mr. Braddock and I go way back."

Downing eyed her, then turned on him. "That true, Braddock?"

Embarrassment lashed him. "It's been a while, Maya. What're ya doin' here?"

She gave him a sad smile as she peeled off the first glove. "I came here hoping to catch the medicine show before it left town. You know how such attractions speak to my love of show business." She meticulously tugged each finger of her second glove, loosening it from her hand. "I missed it but stayed the night. I was readying my horse for my return trip when the sheriff brought Trouble and Mischief into the livery and instructed the hostler to keep them. As soon as I saw them, I knew you had to be somewhere near, but it took time to discover where." She gave the sheriff an unsure look, then closed the distance by half, tugging her second glove off as she did. "I never dreamed you'd be arrested. Why are they holding you?"

Behind her, Downing began to speak. "Mur—"

"A misunderstandin'." He glared at Downing before returning his focus to Maya. "Just a misunderstandin'. We'll get it sorted out."

Sorrow pooled in Maya's eyes as she tucked the gloves away and marched right up to the cell bars, extending her hands to him. "Is there anything I can do? Do you need money? I've told you, Papa has means."

She'd made no secret of her father's money. Those means oozed from every pore. What she'd ever seen in him, he couldn't fathom.

He grinned at the familiarity of her small hands in his. His left thumb instantly sought the large oval birthmark that marked the back of her wrist, similar to how cream-laced coffee might stain a muslin tablecloth.

"I don't know what I need yet. It's all too new. But thank you."

"I should stay in town, make sure you're looked after and have the help you need."

She pulled her hands free and turned, eyeing the chairs near Downing's desk.

"May I, Sheriff?" She started for the blocky wooden seat, but the lawman gave a sharp shake of his head, stopping her in her tracks.

"Not now, missy. I got things to do. You need to go." He hooked a thumb toward the front door. "Ain't nobody stayin' here but him." Downing stabbed a finger toward the cell. "Leastways till I round up a deputy to sit with the ornery cuss."

"You ought to go," Rion called to Maya.

"I won't leave town."

"Go back where ya came from, durn it." Women he knew were turning up dead. "Please head home, Maya."

She turned to Downing. "Once you find your deputy, may I keep Mr. Braddock company?"

"That'll depend on Braddock and the deputy. Now. . .out." He waved toward the door.

Again, she turned Rion's way. "I'll be back. Are you sure you can't think of anything you need?"

Stubborn woman!

"No." Yes. He needed to get out of this cell and take his life back, but Maya wasn't the one to ask for *that* kind of help.

She bid him farewell, and Downing opened the door for her. Once again, the young reporter woman shouted from the shade of the tree outside.

Once Maya left, Downing swung an oily grin his way. "And

who was that, Braddock?"

"Just an old ghost hauntin' from my past."

His smile deepened. "Doesn't seem she thinks that."

A shiver gripped him. He needed to tell Maya *and* Calliope to stay far away. Women he knew were winding up dead.

If she'd held any humor for her circumstances, Lu had lost it an hour ago when the midmorning sky had darkened and thunder began to rumble. In the last few minutes, cold, fat raindrops had begun to splatter the ground, soaking her in the process.

"Sheriff!" Her voice had grown hoarse with all her shouting, but still he didn't come.

"Somebody! Help!"

Anybody. . .

The pace of the rain quickened, and she darted out from under what little protection the pine tree offered and scooped a palm-sized rock from the ground. Hurling it, she watched as it arced too high and hit the roof of the building, rolling a few inches before it stopped. She huffed but picked up a second and tried again. This time, the stone flew true and hit the door with a thud. Blinking water from her eyes, she waited. And waited.

As she searched for another stone to throw, a mighty flash traced across the sky above, lighting everything in an eerie glow. At the same moment, a thunderous boom exploded around her. Heart hammering, she pulled into a ball, her arms over her head, and a scream tore from her chest.

"Please! Help!"

"We're coming!" distant voices shouted back.

Lu huddled, trembling, both from the frigid raindrops and her own fear. Soon, sloshing footsteps hurried her way, and at the same time someone darted up beside her, a rectangle of yellow light fell across the soggy earth between the building and her. She looked up to find the face of the petite woman who'd left the sheriff's office that morning, now shadowed by a western hat that dripped a curtain of water.

"We'll get you inside. We're getting the keys now."

She nodded, and the other woman wrapped a slicker-clad arm around her, trying in vain to shield her from some of the pelting drops. Just a moment later, more splashing footsteps, and the woman's earlier companion unlocked the cuff from around her wrist.

As soon as he got the shackle open, they all dashed to the log building's wide porch. Lu barged through the open doorway, searching for the sheriff. The only one in the place was Braddock, watching from his locked cell.

"You all right, miss?" His eyes were wide, maybe even spooked, as he stared at her.

Another bright flash filled every window and door, and a heart-stopping boom went off, louder than the last.

"Get inside!" The man shoved her and the other woman farther through the door. When it clapped shut, she yelped, trembling as water cascaded from her clothes.

The other woman came alongside her, shrugging out of her long raincoat. "Are you hurt?"

Lu stared around the room, fear wrangling with anger. "Where is that chicken-livered sapsucker?"

"Downing went out the back about an hour ago, miss." Braddock hooked a thumb to indicate the only door on the back wall. "He often ties his horse back there durin' the day. I told him to let you loose first, but. . ." He shrugged.

Her gaze darted toward the door, and she slopped her way to it. Behind it was a darkened storage room with boxes and crates, a rack with several long guns, and on the far wall, another door leading to the outside.

"I'll see if Downing has any towels or blankets you can use to dry off."

Lu shuddered. "Please!"

The little woman hurried toward the storage room, and her companion checked the supplies on the shelves above the pot-bellied stove. He pulled down the big coffeepot from its hook.

"I'll start some coffee." Still clad in his long oilskin coat, he hurried outside and filled the pot from the rain barrel.

Inside the room, a match flared, and the woman looked around then lit the lantern hanging beside the door. "I don't believe I got your name. I'm Kezia Jarrett, and he's Stephen Nesbitt." The woman indicated her companion outside.

A fresh chill grabbed her. "Lucinda Peters."

"How'd you come to be chained to that tree?"

"That idiot, Downing, put me there. I got in a tussle with him about interviewing either him or the prisoner, and the ill-tempered bully chained me to the tree."

Miss Jarrett gaped. "On what charge?"

"None." She wrapped her arms around herself as more chills set in. "Just to make a point."

Glancing around, Miss Jarrett pulled supplies from shelves until her arms were loaded. She laid them on the floor within easy reach. "I've found a towel, some blankets, and. . ." She perused another box. "They aren't exactly fitting for a woman, but—" She shook out a pair of trousers and a shirt fit for a small man. Miss Jarrett sniffed the fabric. "They smell clean enough."

"Anything's better than these."

Once she tossed them atop the towel and blankets, Lu shut herself inside, checked that the back door was locked, and fought her way out of the sopping layers.

"Thought Downing said he was gonna send his deputy

whilst y'all went searchin' for Miss Hattie." Braddock's hushed voice carried easily through the thin walls of the storage area.

Muffled footsteps crossed the room. "He deputized me and went on his own." A growl tinged Mr. Nesbitt's voice.

She dried herself, straining to hear anything further.

"Rion," Miss Jarrett spoke, "we need to talk about the night she disappeared."

So his first name was Rion. . . Rion Braddock.

Lu pulled the shirt over her head, rolling the sleeves so they fell at her wrists.

"Like I told Downing, I don't know anything. I left your boardinghouse and went straight to the base of the game trail, then on up to the cave. Didn't see no one. Didn't stop nowhere. And there weren't anyone in the cave to vouch for me."

"Do you know where Annie Tunstall lives?" Again, Miss Jarrett asked the question, giving Lu pause. "Have you been by her place at all?"

She stepped into the trousers without unfastening the waist, which was huge around her slender frame. She looked for something she might use as a belt, to no avail, so hiking them as high as she could, she knelt and rolled the legs.

"I don't know anyone named Tunstall or where such a family lives." Braddock paused. "What part of town?"

Lu couldn't make out the answer.

"Ain't been in that direction in days. I been around the meadow where the medicine show was, over to the boarding-house, and the roads in between. That's it."

"How are your tracks in that barn if you weren't?" Again, Miss Jarrett spoke.

"You two are the detectives. You tell me!"

Both Mr. Nesbitt and Miss Jarrett. . .detectives? Was that meant as a mocking barb or a statement of fact? If the latter, detectives for whom? What detective agency would be interested in the disappearance of Hattie Ingram or the murders of two others in Cambria Springs?

Oh, goodness. Too many details. Too many questions. She needed her journal. . .

With a firm hold of her pants, she eased out the door, the strong scent of coffee meeting her as she did. "Pardon. I don't mean to interrupt."

Mr. Nesbitt's eyebrows arched at her appearance, and Miss Jarrett stepped out of the open cell to peer her way.

"Would anyone have any twine or rope for a belt?"

Rion Braddock also came to the cell door and suppressed a grin, then disappeared back into the space.

Silent, Mr. Nesbitt went to the desk and riffled through the drawers, but after a moment, Braddock called out.

"C'mere, miss."

Barefoot, she padded to the cell door where he met her with a faded red bandanna he'd rolled. He held it out to her but realized she'd not be able to tie it so, awkwardly, he nodded toward her middle.

"Can I?"

Her face grew hot, but she nodded, and the big man bent intimately close as he threaded the old bandanna behind her and tied it in a knot at her waist.

"That work?"

She loosened her hold on the pants and nodded. "I think it does. Thank you." Self-conscious, Lu stepped back. "I appreciate it, Mr. Braddock."

The man acted as if he might speak but simply nodded, then almost dove for the far side of the cell.

When Lu turned, Miss Jarrett stood nearby.

"I think the coffee's about done, miss, but if you don't mind, would you drink it out on the porch so we can speak to my brother in private, please?"

Brother. . . Kezia Jarrett and Rion Braddock were related?

Mr. Nesbitt had paced to the stove and was pouring cups of coffee.

"If you don't mind, I'd like to collect my journal." She pointed to the floor of the second cell where it had landed hours earlier. "Then, I'll return to the storage room and wring water from my clothes. They're completely saturated."

Mr. Nesbitt carried two cups over and handed one to Miss Jarrett and the other to her. "That'll be fine, miss."

"Thank you." She padded into the other cell, collected her things, and returned to the other room.

With the coffee to fuel her, she quickly jotted notes, straining to hear more. However, the three kept their voices low, preventing her from hearing as easily.

Using a wooden pail she found, Lu wrung out as much water from her own clothes as she could, then laid them out to dry wherever she could find space. Unable to hear much, Lu draped a blanket around her shoulders and worked at finger-combing the tangles from her hair, hoping she might eventually glean more nuggets.

CHAPTER 3

That little woman could talk the ears off a cornfield!

Sheriff Downing had left no instructions regarding Lucinda Peters' release, so after their long conversation that morning, Rion found himself with a jail mate. Trenamen had locked the woman in the far cell before he and Calliope had gone to interview the Tunstall woman and her boy again and to aid in the search for Miss Hattie. What should've been a quiet day with plenty of time to think of how to escape his present circumstances ended up being a day of Lucinda Peters' chatterboxing, particularly when he'd turned his back on her and begun tearing his bedsheet into thin strips. He'd done his best to ignore her questions, eventually playin' possum to get her to hush. It worked, right up until a key turned in the front door's lock. Then, Rion ceased his playacting and sat up.

When the door opened, it wasn't Downing. Not even Trenamen. Instead, Calliope entered with the same basket the sheriff had brought earlier, though it looked heavier than before.

"Afternoon." His sister smiled. "I've brought supper."

She swept in, hefted the basket onto the desk, and then drew the burlap curtain back from the front window.

Rion squinted against the late-afternoon sunlight, noting Trenamen talking to someone in the street outside.

"Dutch sent over stew." Calliope pulled food from the basket—two servings this time. She carried one to Miss Peters and, a moment later, brought Rion his bowl.

As Rion sat again on the cot, Trenamen clomped up onto the porch and, after taking a moment to scrape mud from his boots, entered.

Rion busied himself with stirring the hearty stew, then spooned a big chunk of meat into his mouth.

"Braddock, you up for a visitor?"

He glanced up as Maya emerged in the doorway.

"Rion!"

He stalled after one chew then rolled the bite of beef to the other side of his mouth. "Maya. Thought I told ya to—"

"I told you earlier—" She hauled the nearest chair toward the bars and sat. "I'm not going anywhere. Someone has to keep your spirits up."

He chewed a few times, then swallowed hard. "My spirits are fine."

"They couldn't possibly be. Word is, you're facing some serious charges."

As if reminding him would help.

"Where are you stayin' these days, Maya?" He spooned another bite into his mouth.

Grinning, she waved a hand. "You know me. I'm always on the move—wherever I can find a play to act in."

Yes, that had been her reasoning for ending their relationship years ago—though he'd always figured it was more that she—a woman of means—eventually grew bored with his simple, even backward, ways.

"So you're an actress?" Miss Peters called from down the way.

"I am—as is my whole family. Maya Fellows." She stood and curtsied in Miss Peters' direction, then faced him again.

"Since you asked, Rion, I was most recently in a production in Denver, though it ended several weeks ago, so I've been traveling since then."

"Where else have you acted, Miss Fellows?" Miss Peters asked.

"Oh, goodness. Where haven't I? I've crisscrossed the country many times. I've acted in New York, Omaha, Denver, and San Francisco, and everywhere in between. I've played everything from fine English ladies to southern belles. Grieving young widows to impressionable girls still under their parents' care and tutelage..." She spoke the last words in a range of appropriate accents and affectations.

"You're very talented." Calliope almost gushed as she approached. "And how do you know Mr. Braddock?"

He shot Maya a warning look with a tiny shake of his head, but when she only grinned at his sister, he braced himself for the retelling of the tale.

"We met in a cemetery." She giggled.

"A cemetery!" Calliope and Miss Peters both gaped.

Heat washed through him. "Maya, that's enough!"

"It's not quite as bad as what it sounds." Maya turned toward his sister. "We met years ago during a dark time. My brother had died weeks before, and I'd gone to the cemetery one afternoon to visit his grave. But in my grief, I stayed too long and found myself in the awkward position of having to walk myself home after nightfall."

"Maya!"

"Rion was also in the cemetery. Had been all day, in fact—hidden, watching for one of the men he was trailing. He found me instead and insisted I not leave to walk home in the dark—that it was too dangerous to be out alone. He promised if I'd wait for him to finish his business, he'd escort me safely. I had no idea what that business was until he knocked a man senseless with a shovel, tied him up, and tossed him in a grave they'd been digging late that afternoon. Then he saw me safely to my door and even returned to check on me the following day."

Calliope stared, slack-jawed, then turned to him, fighting giggles. "You're full of surprises, Mr. Braddock." She focused again on Maya. "Didn't that frighten you?"

"Actually, miss, I felt very safe. It was all very exciting."

Another wave of heat crawled up Rion's body. "That's enough, Maya."

The little busybody in the third cell set her bowl of stew aside and took up her book and pencil. "Where did this happen?"

"Denver."

He glared in Trenamen's direction. "Get her out of here!"

Joe grinned at his expense but did start toward Maya. "All right, miss. I think it's time—"

"Please don't make me go." Tears welled as she cast a sideways glance at Trenamen then hurried to the bars and pinned Rion with a pleading look. "I'm worried for you. As much as anything, it will help *me* to be here with you, Rion." She produced a lacy handkerchief as she started to cry softly.

Trenamen paused and shot him a questioning look.

Rion waved the man away, set his cooling stew aside, and then went to the bars himself. "I'll be fine, Maya. They ain't got nothin' on me that can't be overcome with the truth."

If only he believed that.

"They say you murdered a waitress, a prostitute, and a spinster woman with some difficulty walking."

"We have hope Hattie Ingram is still alive," Calliope called. "We're hoping we'll find her quickly."

"It almost makes one frightened to walk these streets."

He pried her hands from around the bars and held them.

After one long look into her eyes, he focused on the birthmark on her left wrist to keep her tears from catching him off guard again. "That's why I'm askin' ya to go, Maya. Where's your father right now?"

"California."

"And your brother?"

"Charles is with Papa. They're playing a father and son in a show in San Francisco."

"Then go back to Denver and stay with your friends." He cupped her cheek. "Promise me."

She pulled away, rubbing her jawline. "You're still trying to send me away."

"For your own good, Maya. I'm poison to pretty gals like you right now."

Feeling something sticky on his palm, he found a flesh-toned substance marring his hand.

Her cheeks turned crimson, and she reached to wipe his palm with her handkerchief. "Sorry. Removing all the makeup we wear to combat the gas lighting in the theater has left my skin irritated. I wanted to look my best when I saw you, so I covered some of the blotches before I came."

"You look right pretty. Now, promise me you'll stay with your friends in Denver. Please."

She blew out a loud breath. "Fine. I'll go. But I'm not pleased about it."

Thursday, June 26, 1873

Howling wind and thunder split the silence. Lightning flashed, startling Lu from sleep. Her heart pounded as memories of fat raindrops pelting her rushed back. Where was she? She reached out and touched the thick log wall beside her, then cautiously looked around. Lamplight flickered from a desk near the far wall, bringing everything into focus.

The jail...

Sheriff Downing hadn't returned, and Deputy Stephen Nesbitt had not taken her word that she wasn't truly under arrest. She hadn't minded being locked in the cell to interview Rion Braddock, but she'd not expected to spend the night. Especially such a blustery night as this. If she'd gleaned more than the handful of minor facts—if Braddock had bothered to answer even one of her questions throughout the day—she'd have felt a lot better about staying the night.

The man was an immovable, unshakable wall of silence. He'd either sat on the end of his bed tearing up a perfectly good sheet—was he that frustrated?—or he'd slept.

From the direction of his cell, something shuffled, and his soft grunt drew her ear. Lu rolled over, head resting on her arm, and peered through the bars. His cot was empty. She sat up, searching the shadows.

There. He squatted in front of his cell door, fiddling with something, though his big frame blocked her view. A moment ticked by before he rose and gave something a hard pull. The cell door rattled. Seemingly satisfied, he crossed to the edge of the cell nearest to her. Again, he fiddled with something, this time his big body shielding the light of the lantern Deputy Nesbitt had left burning, leaving whatever it was he was doing in shadows. When he finally did move, allowing her a view of his handiwork, there was a rope strung between the door and the nearest heavy logs that held up the roof. Where had he gotten the rope?

She squinted, but unable to see, she padded barefoot to the closest edge of her own cell.

Oh! He'd braided the strips of his bedsheets into a makeshift rope.

Braddock threaded the end of the rope through. . . ? She squinted, trying to make sense of what she was seeing. Through what? Some kind of loop. He shifted just enough to reveal what looked like a slipknot in the rope only a foot or two from where it was tied to the door. Tugging the whole length through, he gave a hefty pull. The cell door rattled, wood creaked, and the rope grew tight.

Suddenly uneasy, she eyed the log support. "What're you doing?"

Startled, he whipped around with a loud exhale, releasing all the tension from the rope as he clapped a hand over his heart.

"In the name of Juniper, woman! You about scared me to death!"

Lightning flashed and loud thunder followed.

"What are you doing, Mr. Braddock?"

"None of yer business. Go back to sleep!"

How could she possibly sleep now? Yet he glared at her until things grew awkward, and she padded back to her cot, pulling both trade blankets she'd been given into her lap.

Once more, he leaned back, pulling the loose end of the rope through the slipknot until it grew taut like a bowstring. Keeping the pressure on with his right hand, he stretched again toward the big timber support and looped the loose end around the log a second time, fed it through the slipknot again, and threw his body weight into drawing it even tighter.

The door rattled and strained with a metallic protest, and the log groaned like an old wooden ship tossed on rough seas. Lu held her breath, eyeing the ceiling to be sure it wasn't going to fall in. This time, he gave the rope several mighty tugs, and even the fabric squealed with the tension placed upon it. When he released it, he made no effort to hold it with one hand. It seemed to hold itself, allowing him to go and rattle the cell door. Producing a sheathed knife from his pocket, he tried to insert the blade between the door and its frame but found no success, so returning, he pulled on heavy leather gloves that he grabbed from his cot, circled the rope around the log and back through the slipknot again, and pulled as if he were trying to lift a several-ton boulder. Metal ground, the log creaked, and the makeshift rope screamed its protest. To her amazement, the door appeared to bow under the torque.

When Braddock padded to the door this time, knife in hand, he easily inserted the blade between the door and the frame and, with a couple of prying movements, released the door with an ear-piercing scrape. Immediately, all the tension on the rope gave way, and the end looped around the timber fell loose to the floor.

He darted back to his cot, pulled on his boots and hat, and unrigged the rope contraption. Coiling it in long loops, he rolled it into his blanket, slung his saddlebags and canteen over his shoulder, and strode from the cell. At the desk, he picked the lock on the drawers with the same knife and, opening one drawer after another, eventually set the large key ring on the desktop. Then, riffling through some of the other drawers, he pulled a gun belt from one, uncoiled it, and swung it around his hips. He checked the loads and thumbed bullets from the loops on the belt into the empty cylinder, then reholstered it. He stashed various other knives on his belt, in his saddlebags, and even in his boot. Then, scooping up the key ring, he crossed to the front door and fumbled through the keys until he found one to fit.

Only then did his gaze stray in her direction. She pulled her two borrowed trade blankets closer across her lap as if they might somehow protect her from the big man whose face was cast in eerie shadows. He rattled the heavy keys again and went to her door.

"You belong here even less than me." His voice was a low rumble, mildly gruff, but not unkind. "You want to leave, you leave. If you stay, you didn't see nothin'. You just woke up and the door to your cell—and the jail building—were open. Understand?"

At her silent nod, he found the key to fit her door. The tumblers rattled, he popped the door open, and after depositing the keys on the desk, he walked to the door. As he jerked it open, lightning flashed again, illuminating his frame in the doorway just before he disappeared into the night.

For the space of several breaths, she stared at the darkness beyond. The damp night air crept in, chilling her, and she blinked in wonder.

Rion Braddock had somehow overcome the iron bars and escaped, as if it were easy.

Oh! The subject of her story was getting away!

She lunged up, snatching her journal, both blankets, and the canteen Deputy Nesbitt had given her, and scurried into the back room. Spreading one blanket on the floor, she situated her clothes and belongings onto it, rolled it into a long roll, and tied it across her body like a thick sash. Stepping into her still-soggy shoes, she laced them, tossed the other blanket around her shoulders, and went to the front door.

The sliver of moon was cloaked behind storm clouds, leaving only the frequent flashes of lightning by which to navigate. Lu went back for the lantern, pulled the door closed so as not to draw undue attention to the building, and charged down the muddied porch into the street. The wind blew, lightning flashed, and low thunder rumbled. She craned her neck to see into the distance.

Braddock was nowhere in sight. Like a ghost disappeared in the mist.

Lord, where has he gone?

Exiting the door, he'd turned left. . .

If what she'd heard in conversation that day was true, he had two fine horses he'd want to take. The livery would be a safe bet. And he would intend to be out of there as quickly as possible. She must hurry!

CHAPTER 4

Rion slogged through the muddy streets, staying in the shadows as much as possible, especially with the lightning. Rather than enter the livery's main door, which was closed at this time of night, he circled around, jumped a livestock pen fence, and entered through the back entrance.

The heavy rain that had fallen since the previous day had done him a favor. As wet as the streets still were, he wouldn't leave obvious tracks marked by the crescent shape in his boot heel. But just inside the livery, he traded his boots for his moccasins. They'd keep him from leaving tracks inside the barn—and allow him to move in relative silence.

His horses were in side-by-side stalls. He led Trouble out first, tacked up, and tied his meager belongings behind the big black's saddle. Mischief took even less time, considering the gear he usually tied behind his brown horse's saddle was stashed somewhere he couldn't take the time to find. He led both horses out the back, circled around the pens, and slipped into the darkness, hopefully unnoticed. Finding a secluded place between darkened buildings, he paused.

Where to go?

Far from here. Maybe Texas or California—he could

reconnect with the other fellas he'd escaped from Garvin with years back.

Yet the idea didn't sit right. Not after findin' Calliope—and maybe Andromeda too. But how could he stay? If he did, his neck would get stretched.

He *had* to go—but where?

The cave above town was off-limits. It would be the first place Trenamen and Calliope would look. He needed to go somewhere unexpected.

Lightning flashed, and thunder followed only a second later. Behind him, Mischief shifted and stomped, releasing a distressed whinny.

Not like him to be bothered by a storm. . .

Rion glanced back. "Ho, boy. It's all right."

The brown horse settled again after a second, and Rion faced front, drumming his fingers on his saddle horn. After a moment, sounds of a horse splashing down the street sounded. Rion twisted to see a man on horseback, holding a lantern—though he couldn't make out the rider's features. Waiting several breaths, he faced front, and as another flash brightened the sky, Rion nudged Trouble into motion. The thunder cracked extra loud, echoing between buildings. Behind him, Mischief sidestepped and pulled on the reins in Rion's hand, releasing another whinny.

He whispered a curse and urged Trouble to go before that other rider turned back to investigate.

What in blazes was wrong with Mischief? He was more easygoing than Trouble, but the lightning and thunder had the horse riled. Maybe he'd head down the mountain, get himself to the little spot he knew where he could rest an hour and plan his direction. He turned east, walking Trouble slowly, and eventually found the street he wanted, thanks to the flashes of lightning. Strangely, Mischief didn't react to them, not since they'd begun moving.

Maybe bein' between the buildings had spooked him. . .

Turning off, he found a path that would take him cross-country. It'd be harder travel, for sure, but he'd be too easily spotted on the main roads.

At the path's entrance, Rion shoved aside several low branches overhanging the path's mouth. Ducking around those, he urged Trouble forward and released them. As the branch snapped back, a startled gasp ripped through the relative quiet.

Heart pounding, Rion jerked his pistol from its holster even as he threw himself out of Trouble's saddle.

"Who's there?" he growled.

"Me," Lucinda Peters' familiar voice answered—from the direction of Mischief's saddle.

"How the—" She was on his horse? "How'd you get up there?"

"Easy. When you stopped between buildings, I came up on your horse's right side, between him and the building. . .and waited for an opportunity when the thunder would cover the creaking of the saddle while I mounted."

He swore under his breath. The cunning little—

Rion hoisted the pistol toward the sky and cocked it for effect. "Get off!"

"I'm going with you." Her voice quavered.

"Not on your life! Get down—and walk yourself back to town, woman."

There was the slightest pause. "If you force me to go back, I'll sound the alarm—wake the whole town, and tell them that you've escaped and what direction you went."

Rion gritted his teeth. She'd be just that sort. Any woman fool enough to march into Downing's office and shut herself in a cell to get his story would probably pound on every door until she got the town up and searching for him.

"You are a pain in my backside, woman! You're gonna slow me down, get me caught again."

"I'm from strong stock. I'll keep up."

"I don't need no company!"

"I doubt you do. You're all too comfortable on your own. But I can help you clear your name."

His racing thoughts stalled. "What're you talkin' about?"

"Too much evidence points straight to you, so either you're the most inept murderer in the world or you're not guilty. I'll help you prove the latter. . .if you let me tell your story once we're done."

Rion swallowed hard, uncocked his Colt, and holstered it again. "You durn well better keep up, or I'll leave ya in these woods. On foot."

"Yes, sir. I agree to your terms."

Lu fought the urge to let loose a loud whoop. "I took the lantern from the desk before I left, if you want it."

He paused. "Where is it?"

"Here." It rattled as lightning flashed.

He muddled toward her, and when he finally reached her, their hands brushed in the exchange.

With a sharp inhale, he drew back suddenly, nearly fumbling the lantern, though more lightning showed that he caught it in time. Thunder boomed, and she fought down a shiver as it sparked memories of being trapped in the thunderstorm the previous morning.

"Thanks." He turned toward his horse. "All right, miss. Shut your yap, stay low over Mischief's neck, and I'll lead, leastways till we get some distance out from town."

She tugged the blanket tighter around her shoulders and took firm hold of the saddle horn. "I'm ready."

Beneath her, the horse began to move, and for a solid hour, the only sounds were those of their mounts and the world around them. Thunder, steady hoofbeats, dripping trees, splashing water, sucking mud, the soft rustling of the underbrush, and the occasional night call of coyotes in the distance.

Lu drowsed in the saddle, her hand firmly affixed to the horn, when finally Mr. Braddock lit the lantern. The yellow glow on the trees around them teased her awake.

From his horse's back, he stared. "Exactly how old are ya, miss?"

"That's a rather impertinent question." Particularly to wake up to.

"I mean no disrespect. But they're thinkin' I'm the man what killed a slew of women, and they'll be thinkin' I kidnapped you. So—am I lookin' at facin' the kidnappin' of a grown woman or a little child? 'Cause ya don't look much over fourteen to me."

"I might *look* young, Mr. Braddock, but most would deem me a spinster." At twenty-five, perhaps she was just entering her spinsterhood, but she was a spinster nonetheless. Papa and her brothers had done their level best to change that fact, pushing one eligible bachelor after another at her—but if it meant returning to boring days of keeping a man's house and looking pretty, she was just fine with spinsterhood.

"All right, then." He clucked his tongue to get the big black moving. Her horse followed at the tug of his reins.

"How old are you?" she called.

He was silent for a moment, then cleared his throat. "Reckon maybe about twenty-five. Somewhere around there."

"You don't know?"

"Not rightly, no."

Her jaw slack, she stared at the broad shadow that was his back. "How do you not know your own age?"

"Easy. Ain't nobody made a fuss over my birthday since—" He fidgeted. "It's been some years, and I lost count."

Lost count? How could he just lose count? Was it not a matter of simple arithmetic?

But perhaps it was better to let that pass for now. "I'm...sorry."

For several more minutes, Rion led her horse, but finally he turned up a path and doubled back the way they came for a short distance. Then, out of nowhere, a cave appeared to their left.

Mr. Braddock paused before they reached it and dismounted. Drawing his gun, he paced forward, checked the cave, and walked back to lead both horses toward it.

"I was gonna rest here an hour or so, but it's best I leave you here and go on."

"Go on?!"

"You'll be safe here till daylight, and you can make it back to Cambria Springs by noon."

"Now just a minute."

"Please tell Call—Kezia Jarrett I'm safe."

"I told you I'd help clear your name in exchange for getting to write your story."

"You didn't actually think I'd let you ride with me, did ya? Bein' on the run ain't no life for a lady."

Her frustration flared. "Don't consider me a lady. Consider me a dime nov—" She snapped her eyes closed, then stiffened her spine and glared at him. "A reporter. I go where the story leads."

He narrowed a glance. "Ain't neither one good, but which is it? Dime novelist or reporter?"

Heat washed through her. It was hard enough to get anyone to take her seriously without putting a fly in her own ointment.

Defiant, Lu folded her arms across her body. "A dime novelist trying to become a reporter."

He released a sardonic chuckle. "Why're you doin' this, miss? Shouldn't you be married or somethin'?"

"Married, my foot!" What impudence! And how like a man to think that marriage was the answer to every woman's problems! "My father and brothers tried to force several different men on me, and I want none of it." Not after she'd learned what it meant to be strong, resourceful, and self-reliant taking care of Papa after that Yankee bullet robbed him of the use of his legs. "Now, your story could give me the break I need, so let's talk."

He rolled those brown eyes. "I don't reckon so." He mounted the black again and gathered the other's reins. "Wait here, miss. Once the sun dries the path some, the walkin' will be easier. Just head back the way we came. You'll make it to town without skippin' two meals."

CHAPTER 5

Rion reined Trouble toward the larger pathway, Mischief following.

Lu Peters' voice rang out in the predawn. "So who do your sister and her. . .partner. . .work for? What agency?"

Now how did she know—?

He drew Trouble to a stop and, twisting in the saddle, glared at her.

"What're you talkin' about?"

"They're detectives, aren't they? Your sister Kezia and Mr. Nesbitt. Though Kezia's not really her name, is it? You nearly called her something else just now."

But he'd said nothing about her working for the Pinkertons. Had he? Did he talk in his sleep during the few moments he'd actually rested?

"Where are you gettin' this?"

"Same place I got the information that Miss Mary Redmond was a friend of yours, and maybe more."

He dismounted and marched up to her. "What're you talkin' about?"

"You ignored all my questions until I said her name. Who was she to you?"

"That ain't your business."

"And what about your visitor—Maya Fellows?"

His hackles rose. "You leave her out of anything you write. She ain't involved."

"So who is she?"

The little woman was graspin', tryin' to keep him there. He smiled. "Ain't none of yer business." He returned to Trouble's side.

"Like I said before, either you're the most inept murderer in the world or someone has set you up."

He paused with his foot in the stirrup.

"I'd like to help you discover who that is. Now, I've gathered from your whispered conversations with your sister that these murders have spanned the last five years. She tucked a list of the deaths in your breast pocket yesterday. Why don't we take a look. Maybe we can ferret out who the likely suspects are."

He lowered his foot and touched his shirt pocket.

"Yes, that one."

She'd seen Calliope slip that to him? He'd been sure she was turned away.

As if reading his mind, she continued. "I almost missed it. She was very sly, moving in to kiss your cheek before she left last evening and whispering that she'd written you the list."

Heat crawled up his spine.

Miss Peters approached, watching him intently. "Why are your cheeks flushed, Mr. Braddock? You didn't think I'd noticed that tender moment between you and your sister?"

After years of separation and only being reunited for a day, Calliope's unexpected peck on the cheek had surprised him—and felt too personal for his liking. Maya was the last woman. . .the only woman. . .he'd let so close, and she'd wounded him when she ended their courtship to take a part in a play in a city far away.

Granted, there was a big difference between a romantic interest gone awry and his baby sister reentering his life, but circumstances of his past hadn't left him with a whole lot of trust—for anyone. "Not exactly that, miss, but it don't matter."

"Have you read through it yet?"

"Don't figure I need to." He stretched to alleviate the knots forming in his neck, then stared into the distance. "I didn't kill nobody."

She looked as if he'd gone cross-eyed. "That would've been the first thing I did. Look at the list and start trying—"

"Well, that's the difference between you and me, ain't it?" He towered over her. "Ain't just one way to investigate a matter."

She drew back, confusion marring her pretty features for an instant before her eyes lit.

"Oh." A little breath whooshed out of her. "You don't read, do you?"

The whispered words struck like a volley of arrows. "Of course I read!" He glared. "My father was a professor at a big college back in New York. Taught languages—Greek, Latin, Hebrew."

Her lips parted. "Don't get so riled, Mr. Braddock. I'm not calling you stupid. Any man able to so easily overcome a cell door like you did—and with only an improvised rope—is *not* a stupid man. Rather, he's a brilliant one!"

"Brilliant... Right." Now she was just toyin' with him.

He reached for the saddle horn, ready to mount and be off before things went anymore sideways.

"Please." She caught his arm, and just like when she'd handed him the lantern an hour ago, her touch sent a shock through him. A startling and pleasant one.

Jerking free, he took a big step back and stared. If he got out of this without getting his neck stretched, he really needed to go to town more, be around people. This solitary life was beginning to play tricks with his mind.

"I'm sorry. I didn't mean to embarrass you. And if I'm wrong and you do read, then forgive my misperception. It's just that you. . .you said you'd lost track of how old you are, and then you were flustered at me knowing and asking about the list, so I thought—"

"I'm simple." Shame washed through him afresh as he struggled to breathe.

"—you're a very intelligent man who has difficulty deciphering the written word."

The fact that she wasn't laughing like others had when they'd learned his secret loosened his tongue ever so slightly.

"The marks jumble on the page. I struggle to follow 'em."

She smiled, compassion in her eyes. "I can help with that—if you'd let me."

He eyed her a moment then glanced heavenward as the morning sky brightened. Fishing the folded paper from his shirt pocket, he handed it over.

"Read it whilst we ride. They'll be discoverin' before long that we're gone, and I don't want 'em catchin' us."

As daylight broke, the path became much more visible, and the mud dried some, allowing them to make better time, though Mr. Braddock was obviously concerned about their tracks. He purposely chose difficult paths and rocky areas, and he backtracked to cover their horses' hoofprints when they couldn't find any way around the mud.

As they rode, Lu looked over the list and formulated questions. However, when she rode alongside him and started asking them, he scowled and put his finger to his lips. It was only as they stopped around noon at a partially caved-in mine shaft that he finally said anything.

"We'll stop here to rest." He kept his voice low.

"For how long?" She needed to eat. Surely he did too, although she had no provisions and he had only the contents of his saddlebags. Besides that immediate need, sleep pulled at her.

"That'll depend on who's followin' and how close. We'll try to stretch it for a couple hours, but be ready to move if I say so."

She nodded. "I will."

They dismounted, and he loosened both horse's cinches.

"Can we talk about your list now?"

"Gimme a few minutes—see if I can't rustle up somethin' to fill our bellies. You know how to make a fire?"

"It's not hard, Mr. Braddock."

"And you know to look for dry wood, don'tcha?"

Of course. The wet stuff would smoke terribly—if they even got the flames to light the sticks. "I'll do my best." She wrinkled her nose. "There was a lot of rain yesterday, you know."

"Hadn't noticed." He returned a playful smile and a wink. "Get what you can carry. I'll bring some too. Build the fire inside the mouth of that mine shaft. It'll help disperse the smoke. And keep it small. Easier to put out in a hurry."

They went their separate ways, and soon she returned with an armload of wood and got busy building the fire. He returned a bit later with three squirrels, which he skinned, cleaned, and put over the flames. Only then did he turn to her.

"So. . .what about this paper from Kezia?"

The way he said his sister's name—as if he struggled to recall it—made her think again that it wasn't her real name. But she'd thrown that bait out, and he'd ignored it. No sense harping.

Lu pulled the list from the cover of her journal and moved closer.

"So the first murder was a senator's daughter in Chicago, May of 1868."

"Yeah, and my sister said that happened around the time

they named U. S. Grant as the presidential nominee."

"Exactly. That's what it says here—and that you were in Chicago at the time."

"Right, but I didn't kill no one." His tone grew defiant.

She acknowledged his declaration with an emphatic nod. "Understood. The second murder happened in St. Louis, just short of one year later. And Miss Jarrett's notes say you were also there at that time. You recall it because of everyone celebrating the Transcontinental Railroad's completion."

"Yep. And I didn't kill her either."

Again, she nodded. "Let's save some time. I don't believe you've killed any of these women—so there's no need to say so."

"All right."

"For the next several list entries, there's no note on your whereabouts."

"She didn't tell me about them."

"The third is a—a soiled dove. Alice Haskins. She went missing between Christmas and New Years in Omaha."

"Let me guess." A hard edge filled his voice. "Three Christmases ago?"

Lu copied details into her journal, not wanting to miss anything, then returned her attention to the list. "Yes. Eighteen seventy. How did you know?"

Glowering, he fed another stick into the fire, then turned the meat.

"Mr. Braddock?"

He heaved a breath. "My sisters and I were orphaned young—I was about ten when it happened. We got put on one of them orphan trains and adopted to different families along the line. The fella what took me in—Ellwood Garvin—he was. . .evil."

"I'm sorry," she whispered as she scrawled that name into her book.

"There was five of us boys stayin' with Garvin, and we all escaped together years back. Two of 'em live here. Dutch, the café owner in Cambria Springs. And Seth. Seth married a pretty little gal about three years ago. Her family was from Omaha, so at Seth's request, I rode the train with him and Lena to see her kin at Christmastime. We stayed about a week."

Both fell silent as Lu jotted notes and he fumed.

His was a difficult history. Orphaned. Adopted by an *evil* man—though what made him evil wasn't clear. It seemed the escape happened long ago. Had he had a family since then? She ought to ask, but if she pushed too hard, he might jackrabbit on her.

Finally, she pulled the list out again. "Victim four was Kathleen O'Malley, murdered in Denver that next summer."

He raked a startled glance her way. "The singer?"

"That's what the list says. Did you know her?"

"Maya took me to one of her concerts once. She'd do shows in Denver pretty often, so if I wasn't huntin' a bounty, I'd go. But I didn't *know* her. Never said a word to her. I just liked her voice. It was real pretty."

"And you would've gone to her shows often?"

"Every night she was in town, if I could."

Lu copied the details down. "I'm so sorry."

He turned a hard look her way. "Who else?"

"Norma Varden from somewhere south of Cheyenne, Dakota Territory."

Mr. Braddock swept his hat off and ran his fingers through his dark hair. "Sometime after June last year, right?"

"You knew her?"

He nodded slowly. "A fella I was huntin' up that way caught

me by surprise. Shot me in the leg with an arrow. Wasn't long, and I was in a bad way. Mrs. Varden found me and took me back to her place. She, her man, and their twin girls nursed me back from the brink. Let me stay on till I was healed up. June last year." He shook his head. "Those poor girls."

What could she say? Every one of these murders was heart-breaking—and it must be especially hard recognizing that his association with each one had possibly cost them their lives.

"We'll find out who did this, Mr. Braddock, and they'll pay for every life."

He clamped his eyes shut. "That don't bring back little people's mamas. . ."

"No, it doesn't."

"Who else?"

"The three from Cambria Springs. Mary Redmond. Sweet Serafina, and now Hattie, all this year."

"And I had some contact with all of 'em." He huffed a breath. "Makes me look guilty as sin."

"Therein lies the problem. *Everything* points to you. Since I met you, you've been careful. You didn't leave the rope you used to overcome the cell door. I know you didn't intend to keep me with you, but you didn't leave me in town to point the way to you. Now that the ground is drying out, you've been meticulous about covering our tracks. You made sure I knew to look for dry wood. Yet whoever killed these women has *tried* to point to you."

"Not sure I'm followin'."

"For instance, I overheard your sister say something about a distinctive boot track at the most recent murder—and from the scene of Hattie's disappearance. Yet you're wearing moccasins."

"I always wear moccasins when I'm on someone's trail. They're quieter, more comfortable. They don't leave tracks."

"Which proves my point. Someone is setting you up. Who, from your past, has enough against you to go to such trouble?"

"Ellwood Garvin comes to mind. He's hateful enough."

"That's the man who adopted you."

Mr. Braddock nodded. "He's accused me of stealin' from him. . .among other things."

Lu scribbled in her book. "Who else?"

He turned the meat again. "Like I told my sister, I'm a bounty hunter. Folks hate my guts for puttin' 'em in jail—or getting their kin's neck stretched."

"You've been a bounty hunter for more than five years?"

"Me and Seth collected my first bounty back. . ." He scowled. "Not long after we escaped Garvin's place. Before I was a full-growed man."

"All right. You've been at this long enough. Do you recall the men you've caught over the years?"

"Some, yeah. Not all."

Her hopes faltered, though his brown eyes suddenly lit.

"I keep the posters on the ones I'm lookin' for in my saddle-bags. And after capturin' 'em, when I get back this way, I drop 'em at Seth and Lena's place. Seth promised he won't get rid of none of 'em."

"And where does Seth live?"

"Up the mountain. We'd have to ride past Cambria Springs, and we might run smack into a posse if we do."

"Mr. Braddock, we need those posters."

"You best rest up, then, 'cause this ride ain't gonna be easy."

CHAPTER 6

Cambria Springs, Colorado Territory
Friday, June 27, 1873

It was a huge risk, returning to Cambria Springs before heading to Seth and Lena's place, but he and Lu Peters needed provisions, and besides Seth, Dutch was the only one he could count on. So he'd left Miss Peters and the horses and slipped into town on foot.

Despite the late hour, the glow from the café windows told Rion his friend hadn't yet gone to his small upstairs apartment for the night. Either he was still cleaning his kitchen or was cooking to make breakfast easier to serve.

Rion didn't have time to waste.

Leaving the alley across the street, he ducked onto the street, keeping to the shadows where possible. Reaching the far side, he hurried between buildings a few storefronts down and backtracked to the back of the café. There, he shimmied up the drainpipe that ran beside the second-story window. With effort, Rion slid the lower pane up and pulled himself partway into the sparse room.

As he did, lamplight bobbed up the steps, and he met Dutch's eyes.

"Howdy." Rion's grasp faltered, and he slipped back.

Dutch hurried over and hauled him the rest of the way in the window by his belt. They both tumbled onto the floor, and as quickly as he could, Dutch untangled himself and slammed the window shut.

"What in blazes are you doin' here? There're two posses gunnin' for you, and I wouldn't be surprised if there's folks patrollin' the streets."

Rion shot him a sheepish grin. "Two posses?"

"One went up the mountain, one went down."

"And you're not with either one?"

"Nobody asked. Reckon they know we're friends—which is why you ought not be here. They're probably watchin' the doors."

"Which is why I came through the window."

"And that's not suspicious?"

"I need your help. Food. Rifle. Ammunition." Shaking, both from the exertion and the near fall, Rion settled himself in a nearby chair.

"Tell me you didn't do what they're accusin'."

"You know me better'n that." And it rankled that his adopted brother even asked. "I'm tryin' to prove my innocence."

"Well, you're lookin' pretty guilty, escapin' jail and all."

He scrubbed a hand over his beard.

Dutch pulled a small stool over, staring at him with concern. "You all right, Ri?"

"Would you be if someone was makin' you look like a monster, killin' women for sport?"

"Don't reckon so." Dutch looked him in the eye. "What about the woman that was in the jail? She with you?"

"She's nearby and safe."

"Ri, you need to be careful. They still haven't found Hattie Ingram, and if she eventually shows up dead and you're caught with another woman in tow, they're gonna—"

"I know!" He clamped his eyes shut. "I had no intention of takin' her, but the durn woman climbed up in Mischief's saddle without me knowin' it, and..." He waved a hand. "Never mind. You got any of the stuff I mentioned?"

Dutch glared as he rose. "Stay here." He headed downstairs, this time without the lamp, and returned minutes later with a canvas bag. Settling it on the stool, he reached in and produced a fabric-wrapped bundle.

"I figured you might be stoppin' by, so...there's a slab of salt pork, a few day-old biscuits, some fresh corn dodgers." He unknotted the fabric to reveal the fresh batch. "A mess of pemmican. Some rags and bandages, in case... And help yourself to my rifle and whatever I got in the way of ammunition."

Rion went to the cabinet where Dutch kept his guns and pulled down the rifle, checked it, and drew out two boxes of rifle cartridges, as well as two boxes for his Colt. Pacing back, he tucked them into the bag.

"Thanks." He gave Dutch a solemn nod.

Dutch tied the sack. "Now, you do me a favor. Keep yourself alive. I ain't in the mood to lose a brother and one of my oldest friends."

"I'm doin' my best."

He rose, gave his friend a firm handshake, and started for the window, though Dutch caught his arm.

"I'm gonna turn down the lamp, like I'm headin' to bed—in case anyone's watchin' my place. Wait about ten or fifteen minutes, then slip out the downstairs window. Side of the building, in the storeroom at the back. You know where I mean?"

"Yeah." Rion grinned. "That's a lot easier than shimmyin' down your drainpipe."

"A lot less dangerous too."

"Thanks, Dutch." Again, he shook Dutch's hand, and the other man pulled him close, gave him a hearty slap on the back, and then stepped back.

"Be careful."

⌒

What was taking so long? Lu paced, darting worried glances toward town. Mister Braddock should've been back by now. From her vantage point in the trees, she could sometimes see movement around the distant lights flickering in town, but she was too far away to discern what was causing the wavering.

Lord, please don't let him have been captured. Bring him back safely with the provisions...

Both Trouble's and Mischief's ears pricked, and heated voices sounded from some distance away. She listened, unable to make sense of the sounds, other than someone seemed to be calling out or—

A distant gunshot and a muzzle flash split the quiet darkness. Lu's heart galloped. *Oh, Lord!*

She tightened the cinches on both horses' saddles and climbed onto Mischief's back, holding tight to Trouble's reins. In the distance, more shouting. Lights flooded the street. Her breathing shallow, she watched as mayhem erupted. People called to one another, and lights illuminated windows up and down the street.

"It's Braddock!" someone shouted.

What should she do? Go, and leave Mr. Braddock to find her? Wait, and risk being captured herself—potentially labeled an accomplice? If she knew where Seth lived, she could try to meet him there, but he'd not told her. He'd only said to be ready to leave in a hurry.

Oh, Lord Jesus—help. Help us both! Mister Braddock is as much a victim as the women he's accused of killing!

"Lu!" His hushed call from some nearby place gave her a jolt, and she jerked toward the sound. "Get on Trouble!"

Trouble? That was *his* horse.

"He went this way!" someone slurred. Shadowy forms raced past the lit-up windows.

No time to question. . . She slid from Mischief's saddle and mounted the larger horse. As her backside contacted the leather, he appeared.

"Take this!" He shoved a rifle in her hands as he looped something heavy around the saddle horn. Then, without a word, he swatted her left shin, and when she drew her foot from the stirrup, he climbed up behind her. His body wrapped around hers, his mouth near her ear. "Don't lose hold of that rifle."

She nodded, mute.

He spurred Trouble into motion, and Mischief's reins pulled tight in her hand. Behind them, voices called and more gunshots pierced the night, one spattering tree bark in her face. She yelped, and Rion wrapped himself tighter around her, navigating deeper into the trees.

Sounds of a mounted pursuit crashed behind them. Rion said nothing, though his labored breathing gave away his stress. He reined Trouble down a dense path, his arm circling her waist.

Despite the pursuit, she sank into his embrace, one hand wrapped tight around Mischief's reins and the other around the rifle.

Lord, please—put distance between us and our pursuers.

They rode, the sounds of the chase not stopping. Sweat slicked her skin under the man's shirt she still wore. Rion silently guided Trouble up the path, breathing hard. On occasion, he glanced back, his grip loosening. Each time, she was thankful when he faced front and reasserted his hold.

After one such check, he spurred Trouble into a faster pace and, coming out on a little rise, immediately reined the horse to the left and down a narrow path, putting a tall, rocky outcropping between them and their pursuers.

"Get down," he breathed before sliding from behind her, taking the rifle as he did.

As she dismounted, he paced the wide spot on the path, then hurried to where she held both horses. Taking Mischief's reins, he did *something*—she couldn't tell exactly what in the darkness—and dropped the horse on its side.

"C'mere. Quick."

She went to where he lay across the horse.

"Stretch yourself out across Mischief's neck. Cover his nose, and speak real soft to him."

"What're you going to do?"

"Hide Trouble. Quick, or they'll catch us!"

Again, without questioning, she followed instructions. She stretched out next to Rion, across Mischief's neck, and as Rion rose, the horse remained remarkably calm.

"Easy, Mischief." The horse's ear flicked, but he made no sudden moves or attempts to get up.

Focused on keeping the brown horse calm, she didn't see where Rion and Trouble went. Minutes later, the men pursuing them rode up to the rocky outcropping, one calling to another. Mischief did stir then, straining as if he wanted to react, though she laid a hand on his soft nose and breathed a brief prayer in his ear.

"Lord, keep us calm and make us invisible like You did Peter when your angel led him out of prison in the book of Acts."

The horse settled despite the chaos on the other side of the rocks. The men called to one another, words slurring as they debated what direction to go.

At one point, one rider rounded the outcropping, stopped ten feet from them, and peered into the darkness, eventually tipping something to his lips. His shadowy form swayed in the saddle, and his horse pranced as the man nearly tumbled off. Lu trembled as she kept her hand over Mischief's nose.

"Burl!" another called. He must have twisted in his saddle, based on the creak of the leather. "He went this way."

The man reined his skittish horse around to rejoin his party.

Lu didn't move, listening to the posse crash up the path beyond her.

Lord, keep Rion safe.

In the distance, tree branches broke, and a heavy thud met her ears. She cringed.

"There! I hear him."

A gunshot rang out, and Lu buried her face against Mischief's neck, trembling as her thoughts ricocheted to what her father had told her of being trapped in the woods, enemy soldiers all around him, after a bullet severed his spine.

Lord, is this what Papa experienced? How often she'd imagined it—but until this moment, she couldn't grasp the reality.

"He's gettin' away!"

Their hoofbeats and hollering faded, and she eventually looked up, her heart pounding.

Lord? Was it safe?

She held her breath and listened. When she was sure they were well beyond hearing range, she rolled off Mischief's neck, and the big horse climbed to his feet, though she remained on the ground, trembling too much to stand. A minute later, the brush rustled, alerting her that someone was coming. Tears streaked down her cheeks.

"Lu?" Rion's familiar whisper split the stillness.

A sob lodged in her throat, though she fought it from escaping.

"Lu." He kept his voice low. "Where are you?"

Gulping a breath, she attempted to stand. "I'm here."

He was next to her before she realized it, lending a strong arm to help her up.

"You all right?" His voice was thick.

"Yeah. Just—" *Scared.* But if she said it, he'd dump her like he'd planned at the cave.

"I'm sorry." He pulled her into a hug, and his one strong arm circling her did wonders to calm her racing heart. As she attempted to bury her face against his shoulder, he released her all too quickly. "I was tryin' to keep myself between you and those drunken idiots and their guns."

She swiped at her cheek, feeling something warm and sticky as she did. As she pulled her hand away, it was wet. *Oh, Lord Jesus.*

"Are *you* all right?"

Turning, he faced Trouble as he slid the rifle—which he'd taken from her at some point, she wasn't sure when—into the scabbard. "Mount up. We need to git, before those fools figure out they're chasing a rock I threw."

"Rion." She caught his arm, and he grunted, her hand coming away even more sticky.

"You've been shot."

"It's nothin'."

"Hogwash!" She dug deep for the calm she'd once possessed as she'd cared for Papa after his injuries brought him home from the war. "We need to take care of—"

"I crammed a cloth in the holes for now."

"Holes—plural?"

"I appreciate your concern, but we need to put some distance between us and those fools—and quick. Then we can worry about dressin' any wounds proper. Now, mount up."

He swatted her hip, and she scrambled to mount Mischief, though after what just happened, she would've preferred the comfort of riding with him again.

CHAPTER 7

Saturday, June 28, 1873

"Rion. . ." Lu's soft call from afar off drew him, though he couldn't make himself respond.

Not good. Everything hurt. A chill swept him.

"Rion."

Was she all right? Her voice was small but urgent, like she was calling from a great distance. She sounded terrified. . . He should hold her, soothe her trembling, but—

"Rion."

Something grabbed his left arm, and his eyes flew open. He reached for his pistol, but pain ripped through him, causing him to sag, left hand braced against the saddle horn.

Beside him, Lu sat in Mischief's saddle, staring back with a mix of fear and worry.

"You passed out sometime after we cleaned your wounds."

He vaguely recalled her demanding they tend to the bullet holes, but afterward, he'd insisted they get back on the trail.

"I have no idea how, but you stayed on your horse, so I kept us moving."

He glanced around, trying to make sense of his surroundings.

There was light—was it dawn, maybe? They were still in the trees, but...

"Just over that rise, there's a large lake down below. I think we're northeast of Cambria Springs."

Then they were headed in the right direction. But how far had they gone?

"Where do your friends live? How far?"

His eyes shut again, and he shook his head. "I don't know—"

"Rion!" When she jostled his arm, he looked up.

Releasing the saddle horn, he retrieved his canteen and managed to free the cork stopper and down some tepid water. Replacing it, he met her concerned gaze.

"Show me the lake."

She walked Mischief toward the top of the incline.

As he urged Trouble to follow her, a stiff breeze blew, and a full-body shiver gripped him.

God, if You're listenin', I'm in a bad way. Please help.

They needed to stop, build a fire, boil water, and clean the wounds again—then keep going. But as fatigued and in pain as he was, once he dismounted, it would be a struggle to mount again.

As he moved, his eyelids slid closed, and he shook his head to clear it, jolting himself with pain in the process. He nearly tipped sideways.

Durn it all, Braddock. Hold yourself together.

He righted himself in his saddle, and only a moment later, Lu Peters drew up as a steep, treed slope opened before them. At its bottom, a beautiful, clear lake filled his sight. He drank in the serene view.

Rion bit back a curse.

Dutch had said there were two posses—one that went up the mountain, and one down. The large group breaking camp on the far bank had to be one of 'em. At least fifteen men—and one woman? No, two!—rolled bedrolls or saddled horses while a few others scrubbed plates or pots at the lake's edge.

He clumsily dismounted and shoved Trouble's reins in Lu's hand. "Take the horses back out of sight and tie 'em. Hide 'em in the brush, if you can."

She started to turn, though he grabbed the rifle from its scabbard before she moved out of reach.

Once she departed, he found a vantage point where he could see through the trees toward the posse below, and squatting, he made a tube with both hands and lifted it to his right eye.

"What're you doing?" Lu whispered when she returned minutes later.

"Lookin'."

"I meant with your hands?"

He glanced her way then returned to his former position. "It's...a poor man's telescope. It blocks out all the other sights and helps ya focus on the thing you want to see." He scanned the faces of those in the camp across the lake.

Lu jostled beside him, her shoulder brushing his injured one, jolting him. Irritation compounding his pain, he found that she'd also put her hands to her eye.

"That's...amazing." For an instant she stared, then drew back, rubbed her eyes, and tried again. "Is that Dr. Chellingworth?"

"The medicine show fella?" He furrowed his brow.

"Yes. And—" She gasped. "Elisabeth Gates!"

"Who?"

"The sharpshooter and trick rider from the medicine show."

Rion put his hands back to his eye and stared down at the camp, seeking the faces one by one. The woman was easy enough to spot, her being one of the only females down there. He'd not been privy to her display of skill that Sunday, given he'd walked with Trenamen out to Mrs. Ingram's wagon, but the woman looked vaguely familiar, despite her face being half hidden by her Stetson hat and her mass of fiery-red corkscrew curls. Maybe it was just the bright hair, but perhaps he'd seen her in the background as the others had performed.

The pair stood off to one side, the strange-lookin' Dr. Chellingworth assisting the woman in wrapping her right wrist in a bandage-like cloth, then lacing some type of leather glove or cuff over it.

What on earth...? It was hard to see at that distance, even with the improvised telescope, but it looked as if it slipped over her thumb, wrapped around her hand, and laced along the palm side.

Why would she wear such a thing?

"You said she's a trick rider?"

"Yes—her tricks were astounding!"

Maybe it was a brace to prevent injury—or help heal one. But once Chellingworth had laced the cuff tight, he smiled at the young woman and settled hands on her shoulders in a rather intimate gesture before sending her along with a wave.

Rion scanned the other faces, recognizing men from town. Sheriff Cooper Downing was there. Joe Trenamen. And Calliope. The pair's presence gave him some hope he might get a fair shake, but why were two women ridin' on this posse?

Lu glanced over. "Why are the medicine show people riding with that bunch? I thought they'd moved on."

His shoulder cramping, he eased his arm to his side with a groan and felt beneath his shirt for fresh blood. "Folks don't take to anyone harmin' women out here." Including him. After what he'd seen—and suspected—from Garvin all those years back, he'd had his fill. "Reckon people might come out of the woodwork to hunt the one they think's doin' the harmin'."

Fatigued, he sat, back against a tree.

"We need to check your wounds."

"Just make sure I'm not leakin' blood. With that posse so close, we ain't got time to do it proper." Rion stared at the lake. "I think I know where we are. We're not far from Seth's. Another hour, at most."

⟋

It finally happened. Once they were away from the lake and perhaps halfway to Seth's place, Rion passed out again and, this time, fell from Trouble's back. No amount of jostling or calling his name had awakened him. The single bullet had punched through his shoulder and left a hole, back and front. Both had grown angry and hot. She had no choice. Once she'd wrestled his big frame off the path as best she could, she set out to find Seth and Lena's place, alone. Thankfully, Rion had told her where their house was, so with a fervent prayer for his safety and her own, she rode for help.

After what seemed forever, the pretty little clearing opened ahead of her, just as Rion said it would, and in that beautiful glade was the log house he'd described, smoke curling from the stone chimney, even as the door stood open. In the corral out front, a man brushed down a brown horse, not unlike Mischief. As she neared, he glanced up then stopped, dropped the brush into a bucket hanging from a nearby fence post, and ducking between the fence rails, walked toward her.

"Can I help ya?"

She glanced around. "Would you happen to be Seth Kealey?"

"I am." He nodded toward Trouble and Mischief. "You want to tell me how you come to possess those horses, miss?"

Behind him, a woman appeared in the open door of the log house, holding her rounded belly.

"I'm a friend of Rion Braddock's. He's not far from here,

but he's been shot."

His eyes rounded. "Shot?"

"It's a long story, which I'll explain, but please help. He's in danger."

The man didn't hesitate. He dashed back, saddled his horse, and with a quiet call to the woman, let the horse out through the gate to meet her.

"What's your name, miss?"

"Lucinda Peters. Lu."

"All right, Lu. Lead on."

She headed the way she'd just come, Trouble trailing her, and Seth following close behind.

"Tell me what happened. Did someone Rion was chasin' get him?"

Suddenly overwhelmed, she felt tears sting her eyes. "Rion's being framed for murder."

"Murder?!" He nearly roared. "Of who?"

"Seven women—and the kidnapping of an eighth."

Silent seconds ticked by until she finally glanced back to be sure he was still there. He was, though he'd stopped.

"You weren't joshin' when you said it was a lot."

"You don't know the half of it. There's a posse on our trail—and they're close."

He urged his horse to catch up. "All right. Take me to him, and we'll cover the rest once he's safe."

They finally reached Rion's location. While she watched for the posse, Seth wrestled Rion's unconscious frame over Trouble's saddle. Unable to move quickly, Seth walked the horses ahead of her, and she watched the ground for blood drops as well as any trouble behind them. By the time they reached the house, an hour had passed, and Seth wrestled him inside and onto the table in their small kitchen.

As Lena heated water and gathered bandages, she and Seth unbuttoned Rion's shirt.

"Now explain to me how in heaven's name this man is wanted for—what'd you say?—seven murders."

"Seven?" Lena gasped.

"I'm not sure. I came in partway through. Somehow, Rion reunited with one of his sisters, and—"

"Wait. His sister? Calliope or Andromeda?"

"She isn't using either of those names. I think she's a detective for some agency. I'm not sure which. When I came into Rion's world, Kezia Jarrett—that's the name she uses now—was delivering him to the Cambria Springs jail."

Seth stared. "His own sister arrested him?"

"Yes, but she and the man she was with, Deputy Nesbitt, didn't seem happy about having to do so. They were trying to help him."

As they worked to free Rion from his shirt, Lena brought shears and cut the sleeves from around his arms, and Lu quickly unfolded the story of how they'd met, her own incarceration, their escape, and all that had transpired between then and now.

"Once we realized this might be tied to his bounty hunting, we came here. He said you have the old wanted posters he's collected on."

"Yes, miss. I do. I'll get 'em once we're done cleanin' these wounds. They're in the cellar, near the cot where he sleeps, and the only door's under the table."

"He'll have to look through them anyway. He knows the history. I don't." She heaved a deep breath. "Now. . .how can I help?"

"You look wrung out, hon." Lena beckoned as she waddled toward a doorway at the end of the room. "These past few days couldn't've been easy. Why don't I get you some warm water so's you can freshen up, maybe close your eyes and rest."

She watched as Seth began soaking away the dried blood.

"I feel like I should stay." Just like she'd done for Papa years ago. She couldn't just abandon her post. "There's a posse near, and—"

"Honest, miss. I'm gonna have Lena step away while I clean and cauterize these wounds. Neither of you needs to see that."

She didn't want to—but she'd done plenty of difficult things in caring for Papa, and if needed, she could again.

"Rion and me—we've been lookin' after each other a long time. Let me handle cleanin' him and gettin' the bleedin' stopped. Once that's done, I'll leave it to you gals to bandage him and whatever else needs doin' while I try to cover y'all's trail. All right?"

She couldn't force herself from the spot until Lena waddled in carrying a heavy basin and ladled hot water from the pan on the stove into it. Seeing her struggle to manage the full basin around her big belly, Lu took the bowl and followed her into the next room. The space contained a bed, a hope chest, and little else but the washstand. Lu set the heavy bowl down.

"Have you anything more fittin' to wear, miss?"

Lu glanced at the men's trousers and the oversize shirt, still belted at the middle by Rion's bandanna. "I have my clothes wrapped in the blanket tied behind Mischief's saddle, but they were drenched when I traded them for these. I've no idea what shape they might be in now."

Lena nodded. "I'll put Ri's horses up and get your things. If need be, I'll find ya somethin' of mine to wear. I got dresses I haven't worn in about seven months now." She rubbed her large belly.

"Thank you. You're very kind." Lu nodded, and Lena exited.

For a moment, she could only stare, unable to believe she was safe. How long had it been since she felt that security? At the very least, since before Sheriff Downing chained her to the tree. But really, years—with only a taste of it here or there. One of those tastes was being told she could rest while Seth and Lena stood guard. Another had been as Rion Braddock rode behind her, his body shielding her to keep her safe

No one had ever acted so selflessly for her. She wasn't sure how to take that. But from that experience grew a tenderness in her heart for Rion Braddock that she'd never felt for any man before.

CHAPTER 8

Sunday, June 29, 1873

Between the cool darkness, the earthy scent, and the strips of light showing between the planks above, there was no mistaking his location. Seth's cellar. How had he gotten here? And when?

Light flooded down the stairs, signaling that the trapdoor was open. With effort, Rion sat up, though the movement brought lancing pain and dizziness.

"What in the name of Juniper?" He probed his shoulder, where most of the pain centered, and found himself shirtless and bandaged. Right. He'd been shot trying to slip out of Cambria Springs and make it back to—

Lu!

Cradling his right arm against his body, he eased to his bare feet. Drawing the wool blanket around his shoulders, he maneuvered around the shelves of jarred and canned goods and made his way upstairs slowly. Weakness pulled at him. Even that little effort drained him. When he reached the third step from the top, he tugged the blanket around him and sat on the floor, legs still inside the opening.

"Well, howdy." Seth, seated at the table now shoved against the wall, grinned at him over a mug of coffee. Beside him, Lena also smiled. At the other end of table, Lu Peters, dressed in a pretty brown skirt and a white blouse with some sort of delicate pink edging at the cuffs and collar, stared back.

"Howdy." He couldn't pull his gaze from the pretty sight of her in her womanly attire.

Lu offered a faint smile, her gaze fixed as well. "Morning."

"Need help gettin' to the table?" Seth called.

Eyes still locked on Lu, Rion cocked his head. "How'd I get here?"

"You don't remember?"

He shook his head.

"From what Lu tells us, you had quite a night." Lena's cheery voice didn't match the hazy images in his mind. "We hear ya nearly got yourself caught in Cambria Springs. . ."

He recalled that part, and the searing pain of the bullet that knocked him off his feet before he reached Lu and the horses, but after that. . .only a few ghostly images or recollections.

"We got away, but you were shot, so you pointed and told me Seth and Lena lived up this way. When you passed out, I took the lead and kept going until we stumbled on the posse."

He swallowed. "We ran into the posse?" How could he not recall *that*?

"Not directly. Across the lake."

The lake. . . He didn't recall being near any lake.

Seth cleared his throat. "You know, Gartner Lake, a few miles from here."

He nodded, eyes pinned on Lu.

She shrugged. "You told me how to reach Seth and Lena's place, so when you passed out and fell off Trouble partway there, I brought Seth back to get you."

"You coulda gone for the posse just as easy as here."

"I could have, but I meant it when I told you I'd help clear your name."

He heaved a big breath, sending another jolt through his right side. Once it passed, he nodded at her. "Thanks."

She grinned, and he was caught again by how pretty she looked.

"Did you do something to your hair?"

Her cheeks flushed, adding to her prettiness. "I washed it, let it dry, and pinned it up."

He was vaguely aware that Lena and Seth exchanged a glance then rose and left the house, shutting the door behind them.

"Looks real nice that way." With her hair pinned up, she still looked young, but she'd pass for Calliope's age, at least.

Lu joined him, sitting to his left with her legs dangling into the cellar opening, her knee rubbing against his. "How do you feel?"

"Weak as a newborn kitten."

Settling her small hand on his forehead, she slid it toward his temple, the gentle touch sending a shock through him like before.

"At least your fever's gone. You lost a fair amount of blood."

Lu tried to pull her hand back, but he caught it against his cheek. "Your touch is real soothing."

After an instant, she pulled away, though he settled his hand near hers in the space between them.

"I suppose that's a compliment."

"Did it sound some other way?" He wouldn't put it past himself, his thoughts addled like they were.

She chuckled. "I've had lots of practice. My father was wounded in the war and returned home without the use of his legs. My stepmother, Viola—a selfish, unfaithful woman interested more in Papa's money than in him—decided caring for a cripple wasn't the life she wanted. She abandoned us. For nearly three years, I was the only one Papa had, so I became quite adept at wound care and remedies."

He gaped. "How old were you?"

"Just fifteen when Papa returned. I was nearly eighteen when the first of my brothers returned at the end of the war and took over."

"I'm sorry." He squeezed her hand but released it just as quick. "That's a big burden for a young girl."

For a moment, she seemed to study their hands there, side by side. "I did what I had to."

"I'm sure your pa appreciates it."

"I don't believe Papa does."

"Why?" Why *wouldn't* he? There'd been no one in Rion's life to offer gentle ministrations, concern, or soothing words, so Lu's tenderness was a welcome change.

"Oh, in the midst, Papa accepted my help readily. Even demanded it. I became quite good at anticipating his needs and answering them. Not only did I have to learn wound care and remedies and how to keep him happy, but I also learned how to accomplish things in the dangerous world beyond our door." She flicked a glance his way, eyes brimming and cheeks flushing. "That's why I marched into the jail and locked myself in the cell beside you. I long ago found the best way to get what I needed was to make such an annoyance of myself that people would give me what I wanted just to get rid of me." Her eyes took on a haunted look, and her voice dropped. "Most of the time, it worked."

He swallowed hard. "What about when it didn't? Did somethin' bad happen? Somebody hurt ya?"

"I—" She folded her hands in her lap. "I got in a few scrapes, and there was one very close call, but by the grace of God, I got out of them all."

She swiped at her cheek, but not before a tear splattered on her brown skirt.

"I'm glad." He caressed her arm with the back of his hand. The idea of anyone hurting her unsettled him—whether in the past or now.

Especially now.

"Anyway, I don't think Papa knew how to appreciate my care. He needed me, and I rose to the occasion, but once my brothers returned from war, Papa tried to force me back to my former position."

"Which was. . . ?"

"Look pretty and attract the eye of a rich businessman Papa could join forces with. Apparently, I was to be married off to cement *Papa's* future, with no concern for my desires. But after proving to myself how much I could accomplish with almost nothing, I wasn't about to go back to being the girl-child raised to be seen, not heard. I didn't want to be anybody's pawn. So as Papa and my brothers were negotiating my marital future, I left. I'd survived Kansas during the war while caring for my invalid father. Surely I could survive out here with only myself to care for."

"You're brave," he whispered.

She adjusted her position and smoothed her skirt. "More like stubborn."

He locked gazes with her. "Tenacious."

"Bullheaded." She tapped her chest with a frown.

For an instant, he drank in the pretty hairstyle, the feminine clothes, and the expressive eyes filling with tears again, and then he grasped her hand. "Beautiful."

She offered him an unsteady smile and settled her hand over his.

The front door squeaked open, and Lena scurried in.

"Sorry to break this up, but y'all need to get in the cellar. Now. The posse's comin'."

Lu's heart, already pounding, beat all the harder as Rion jerked back to look at Lena.

"Go on. Let me get the trapdoor closed and everything back in place."

Moving carefully, Rion stood and reached for her hand. Lu slipped her fingers into his big palm and followed him.

"Your guns and gear are all down there, Ri. On the shelf nearest the bed."

"My shirt?"

"It's beyond repair. You got a spare?"

"I do."

Lu gasped. "Wait! I need my things!" She dashed up the steps, into the bedroom, and grabbed her skirt, blouse, and petticoats from where Lena had deposited them after a good washing. Returning, she grabbed her journal from the table and rejoined him.

With a solemn nod, Lena lifted the heavy trapdoor from where it was folded back against the floor planks. "Get yourselves hid."

"What about Trouble and Mischief?"

"Seth got 'em tucked out of sight among his herd up the mountain. Now, go. Hurry. Hide."

Lena shut the trapdoor, sealing them into darkness. Rion fumbled with something, even as Lena rolled out a rug and moved the table in place above.

Light flared, and Rion cupped a match in his big hands.

"You all right?"

She swallowed, whispering in hopes of hiding her fear.

"What if they come down here?"

"They won't see us."

"Lena just sealed us in! There's nowhere to go."

As the match burned toward his fingers, he touched it to the wick of a lamp on one of the shelves, adjusted the wick, and then padded toward the bed.

"C'mere." He grabbed his saddlebags, the bag of provisions from Dutch, the canteen, and his gun belt and rifle, and tossed them all on the rumpled bed.

As she approached, he fished a Henley shirt from his saddlebags and pulled it over his head.

Seeing him struggle to get his injured arm into the sleeve, she dumped her things and stopped him, pulled the shirt from over his head, and helped him thread his injured arm through the sleeve first.

"Thanks." Cheeks flushing, he pulled the shirt on then slipped into his moccasins. He snatched a thick stack of papers from under a couple of cans, rolled them, and tucked them in the bag Dutch had given him. Rion pushed the rifle, the saddlebags, and a blanket into her hands, gathered the rest of their things, and waved.

"Over here."

Her skin crawled. There was no obvious outlet, but he led her around the staircase to the wall where several big burlap sacks leaned against it.

"Do you trust me?"

She barely knew him. Yet since she'd first made his acquaintance, she'd watched him escape a jail cell with only an improvised rope, rustle up a three-squirrel dinner without firing a shot, escape a band of drunken idiots with guns, and navigate the mountainous terrain while wounded.

"I trust you."

"All right, then." He set his things down, lifted two heavy sacks aside, stifling a groan as he did, and revealed an opening with light visible on the other side. Rion extinguished the lamp, then returned.

"We're gonna hide in here. You'll have to crawl on your belly for a few feet to make space for me. As little as you are, you ain't gonna feel too cramped. Me, it's a tighter fit."

She peered inside, heart thundering at the cramped quarters.

"You don't have to crawl all the way through—just enough for me to get in. On the other end, the openin' is blocked by rocks, but not so blocked you can't see out. If the tight quarters get to you, you can crawl down there and peek out. But don't move the rocks. That's just on the side of the house, and the posse might be swarmin' around here."

Above them, muffled voices sounded—Seth's and another man's. Sheriff Downing's, maybe. Whoever it was, the posse—or its representative—had come right up by the house. She couldn't make out their words, but the tone sounded conversational. . . for now.

"You go first," she whispered, pointing toward the hole.

He shook his head. "I'll need to wrestle the sacks back in place so it ain't obvious there's a passage out of the cellar." He touched her cheek. "Ya just said it yourself—if you could survive wartime Kansas while carin' for your injured pa, you can do this. You're brave. . .and I'll be right behind ya."

Oh, Lord Jesus. Why was it easier to believe when looking into his eyes?

She fed their belongings into the hole, then crawled in after them. Inching forward, she eased saddlebags, then rifle and blanket full of her clothes, forward, keeping them from scraping across the floor. Progress was slow in her borrowed skirt, her feet tangling in the fabric repeatedly. As strange as they were, she'd welcome those trousers for this endeavor. Glancing back, she saw Rion slide in feetfirst, as promised.

The narrow channel rose with a slight uphill tilt at first, and when she finally reached a point where the soft glow of morning sunlight greeted her from a small wall of stacked rocks ahead, she stopped.

Her neck and shoulders ached from dragging herself, and the tunnel's roof was low in places. If she was uncomfortable, how much worse was it for Rion? In the narrowest of places, he might very well have gotten stuck.

Pressing herself to one side, she peered back, though the light didn't reach him easily.

At one point, she thought she heard the creak of the wooden trapdoor or perhaps the stairs. In response, she recognized the sound of his pistol pulling free of its holster. Her heart pounded, and she eased the rifle up close. Minutes ticked by, and muffled voices sounded behind her—Seth's and another man's.

Lord, protect us, please!

The voices faded, and the same wooden creak sounded. For several minutes more, all she heard was a slight shifting on Rion's part, the heavy exhale of a hurting man.

Lord, is it safe yet?

Dust motes floated in the sunlight trailing in between the stacked rocks ahead. Time stood still, and her mind wandered to what might be on the other side of those rocks.

Freedom.

Fresh air.

Space.

A large shadow.

Her mind snapped to attention, and she squinted at the darkness that had blocked out the sunlight. She gripped the rifle, finger near the trigger guard. She hadn't asked Rion, nor had she checked for herself to see if the gun was loaded. And there was no use calling back to him for cartridges now.

Lord, protect us. Please.

"Have you found her yet?" The sharp whisper echoed through the passageway at her.

"Still lookin'."

The whispery voice swore, and a scuffle ensued. "Tell me again how you lost a crippled woman! An *injured* crippled woman, at that!"

Her jaw hinged open. *Oh, Lord! They mean Hattie Ingram!* She was still alive? *Save her, Father, please.*

More swearing from the other voice. "Quit pushin' me around."

Father, who are these people?

As quietly as possible, she inched toward the tunnel's end.

"I'll do more than push you 'round if you don't find her and finish her."

"What do you think I'm doin'?"

"Not enough, you fool. Now get out of here, before you're seen."

One of them hissed another bitter curse, and before she could reach the wall of rocks and peek through one of the openings, the shadow disappeared, allowing the light to stream back in. She squinted, momentarily blinded.

By the time her eyes adjusted, hoofbeats retreated in two different directions—some toward the front of the house, and some toward the back.

And she'd seen exactly nothing!

CHAPTER 9

Something jostled his left shoulder, and Rion jerked awake and cocked his Peacemaker.

"Whoa!" Seth clamped a firm hand around his, where it and the Colt rested on his chest. "Give me the peashooter. The posse's gone."

Rion shifted his hand from the weapon. "I heard you talkin' in the cellar. Wasn't sure if I got the bag back in place."

"You did all right." Seth took the gun and eased the hammer back in place. "Sheriff Downing told his deputy to check down here. Stephen Nesbitt—and he had a woman named Kezia Jarrett with him?"

He wobbled a grin at Seth. "That's my sister. Calliope. Nesbitt's her partner."

Seth nodded. "Lu said somethin' about that. Been itchin' to ask you. I want to hear about this, but let's get you both out of that tunnel first."

That sounded good. After all the wrestling and movement, the pain hadn't relented. At least not until he'd fallen asleep. Or had he passed out?

Seth helped him wiggle free of the opening before assisting him back to the bed. As he sank to the mattress, a shiver grabbed him.

"Is Lu all right?"

"Goin' to get her now. Be right back."

Seth retreated, and Rion tried to watch for her to emerge, but his eyes were heavy. A wave of pain racked him. He stretched out across the mattress, and when he next opened his eyes, Seth had returned, Lu beside him, both with arms full of their belongings. When his eyes fluttered open, she deposited her things on the nearest shelf and squatted beside him.

"Are you all right?" She settled a gentle hand across his forehead.

"I'm spent—but I ain't hurt. No more than before, anyway. How 'bout you?"

She looked like she might speak but glanced up at Seth first. At his nod, she returned her focus to him.

"I heard something while we were hiding."

Lena came partway down the steps, balancing a tray between one arm and her rounded belly. When she cleared her throat loudly, Seth hurried to take the tray and assist her the remainder of the way down.

"What'd you hear?"

"Two people were talking outside the far end of the tunnel. They were whispering, and I was far enough from them that I couldn't see anything, so I'm not certain whether it was men or women."

"There was only your sister and the one other woman in the posse," Seth called.

He rubbed at the pain. "What'd they say?"

"It was a short conversation—about Hattie. One was angry that the other had lost her. He wanted to know how he'd lost an *injured* crippled woman, he said."

"Injured. Not dead."

"Yes." Lu nodded.

Slow as his thoughts were moving, they shot down the path she'd pointed him to. "If they're talkin' around here, maybe she's nearby."

Lu nodded. "I suspect so. The one said to the other to *find her and finish her.*"

Lena leaned into Seth's side. "That poor woman."

"We gotta find her." Rion tried to sit up, though Seth was quick to restrain him, even while balancing the tray.

"You're not goin' anywhere. You need to rest, at least for a few days. Get some strength back."

"But—"

"Rion, he's right," Lu whispered, settling a hand on his forehead once more.

Yes, Seth was right. This conversation was sapping his strength—fast. He was in no shape to sit a horse or search for Miss Hattie. But after the kindness the Ingrams had shown him, allowing a stranger to sit with them at the medicine show, he owed it to them to find her.

Besides, she might be able to identify the real culprit.

He peered up at Lu as she hovered nearby. "You're sure you don't know who was talkin'?"

She shook her head. "Before I could crawl to the end of the tunnel, the conversation was over, and they'd left."

Lena's jaw hinged open, and she looked at each of them. "Wouldn't that mean whoever was talking is part of the posse?"

Lu shook her head. "One told the other to leave before he was seen. I think one may have been—the one calling the shots. But I'm not sure the other is."

A shiver gripped him. "Can somebody get me a blanket?"

Lena snapped to work, freeing the two blankets from all the gear they'd taken into the tunnel with them and spread them over him. "I made you some broth, and I expect you to eat at least half of it." She jabbed a finger at the tray Seth held. "It'll help get your strength up. And I brought you some whiskey for your pain."

He wasn't one for strong drink, but hurting as he was? "I'll take the whiskey first."

It wasn't long before Rion was asleep, having eaten only a little of the broth. As much as Lu wanted to sit with him, she followed Seth and Lena upstairs.

"I feel terrible that I didn't see more."

Lena turned a startled glance on her. "You shouldn't. That was a difficult situation."

"You've got a whole lot more information now than you had an hour ago. And there's hope that Miss Ingram's still alive."

Lu shook her head. "Are there other people around—other homes?" With the fear-inducing circumstances and pace they'd had to keep getting to Seth and Lena's, she'd not taken time to look for other houses.

"There's a few who live not far below Gartner Lake." Seth's expression was grim. "There's not many of us above it."

"There is—" Lena cocked an eyebrow in her husband's direction.

He nodded.

Lu stared at the pair. "Who?"

"Ollie Sapey." He rubbed a hand over his hair. "A cantankerous old woman. Not long after Lena and me got married, we started buildin' this place. I was out huntin', came up on her place, and she gave me a strong warnin' to stay away. Said it'd be the only warnin' I was gonna get. I left. Didn't want trouble. But a few weeks later, I was out again, somewhere else, and the old biddy came out of nowhere and about blew my head off with her shotgun. She's an ancient woman, a recluse who, I reckon, don't like having neighbors."

"Do you suppose she might've seen something?"

"It's possible. She seems to have a way of knowin' what's happenin' on this part of the mountain. She moves like a ghost. I originally stumbled on her house unawares. The place is built right into the side of the hill, so it's easy to miss until you're on it. When she took the shot at me, I was in another area entirely."

Lena stepped nearer and ducked her head. "I didn't tell you, but she gave me the same warning not long after your run-in with her. And a few months back, I was out foraging things for a meal—three months ago, maybe?—and the old witch took a shot at me too."

"She what?" Seth roared the question. "You shoulda told me!"

"I didn't want trouble. This mountain's big enough, we can all live on it—"

"Not if we don't know what she considers hers!" He shook his head. "Takin' a shot at my wife—carryin' my child! I oughta go on over there and—"

"Get your fool head blown off? Then where would this baby and I be? You'll do nothin' of the kind, Seth Kealey."

Lu focused on the floor, thoughts spinning. "But maybe I can. . ."

Seth stilled in his fuming. "You can what?"

"Go over to this Ollie's place."

He looked at her as if she'd suddenly gone cross-eyed. "To what end? So she can shoot at you? I don't think so! For one, you don't need to be out roamin' the countryside with a posse huntin' you and Ri. For another, I saw the way my brother looks at you. . .and I don't want to face him if somethin' happens to you when I coulda prevented it."

"Hear me out. This woman gave you each a verbal warning,

and only on the second encounter did she actually fire at you. If she follows suit, then I could go under cover of night when she'll be less likely to see me coming, and I could get to her door."

"No!" Seth belted the word.

"If I can get there, I can ask if she knows anything about Hattie. If she knows everything that happens on this part of the mountain, maybe she saw something. Maybe she'll help us if we tell her a man's life hangs in the balance!"

"And maybe she'll decide to shoot on sight and not give a verbal warnin' like she's done before—and I'll be left explainin' to Ri how I let you get yourself killed. Or, you stumble on the posse, and they figure out you and Ri are about these parts—and you're both caught. No! It's a bad idea."

Lena laid a hand on his arm. "She might be on to somethin'."

"It's a fool-headed notion."

"No. Listen. Once night falls, you take her in the direction of Ollie's place. She won't see either of you, and you can keep an eye open for the posse while Lu does what she needs to. Now, when Ollie took that shot at me, she proved she is either one heck of a terrible shot or was purposely tryin' to miss me. I'm a little woman, and she aimed a good ten feet above me. You said the same when she took the shot at you—she shot high, rainin' tree bark and such over you."

Despite his silence, it was obvious Lena's words had Seth thinking.

"I doubt she really intended to hit either of us. It was another warnin'. Maybe there's a softer side to her than we think. . ."

"That's an awful big *maybe*."

"And what if Hattie is alive and Ollie knows something?" Lu whispered. "We could potentially clear Rion's name. . ."

Seth folded his arms as a muscle in his jaw popped. "What if she doesn't know anything at all?"

Lena smiled the smile of a woman who knew she was about to win her point. "Then what have we lost?"

He shifted his feet, glanced at each of them for an instant, and then shook his head. "I'll think on it, let you know by dusk."

A thrill wound through Lu's chest even as Lena stood on tiptoes and reached to peck her husband on the cheek. It was more than she thought Seth might agree to...

"Thank you," Lena whispered.

He grunted then brushed past her and marched into the yard. Once he was gone, Lena patted Lu's arm.

"Don't you worry, hon. He'll say yes. Just you watch and see."

CHAPTER 10

Water dripping. No, cascading. But only for a moment?

Rion blinked his eyes open and tried to orient himself. Still in Seth's cellar. He blinked a time or two more as Lena's face bobbed into view above him, and something hot and damp probed his shoulder.

He gasped as pain jolted up his neck and down his arm. Lena pulled back, and he breathed until the worst of the throbbing subsided. Then he squinted at her.

"Hey there, sleepyhead." She grinned.

"Howdy."

"Time to clean your wounds."

"I gathered."

"I know it hurts, but there's some infection, and we need to stay ahead of it." A sympathetic smile curved her lips. "You want the whiskey before I continue?"

He never had liked being drunk—not after seeing how Garvin acted after pickling himself in a bottle most of the time. The man was vile, and Rion wanted to be nothing like him.

"I'll try it without."

"You sure? You took some before."

He gave her a tiny nod. "The pain's not quite as bad. Either that or I'm getting used to it. Just give a warning before you jab me again."

Her expression turned grim, but she nodded. "All right." She must've dipped a rag or something into water, because the same cascading sound came an instant before she met his eyes. "I'll be as gentle as I can."

He nodded, and this time, bracing himself for her touch, he endured the jolting pain with gritted teeth, several stuttering breaths, and one long groan once it was done.

"Lu suggested we try a sugar poultice to draw out the infection, so I'm goin' up to the kitchen to ready that. Shouldn't take more than a few minutes."

"Where is Lu?" She'd been at his side throughout the day whenever he'd awakened, though she was conspicuously absent now.

"She and Seth had an errand to run."

"An errand?" Unless he'd lost a whole lot of time, it was still the same day the posse showed up. "What's that mean?"

"Don't concern yourself with it. Just rest. Seth'll keep her safe."

Lena rose and headed up the steps, leaving him alone with his thoughts.

Seth and Lu had gone on an unknown errand; but with the posse close by, how safe was that? Something about it didn't sit right. He trusted Seth completely, but Lena's comments set his teeth a little on edge, particularly how she'd said Seth would make sure Lu was safe. So there was some danger to this errand. . .and Seth was the one protecting her.

It ought to be *him*, not his brother.

With a huff, he fluttered his eyes open. What was he thinking? He couldn't even take care of himself at the moment, much less a woman full of spunk and daring like Lucinda Peters. Even without two holes in his shoulder, he didn't have the means. No proper home. No belongings but the clothes on his back, his two horses, and what little he could pack on them. Not to mention the fact that the life of a bounty hunter wasn't favorable for keeping a woman happy. He'd proven that with Maya.

He scrubbed his face with his good hand. How in the name of Juniper had he gone from not wanting little Lu Peters around to desiring to protect her—and even depending on her to save his life?

"You're a durn fool—"

"I am?" The wooden steps protested with a squeal as Lena descended. "Or did you mean someone else?" She crossed the cellar and settled herself in the chair beside him.

"Talkin' to myself. Not you."

She pressed something warm to his shoulder, both front and back, and wrangled for a moment with a roll of bandages. "Why're you callin' yourself a durn fool?"

"I'm thinkin' things I got no business dwellin' on."

"Like?"

His cheeks warmed, and he couldn't bring himself to meet her eyes.

"Ooooh. You're thinkin' on a little brown-haired beauty, are ya?"

Rion glanced away, all too aware of her knowing smile.

"Seth and I really like her. She's whip-smart and sweet as pie, and she's obviously very attentive to you."

He adjusted his position, regretting the movement when pain crackled through his right side. Once it subsided, he shook his head a little.

"I got nothin' to offer a woman."

"That didn't stop you with that actress woman—what was her name?"

"Maya Fellows."

"Yeah." She pursed her lips as she continued her bandaging.

"Not that it matters now, but we never did like her."

He attempted to turn his face her way, but she tipped his chin the other direction as she wound the cloth around the poultices.

"You didn't say nothin'."

"Would you have listened if we had?"

Probably not, as he thought about it. "What didn't you like?"

"For one, you met her in a cemetery. That's...unconventional, if not disturbing."

A sarcastic laugh bubbled out before he could stop it. "Yeah, and I met Lu in jail."

"She told us. Still unconventional but not near so unsettling." She tied off the bandages, pulled the blankets up over him, and tipped his chin back in her direction. "None of us had any peace about Maya. She seemed a little too interested in you."

"What's that supposed to mean?"

"I don't know if I can explain it, but we all felt it. Even Dutch." She exhaled and settled a hand over his through the blanket. "Maybe it's that we all felt like she thought herself better than you. I don't know—there was just an air about that woman that didn't sit well."

"All right. But Lu *does* deserve better than me."

"Stop it. That's not what she's thinkin', I can promise you. And even if she was somehow better than you, she doesn't see herself that way. Seth and I think she's perfect for you."

He rolled his eyes closed. "That don't change the fact I got nothin' to offer a woman." Any woman—Lu, Maya, or otherwise.

Her vise grip clamped around his bearded jaw, firm enough to grab his attention. He flung his eyes wide to find she was staring right through him.

"Then change that, Orion Braddock. Don't you recall, Seth didn't have nothin' either. He was huntin' bounties right alongside you. Then he met me, decided he wanted a different life, and caught that herd of wild horses to break." She loosened her hold on his jaw.

He pulled his face free of her grip and rubbed his beard. "Don't forget. I'm a wanted man."

"Yeah, and Lu's workin' on findin' Hattie Ingram and clearin' your name as we speak. But I'll agree with you in one thing—you are a durn fool if you keep bounty hunting and let Lu Peters walk out of your life."

⁓

"You stick close."

Lu nodded at Seth, feeling awkward wearing the men's trousers and shirt again, along with a pair of moccasins Seth had made Lena some time back, and an old hat pulled low over her face. In the dark, they hoped she might pass for a boy if they happened to come across anyone.

They walked in silence, headed toward Ollie Sapey's place. Seth's attention roved over the trees and brush, and at certain moments, he'd pause, at first she thought so she could catch up, but after the third time, she realized that each time, he discreetly touched his finger to his lips and paused, listening. When he started again after that, he veered down a narrow trail where the brush pushed in and, in a thick spot, turned and caught her.

"Stay here." He barely breathed the words. "And if anyone other than me approaches, shoot 'em." He handed her the pistol from his gun belt, butt first.

"Where are you going?" She looked around, but the brush stood too tall for her to see her surroundings.

"I'll be back. Stay down." Rifle in hand, he disappeared down the path, out of sight.

Lu gripped the pistol and listened, a whispered prayer on her lips. Minutes ticked by, and nothing but the sounds of nature broke the stillness. At least until a sickening thud of wood against bone carried to her ears. She cringed and covered her mouth. After the initial shock passed, she crept in the direction that Seth had gone, eventually making it to where she could see a man's silhouette wrestling another fella onto the back of a horse, similar to what Seth had done with Rion.

He lifted him over the saddle and, centering his weight, used something to tie the man in place. Then, leading the horse to a wide path, he took it some distance until he was out of sight. She waited, unsure what to expect; but some twenty minutes later, Seth returned with only his rifle in hand.

"What'd you do?" She handed him the pistol as he rejoined her.

"I figured Sheriff Downing might've left a posse member watchin' the house." He nodded in the direction where he'd found the fella. "I was right. I knocked him out, tied him over his saddle, took his horse to the big path leadin' to the lake below, and gave him a smack on the rump. He'll have to wake up, get himself unbound, and figure out where he is before he'll be much threat to us. Now, let's git. I don't like leavin' Lena too long in her condition."

Seth led her a few miles through the trees, eventually coming to another small glade. At the edge of the trees, the darkened surface of a tall rock wall showed in the partial moonlight, and at its base sat a small house built right against the surface. In the stillness, crickets serenaded the night, and golden light poured across the darkness from the two small windows at the front of the earth-berm house.

"That's Ollie's place. For all our sakes, I don't think it's wise I go any farther, but I'll be ready to shoot if things turn ugly. So do your best to stay clear of her. I don't want to hit you."

Lu stared, heart pounding. Had she really thought this

was a wise idea? What if Seth was right—and Ollie did take a shot at her?

Lord, I'm about to talk myself out of this. Help me muster my courage! Go before me, send angels behind me, and let nothing touch me. Please.

She inhaled deeply, fixed Rion firmly in her thoughts, and walked toward the door before she could change her mind. Her heart thundered, and her skin crawled, but she forced one foot in front of the other.

At the door, she raised her hand to knock.

Jesus, I put my trust in You. If it's my time, take me quickly. If it's not, let me glean some information on where Hattie Ingram is. Something to help Rion!

Before she could knock, the faint rustle of grass came from the left side of the house, and the shadowy form of a woman with a shotgun, open at the breech and cradled in the crook of her elbow, appeared. Faint moonlight glinted on her short-cropped white hair and the gun's barrel as she fed shells into each of the side-by-side barrels.

"Who are you, and what do you want?" Hers was a gravelly voice with little softness.

Trembling, Lu raised her hands, her mouth turning to cotton. "Are you Ollie Sapey? If so, I mean no harm."

"Again, who are ya?"

"Lucinda Peters. I'm from Cambria Springs."

"You're a long way from home. What're you doin' at my door?"

"I only want to talk."

"Not big on conversation. Git to your point."

"I'm looking for a woman—Hattie Ingram. She was taken from town, and I have reason to think she's somewhere around here. I need to find her."

"I don't know nothin' about no woman."

"She's got old leg injuries that make it hard for her to walk, but she may be suffering with more recent inj—"

"Already told you and that bunch of men what came ridin' round this morning, I don't know nothin' about no woman! Now, git off my land, and don't come back or I'll unload on ya."

"Are you sure, ma'am? A man is being falsely accused of kidnapping and murder. If we can just find Hattie, we can return her to her kin and clear—"

The woman stormed closer, coming within feet.

"You deaf, girl? I meant what I said!" She snapped the shotgun closed, cocked the breechloader, and fired into the air. "Now, git!"

Lu's heart launched into a thunderous gallop as she turned and ran, ears ringing from the close blast. She fell, shoved back to her feet, but stumbled again.

Behind her, the woman laughed, the sound muffled by the clanging in Lu's head. Fear enveloped her, urging her to run. Get away from the danger. Reaching the trees, she slipped into their cover and raced on.

Some distance beyond, someone caught her from behind. She screeched, the sound strangling in her throat as she flailed and fought.

"Lu! Lu, it's me—Seth!"

The muffled-but-familiar voice sliced through the ringing like a sunray in the fog.

"C'mon now. Calm down. I got ya. Nothin's gonna hurt ya."

Gasping, she braced her hands against the nearest trees.

"That's it." His grip loosened, and he ducked around in front of her. "Breathe." He swept the hat off his head and inhaled through his nose.

She whimpered, repeating the action, though it took her several tries to fill her lungs.

"Good. Keep breathin'." Again, he inhaled and released the

breath. "You're all right. Ain't nothin' gonna hurt you."

She sagged against him, her knees going soft then, and he eased her to the ground. For a couple of moments, she trembled as she fought to hold back the flood of emotion that threatened to spill over as her calm returned.

He finally crouched in front of her, taking her by the shoulders. "You all right?"

She couldn't bring herself to answer except with a slight nod. After another minute, he hooked a thumb toward his place. "C'mon. Let's get you home. Maybe Lena can help you."

Only she didn't want Lena's comfort. Or Seth's.

He guided her down the trail, allowing her to lean on him at first. As they walked, her strength gradually returned, though she still couldn't bring herself to speak.

Once they arrived, Seth lit a lamp in the kitchen, and she made a beeline for the cellar. As Lu approached Rion's bed, Lena looked up, startled.

"Are you all right? You look like you've seen a ghost."

At the sound of Lena's voice, Rion's eyes fluttered open, and he glanced at the three of them. "What happened?"

Seth piped up from behind her.

"I took her to our neighbor's place a few miles away to ask if the woman knows anything about Hattie Ingram. But Ollie ain't the friendliest of women, even on the best of days, and like she's done with me and Lena, she turned a gun on Lu."

Rion glared. "You took her there, knowin' the woman's turned a gun on you both?"

"Don't be angry at him," she whispered. "I pressed him. If we can just find Hattie—"

"You shouldn't've done that." With effort, Rion pushed himself up and swung his legs over the bed. "You coulda been killed."

"I was trying to help you."

He pushed unsteadily to his feet. "By puttin' yourself in danger."

"We've been in danger since the moment we escaped the jail. I was hoping to put an end to it so we can stop running." So they could see what more normal moments, not fraught with dangers and concern, might be like. "I was trying to clear your name."

His brown eyes grew even darker as his ire registered in his face. "Maybe I don't need your help. I'll worry about clearin' my own name."

The words struck like the stings of a hundred angry bees. He didn't need her.

Rion shifted to glare at Seth. "And you! Would you have let your wife do somethin' so dangerous?"

After her encounter with Ollie, she'd wanted nothing more than to see Rion. To hear his voice and let his big presence bring some calm to her still-racing heart. But he'd just made it very clear.

He didn't need her. . .and he didn't want her.

So why did she want him?

Eyes brimming, she spun and raced up the steps into the kitchen. For an instant, she paused there before she dashed out into the yard—and stopped short as two riders dismounted.

CHAPTER 11

Whatever words Rion was about to speak died on his tongue as Lu bolted from the cellar.

For an instant, they each looked after her then at each other before Lena shook her finger at him.

"Lucky for you, you're injured, Orion Braddock, or I might just grab you by your chin hairs and drag you upstairs to apologize." Lena started up the steps, shaking her head. "That woman was trying to save your life, at her own peril."

That was the problem. She was putting herself in danger on his account—and he couldn't live with himself if something happened to her.

Once Lena had gone, he tottered toward the shelves a couple feet away, steadied himself, and turned again toward Seth, his immediate anger quelled somewhat.

"Why don't you lie down before you fall over." Seth nodded to the bed. "I'll see if we can't coax her back down here to talk."

"You've done enough tonight. I'll go talk to her." He needed a change of scenery anyway. The tight quarters and grim darkness in the windowless cellar were wearing on him.

Right arm cradled close to his body, he started toward the steps, far more unsteady than he liked. But Lena was right. There was something special about Lu, and he needed to apologize for whatever fool thing he'd just said to set her off.

"You're one stubborn cuss, you know that?"

"It's what's kept me alive all this time." He took the first few stairs, and as his head and shoulders emerged through the hole in the floor, he found Lena frozen a few paces beyond, staring out the open door, and Lu just outside, her back to the cabin.

"We saw you and Mr. Kealey leave and return, and you didn't seem to be under any duress. Are you well, Miss Peters?" a female voice asked.

A familiar female voice. . .

Calliope's voice.

How many people had she brought with her? The whole posse? A few? Just Trenamen? Or had she come by herself?

If by herself, he'd have something to say about that to her partner. After all, there was a murderer on the loose— the *real* one.

Coming from behind him, Seth took the stairs by twos and barged past him, past his wife, and straight out the door.

"Mr. Kealey."

This time, it was Trenamen's voice. So there were at least the two of them. Were there others?

"I see you've found Lucinda Peters. Is Rion Braddock here too?"

The thought of ducking back into the cellar and tucking himself away in the tunnel flashed across his mind, but he couldn't gather his belongings, get them stashed, and hide himself quickly enough. And that would leave Lu hanging by herself, which he didn't want to do. She'd stuck by him through this whole mess. He wasn't about to abandon her now.

Mustering his strength, he climbed the remainder of the stairs and came to stand near Lena in view of the open door. Beyond Lu stood Calliope and Joe, both beside their horses.

The sight of his sister sent a shot through him—both happiness and dread—and he stifled a groan as weakness caused his head to swim.

He met her eyes across the distance. "I'm here."

Lena dragged a chair over. "Sit."

He didn't argue.

In a flurry of activity, Calliope and Joe Trenamen hurried inside, Seth and Lu crowding into the kitchen after them. Seth closed the trapdoor to the cellar to make more room.

Calliope marched up to him, worry marring her pretty features. "Look at you." She took his face in her hands. "You're hurt!"

"Evenin', Calliope." He blinked heavily and tried—probably failed—to smile. "I was shot. Once. Bullet passed through my shoulder. I'll be well enough soon." He tried to sound confident, but the fatigue pulling at him said otherwise. Hopefully, another day or two of decent sleep would help.

She released him and looked around at the others. "Is he right?"

"The bullet didn't hit any vital organs, miss, but he's hurtin' plenty," Seth started. "We're workin' to get rid of some infection. What he needs most is time and rest."

Trenamen turned to Lu, who'd positioned herself about as far from Rion as she could get, near the doorway to Seth and Lena's bedroom. "And are you all right, miss?"

She gave a defiant lift to her chin. "I'm fine. Unharmed."

"Did he kidnap you from the jail?" Trenamen jutted his chin, now sporting a few days' growth of a beard, in Rion's direction.

Irritation clawed his belly like a trapped cougar, though he had no strength to address the needling question.

Again, Lu's posture seemed to stiffen. "He didn't force me to go anywhere. I came to get a story."

"I'm glad for that." Joe turned his way. "Were y'all here this morning when the posse came?"

"We were." He shifted, trying to ease the ache that sitting up was causing. "Wasn't a good time to talk."

"Doesn't look like now's much better."

"Not particularly." He glanced toward the windows. If only he could see out into the darkness beyond. "You let me rest awhile, and I'll talk to you and Calliope. But if that posse's ridin' this way, I'd rather know it, and I'll excuse myself, so long as I have your word Lu won't be held responsible for anything. She's innocent in all of this."

Calliope shook her head. "You look in no shape to excuse yourself anywhere but back to bed. Besides, the posse's miles from here."

"Then why're you here? I thought y'all were ridin' with that bunch."

"Sheriff Downing said you were friends." Calliope motioned to Seth and Lena, then him. "So we followed a hunch that you'd be somewhere about. We asked to stay behind and watch the house. We knew we were right when we kept seeing your boot tracks all around."

"What?" He rubbed at the intensifying ache in his shoulder. "My boot tracks?"

"You know, that crescent-shaped scar in the right heel?"

"What're you talkin' about?" He shook his head, his eyes growing suddenly heavy. "I can't be leavin' tracks everywhere. I traded my boots for moccasins just inside the Cambria Springs livery, and I haven't worn 'em since."

"Look," Seth called. "I understand y'all are detectives or somethin' and you've got a case to investigate, but it's been a hard day here. It's late. Maybe we could wait until mornin' when we're all a little more rested?"

Rion tried to shake his head. He needed to understand what

Calliope was saying. How were his boot tracks everywhere?

"I think that's a wise idea." Trenamen hooked a thumb toward the door. "You mind if we stay? Put our horses in your corral? We'll sleep outside if we have to."

"Like Rion said, so long as you promise that posse's not comin', you're welcome to stay. Lena can give instructions on where."

At Trenamen's and Calliope's agreement, Seth opened the door to the cellar again and helped him up.

"C'mon. I want you downstairs in bed before you pass out on me. You're nearly an immovable boulder once you go out."

Rion glanced Lu's way as Seth guided him down the steps, though she quickly averted her gaze.

This night hadn't gone well. Maybe things would look different in the morning.

⌒

Monday, June 30, 1873

Lu paced out of the bedroom, which she'd shared with Lena and Calliope, once again dressed in her own feminine attire. The strong scent of coffee and frying bacon met her, and she looked around at the faces. Seth and Deputy Nesbitt—or whatever his real name was—sat at the table, deep in conversation. Lena and Calliope stood at the stove, chattering softly as they cooked.

Rion was the only one not present. He was probably still asleep in the cellar. It was the best thing for them both, considering she needed to go down there and see if she could find her journal. She'd not seen it since they'd hidden in the tunnel the morning before, and she had many thoughts to capture in its pages. But she didn't want a discussion with him. The sooner she could return to her small rented house in Cambria Springs and forget about Rion Braddock, the better.

Nodding to the greetings of the others, she walked through the room and downstairs, the steps squeaking as they often did. She cringed and attempted to avoid the worst creaky spots. At the first shelf, she found the box of matches Rion had used the previous morning to light the lamp and, walking deeper into the cellar where they'd stashed all their belongings, lit a match.

There. Her journal peeked out from under his saddlebags and rifle. She tugged it free and shook out the match, preparing to turn back.

"Lu?"

She cringed at Rion's voice.

"You're dreaming," she whispered. "Go back to sleep."

He chuckled, the rich depth of the sound tugging at her heart. "I'm not dreamin' and I'm not delirious. I know it's you."

"But you should still be asleep."

"I actually feel a little better. I think the poultices helped."

Of course they had. She'd seen them work wonders on her father. "Good. I didn't mean to disturb you."

She deposited the matches in their place and headed for the stairs.

"Please stay. I need to talk to you."

A big knot formed in her throat, and she shook her head. "You made everything very clear last night." She hurried up the steps, pausing long enough to ask Lena and Calliope if they needed help with the breakfast preparations. Upon their negative answer, she excused herself back to the bedroom to write her thoughts.

Kicking off Lena's moccasins, which she'd donned to run downstairs, she sat on the bed and pulled her pencil loose from the spine. The lead was broken. She puffed out her cheeks in frustration, laid the journal aside, put the moccasins back on, and padded to the other room.

"Would one of you happen to have a knife I could use to sharpen my pencil?"

Both Seth and Deputy Nesbitt looked up, and Seth took the pencil and produced a small pocketknife. Before he even got the blade open and began to shave the wood down, Rion emerged from the cellar.

"I need a word with you, Lu. Please."

Seth innocently worked on the pencil, acting as if he'd not heard a thing. Deputy Nesbitt watched with curiosity. And near the stove, both Lena and Calliope had turned. Rion grabbed her hand and pulled her toward the bedroom.

Still shirtless and bandaged, he looked much more in control of his faculties than the previous evening. She attempted once to pull free of his grip, but it was strong, and he walked with a purpose that he'd not had the day before. Reaching the bedroom, he drew her inside and shut the door.

"Are you trying to embarrass me?" she whispered when he finally let go and faced her, his back braced against the door.

"Embarrass you?" His brow furrowed. "No. I'm tryin' to apologize. I said some things last night that either I didn't mean or they didn't come out like I intended 'em."

She stared.

"I may not be the brightest man in the world, but I reckon it's not usually a good thing when a woman you're talkin' to runs out on the conversation partway through, cryin'."

Her eyes stung again with unshed tears. "Not typically, no."

"I'm sorry. I woke up last evenin' and found out Seth had taken you on some kind of. . .errand, Lena called it. And the way she said it, it made me realize you could be in danger. I didn't like that. And to hear some old woman took a shot at you while you were tryin' to clear my name? And my brother let you go there, knowin' that was a possibility? I *really* didn't like that. Between those things and how addled my thoughts were, I said I didn't need your help."

"You don't." She swiped away a tear before it streaked past her cheekbone. "Since we met, you've proven over and over how capable you are. You'll figure this out too."

He heaved a breath. "Reckon I'm not makin' my meanin' very clear, then. What I'm tryin' to say is, I misspoke. Lucinda Peters, I *want* your help clearin' my name. I just want you safe while we're doin' it. And if you're gonna put yourself in danger, *I* want to be the one beside you. Not Seth. Not Lena. Not Calliope or Joe or anyone else." He tapped his chest. "Me."

She eyed him as she brushed away another tear.

After a moment, his brow furrowed. "Have you got anything to say?"

"Let me make sure I'm not continuing to misunderstand. Do you mean this about our current task of clearing your name, or does that extend beyond that point?"

"Well, now, I reckon that's gonna depend. We fail to clear my name, and my neck's probably gettin' stretched. We succeed, and..." He grinned with a faint, one-shouldered shrug. "I kinda like the idea of a partnership. You in?"

Lu stood a little straighter, pressed her lips together, and nodded. "Under those terms, I think it's in my best interest to be sure your name gets cleared."

With his left hand, he tugged her to his side, and she pressed in, careful not to jostle him or lean too heavily. They stood like that only an instant before a single, sharp rap came at the door and, startled, she pulled free.

"Breakfast," Seth called.

Rion shook his head then nodded toward the door. "That one always did have bad timing."

Cheeks flaming, she giggled.

When Rion opened the door, Seth looked them both over, then tossed one of the blankets from the bed downstairs at Rion.

"Why don't you cover yourself, and let's eat."

"Yes, sir."

Seth motioned her out ahead of him, and with one more smile in Rion's direction, she exited.

CHAPTER 12

By the time Rion got the blanket wrapped around himself and joined the others at the table, pain and fatigue nipped at him like an annoying goat nibbling at his shirt hem. But it was a durn sight less than the night before when he almost couldn't keep his eyes open or string two thoughts together.

"Mornin'." He took the only empty seat, right beside Lu.

"Mornin'." Lena grinned from her spot beside him.

Across the table, Joe and Calliope smiled and nodded in greeting, and once Seth asked a blessing over the meal, Rion pinned them both with a look.

"So how much trouble am I in?"

Trenamen's brows rose as he reached for the plate of bacon. "You already knew the deck was stacked against you, and then you had the fool notion to break out of jail and take an innocent woman with you. It doesn't look good."

"First of all"—Calliope helped herself to a couple of flapjacks then looked at both him and Lu—"I'm happy you're both alive—and relatively unharmed." She handed the plate on to Lena and pinned him with a hard look. "But why didn't you stay in the jail? We told you we'd do everything we could to help you."

Rion debated before speaking, not wanting to hurt his sister's feelings. "I don't mean these words to be as harsh as they'll probably sound, Calliope, but after however many years apart, I didn't know if I could trust you. Lord knows I wanted to, but right from the first, you hid who you really were. I understand why, but that don't take away the fact you did. And when you clued me in to your true identity, the first thing you did was start revealing all the murders you think I committed, started makin' a case for why you need to lock me up." He stabbed a single flapjack from the plate Lena held out toward him, plunked it on his plate, and passed the serving dish on to Lu. "Would you trust you if you were me?"

The words obviously struck a tender place if his sister's squirming was any indication, but she quickly stilled herself. "For the record, I don't believe you've committed any murders. But I had to take you in. All the evidence was pointing straight toward you."

"Yeah. Well, that didn't build my trust, and I could see real clear how stacked the deck was." He nodded in Trenamen's direction. "So I figured I'd do better on my own. I let you do your job—and then I escaped so I could do mine."

Lu laid a hand on his left forearm, stalling any further comment. "Forgive me. This may seem a bit off the beaten path of the conversation, but you said something last night about Rion leaving boot tracks all over. That's how you knew he was here."

"That's not exactly what we said." Trenamen poured himself coffee and offered some to Calliope. "Sheriff Downing pointed out y'all are old friends." He indicated Rion and Seth with the fork in his hand.

"Not just old friends. Brothers," Seth corrected, mimicking Joe Trenamen's motion. "We were taken in by the same ornery bag of bones off two different orphan trains."

Understanding dawned in both Joe's and Calliope's eyes.

"Thank you for that clarification. Because of your connection to each other, we asked if we had Downing's permission to stay behind and watch the house, expecting you might show up. Then, we started seeing the tracks around here—some of 'em pretty thick in places, like you were hiding and watching the house as well."

Rion looked at Lu, and they both faced front. "I tried to say it last night. I haven't worn those boots since the night I escaped the jail. I changed to the moccasins I'm wearin' now just inside the back door of the town livery. Those boots ain't been on my feet since. Where are these tracks, and how old are they?" Not that he could've left them anyway—he'd not been up to see Seth and Lena in a couple of months. Any track he would've left would've been obliterated by the elements long ago.

Confusion marred Joe's eyes. "They were fresh. Since that big rain that came through a few days ago."

"How many other posse members did Downing leave to watch my place?" Seth asked.

"Just the two of us. Why?"

Seth's eyes closed. "I found a fella watchin' the place last night an hour or so before y'all made your presence known. I figured Downing woulda left someone watchin' us, and I thought that was him. I knocked him unconscious, tied him over his saddle, and sent his horse wandering toward Gartner Lake."

Rion leaned forward to peer around Lu. "Did you recognize him?"

"Unfortunately, not well. . .not in the dark."

"Show me where you found him." Trenamen nodded toward the door.

"Right now?"

Trenamen started to nod, but Rion cleared his throat. "Why don't y'all wait a minute. Lu." He nudged her elbow with his.

"Maybe now's a good time to tell them about that conversation you overheard."

Looking a little uncomfortable, she nodded. "While the posse was here yesterday, we were hiding in a—" She darted a glance at Seth.

He hooked a thumb toward the trapdoor. "There's a tunnel that connects the cellar to the outdoors, about ten or fifteen feet long."

Lu returned her attention to Joe and Calliope. "We were hidden in the tunnel, and I overheard a whispered conversation from the outdoors end. I think it was two men, and I think one was with the posse and one wasn't."

She detailed the facts of the conversation, which left both Calliope and Joe mute for a moment after she'd finished.

"I know Miss Hattie's a friend of yours, so I'm sorry for the unpleasant news about her. But I thought you ought to add that into whatever case you're buildin'. It's not me—but whoever it is might be on that posse."

Joe seemed to ponder the information. "Between all of us, Callie and I have wondered if Sheriff Downing isn't involved somehow."

Beside him, Calliope nodded.

"Once we're done eating, I want to see your boots." Joe nodded to Rion, then shifted his focus to Seth. "And I'll ask you to take me out to where you knocked the fella unconscious last night—as well as where that conversation would've happened. This isn't makin' sense yet, but I feel like it's about to."

⌒

After Rion finished his light breakfast of a single buttered pancake and a little coffee, Lu changed the dressings on his wounds and reapplied the warm sugar poultices, which had seemed to work wonders overnight. Then, he'd returned to bed and slept several more hours.

In the meantime, Seth and Joe went out to look at the areas Joe had asked about. They'd returned long enough to say they were saddling their horses and going to take a ride. Lu had wanted to go down and sit with Rion, to stay close and ponder what had happened earlier in the private moment they'd shared, but Calliope had requested both she and Lena stay and talk with her—as much about the man Rion had become since they'd separated as about the case. Lena was much more helpful with that topic than she could be. She was only just getting to know him herself—though she found it both enlightening and entertaining to hear stories of the real Rion Braddock. She'd scribbled details furiously from Lena's stories into her journal.

When Rion emerged from the cellar again a little after noon, sleepy-eyed and hair mussed, he carried a thick stack of wanted posters and the dark blue Henley he'd worn briefly the morning before. As he deposited the posters on the table next to her, he yawned and blinked and, heading toward the stove, struggled to straighten out his shirt and tug it on. Seeing the posters contrasted against his sleepy fumbling, she was reminded of a bear just waking from hibernation. It appeared cuddly and harmless, but hidden beneath was a fierceness and skill for protecting what he saw as his.

And he'd said he wanted to protect her...

"Where are Joe and Seth?" He poured himself a cup of coffee, pausing a moment to take a sip before returning to the table and easing into the chair next to her.

Calliope motioned. "They went to look at the boot tracks and, from there, took a ride."

He took another sip. "Thought they left when I went to lie down."

"They did. I would've expected them back already."

"Any of y'all concerned they're not back yet?"

Lena nodded. "I think their purpose was to see if they couldn't track down the fella Seth knocked senseless last night."

"That's right." Calliope exhaled deeply. "They found what appeared to be your boot tracks, both where the tunnel ends over here"—she pointed toward the side of the house—"and where Seth found the fella watching the house. They have the same crescent mark, in almost the same spot in the heel—but the boot tracks are smaller than yours by about that much." She indicated about half the pad of her thumb. "A little narrower too."

Lu's brows shot up, and Rion paused with the coffee cup nearly to his lips.

"So you're tellin' me someone else has a pair of boots just like mine. . .with the same scar in the right heel?"

Calliope nodded. "It appears so."

He set his mug down hard, sloshing coffee over the edge. "Now do you believe me?"

Lu snatched the wanted posters away from the spilled coffee and rose to grab a towel.

"I've told you more than once." Calliope stared him down. "I believe you. But this isn't enough to clear you. Not yet."

Lu returned and dabbed up the spilled coffee.

"It's enough to prove someone's framin' me!"

Lena cleared her throat. "Rion, it's a start. Can you think when that mark first appeared in your boot heel? Or how it got there?"

He closed his eyes and rubbed the heel of his palm against his left eyebrow. "I don't know. It was there from the time I got the boots."

"So you bought them like that?" Lena raised an eyebrow. "Was it a mark the boot maker made?"

"I didn't buy 'em new. Somebody gave 'em to me."

At Lena's quizzical look, he continued.

"I hadn't collected any decent bounties in a while, and my boots were worn thin. Fallin' apart, actually. Somebody had a spare pair and told me if they fit, I was welcome to 'em."

Calliope frowned. "Who?"

Jaw clenched, Rion shook his head.

"Does that bear out with the evidence at the various murder scenes?" Lu took her seat, leaving the towel in case it was needed again. "Were these boot tracks at the other scenes, or only these last few?"

"Without being able to refer back to the case notes, I'm not sure. Joe's worked this case since the first murder five years ago. I came into it much more recently."

"All right. Then let's go back to why we came here." She pushed the stack of posters at him. "Who has a grudge against you? Ellwood Garvin and who else?"

As if to shake off the vestiges of sleep, Rion rubbed his eyes again then started to leaf through the posters.

From across the table, Calliope took one of the posters from the stack. "What are these?"

Rion snatched it back, returning it to its place. "It's history. My history. Who I've tracked, caught, and collected on in my bounty hunting. Every poster's in order of when I turned the fella in, so please don't go grabbin' things and puttin' 'em out of order."

"All right." She came around to stand behind her brother.

"Calliope, the murders date back to. . . ?" Lu raised an eyebrow.

"May of 1868."

"So you'll want to look at those bounties you collected on prior to that, since whoever is doing this has been setting you up from the first murder."

"Right." He took another swallow of his coffee, set the mug aside, and leafed down through the stack. Finding the right place, he turned to the posters in question and started going one by one again.

"This one was hung, so it's not him." He turned to the next page. "Jailed. . ."

Lu laid a hand on the page before he could flip it, then turned the previous poster over again. "Do you know anything about this man? Did he have family—someone who might want vengeance because he was hung?"

"That's a tall order just after I woke up."

Lena rose and checked the coffeepot, then carried it over and topped off his mug. "I'll make more if I have to. . ."

He blinked, took a sip, and looked again. "I don't remember any family with this one." He moved on, going poster by poster. On the sixth or seventh, he paused, his brows arching.

"This fella—Dunwitty. He had an ill-tempered mama and an equally foul-mouthed wife. They threatened to come after me as I dragged him away."

"That's something." Calliope drew up a chair and sat on his left side. "Have you seen either of them since?"

"Not that I recall, no. But I've been in a lot of places in the last five years. They coulda been in some town somewhere."

"Lu, would you write his name down so we can look into it further?" Calliope asked.

Lu jotted it into her journal.

"But it's not just seeing them once, is it?" Lena eyed them all from her place at the end of the table. "Whoever has been doing this has been setting him up across a long time."

"That's right." Calliope nodded.

"But if we narrow this stack into a shorter list"—Lu tapped the posters—"we can work on narrowing it even further into who had the means to do such a thing."

As Rion flipped to the next poster, Lena turned Dunwitty's poster so it stuck out from the stack for easier finding.

After a couple more, he tapped a page. "Walt Esper escaped jail. He was facin' a hanging, and his friends broke him out. Ain't seen him, but he might have a grudge."

Lu jotted the name, adding notes to remind her why each name was of interest.

He waded through more pages, pointing out Jimmy Albey, whose son had made a lot of strong threats; Edward Hunney, who'd threatened that his family would make Rion's life a misery; Clyde Page and his gang, who'd leveled a lot of threats; and Al Langer, whom Rion had shot in the course of capture and who had nearly died.

"Langer's probably out by now. I don't recall that he had a long sentence."

Lu pointed to the date scrawled somewhere on the page. "These are the dates of when you turned them in?"

Rion nodded. "And if there's a second date, like on this one"—he pointed to a different poster—"it's the date of death. Usually a hangin'."

She jotted the date beside Langer's name, then went back through the stack to log the dates on the other five as well.

Calliope stopped him before he continued his perusing. "If I had to guess, we've gone far enough back. This one is more than a year before the first murder."

"If you say so." Rion took the last swallow of his coffee and gathered the posters back into a pile, leaving the few turned out as Lena had done. "I'm gonna go lie down again."

His sister rose and moved the chair so he could get out. "Do you mind leaving those so I can show Joe when he returns?"

"I don't mind." He pushed to his feet, rubbing his shoulder as he did.

Rion gave his sister a hug as he passed her, and as he started down the steps, he caught Lu's eye. "You mind comin' down and keepin' me company until I fall asleep?"

He didn't have to ask twice.

CHAPTER 13

"I consider myself a better-than-average tracker, and I struggled to follow his trail." Arms folded, Seth leaned his hip against the kitchen counter and stared at Rion as Lu checked his wounds and changed the bandages.

Rion shot his brother a teasing grin. "Oh, quit your joshin'. You're average at best."

Seth grabbed the dishcloth from the counter and launched it at him, Rion barely batting it aside, left-handed, before it hit him in the face. The damp cloth landed on the table, fluttering several of the wanted posters from the stack as Calliope showed Joe those he'd pointed out earlier.

"Boys!" Calliope gave them a mock glare, then set the cloth aside to straighten the pages. "Somebody gets fussy when these papers are out of order."

Rion wrinkled his nose at her, and she wrinkled hers right back, both chuckling as she did.

"Anyway, it was a long, frustrating day with little to show for our efforts." Seth received a freshly washed plate from Lena beside him and turned to dry it.

Once his back was to the room, Rion snatched the damp cloth and hurled it, again left-handed, hitting Seth square between the shoulders.

The room erupted in laughter, and Seth spun to face him.

"Well, somebody's obviously feelin' better." He scowled Rion's way.

"After sleepin' most of the last few days, I am—thank you very much. But that wasn't me. It was Joe." He hooked his thumb in the other man's direction.

Joe jerked his gaze up, first at Rion, then Seth. "Leave me out of this. I'm working. . ." He turned again to the wanted posters, only to be hit a moment later in the ear with the cloth.

More laughter ensued as Joe scooped up the cloth, ready to hurl it, though seemingly torn on whether to pitch it in Seth's or Rion's direction. Deciding, he tossed it at Seth, who ducked. The cloth landed in the pan of sudsy water where Lena was washing the dinner dishes, splashing water over her and the counters.

Mouth agape, she stood for a moment then fished for the cloth, but before she found it, a soft knock sounded at the door.

The laughter died, leaving the room eerily silent. For only an instant, they all stared. Then Seth hurried to jerk the trapdoor open.

"Downstairs. Now!" He mouthed the words, and both Rion and Lu grabbed whatever they could of their belongings and darted into the dark cellar, Lu following him with partially applied bandages trailing between them.

At the base of the creaky stairs, they looked up, and Seth put his finger to his lips and closed them into the dark.

"Finish this. Quick." Rion tugged on the bandages.

Lu continued to wind the remainder around him.

Above, footsteps sounded and the door opened.

"Can I help you?" Seth's voice broke the stillness.

Lu tied off the bandage, and as she did, he grabbed her hand and pulled her toward the end of the cellar where the cot sat. Setting his shirt and her journal on the shelf, he felt for his gun belt, hanging from the corner of the shelf, and drew his pistol. As quietly as possible, he checked the cylinder and found it just as he'd last left it: five bullets, with the hammer resting on an empty chamber. He eased the cylinder closed and, feeling for her arm in the darkness, pressed the pistol into her hand.

"Hold that, and don't go anywhere."

"Shouldn't we get in the tunnel?" she whispered.

"No time." He tugged his shirt over his head, then pulled the gun belt down from its place. Before he could swing it around his hips, the trapdoor lifted again. In one motion, he tossed the belt toward the bed and pulled Lu behind him.

"Rion?" Seth came partway down the steps, then bent to peer into the darkness. "You ought to come up here."

"Is it safe?" He hissed the words, loud enough only he and Lu would hear.

"There's no danger."

He released a breath, and tension drained from his muscles.

Behind him, Lu pressed one hand to his back, her head resting against him. With the other, she pressed the pistol to his right side. He took the gun, turned, and tugged her against him.

"You all right?"

She nodded. "My heart's in my throat, but yes."

He squeezed her a little harder, then released her and eased the Colt back into its holster on the bed. When they started toward the stairs, Seth stepped back up to the main floor and held the trapdoor open for them. As they emerged, Rion found a woman, probably in her middle fifties, with short-cropped white hair, clad in trousers and a man's coat and shirt. He glanced at the others in the room, eyes settling on Seth.

"Who's this?"

Seth set the door back in place. "Our nearest neighbor, Ollie Sapey."

At her name, Lu inhaled sharply, and she trembled beside him. He squeezed her wrist.

"The woman Lu went to see last night?" He scowled in her direction, ready to tear her head from her shoulders.

Seth seemed to find his voice then. "Yes. But she's come in good faith today."

Her light eyes flicked toward the door. "I got the woman. The one you asked about last night?"

"Hattie!" Calliope gasped.

Joe looped a protective arm around her shoulders. "Is she all right?"

"No. She was stabbed. A few times. They were shaving her hair when I rescued her."

"They—" Rion breathed the word, but Ollie had already pressed on.

"I've been nursing her, but she's unconscious and not well. I didn't know who she was. Didn't really know who y'all were. But if she belongs to somebody, she needs to go back to her kin so's I can get back to livin' my life."

Rion glared. "You saw who did this?"

She gave a defiant shake of her head. "One, a tall, broad-shouldered man about your height, dark hair, and a beard. In the darkness, I coulda mistaken him for you—but there were subtle differences. Not sure how to describe it. . ."

Irritation clawed at him.

"The other person I saw was smaller. I didn't see that one as well."

"When did this happen? Where?"

"During that heavy rain a few days back." She turned toward Seth and Lena. "I heard screams coming from the direction of that old mining shack west of my place. Then they stopped. I went out in the storm to look for who was in trouble. Was about to give up when lightning struck a tree and split it in half, then three horses came racing by. Not long after, the two I described came huntin''em. I went into the shack and found the woman, so while they were chasing their horses, I took her."

Seth shook his head. "I know that old shack you're talkin' about. That's an awful long way to reach your place. How'd you carry an injured woman that far without leavin' a trail?"

"Ain't none of your business. I got my ways."

Rion's thoughts spun with all the information. "Can we see her?"

"You asked for her last night. Come get her."

⌒

Wednesday, July 2, 1873

Lu sat beside the bed in the cellar, now occupied by Hattie Ingram, as she tended to her wounds.

"Her fever seems better," Calliope whispered from beside her.

Lu smiled. "The fact that she's still alive and fighting is a testament to how much Ollie did for her. If she's made it this far, I choose to believe she'll pull through."

Calliope nodded. "Hattie is a fighter. She was the only survivor of a house fire when she was just a wee thing, badly burned. But she survived that, and I do believe, if she's still here, she'll make it through this too."

Hattie groaned as Lu cleaned the largest of the wounds, and for a moment, her eyes fluttered open.

"Calliope." Lu tapped her new friend's thigh, and Callie leaned over and smiled at the injured woman.

"Hattie, it's Kezia." She brushed some of Hattie's unshaved hair back. "Can you hear me?"

She blinked and seemed to make eye contact, a tiny smile curving her lips.

"That's right. You're safe, and we're going to get you back home soon, all right? To the boardinghouse and your mother." She nodded, and Hattie's smiled deepened. "Just rest now."

Hattie held her eyes for a couple of seconds, then let them close again.

Lu grinned at Calliope. They would need to get Hattie back to Cambria Springs—very soon. But after the move from Ollie's place to Seth's had set the worst of her wounds to bleeding again, they'd decided to wait a day or two to see if they could get her stronger before making that bigger journey. In her estimation, one more day and Hattie might be ready.

"I need to go upstairs and prepare more tea and poultices. I'll be back soon." Lu covered Hattie, then rose.

Making her way up the steps, she found Rion and Joe in conversation at the table. Lena was nowhere in sight, but the door to the bedroom was closed. Movement outside the window drew her eye to the corral, where Seth worked with one of his horses.

"How's Hattie?" Joe asked.

"She woke up for a minute, made eye contact with Calliope, and seemed to react favorably when she heard we'd be taking her home soon."

Rion grinned and rubbed at his shoulder. "That's an improvement, right?"

"A small one, but yes." She motioned toward his shoulder. "Is it hurting you?"

"Itchin' like mad."

She patted his other shoulder as she walked past. "That's a good sign too. Where's Lena?"

"Resting. Seth thinks the baby's comin' soon."

Lu stopped short at his matter-of-fact announcement. She turned back. "*How* soon?"

"I don't mean today—but a week, maybe ten days. When

do you reckon Hattie might be ready to move?"

She glanced to the bedroom door then toward the cellar. "She might be able to make it today, but I was thinking tomorrow or the day after would be better."

"That'll probably work."

She'd overheard some of their conversations in the days since they'd arrived. Seth and Lena had planned to head into Cambria Springs before her time came so that she was near women who could help with the birth.

She blew out a breath. Neither she nor Calliope had any such experience.

"Don't worry about it. I'm sure it'll be fine." He grinned. "Seth's assisted plenty of foals into the world."

"Foals?!" Her jaw cracked open.

Both men chuckled, and Rion acted as if he might speak, but before another word left his mouth, Seth hurried through the door.

"Posse's comin'."

The mirth trickled off Rion's and Joe's faces, and Rion stood.

Her mind jolted. What did she need to gather? "I have to get my journal and the other set of clothes."

She started for the bedroom, but Rion caught her wrist. "No."

"What?" She darted a look toward the yard, then back to him.

He turned on Seth and Joe. "It's time y'all go to town. Take Lu with you, please, and get Miss Hattie home."

"No!" She tried to pull free of his grasp. "I'm going with you."

He shook his head. "You're not."

"What're you plannin' to do?" Seth's voice reflected his concern.

"Now that I'm stronger, I'm gonna take a crack at findin' that fella leavin' the boot tracks."

"Braddock, I need to lock you up!" Joe balked.

"You have my word that I'll turn myself in, but I need to find that fella, and I'm feelin' up to the task now."

"I'll go with him," Lu whispered, mind reeling with the sudden change. "And I'll—"

He spun to face her. "You're not goin', Lu. I need you to go with Hattie. You're makin' a difference for her. Aside from the fact that she doesn't deserve to die, I need her alive to say I wasn't the one what took her. And I need you to tell my story. *Our* story. Please."

The intensity in his brown eyes sparked something in her, and despite the ache in her chest, she nodded.

"All right. I will. But promise me you'll come back to me."

He cupped her cheek with his hand. "There's no doubt." He bored a glare into Joe Trenamen. "And when the time's right, I'll find you and Calliope, and I'll turn myself in. I want this done. I want my name clear."

"All right." Joe nodded. "I'll give you ten days—and if you don't do what you said, I'll be on your trail."

"Rion, you don't have much time. Go!" Seth motioned toward the trapdoor. "I'll get everyone together and we'll go to town. You hide until we're gone. Trouble and Mischief are up the mountain with the herd."

With one curt nod, Rion headed for the stairs, and Lu trailed him down to the cellar.

He moved the burlap sacks aside, then stood to face her.

"What about your things?"

"After the night Ollie came by, I stashed everything inside."

Fighting tears, she slipped into his arms. "Please be careful! They could've killed you before."

"You have my word—and if I promise somethin', I do it. So I'm promisin' you now, Lucinda Peters, you're gonna see a lot more of me, and not too far off in the future."

He brushed his lips across her forehead and, releasing her, wiggled into the tunnel, feetfirst. She took one last look at him and, as a loud knock came at the door above, moved the heavy burlap sacks into position again.

Part 3

ON THE CASE

CHAPTER 1

Colorado Territory
Saturday, July 12, 1873

"Ladies and gentlemen, please make room," the conductor's voice boomed from the head of the aisle. "We have a very full train heading into Denver."

The announcement drew Andie McGovern's attention from the thick tome in her lap. The conductor disappeared, appearing again outside the train car. Passengers jostled past, some filing off, some on, while others changed seats. A family of four hurried across the busy platform, the man rushing toward the conductor. After a brief conversation, they were waved inside.

As they rounded the corner to the main aisle, the mother, guiding a boy and a girl, looked down the length of the car. Andie glanced across the way. If she moved to where the dusty cowboy lounged with his hat over his eyes halfway down the car, she could free up four seats for the family to sit together. Otherwise, they'd have to sit in pairs, separated by several rows on opposite sides of the car. Andie rose, retrieved her colorful carpetbag, and, book clutched in her arm, motioned for the family to take her place.

"Thank you kindly, miss." The woman guided her children

to the seats, and Andie moved down the way.

"Excuse me, sir."

The dusty man didn't stir. Instead, he sat, arms folded across his chest, head against the window, face obscured by his hat, and long legs stretched so that his feet rested kitty-corner on the opposite bench, blocking the entire red velvet seat. A long brown duster and saddlebags occupied the space next to him.

One man occupying four seats. Papa had warned before she left St. Louis that life in the West may seem rather uncouth comparatively.

Andie cleared her throat. "Pardon."

He still didn't move.

Setting her bag down, she tapped his thigh with her book.

He jerked the hat from his face and, scowling, reached toward the holstered pistol she hadn't noticed against his right thigh. Her heart thrummed. Andie drew back with a sharp gasp, clutching the book as she grabbed her carpetbag.

The man's face blanched, and he rose to catch her elbow. "Whoa, now. Sorry." He locked his intense blue eyes with her. "So sorry. You all right?"

"Fine." Except her knees had gone soft and she trembled.

The man's cheeks reddened. "You startled me."

And he'd *terrified* her!

"Release me, sir," she whispered.

Eyes widening, his grip loosened. She pulled free and brushed at her sleeve, then hurried to one of the few empty seats at the far end. Only as she beelined for it, a man entered from the opposite end and inquired about it. The passengers around it nodded, and the man sat.

Gaze roving, she saw another seemingly empty place—much closer—but as she neared, it too was occupied. A knot lodged in her middle. Turning back, she realized the only seats. . .no, *seat*—a couple had taken those across from the man—the only *seat* available was beside the long-legged cowboy.

Lord Jesus, please. . .must I sit next to him?

But there were no other places.

Uneasy, she returned the way she'd come. When she reached the empty seat, she paused, glancing once at him and immediately averting her eyes.

"Is this seat taken?"

Blue eyes drew her to look again, though she did so only long enough to see his embarrassed smile.

"Now it is, miss. Welcome back. And again, sorry for frightening you."

Without acknowledging him, she put her carpetbag between them as a buffer, then sat as close to the aisle as she could.

The other couple offered pinched smiles as she settled her book in her lap and tried to read. Flustered as she was, she couldn't force her mind to focus.

Who was this man? An outlaw? A gunman? As quickly as he'd reached for the pistol at his side, probably the latter. Would he rob the train? She'd heard of such events.

Oh, Lord, perhaps I should have had Freddy escort me all the way to Denver.

Papa would've preferred it, but it seemed silly to have her cousin travel out of his way when, in a few hours, she would reach her meeting point with Calliope. Of course, she would've preferred Papa accompany her himself. His calming presence and legal expertise would be welcome on this trip. Once more, she gave the man a sidelong glance then focused on her book.

Lord, have I made a grave mistake? Protect me, please.

The train pulled out, and the conductor made the rounds. As he reached her, she closed the book's cover.

"How long until we reach Denver?"

Removing his pocket watch, he clicked open the cover. "About an hour and a half, miss."

"Thank you."

He checked the tickets of the others seated with her and moved on.

An hour and a half sitting next to a possible outlaw—an uncomfortable proposition after he'd left her embarrassed and on edge. More importantly, an hour and a half until Calliope would meet her. After fifteen years, she could wait that much longer, even if next to a man of questionable integrity and character.

So long as he didn't rob the train. . .

She opened the cover of her book to remove Callie's telegram, but her stomach knotted. It wasn't there!

Clapping the cover closed, she swept the layers of her dress and petticoats this way then that as she searched the floor. Not seeing it, she stood and checked the seat, but it wasn't there. She peeked down the aisle.

"Lose something, miss?" the cowboy called.

Again, she opened the cover of her book and leafed through the first few pages. "An important letter."

"You stored it in your book?"

Her temples throbbed as she deposited the tome on her seat. "In the front cover." She charged up the aisle to her original seat.

"Pardon. I've misplaced a telegram. Would you happen to have seen it?"

"I'm sorry, miss. No." The gentleman shook his head.

Her head spun. Where could it have gone?

"Thank you." She forced a smile, though it likely looked as if she had a stomach cramp.

She turned, ready to walk the aisle, but as she did, the cowboy caught her eye and held up Callie's message.

Andie stormed back and snatched it away. "Where did you

get this?" She hissed the words.

The man's brows shot up. "I found it in the *front* cover of your book, there." He smirked at the thick volume. "Considering you were readin' the durn thing upside down, miss, you only looked in the back."

Her cheeks flamed as the other couple stifled smiles.

"And as a matter of record, I didn't read it. I simply found it—exactly where you said."

The gent facing them nodded. "He's tellin' the truth, miss. I watched him turn your book over, and it was right there. He ain't had time to read it."

If only she could crawl into a hole somewhere. "Forgive me." The words grated like sand in her throat, and meeting his. . .incredible. . .gaze was worse, considering his smirk. "I shouldn't have snapped at you. Thank you for finding it."

He nodded. "I figure we're about even, miss. I scared the bejeebers out of you. You snapped at me. It's a wash. Maybe we could start over. . . ?"

So much for Papa's warning of the uncouth West. Thus far, she'd been the ill-mannered one.

"I think that's wise." She nodded. "Thank you."

He shifted toward her. "My name's Daniel Littrick. And you are?"

"Andromeda Braddock McGovern." Why she felt compelled to add the *Braddock*, she couldn't say—except that on the verge of reconnecting with her younger sister and older brother, she was feeling nostalgic for her birth surname, like she had in the year immediately after her adoption.

That annoying smirk returned. "Quite a mouthful, there. Didn't your parents like you?"

The storm clouds of embarrassment and shame that had just started to break came crowding back in. "What kind of a question is that? Of course they did!"

He chuckled. "It's just…that's an awful big handle for a pretty little thing. Kinda like that thick ol' book you're tryin' to read."

Jaw clenched, she clutched the book to her chest. "What an insufferable thing to say! Every part of my name is full with personal meaning. And as for my literature choices, I've read this book—and others just as large—many times through. Unlike you. You're probably illiterate." She scooted toward the aisle, as if she could get any further away. "Now I'll thank you, Mr. Littrick, to mind your own business and not speak to me again."

⌒

Heat like that of a desert at high noon crawled up his neck. Had he honestly just asked a total stranger if her parents didn't like her—because of her long name?

What had possessed him?

He knew.

From the instant he'd been startled awake and nearly drew down on her, he'd been on his proverbial heels and tryin' to find his balance. He'd tried to tease his way to better footing. His last comments were meant simply to be funny. Durn it, he should know better. Get him around a pretty gal and he'd forget his expensive college education and run on at the mouth like the village idiot.

"Guess I've done stuck my foot in it. Forgive me, miss. No disrespect intended." He exhaled. "Won't bother you again."

Settling his hat over his eyes again, he huddled against the window, arms folded.

Honestly, his problem hadn't begun when he was startled awake. It stemmed from why he rode the train to begin with. After three trips to Cheyenne in six months—one to see his youngest brother married, another for the births of his older brother's and his only sister's first children, and the last to move his father and business partner to be near their expanding family—he was plain irritated. He was the only kin left in the Colorado Territory...and the only one left to run a business he'd not been interested in starting. Oh, he could pull up stakes and move, but after years away at college, the thought of starting over held no appeal.

So his failed teasing over Miss McGovern's name had come because of some prickly areas within himself. He'd acted the fool, and she thought him a scoundrel. Did it honestly matter? She was headed to Denver. He'd head to parts beyond once they unloaded his paint horse, Briar, from the stock car. . .and he'd probably never come across her again.

He could live with that.

Although her choice in reading had given him pause. Few outside of academic circles or with a bent toward politics read Sir William Blackstone's *Commentaries on the Laws of England*—and even fewer women. He would've thought her more the *Godey's Lady's Book* sort, with her fashionable green dress and perfectly coiffed hair. She reminded him of the women he'd met back east while attaining his degree. The same sorts who'd poked fun at his colloquial turns of phrase or simplistic Western sensibilities.

Daniel shoved aside his thoughts, and the rhythmic rattling of the car and the darkness under his hat set him drifting again. When he roused, it was to the conductor's announcement that they were approaching the Denver station. He straightened, clapped his hat on his head, and gathered his duster and saddlebags.

Beside him, Miss McGovern flipped a page and read on. He watched, impressed at how quickly she turned the next page. She obviously wasn't laboring to understand. . .which was a relative feat. His first time through the four volumes had taken him weeks to ponder and understand.

He cleared his throat, and she glanced his way.

"Blackstone's no light read, miss."

Her lips curved into a frown. "And your point is?"

He furrowed his brow. "That *Commentaries on the Laws of England* can be difficult."

"You're familiar with Blackstone's writings."

"I've perused the pages a time or two."

"And that makes you an expert?"

"Didn't say that. Just that such a book takes some effort."

"And a woman couldn't possibly grasp such difficult meanings—is that it?"

He rubbed at his forehead beneath his hat. Yep, he was most certainly the village idiot.

Am I ever gonna learn, Lord?

He'd tried, for durn sure, but the lessons never seemed to stick.

"Forgive me, miss. I'll just leave you to your reading. Sorry for the interruption."

Her cheeks turned as red as some of the flowers in the weave of her carpetbag. "I suppose I was rather rude."

"No." He let his contempt drip from the word. "Surely not you. I should know that a refined lady such as yourself wouldn't spare a moment to converse with a dirty, know-nothin' saddle tramp like me. Forgive me for wasting your precious time."

This time, her lips parted in shock, and he reveled too much in the shamed look in her brown eyes.

He set his face toward the window as Denver came into view. As they neared, the train slowed. Beside him, she was more subdued, perhaps not so full of herself as she tucked the book away. She peered past him toward the train platform as it came into view, as if searching for someone. As she craned her neck, a smile broke across her face. The *snap* of the carpetbag's clasp drew his attention as she closed it and drew it into her lap, brushing it where it might have contacted his leg. He rolled his eyes.

She was obviously itching to see someone. Who was there to meet this uppity shrew? Not that it mattered. . .but who would put up with such behavior?

Thank goodness, once the train stopped, he wouldn't have to. He'd collect Briar and be on his way. He'd never cared for being sharp-tongued and rude, especially to a woman, but sometimes, folks just needed a dose of their own medicine.

It was for the best.

Once the train rolled to a stop, Miss McGovern rose, her bag held tight, and allowed the couple across from them to step into the aisle as others rose to disembark. She scowled as she motioned for him to slip into the walkway.

"No thank you, miss. I'll wait till you're clear. Wouldn't want to stand too close. Something might rub off. . ."

Despite how she lifted her chin in disgust, he wasn't about to take the prodding words back.

CHAPTER 2

How rude! Andie clamped her jaw tight and averted her gaze. Good riddance.

The line moved, and Andie glanced toward the platform where the young woman with the medium-brown hair stood beside a tall, handsome fellow. That had to be Calliope and her beau, Joe Trenamen. Calliope had said that she'd wear a blue dress and that Joe would be in a brown shirt. While the woman wore a decidedly western skirt and vest, the outfit was blue, and the man wore brown.

People began to disembark. She shuffled forward, heart pounding as she fought to keep sight of Calliope and Joe. When it was her turn, a porter took her bag, then helped her descend. Before she'd turned to receive her bag, the couple she'd spotted headed her way, hope in the young woman's eyes.

She hurried toward them. "Calliope?"

"Andromeda!" Tears filled her sister's eyes as they threw their arms around each other.

"Oh, Lord Jesus, thank You." She held tight to her sister.

"I can't believe I finally found you." Calliope clung to her, weeping, and Andie's own eyes were far from dry.

"Miss, would you like me to hold your bag?" At the man's question, Calliope pulled back.

"Joe. She's here." She looked at the handsome fellow as her tears flooded again.

He looked plenty pleased as he nodded. "Welcome, Miss McGovern. Glad you could make it. I'm Joe Trenamen, Callie's partner."

"And beau," Calliope whispered.

She nodded. "Please, call me Andromeda—or Andie."

"All right. . .Andie. May I take your bag?"

"Thank you." Andie handed it off, then turned to her baby sister.

She was a baby no more. Gone was the six-year-old child. A grown woman stood before her—with braided, medium-brown hair, and dressed in that long blue skirt, white blouse, and matching blue vest, with a hat not unlike the one Mr. Littrick had slept under.

"Look at you. You're beautiful."

"So are you." Calliope looked her up and down. "I've dreamed of this day for so long." Once more, she launched into Andie's arms and, laughing, hugged her tight.

Around them, folks looked on as they giggled and cried.

Finally, Calliope dabbed away the dampness under her eyes. "The only thing that could make this better is if Rion was here."

Andie sobered. "Have you found him yet?"

Joe pressed nearer. "They're getting the baggage unloaded." He waved down the platform. "Do you have anything more to collect?"

Several cars beyond where they unloaded crates, trunks, and mailbags, someone led a beautiful paint horse down a ramp from one of the boxcars. Mr. Littrick—now clad in that brown duster—waited with a saddle slung over one shoulder and saddlebags dangling from the other.

Yes, he was very much that saddle tramp—though not an unhandsome one.

She shook off the thought. Good looks couldn't overcome a sharp tongue and black heart.

"One trunk."

They headed down the platform, and she led Joe and Calliope to her piece. Joe handed her carpetbag back and went to secure a porter's help getting her luggage moved to their wagon.

Within minutes, the trunk was settled in Joe and Calliope's wagon, and they climbed onto the wagon bench to head to the mountain town of Cambria Springs.

"Was the trip uneventful?" Callie asked.

"Yes, until the final few hours." She related the story of encouraging her cousin to depart the train before seeing her all the way to Denver, then changing seats and winding up beside the disagreeable cowboy. "I'll admit I was far more anxious about traveling after my cousin Freddy and I separated than I anticipated. So perhaps I was too quick to assume he had ill intentions. But he wasn't helping matters."

"Sorry for the uncomfortable situation." Joe flicked the reins over the horses' rumps. "He didn't hurt you, did he?"

"Only my pride. The only time he touched me was when I first encountered him." Her cheeks warmed. "I woke him suddenly, and he reached for his gun, which—honestly—scared me. I backed up a step and he took my elbow, probably to keep me from running away."

Calliope giggled. "Welcome to the West."

"As I understood from our correspondence, you've not been here long yourself."

"I was here in Denver for a few months before going to Cambria Springs a month ago."

"And how did you became a Pinkerton?" She asked the

question in a hushed tone, as if to keep anyone else on the Denver street from hearing.

A coy smile overtook Calliope's features. "The day I was adopted, I was so distraught at being separated from you and Rion that I jumped from our moving wagon into the middle of the busy, muddy Chicago street. I was determined to get back to the train station to find you both. Horses and wagons veered all around me. It was mayhem."

Andie's breath caught. "You could've been killed."

"Yes. A man galloped up on a horse, plucked me from the mud, and ushered me safely out of the street. It was Allan Pinkerton. He saved my life. As I grew, he kept some small connection with my adoptive parents, and I was quite taken with him and his agency. So when I learned that he hired Kate Warne and other women as detectives, I determined I'd be one."

"That's so brave! I think courage must've skipped me."

"Why? You've defied tradition to become an attorney. That's daring."

Andie shook her head. "My father humored me. From the day he and Mama adopted me, Papa was so gentle and supportive. I couldn't spend enough time with him, so after school each day, I went to his office to file papers or take notes for him. Sometimes, I'd sit in the courtroom as he tried cases. I wanted to know everything he was doing, and he patiently answered every question. As I grew, the questions became more detailed, and he got the ridiculous notion to have me train for the law. So I did. He's affirmed me as a full-fledged lawyer, and I've helped him prepare cases, but I've never taken the lead on anything. I doubt I'd even be allowed."

Calliope and Joe glanced at one another, and Joe spoke. "Not only would you be allowed—it's desired. We need a lawyer."

Her stomach clenched. "For what?"

Calliope's face shadowed. "Rion."

"So you have found him?"

Nodding, Callie's face paled. "I convinced him to come in and allow himself to be arrested."

"For what?"

"Murder."

Andie snapped her eyes shut. *Oh, dear Jesus, no.*

⌒

Happy to be back in the saddle—and especially away from haughty Miss McGovern—Daniel turned Briar toward home, though he had one short stop to make first. He rode through the busy streets, navigating to the cemetery at the edge of town. There, he turned in and rode across the wagon path toward Ma's grave near the center of the sizable graveyard. Dismounting, he tied Briar to the nearest tree and strode to her plot.

"Hey there, Ma." He swept his hat off and held it against his chest. "It's been a while." He cleared his throat. "Too long. Honestly, I've been avoiding coming here of late, and I shouldn't have."

It wasn't harming Ma any—and holding on to hurt feelings when he was the only one affected made him feel all the more like a donkey's backside.

"Sorry." He cleared his throat. "You always did say I could be stubborn as a mule. Guess I've been letting my mulish parts show." He clapped the hat back on his head and sat at the foot of the grave. "I just—I dunno, Ma. Reckon I figured at twenty-five my life would look different. I got the degree you begged me to get, but I can't support myself with that alone. And Pa and I were supposed to be partners in a land surveying business, but Caleb, Wes, and Helen all settled down in Cheyenne. Grandbabies started coming, and Pa moved up that way too."

He rubbed at his chest, as if to ease the ache he felt. "Again, maybe I'm being headstrong, but after spending years back east. . .after not being here when you made your exit. . .fighting to set up my practice and the surveying business and get both off the ground. . .I don't want to pull up stakes and start over in Cheyenne."

Across the cemetery, a woman on a fine mahogany bay trotted up and, before she'd even stopped the animal, slid from the saddle. The horse trotted past, and she whistled, causing the mount to return. The gal stroked the horse's nose then retrieved a blanket from behind the saddle and spread it near a headstone.

"As I was sayin'. . ." He focused on his mother's marker. "I'm not happy doing either job. Surveying is what Pa wanted. Lawyering is what you wanted." He shook his head. "Guess I've been busy enough chasing everyone else's dreams for my life that I don't know what my own are." Yet it was a shame and a waste to have paid for a college degree, not to use it.

"I feel stuck, Ma. Kind of wish you were around to talk to—but if you were, I couldn't talk to you about this, because I'd probably hurt you when I said I don't want to be a lawyer." How brave of him to say it all now—years after her death. Why couldn't he have said it before?

He shook his head. "In other news, I met a woman. Sat next to her on the train. She seemed smart. Pretty. . ." Real pretty. "But she was an absolute spitfire. Sharp-tongued, objectionable, ill-tempered. I know you always hoped to see your children married off, but if this is what the world has to offer, I doubt it'll happen for me."

Daniel rubbed his hands down his thighs. It was time he lived his own life, chased the things he wanted to pursue, without worrying if he pleased his parents.

It sounded easy, but it wasn't. It would take money or skill to start over. He had little of either.

"Guess I've got some soul-searchin' to do. Reading the scriptures." After all, he ought to include God in his decisions.

A pang lodged in his chest.

No. He ought to seek God for answers, not consult Him for an opinion on his own plans.

Sorry, Lord. I've poured my thoughts out more to my deceased mother's grave than seekin' Your wisdom. Forgive me. That's backward. And thank You for the conviction. What do You say I should do?

Minutes ticked by, and he listened. Yet all he heard were birds chirping, bees buzzing, and wagons rumbling as they passed outside the graveyard.

Across the cemetery, the woman rose from her blanket and peered toward the road. After an instant, she headed toward the property's edge, waving and calling out. When the wagon didn't even slow, she whistled for her horse and swung into the saddle. Spurring the horse, she rode after the three sitting shoulder to shoulder on the wagon bench.

CHAPTER 3

"Rion's wanted for *murder*?" Andie's words barely sounded above the rumbling wagon wheels.

Calliope nodded. "And kidnapping and attempted murder. Will you defend him in court?"

She gawked. "I—I—He's not guilty, is he?"

Joe glanced her way. "He's being framed."

"Framed?"

"He needs a good attorney." Calliope's weighty stare nearly chilled her to her core. "He needs you."

"I—" Calliope had mentioned there was trouble, but Rion. . .wanted for murder? "Oh dear."

At the same moment she stammered like an imbecile, Calliope's gaze flew to some point, and she swatted Joe.

"Is that Maya Fellows?"

Joe glanced toward the cemetery on Andie's right, and he frowned.

There, a woman atop a big horse charged along the low stone wall surrounding the graveyard, flailing one arm, trying to flag them. Joe drew the wagon to a stop, though the woman galloped on for some distance, headed straight toward a tree's low-hanging limbs. In horror, Andie gripped the wagon bench with one hand, Calliope's wrist with the other, as they all watched.

At the last moment, the woman faced front to see the huge obstacle, and she ducked. Her top hat flew off, and her horse slowed. Heart pounding, Andie held her breath. Surely they'd see an empty saddle or the woman badly injured. But when she emerged on the far side of the tree, the only difference in her appearance was her hat was missing and her braid had uncoiled itself from its bun.

Joe flicked the reins and moved toward the tree. "Are you all right?"

The woman faced them again, one hand over her heart. "That was nearly a disaster."

Calliope leaned around Andie. "Are you hurt, Miss Fellows?"

"Thankfully, no. Although I'll need to repin my hair."

"What in heaven's name were you doing?" Joe scowled.

The woman laughed. "Trying to get your attention. How is Rion?"

They all gaped. When Joe noticed another wagon coming in the distance, he motioned. "We'll come talk to you so we don't have to shout."

At her nod, Joe wheeled the wagon in the opposite direction.

"Let's mind what we say, Joe." Calliope glanced at him.

"Agreed."

"Who is this person?"

Calliope smoothed her skirt. "Maya Fellows—a former. . . interest. . .of Rion's. When she heard he'd been arrested, she appeared at the jail, offering help."

"Our brother's in jail?"

Joe shook his head. "He escaped from jail. He's on the run."

"Oh, Lord Jesus, help." She cradled her head in her hand. "Please start at the beginning."

By the time they neared the cemetery entrance, another rider had approached Miss Fellows from within the cemetery and held her hat out.

That dratted long-legged cowboy—Daniel Littrick. What was he doing there?

Joe pulled through the open gate, parked, and climbed down as Miss Fellows and Mr. Littrick led their horses in their direction. While Joe assisted Callie down, Mr. Littrick chuckled at something Maya Fellows said, the sound rich and warm.

Andie crinkled her nose. The man was flirting. . .and Miss Fellows' coy smiles and occasional giggles seemed to egg him on.

She glanced at her top hat and, with a perplexed look, laughed at the mangled brim. "I suppose that was much closer than I realized."

"Like I said, it was a spectacular display of good fortune or superior skill. Not sure which. All I know is I expected we'd be rushing you to the nearest doctor for a serious head wound, but all that needs surgery is your hat brim." Mr. Littrick touched the floppy piece, which had come unattached from the body of the hat, except for a one-inch length that still held it all together.

Again, she giggled. "Call it pure, dumb luck, Mr. . . ?"

"Daniel Littrick, miss."

"A pleasure, Mr. Littrick." The woman's smile was so sweet, if she'd held it much longer, her lips might've frozen as all the sugar hardened into cement.

Was Mr. Littrick a natural-born flirt, or was this some show just for her? Not that it mattered. . .

Joe helped Andie down then strode up to Miss Fellows. "You're sure you're unharmed?"

"Yes, Mr. Nesbitt. Thank you."

She leaned closer to Calliope. "Nesbitt?"

"Play along. I'll explain later."

Mr. Littrick squinted Joe's way. "You look familiar. Do I know you, Nesbitt?"

"You live up around Cambria Springs, don't you?"

"I do." He glanced her way, then back to Joe. "Your companion gave quite a tongue-lashing on the train. Hope she's going easier on you than me."

Andie stiffened. "If you'd like to continue this petty feud, I'll oblige you, but I suspect we all have better things to do."

That stupid smirk returned. Oh, how she'd like to wipe it from his face.

"That's enough." Joe held up a hand. "None of us wants trouble."

"No," Miss Fellows cut in. "In fact, I hope you'll understand, Mr. Littrick, but I need to speak with Mr. Nesbitt and Miss Jarrett about my beau. Please excuse us."

"Lu won't appreciate her calling Rion her beau," Callie mumbled.

"Lu?" Andie's head swam.

"I'll explain later." Callie crossed to where Miss Fellows stood.

"Sure." Mr. Littrick gave a slight bow. "Have yourself a pleasant day." He led his paint horse away, riding down the row of graves.

"And you are?" Miss Fellows turned in her direction.

"Needing to stretch my legs. Excuse me." Andie meandered around the wagon and made her way down the same row, reading headstones, calculating ages, and otherwise entertaining herself as she waited. As she walked, one grave draped with a brightly colored quilt caught her eye. She admired the patchwork, then read the name and dates on the headstone. Odd. The date of death was July Fourth—America's Independence Day. The anniversary would've been only days ago.

"Pardon, miss!" Maya Fellows called out.

Andie turned.

"Would you bring my quilt when you come, please?"

She gathered the blanket, folding it as she paced back toward the wagon. Reaching the three, she handed off the quilt.

"Thank you." The woman rolled it and, struggling, managed to tie its bulk behind her saddle. "All of you." She turned specifically toward Joe and Callie. "Please, give my best wishes to Rion when you see him."

They said their farewells, and once Joe helped them into the wagon, they departed.

"What was that about?" Andie asked once they were out of earshot.

Joe slapped the reins. "Maya Fellows is a former flame of Rion's. The very morning he was arrested, she happened to be in Cambria Springs—so she could see the medicine show that had come through town. She offered her help—mainly her pa's money—then regaled us with stories. Rion told her to come stay with friends in Denver. But when she saw us passing by, she had to have an update on how *her beau* is doing."

"And...Lu?"

"Lucinda Peters. She's...ah. . ." Callie blew out a breath. "We have so much to explain."

"Obviously."

What had she gotten herself into?

⌒

The sun sank behind the horizon as Daniel reached Cambria Springs, but rather than heading straight home, he stopped first at the Wells Fargo office near the town square. The door was locked tight, and the shades were drawn. However, the lamp inside was obviously still lit. He dismounted, tied Briar, and knocked.

"We're closed!" came a familiar voice from inside.

"Hector Darden!" He called loudly enough to be heard. "It's Daniel. Open the door."

An instant later, Heck lifted the shade.

"You know I can't." His friend overenunciated his words.

"How long till you're done?"

"Twenty minutes, maybe?"

"You hungry?"

At Heck's nod, he motioned. "Meet me at Dutch's Café when you're done."

Heck nodded. "Sounds good."

"See you over there soon."

It took him every bit of the twenty minutes to ride home, change clothes, get Briar settled in the livery, and make it to the café—though Heck arrived at the same time.

"How are ya?" He grinned. "You look tired."

Daniel nodded. "Long trip. Moving Pa to Cheyenne wasn't the pleasantest way to spend my time."

They took a table in the corner, away from the other diners.

"He's settled, though?"

He waved a hand. "Yeah. Seems happy to be with most of his kids. Of course, there was all kinds of pressure for me to move up there, but. . ." He shrugged.

"Man, you've got to live your own life. Not theirs."

He chuckled. "I stopped by Ma's grave today and came to the same conclusion."

"Good."

Dutch approached the table, his demeanor surlier than Daniel could ever recall. "Evenin', fellas. All I got left at this hour is beef stew or chicken and dumplings. And a few pieces of apple pie."

Daniel and Heck looked wide-eyed at each other.

"I'll take the dumplings—and pie." Daniel's belly growled in anticipation.

Heck grinned. "I'll take the stew. And pie."

"Done. Have it out in a couple minutes." The man retreated.

Daniel looked at Heck. "What's with him? He's usually happier than that."

His friend's eyebrows rose. "Reckon you haven't heard, have you?"

"Heard what?"

"Since you've been gone, Sheriff Downing captured a fella what looks like the one who murdered Miss Mary, who used to wait tables here in the café, and that soiled dove."

"Who'd he capture?"

Heck leaned nearer, dropping his voice to a conspiratorial level. "You know that bounty hunter, Braddock, what comes around here from time to time?"

"Can't say I've met him, but I know who you mean." He thought a moment. "Isn't he some kind of friend of Dutch's?"

"Kin." Heck leaned closer still. "Or close to it."

"So this Braddock fella murdered Dutch's waitress?"

"I get the sense Dutch doesn't believe it's him. But since you've been gone, Miss Hattie—you know, Mrs. Ingram's daughter, the one with the bad legs?"

"Yeah."

"She went missin'. And Downing arrested Braddock for it. Then Braddock escaped the jail and took another woman."

"So he kidnapped two women?"

"The other woman—Lucinda Peters—says she wasn't kidnapped. She's some kind of reporter, wantin' his story, so she rode with him to get it. And Hattie Ingram's been found but in real bad shape. Stabbed a bunch of times, part of her hair shaved like Mary and Serafina. They say she's on the mend, but ain't nobody seen her except those at Mrs. Ingram's place."

"Thank God she's been found! Have they recaptured Braddock?"

"Not yet. The man's in his element out there." He jutted his chin toward the front of the building. "From what I've gathered, he sleeps under the stars or in caves most nights. Always on the hunt for a bounty. Only now, he's the hunted."

"A fine time to leave, huh?"

"You missed a lot."

Dutch deposited the steaming bowls and plates of warm pie as well as two glasses of water on the table and retreated.

"Word is, Braddock was injured. Posse found blood—a fair bit. But they still haven't found him. They think he got help from another friend up the mountain, Seth Kealey, after Miss Peters and Miss Hattie were found at his place. But they've been back for more than a week, and nobody's seen Braddock."

"Is the posse still tracking him?" Daniel blew on his chicken and dumplings.

"Posse started droppin' out and headin' home once the women were found, leavin' just Downing and a couple others." Heck stirred his stew and tasted it, continuing to talk around the mouthful. "With Downing's election later this year, he can't afford to leave the town unprotected."

"True." Daniel took a bite, enjoying the warmth and the taste.

"So he called in the territorial marshal. Whole town's on edge."

He blew out a breath. "Guess I oughtn't leave again if this is what happens when I do."

"So how was the trip?" Heck washed his next bite down with water.

"Pa's settled. Happy. Everyone's pleased havin' him there."

"So nothin' eventful."

"Unless you count today. The train ride home was interesting. . .and then the time at the cemetery."

"Train wasn't robbed, was it?"

"Nothing like that. I sat next to a woman. Real pretty, but—"
He shook his head. "About as pretentious as they come. Thing
that made her interesting was, she was reading Blackstone." He
spooned up another bite of chicken.

"Blackstone?" Heck looked surprised. "As in, Sir William?"

"That's the one. I'd have talked to her about it, but every time
I tried, she insinuated I was too stupid to understand."

"You're only about the smartest fella in town."

"I wouldn't say that." But he did have a college degree—a
rarity out here.

"You tell her you aced law school?"

He rolled his eyes. "I didn't *ace* law school. I passed. And
why? I've got nothing to prove."

"I'd've told her, but—" Heck took a big bite. "What about
the cemetery?"

"Strangest thing. Some woman was there, visiting a grave,
sees someone on the road, and goes charging through the
cemetery on horseback trying to flag the wagon down. About
took her own head off when she about rode into a low-hanging
tree limb. At the last possible moment, she shifted sideways
and just missed it."

"Hoo!" Heck's eyes grew wide. "That had to be somethin'.
How'd she react?"

"That's what was so strange. She almost seemed to relish
the attention." He took a drink. "She wore this top hat, and it
was a close-enough call that her hat brim got torn off, but for
about that much." He indicated the inch that had remained
connected.

Heck looked even more surprised. "She loco or something?"

"Durn if I know. Turns out, she was flagging down the
woman from the train and the couple that came to pick her

up. Once they drove into the cemetery, I went my way." He shrugged. "So all the excitement came today."

"And you come home to all this."

Daniel chuckled. "Maybe movin' to Cheyenne has some appeal after all. . ."

CHAPTER 4

It had been a long day of travel. Once they'd reached the boardinghouse, Mrs. Ingram had graciously fixed them a light supper, despite it being late. The other boarders were cordial and sat in the parlor, passing the time. But everyone filtered off to their respective rooms for the night, leaving only Joe and Calliope with Andie.

"I'm so happy you're here." Calliope leaned her head against Andie's shoulder.

"It feels like a dream." And it had finally come true, though not without some rough patches. Learning of Rion's legal troubles had been an unwelcome turn. Could she defend him in court? She'd never taken the lead before—particularly not in a murder case. In fact, she'd had little courtroom experience, other than watching Papa argue his cases since she was a child. If the timing were better, that's what she would do: ask Papa to defend Rion. But he had several big cases he was scrambling to prepare for, especially since she was now here. To make matters worse, he'd fallen from a ladder and broken several ribs, which allowed pneumonia to take hold. He was on the mend, but it had slowed him down. With all that, she couldn't ask Papa to come. If Rion needed an attorney, how could she not try? Their brother could lose his life if she didn't.

He could also lose his life if she failed. The thought turned her stomach.

Oh, Father! How should I answer this request? I feel unequal to the task.

There would be no trial until Rion was captured again— or turned himself in. Papa's schedule might very well clear before then.

Please, let that be the case, Lord. Rion needs a competent attorney. Not me!

Something struck the window nearest them, a rapid succession of light taps, almost like rain splattering the window. Both she and Calliope looked at the window. Joe also perked up. After several seconds, the unusual sound repeated, then again some seconds after that.

"Callie, turn down the lamp." Joe paced toward the window while she did.

As the light dimmed, Joe peeked into the darkness beyond.

Again, the faint taps came—and Joe cupped his hand over his eyes to see out.

"Oh my word! I think Rion's outside!"

Calliope launched from the settee. "He is?"

Another series of taps came.

"What's making that sound?" Andie also rose to stare at the window.

"I think he's throwing pebbles at our window."

"I'm going out there." Calliope headed for the front door, but Joe whipped around.

"Calliope, no."

She turned on him. "He's my brother." Her voice was an urgent hush. "*Our* brother!"

"Let me check first. I'll make sure it's him and not whoever's been masquerading as him. If it is, we'll all meet at the barn."

Calliope sobered. "You're right. But hurry, please!"

Joe walked past, pausing to kiss her forehead before moving to the front door where his gun belt and pistol hung. He unholstered the gun, unlocked the door, and slipped out.

Calliope hurried back to Andie's side. "If it is him, that would make today perfect."

Excitement warred with dread in her heart. Yes—perfect to meet both her brother and her sister in the same day. But professionally, it would mean she could be forced to defend him in court—and risk the shame of losing his freedom or his life if she failed.

Joe returned minutes later, reholstering the pistol.

"Is it him?" Calliope's voice was still cloaked in whispers.

Joe swung the gun belt around his hips. "It is."

Andie's breath caught, and her head swam.

As he buckled the belt in place, he nodded toward the back of the house. "We'll go out that way. He's heading there now."

Calliope grabbed her hand and almost dragged her toward the back door. They eased past Mrs. Ingram's and Hattie's rooms, and Joe unlocked the door.

Once outside, Calliope bounded down the porch steps and toward the barn, where the door stood slightly ajar. Joe locked the door, pocketed the key, and waved Andie toward the path Callie had taken. In the barn, Joe lit a match, where her sister wept in the arms of a large, unkempt, dark-haired man. He looked her way.

"Andromeda?"

A knot lodged in her throat until she could only nod.

His eyes glistened. "I can't believe it. I've been lookin' for you. For years." One-armed, he hoisted Calliope and carried her to where Andie stood, then pulled her also into the hug.

For the second time that day, emotions broke free, and Andie wept in her brother's arms. When finally the emotions abated, she pulled back.

"Calliope said you were hurt."

"I'm better. Shoulder's still tender, but that happens with a bullet wound."

"Wounds." Calliope overemphasized the *s*. "The bullet went through—here and here." She touched the front of her shoulder, then the back.

Rion glared. "So much for not worryin' her." He grinned. "Wounds. Two. They're healin' just fine. And what about you?" He shrugged. "Tell me...everything."

Something between a laugh and a sob bubbled up, and she shook her head. "We haven't time for everything now. But I'm well. I was adopted by a wonderful, childless couple who doted on me and treated me like their own. I've led a wonderful life."

"Good." His jaw firmed, and for a moment, he looked like he might succumb to his own emotions, though he breathed deeply until it passed. "It eases my guilt, knowin' y'all both led good lives."

Joe cleared his throat. "Rion, I think it's time you turn yourself in."

He shook his head. "I haven't found the fella with the similar boot tracks yet."

"And I doubt you will. If that fella, whoever he is, knows Miss Hattie's been found—"

"How is Hattie?"

"She's mending. And she's said she knows it wasn't you who took her."

Rion nodded.

"As I was saying, if the imposter knows Hattie's in town,

it doesn't make sense for him to keep leavin' boot tracks like yours. If he could've found her, he'd have left boot tracks like yours while he finished the job he started. But when we found her and brought her home, if he was smart, he'd have changed out of those boots."

Rion nodded. "I had similar thoughts."

"All right. So you're not gonna find him. At least, not by his tracks—and probably not easily."

"But I been checkin' on the wanted posters we pulled out. Looked into three of 'em. I got three more to go."

"Callie and I can take that over."

Again, Rion shook his head. "I know the cases, the people. I can get it done faster."

"Not when there are people lookin' for you. You could be shot again. Killed. You've done half the work. Callie and I can finish the rest while you stay in the safety of the jail."

Rion grinned. "I've proved how unreliable those jail bars are."

Joe folded his arms. "And I trust you're not going to again."

Callie tapped his arm. "Rion, Andie's father is an attorney, and so is she."

Andie's heart sank, especially when his eyes rounded. "You're joshin'."

"No—not *joshing*. But—" How could she say this? "I've never tried a case in court. I've only helped Papa prepare his."

"But you could, couldn't ya?" The hope in Rion's eyes was unsettling. "Because I'm in a lot of trouble."

"I—" Her stomach knotted until it hurt. *Oh, dear Jesus.* "Of course I can. I—I will."

He engulfed her with another hug, and she fought the urge to vomit.

"All right. If you and Calliope will keep searchin' and

Andromeda will defend me. . .I'll turn myself in."

She couldn't breathe. *Lord, how can I live with myself if Rion loses his life because I failed?*

⌒

Sunday, July 13, 1873

The itinerant preacher wasn't in town this weekend, so first thing after breakfast, Daniel put on his best suit and headed toward the sheriff's office. Hopefully, Downing would be in so he could get more details on the murdered women. As a lawyer and an officer of the court, there might be work he could do to help the sheriff—and as tight as his finances were after weeks away, any work was welcome.

Rounding the last corner, his steps faltered. A crowd surrounded the log building, filling the porch outward toward the big pine that once served as the jail. He hurried on, weaving his way through the crowd to the door. The door was locked. Sweeping his hat off, he peered in the window.

Another smaller crowd occupied the office, but when he rapped on the glass, a sullen Downing glared his way then beckoned him in. Daniel mouthed, *It's locked*. The sheriff flicked the key and jerked the door open.

"All of you, git!" He flung a hand at the crowd. "Go on now or I'll start makin' some arrests."

"For what?" someone shouted.

"I'll come up with somethin'!" He turned Daniel's way. "You. Inside." He addressed the mob. "Everyone else better be gone next time I stick my head out this door." Once Daniel slipped inside, Downing slammed the door and locked it again.

Aside from Downing was the big bounty hunter, Braddock, Stephen Nesbitt, and Kezia Jarrett, and another brunette woman—childlike in size and stature and with a baby face. But the adoring way she and Braddock looked at one another said she might not be as young as his first glance indicated.

In the corner near the stove, the shrew from the train looked puzzled at him. Perhaps it was the fancier duds.

"Morning, Miss McGovern."

She cleared her throat softly. "Mr. Littrick."

"I'd say it's a pleasure, but that hardly applies to our past encounters."

"At least you've proven you understand the value of cleanliness."

"Well, as the great John Wesley said, 'Cleanliness is next to godliness.'"

She arched a brow. "Too bad you didn't apply that principle yesterday. You were in a most ungodly state."

Heat washed through him. "You know, I wasn't gonna bring it up, but since you broached the topic—you *looked* shiny and fresh, miss, but you smelled a little ungodly yourself."

She gasped, and her face turned a deep red.

"Littrick!" the sheriff bellowed, drawing both his and Miss McGovern's attention.

Braddock now occupied a cell, and Miss Jarrett comforted the youthful woman.

Downing waved him into the storeroom and closed the door after them.

"Yes, sir?"

"I already contacted the marshal to see when we can get Braddock on the judge's schedule." He spoke in a tone only Daniel would hear. "Since he's already escaped once, it needs to be soon. He said it'd be six weeks before they can get here."

"All right?"

"So. . .find me that justice of the peace, Judge Oakwell.

He'll get here sooner."

It wasn't unusual for territorial judges to be booked out for months. Zebulun Oakwell was usually available—but only because he was such a poor judge. "Why the rush?"

The sheriff snorted. "That bounty hunter's a pain in my backside. He won't escape me again."

"All right, but do you mind if I look for a more competent judge? Oakwell's the worst."

"He'll be available. A quick trial's important to me."

Not what Daniel wanted to hear, but he nodded. "Talk to you once I know anything."

The sheriff reached for the door, though Daniel stopped him. "How's Miss McGovern mixed up in this?"

"Who?"

"The woman standin' by the stove?"

"Oh." Downing smirked. "Her." He chuckled. "Considerin' I'm expecting you to prosecute, she's your courtroom opponent: Braddock's attorney."

With that, Downing motioned Daniel out.

CHAPTER 5

"What do you mean, the trial begins Wednesday?" Andromeda's world tipped and spun. "You said it would take time for the judge to make it back to Cambria Springs." Could she even attempt to mount an appropriate defense in such a short time frame?

"It does—and this district's judge was here two months back, so it'll be a while before he returns. But after Rion's escape, Downing wanted a fast trial. He's called a justice of the peace to preside."

How could this be? "This is a territorial matter. He's accused of breaking territorial law, isn't he?"

Calliope laid a hand on her arm. "Andie, I've struggled with this too, being from Chicago. Everything moves slower in the territories. When things move too slowly, people find faster ways to get things done. For instance, a posse made up of local citizens rather than marshals and deputies. Vigilante groups exacting justice without a trial. Or, in this case, finding a faster way to try Rion."

She gulped. "But if the usual processes don't apply in who conducts the trial, how can we be assured they'll apply in other areas?" Could Rion even get a fair trial here, given three women from the town had been affected? Women who were friends or family of the town residents—or in the soiled dove's case, someone from whom many men had sought. . .pleasure. She shuddered.

"It's a hard truth of life in the West." Joe's tone was soothing. "Things aren't as refined as in St. Louis."

No. No, they weren't, and she struggled to grasp it.

Andie took deep breaths to calm her racing thoughts. "All right. If this is what I have to work with, then I'll need every minute between now and Wednesday morning. I need files, notes, witness statements—and someplace big enough to spread things out."

Joe and Calliope both thought.

"Lu's renting a house a couple blocks from here," Callie said. "She might let us use her place."

"All right." Andie shook her hands as if flicking water from them. "And I'll need to send some telegrams." She should notify Papa. Perhaps even from afar, he could guide her.

Joe motioned. "That'd be the Wells Fargo office. But it's Sunday. They're probably closed."

"But Sheriff Downing told Mr. Littrick to send word to the US Marshal this morning."

Callie shook her head. "You two check on whether you can send your telegrams. I'll ask Lu about using her house."

"All right." Andie tried to settle her racing heart. "Since this is all outside of the usual procedures, who would I petition *now* for a change of venue?"

"A what?"

"A new location. To Denver, or. . .somewhere. Given the murdered women were a part of this community, and especially the respect the community holds for Hattie and her mother, I don't know that Rion will get a fair trial here."

"Changing location is a tall order."

"But necessary."

Joe groaned. "It's a mighty big risk. How many people will travel to the new spot to testify? Could work in Rion's favor, in that people who'd testify against him may not show. But it'll work equally against him, when folks like Seth and Lena maybe can't make the trip because her time's so near."

"Out here, people will wantonly ignore a court summons to testify?"

"Some will. In Seth and Lena's case, it wouldn't be brazen disregard, just bad timing, with her baby due any minute. But they're an important piece of your case—explaining that Rion didn't kidnap Hattie. You need them there. And Hattie'll speak for Rion, but she's not strong enough to make an out-of-town trip yet."

Oh dear.

"Besides, don't you usually do that kind of thing in the first days of a case?"

"Of course, but why should the judge travel here only to move the location? If I could request the change of venue now, it could save time, money, travel."

"I see your point, but I think you're stuck."

She probably was. If only she didn't have to deal with it all on her own. Her mind was spinning so fast she struggled to grasp thoughts as they raced past.

Andie glanced across the foyer of the grand house and saw the large family Bible on its stand in the corner. At its sight, her heart slowed ever so slightly.

"Does this town have a church?"

"A church. . ." Joe repeated.

"A house of worship?"

Callie nodded. "It serves as a school most times, and an itinerant pastor comes to town every so often. But yes, and they even open the doors on Sundays so folks can gather on their own."

"Would one of you point me to it? I need to pray."

The only way she knew to combat the turmoil she felt was to fall on God's mercy.

⌒

Daniel sat on the front row of the schoolhouse, elbows on his knees and hat in his hand. He'd folded his suit coat over the bench behind him so he could feel the breeze blowing once he'd opened the doors and windows.

"Father, long ago I committed to You and Ma that I wouldn't approach any trial with a wrong heart. I promised I'd deal honestly, seek the truth, not just to win." Victories in his profession could cost men their freedom—or their lives. He wanted no part of falsely convicting anyone, but if Braddock was truly guilty, then he should pay.

"You lead, please, Father. Let justice be served."

Sheriff Downing's sneering attitude when he announced Miss McGovern would be his courtroom opponent, as well as the cutting exchange he'd had with her that morning, jangled in his mind, standing out like a single ill-tuned key on an otherwise-tuned piano. What was wrong with him? It shouldn't matter if she was rude and antagonistic. His parents taught him to respect women, and he'd been nothing but disrespectful to her.

Heaviness grew in his chest, and he knelt, facing the bench. Settling his hat on the seat, elbows on either side, he started again. "Lord, I don't like how I've acted toward Miss McGovern." He buried his face in his hands. "Reckon she's showin' me the darkness in my own heart, and I don't much like it. Forgive me. I'm embarrassed. I expect more of myself. No wonder I'm the only Littrick who isn't married. I got much to learn—and I'll need the rest of my lifetime to drive those lessons through my thick head."

If he'd said anything he'd spoken to Miss McGovern in his parents' hearing, Ma would've grabbed his ear and dragged him outside to cut a switch. He should be capable of restraining his tongue out of simple kindness.

"Lord, help me mind my speech and my manners. We got off on the wrong foot—and I've danced on her toes ever since. If we're to be thrown together in this trial, please keep me from speaking any more disrespect."

He was a fool. . .

"The village idiot, for certain." He shook his head. "Help me, Lord. I got so much to learn. . ."

He would have continued his prayers, but a sniff from the back of the room drew his ear. Startled, he looked up. There, Andromeda McGovern stared, her pretty pink dress reflecting off her cheeks quite fetchingly.

"Beseeching the Lord, are you?"

Red-faced, he stood. "I'm still clean, miss, so it's a fine time to get next to God."

"And why were you invoking my name, Mr. Littrick?"

Heat flooded his face. "Heard that, did you?" Why had he shaved the two weeks' worth of scruff from his jaw before boarding the train yesterday? If he'd left it, at least there'd be something to hide his embarrassment.

"I did." She straightened. "What's your purpose in speaking my name in your prayers?"

"Just makin' sure my heart's right, miss. Nothin' more."

"Or were you enlisting God in plotting my failure in Mr. Braddock's case?"

"I wish you no ill will, miss. In fact, I was prayin' the truth would come, no matter who wins."

"I'm sure you'd like nothing more than to put a presumptuous woman with the preposterous notion she belongs in a courtroom in her place. Relegate her back to being a wife and mother."

"I had no such designs, but if that's where she belongs. . ."

She sniffed. "Few men believe otherwise."

"Don't you think you ought to get to know a fella first, before you decide what he believes? We ain't all cut from the same cloth. Some of us might surprise you."

"I doubt it."

He cocked his head. "Where are you from, miss?"

"What does that matter?"

"Just tryin' to get a fix on where that uppity manner comes from. You from some moneyed family back east?"

"What would you know about life back east?"

"Considerin' I spent several years in Massachusetts attendin' Harvard Law School, more than you think."

Her face paled, and she settled a hand on her belly before she stiffened her spine and glared. "You are *not* a Harvard-trained lawyer."

"Believe what you want, but I got a head full of knowledge and a real pretty paper with my name on it to prove it."

The way she gulped air, she looked like she might be ill.

"Somethin' wrong, miss?"

"No, Mr. Littrick. All is well enough. But since you're obviously occupying the church, I'll come again later." She stomped out before he could say he was done.

CHAPTER 6

Monday, July 14, 1873

"How are you coming, tracking down the men on the wanted posters?" Andie turned to Joe and Calliope with a pleading look.

Joe crammed his hands in his trouser pockets. "Rion found Jimmy Albey, Al Langer, and Walt Esper. None of them are behind this. We've found news of Clyde Page and his gang. Two are in prison, and most of the rest are dead."

Andie tried not to shudder. "But not all?"

"One's free—but after a bad injury, he couldn't pull off the travel to get all the places these murders have occurred."

She turned the posters over, leaving two face up. "And these?"

Calliope chewed a fingernail. "Frank Dunwitty and Edward Hunney are deceased. See the two dates on the posters?" She indicated the handwritten numbers. "The earlier one is when Rion turned them in. The second is date of death. We're struggling to find the families of each. I don't know if those are false names or if female relatives have gotten married again. We're doing our best."

Andie jotted questions to ask Rion later, then leafed through her other points.

"Has anyone spoken to Ollie Sapey?"

Lu shuddered. "The night we collected Miss Hattie from her, yes."

"Not since?"

Joe straightened from looking at the information spread across Lu's table. "She's a recluse. Seth and Lena say she gives one spoken warning then makes use of her shotgun."

Andie gaped. "She's shot people?"

"Her first shotgun blast is usually into the air. It was with me—and that's what Seth and Lena experienced as well. None of us have been stupid enough to try a second time."

"But she saw the man who she described as similar to Rion but somehow different?"

Joe nodded.

"We need her testimony."

Lu's expression was haunted. "I doubt she'll agree."

Joe folded his arms. "I could try to talk to her."

"Would you?"

"What's most important to you? I can head that way—with no guarantees that Ollie will testify. Or I can keep working on the wanted posters."

"With the trial looming, we may not have time to find who's framing Rion. At least, not as our sole means of saving him. We'll have to prove it in court, and then find the real culprit."

"Lu and I can work on the wanted posters, if you need him to go." Calliope turned a stern look his way. "But if you do, Joe Trenamen, be careful."

He nodded. "When aren't I?"

If she were in St. Louis, Papa had a handful of trusted men who investigated matters, tracking down people, and the like. Here, she had Calliope, Joe, and Lu. Seth was willing, but with Lena's baby due any moment, she couldn't ask him to leave her. And without knowledge of Cambria Springs' residents, she had no one else trustworthy enough to count on. Joe and Calliope had expressed questions about Sheriff Downing, so she hesitated to ask him.

"How's Hattie?" Granted, Andie had been staying at the boardinghouse, but her days had been spent working on the case, so she'd yet to see the woman.

"Stronger every day." Calliope nodded. "She'll speak with you whenever you and Mr. Littrick are ready."

At the very least, her testimony should rule out kidnapping and attempted murder. If she could make a jury doubt he did one thing, they might believe he didn't do any of them.

She scanned her scribbled notes.

"Rion said someone gave him their cast-off boots, and the mark in the heel was there when he acquired them."

"Yep." Joe glanced sideways at her.

"Who gave him the boots?"

Lu, Callie, and Joe all paused.

"I asked, but I'm not sure he ever said. . ."

Her list of questions was growing longer and longer—and time was dwindling.

⌒

Daniel knocked then waited with Sheriff Downing on the boardinghouse porch, praying Hattie Ingram wouldn't be too anxious at being questioned about her ordeal.

"Is this your first opportunity to speak with Miss Hattie since she was found, Sheriff?"

"Yep. She was eaten up with fever and infection when we brought her down. Only conscious for a few minutes at a time. Since we got her back here, Bess has kept her under lock and key."

The door opened, and Bess Ingram smiled. "Gentlemen. Welcome." She waved them to the parlor. Daniel hung his hat on the hat rack before proceeding.

Miss Hattie sat in a tall wingback chair, a blanket pulled to her waist, her long, dark hair loose about her shoulders. Despite the new growth, the shorn patch above her right ear was easily noticeable. The poor woman looked pale, though she smiled. "Howdy, Mr. Littrick."

He returned her grin. "Miss Ingram. Glad you're up and about. I was real sorry to hear what happened."

"Thank you."

"Miss Hattie." Sheriff Downing handed his hat to their host before stepping through the door. "You look a sight better than when I last saw ya."

"I feel better."

Andromeda McGovern stepped off the staircase into the parlor and immediately greeted Hattie with a hand squeeze and a smile.

"Are you boarding here, Miss McGovern?" He'd thought that Mrs. Ingram's rooms were all rented.

She turned, looking far more unwelcoming than he'd hoped. "Kezia Jarrett and I are sharing a room."

Lord, is she always gonna be so aloof and distrusting?

"Please, find a seat," Mrs. Ingram called from the doorway.

They did, and Mrs. Ingram offered them tea or coffee, and when they all declined, she stepped out to give them time alone.

Looking uncomfortable in his dainty chair, the big sheriff leaned forward, settling his elbows on his knees. "Thank you again for meetin' with us, Miss Hattie. Do you remember what happened?"

"Some."

"Please tell us. Any details are helpful."

"I, um. . ." She closed her eyes. "I went to stay with Annie Tunstall for a night or two, and when I went out to feed the barn animals after dark, a man grabbed me." Her eyes fluttered open, distant and unfocused. "I tried to scream, but he covered my mouth with a cloth." Her voice pitched into a fearful tone. "Everything went black very quickly."

Daniel spoke gently. "Take your time, Miss Hattie."

Her chin quivered as if she might weep.

Miss McGovern moved to the matching wingback chair beside her, taking her hand. "You're not alone, and there's no rush. All right?"

The two women focused on each other, and Hattie took a moment to calm herself.

"Miss Hattie?" Downing met her gaze. "Would ya be more at ease if your ma sat with you?"

She nodded, and the lawman rose and returned with Mrs. Ingram, who sat beside Hattie. Miss McGovern returned to the settee, and Downing leaned his shoulder against the doorjamb.

"I don't recall much. I woke up a time or two." She bit her lower lip, fighting for calm.

Daniel prayed, not desiring to see the woman tormented by recounting her ordeal.

"I was tied over a saddle. As soon as the man realized I was awake, he'd put that cloth back over my face, and everything would go black again." She took several deep breaths. "The next thing I recall, I was in a broken-down cabin."

Her voice grew hoarse. "When I came around, I was in a room alone. Beyond the door, people argued. It was dark—and there was lightning and thunder." Tears slipped down her cheeks, and Mrs. Ingram gripped her hand. "Then someone came in." She gulped a breath. "I could see even in the dark he had a knife. I screamed and tried to get away, but—" She sobbed, Mrs. Ingram doing her best to comfort her grown child.

"Why don't we give you a few minutes?" Daniel rose,

motioning the sheriff toward the door. They both stepped onto the porch again. To his surprise, Miss McGovern joined them, keeping the door cracked.

"She's told enough." Downing folded his arms.

"She doesn't need to go into the details of the attack, but I have some clarifying questions about what she's already said." And they knew from Seth and Lena Kealey's statements, as well as Lucinda Peters, that Ollie Sapey supposedly heard her screams and rescued her during that heavy mountain thunderstorm. He hoped to ask about her—among other things.

Miss McGovern peeked back inside. "Thank you for being gentle with her."

"Littrick and me ain't so refined as you, but we ain't monsters. No one wants to see her relive that horror."

Embarrassment flashed in her eyes, and Daniel hurried on, trying to soften the lawman's words. "Especially after all she's endured in her life."

For once, she looked humbled. "I'm thankful. Miss Hattie and I just met, but both Kezia Jarrett and Mr. Nesbitt speak highly of her."

"Everyone in Cambria Springs loves Bess and Hattie Ingram." Downing pulled a toothpick from a pocket and clamped it between his teeth. "If they don't, they ain't good people."

She peeked inside again then opened the door. "They're ready."

As they headed toward their respective places, Hattie hung her head. "I'm so sorry."

"There's no need for that, miss." Daniel shook his head. "You're brave to speak to us."

"I don't remember much more." She leaned her head against the chair.

"May I clarify a few points?"

Hattie nodded.

"Did you see who grabbed you?"

"No, Mr. Littrick. He came from behind."

Miss McGovern cocked her head to one side. "When he covered your mouth with the cloth, did you see his hands, arms, feet? Anything?"

At first, she shook her head. "No." Her eyes went suddenly wide. "But I felt them. . .as I tried to claw his hand away from my face. They were almost dainty for a man. I was able to get my hand around his wrist better than some."

"Was his wrist like mine?" Daniel unbuttoned his shirtsleeve and pushed the cuff up. He wasn't a small man, and his own wrists weren't as meaty as many his size. He allowed her to test his arm against what she remembered.

"Smaller. His were bony in comparison."

"That's helpful, miss. Thank you."

Hattie shook her head. "I recall him dousing that cloth with a liquid before he put it to my face. He had long fingers."

She closed her eyes.

"Are you holdin' up all right, Miss Hattie?"

Blinking, she nodded. "At first, he didn't have me blindfolded, and while I was over the saddle, I saw his back, while he led the horse I was on."

Miss McGovern perched on the settee's edge. "Do you recall either the horses or what he looked like?"

"His horse was a real pretty black—with three white stockings—but there was something wrong with them."

"Wrong?"

She closed her eyes again. "I can't explain it. The fur was. . .cracked or. . ." She shook her head. "The legs were white, but with black showing through underneath. I don't know. I was upside down. My head was pounding. Maybe I was seeing things. Or not seeing clearly anyway."

"And did you see him at all?" Miss McGovern asked.

"He was a pretty big man. Tall. Wide shoulders."

"Is this the fellow you saw?"

Miss McGovern unfolded a paper and showed it to Miss Hattie, who immediately shook her head. "No, it wasn't Mr. Rion."

Daniel came to stand behind Miss Hattie's chair to look at the immaculately drawn image of Rion Braddock, both from the front and the back.

"You're certain?"

Miss Hattie nodded. "The day of the medicine show, Mr. Rion escorted me to the wagon. I held his arm. His arms—particularly his wrists—are too meaty to belong to the man who grabbed me. And from what I saw, the man was probably as tall as Mr. Rion, his shoulders as wide, but he was too lean. Mr. Rion's built more like a bear than the man who abducted me."

Sheriff Downing sat again. "You're sure it wasn't Rion Braddock?"

"Absolutely. I sat behind him at the medicine show, Sheriff. Their hair color, beard, and height might be close, but Mr. Rion was not the man on the horse that day, nor was it his wrist I grasped in Annie Tunstall's barn."

"Now hold on there. You admit the fella what took you drugged you. How can you be sure of what you saw?"

Her face paled, and Mrs. Ingram's features hardened.

The lawman turned Daniel's way. "You best keep prosecutin' Braddock for her kidnappin' and attempted murder."

Daniel's mind flew. If Braddock wasn't guilty of kidnapping Hattie Ingram but someone was trying to make it look as if he was. . .was he guilty of the other murders?

He glared back. "Beggin' your pardon, sir, but I'm prosecuting this case. That's my decision."

CHAPTER 7

Wednesday, July 16, 1873

THE ROCKING J SALOON...

Andie stared up at the sign from across the street. Her stomach soured as she stared at the largest saloon in Cambria Springs. Since the mountain town had no official courthouse, Rion's case was to be held there.

She'd never set foot in a saloon. Worse, she couldn't have Callie, Joe, or Lu by her side because, as witnesses in the case, they weren't allowed in the courtroom until they were called. The best she had was Mrs. Ingram's other boarders.

As if it wasn't frightening enough to face her first solo court case, but to be sitting opposite Daniel Littrick while Rion's life hung in the bal—?

Hung? "Terrible word choice," she chided herself under her breath.

"I'm sorry—what?" one of the women asked.

"Not important."

She led the way into the Rocking J. Even at a little before nine in the morning, spectators filled the room. Cigar smoke tainted the air, and heavy stares settled on them. Several onlookers groaned at their appearance.

Her heart pounded. Walking into a real courtroom knowing she would take an important role in the trial would have been daunting enough, but this? She couldn't be more out of place.

Lord, how do I get through this? I never expected to try a case, much less try one in a saloon. Especially defending my own brother's life. . .

The other women settled at the nearest empty table as she walked to the defense table. She put her carpetbag, full of her law books, notes, and papers, in one of the chairs.

"Pardon, miss," a tall man with an uncanny likeness to Abraham Lincoln slurred as she unpacked her bag. "That table's for the defendant."

"Understood."

"Don't reckon you do. That's where the accused'll sit. And don't think about takin' that place, neither." He indicated the matching table feet away. "It's for the prosecution."

She looked him in the eye with more boldness than she felt. "Let me see if I understand. The big bounty hunter, Orion Braddock, is going to sit here."

"Now you're gettin' it." His leering grin unsettled her.

"Along with his counsel, I presume?"

"Yeah." He tossed back a shot of whiskey and clamped a pipe between his teeth.

Andie cleared her throat. "Then I'm in the correct place, thank you." She began to arrange her things.

Confusion ruled his features. "Are ya settin' up for your man, there, ma'am?"

Again, she paused to look at the odd fellow. "My man?"

"Your husband."

"I have no husband."

"Then, a father or a brother. . ."

"If you must know, I'm Rion Braddock's attorney."

The gent adjusted his glasses and squinted, laughter rippling across the hushed room.

"A woman?" He shoved his shot glass across the bar toward the bartender.

The laughter grew louder.

Oh, Lord. . . Now that she'd said the words aloud, her head spun.

"Congratulations, sir, for grasping the simple truth that I am, in fact, a woman."

"Yeah, well. . .we'll see about that." The bartender refilled his shot glass.

Her heart pounded. "Unless the judge is God Himself, I doubt he'll be able to change my womanhood. Now, good day, sir. I have a case to prepare for."

The man returned a simpering smile, tossed back the whiskey, and leaving the glass on the bar, tottered toward the back of the establishment to the guffaws of the onlookers.

"Good riddance." How could that man already be inebriated at this hour of the morning?

To calm her frayed nerves, Andie opened the cover of Blackstone to read Papa's telegram, which she'd received after sending word home about defending Rion.

Rion has chosen well *STOP*
You can do this *STOP* You are ready *STOP*
Trust what you have learned *STOP*
More importantly, trust God *STOP*
We are proud of you and love you *STOP*

Papa's voice rang in her thoughts as if he were with her. Always the optimist, he found the bright side in every circumstance. If only she had half his positivity. Or his wily ways in the courtroom.

In a flurry, people entered—among them a whole company of men and women. One man among them was unnaturally tall and muscular, another abnormally short. Still another, a woman, untied her bonnet and—Andie's eyes rounded. A *bearded lady?*

Mr. Littrick, entering with a heavily loaded leather case, beelined for the prosecution's table, though he also paused to gape. The woman curtsied.

"Howdy, handsome." She grinned, words dripping with a thick southern drawl. "I'm Annalee Ralston, with Dr. Chellingworth's Medicine Show."

"We're all from Chellingworth's," the tall, muscle-bound man boomed, and the collection of odd folks clapped and cheered.

Mr. Littrick gave a respectful nod. "Well, then. . .welcome to you all."

Sheriff Downing and a couple of deputies herded Rion in. Shackled hand and foot, her brother looked like a caged animal, ready to fight out of the corner he was in—though once he saw her, he seemed to calm some.

Downing prodded Rion to the table and shoved him into the second chair. "You're gonna sit there, Braddock, until Judge Oakwell or I tell you otherwise. One wrong move, and I'll open fire. Understand?"

"We're clear."

The sheriff stationed the others who'd entered with him, one guarding the hallway leading toward the back, one at the main door, and himself seated a few feet from them.

Rion turned her way. "Morning."

"Morning."

The caged animal look returned as he surveyed the room. "You ready?"

Tears stung her lids, but she swallowed them back, opened

the front cover of Blackstone's thick tome, and reread two lines of Papa's message. *Trust what you have learned. More importantly, trust God.*

Her stomach roiled and pitched, threatening to expel her light breakfast. With the addition of the medicine show people, the atmosphere had taken on the feel of a literal circus, but she drew a big breath, clapped the cover closed, and took her brother's shackled hands as unexpected words rang in her mind.

Yea, though I walk through the valley of the shadow of death, I will fear no evil: for thou art with me; thy rod and thy staff they comfort me.

"God's going to walk us both through this, Rion."

Did she believe her own words?

Lord, let it be true today, please!

⌒

Daniel debated greeting Miss McGovern. So far, she'd not looked once in his direction. Without pondering too long on the matter, he crossed the short distance.

"Morning, Miss McGovern."

"Mr. Littrick." She dipped her chin slightly. "Can I do something for you?"

"No, miss. I simply wanted to wish you a pleasant morning." He turned to the bounty hunter. "Mr. Braddock."

Rion glowered.

"How are you, sir?"

"How would you be if the man gunnin' to see you strung up asked such a question?"

"I assure you, sir, I have no designs on the outcome of the trial. I'm after the truth—even if that means I lose this case."

Rion shook his head. "That sounds noble, but I reckon I don't believe it."

"Fair enough. I'll simply have to prove myself."

"Hope you do." Braddock faced front and settled his shackled hands on the table.

Daniel nodded. "I wish you both my best."

"Thank you." Again, Miss McGovern dipped her chin, morning sunlight playing on the curves of her face and highlighting her brown eyes.

She was a pretty woman—when she wasn't belching flames.

He returned to his table, unburdened his leather satchel, and as he was arranging the books, papers, and notes, the court crier stepped from the back and cleared his throat.

"Ever'body rise for Judge Zebulun Oakwell."

Chairs scraped across the floorboards, and the buzz of conversation dulled as everyone stood. Daniel glanced around. The place was packed. Standing room only. Facing forward again, he turned as Judge Oakwell, with his unkempt beard and ever-present pipe, stepped out of the back hallway, glassy-eyed as he took his place behind the table nearest the bar.

Miss McGovern gasped, and when he looked her way, she appeared especially pale.

"Hear ye! Hear ye!" the court crier went on. "Court's in session. All you mulligrubs in the back of the courtroom keep your traps shut and give these fellers up front a chance to talk."

Judge Oakwell looked across the room. "Court's in session." He banged the gavel. "All y'all sit."

Again, chairs scraped and boot heels clicked on the plank floor.

"Except for you." Oakwell jabbed a finger in Miss McGovern's direction.

For a confused instant, Rion Braddock and Miss McGovern looked between themselves, and she moved to sit while he remained on his feet.

"No. Defendant—sit." He stabbed a finger at Braddock. "Defendant's counsel—remain standing." Again, he motioned her upward.

Wide-eyed, Miss McGovern straightened, obviously trembling.

Oakwell glared at her.

"You're dismissed, missy."

She straightened her spine—a move he was realizing she made as she geared up for battle. "On what grounds?"

"In this courtroom, I'm as good as God." His words slurred. "And I ain't puttin' up with shenanigans, like a woman thinkin' she can argue matters of the law."

"You can't dismiss me. Mr. Braddock hired me as his counsel."

"My courtroom, my rules. Now, skedaddle." He waved as if shooing a fly.

Was this really happening? Daniel shot Sheriff Downing a look, but he appeared about as flummoxed as he felt.

"Point of clarification, Judge?" He half stood as he called out.

"What?" Oakwell swung toward him.

"Are you dismissing Miss McGovern because she doesn't understand the law?"

"Women ain't got the means to understand or argue the finer points."

The woman turned an even pastier shade as the onlookers laughed.

"Begging your pardon, Judge, but it's not fair to deny Mr. Braddock his counsel because you fear a woman hasn't the wherewithal to argue his case. If the defendant trusts her, that ought to be enough."

"No woman's gonna make a mockery of my courtroom."

Daniel shoved a hand in his pants pocket. "I object. Mr. Braddock is entitled to the attorney of his choice."

From behind him, one of the medicine show workers shouted, "Let the little gal ride, Judge. It'll be entertainin', at least! And after bein' the entertainment for so long, we wanna be entertained!"

"Hear, hear!" another man bellowed from across the room. "And we'll have us a necktie party once she loses. It'll make for a great distraction."

Drunken chuckles followed, and Daniel shot up a prayer—both for Oakwell to see reason and for Miss McGovern and Mr. Braddock not to listen to the doomsday predictions. He glared at the sheriff.

Oakwell threw up his hands and pitched back in his chair, settling his boots on the table, legs crossed at the ankle. "Fine. In the interest of amusement, Miss McCoven can stay."

His hackles rose. "It's Miss Andromeda *McGovern*, Your Honor."

The judge shrugged. "I was close. . ."

Lord in heaven, please. Let him show some respect.

The man had no business being a judge.

"Your Honor?" she called.

"What?" His glassy eyes held disdain.

"May I have a five-minute recess?"

"We're just gettin' started, missy."

"We could use us a recess too, Judge!" someone shouted from the back. "Seems as good a time as any for fresh libations."

"You're saved, Miss McCoven." Oakwell reached for his gavel. "Five-minute recess, startin' now." He cracked the gavel once, and Miss McGovern darted out the front door.

CHAPTER 8

Queasy, Andie barreled outside and raced to an alley a couple of buildings away. There, she darted alongside the structure and, finding a relatively empty spot between piles of refuse and empty crates, tried to settle her stomach. To no avail. After gulping several breaths, her middle cramped, and she expelled her breakfast into an empty crate beside her. She spit, wiped her mouth, and, embarrassed, leaned against the wall.

Lord Jesus. . .I can't do this!

The disrespect in that room! From both the judge *and* the patrons. She'd seen fiery encounters in Papa's trials but nothing so demeaning as the judge attempting to dismiss an attorney on a baseless matter. Of course, she was the only female attorney she knew. If there were others, would they have been dismissed because of their gender? And. . .she should have kept a civil tongue when the drunken man antagonized her before the proceedings. But how was she to know he was the judge? Judges shouldn't be drunk at nine in the morning—or in their own court proceedings!

She fought back tears.

"Miss McGovern?"

Andie jerked to find Mr. Littrick at the mouth of the alley.

"Please leave me alone." The last thing she needed was that infernal man rubbing her nose in the dirt.

He picked his way through the stacks of crates, the refuse, and other debris to stand beside her.

"Are you all right?"

Avoiding his eyes, she straightened. "I asked you to go."

"I was concerned."

"About me?"

"Yes—for what just happened with the judge and because this isn't the part of Cambria Springs where a beautiful, refined lady like yourself ought to be found. Particularly alone in an alley."

She met his brilliant blue eyes, so full of compassion she couldn't hold her tears back.

"I can't do this." Unable to stanch the words, her cheeks flooded with heat.

He produced a handkerchief and offered it to her. "By *this*, you mean the trial?"

Nodding, she dabbed an eye. "I probably shouldn't confess that to you."

"Because I'll use it to gain some advantage?"

Again, she nodded, dabbing the other eye.

"Would you believe that I have no such intentions?"

"I wouldn't blame you if you did. I've been awful to you from the moment we met."

"Perhaps a little sharp-tongued, *maybe* borderin' on fire-breathing at moments. . ." His teasing grin softened the jabs until she giggled through a sob.

"Like I said—awful."

"Well, the first moment we met went cockeyed because of me. I deserved some of those sharp-tongued comments."

He hadn't. Not like she'd doled out, though he was kind to say so.

"As far as this case, you're not givin' yourself enough credit, miss. Any woman who reads Blackstone to pass the time while traveling across country must have a very sharp mind."

Her tears flowed more freely, and she dabbed at them furiously. The last thing she needed was to walk back in that saloon looking like she'd been weeping.

"Why are you being so kind? You defended me to the judge, and now this."

He tugged at his collar. "You want the honest truth, miss?"

She shot him a coy grin. "No, Mr. Littrick. I'd prefer you lie to me—and make it colorful and unexpected."

He chuckled as he opened the cover on his pocket watch. "That might take more time than we've got." He pocketed the watch again. "Truth is, I never wanted to be a lawyer. I don't much enjoy it. But facin' off against you is. . .a welcome challenge."

"An easy victory, you mean."

"I hope not. I'm rather lookin' forward to you givin' me a run for my money."

"What if you're giving me too much credit?"

"Call it a gut feelin', but. . ." His blue eyes sparkled. "I don't reckon I am."

She fought down her emotion. "I hope I won't disappoint you."

"Keep your sharp wit while you're challenging me on the law, and you won't."

Andie wobbled a smile. "All right."

She dabbed her eyes once more with the handkerchief, folded it, and reached to return it to him.

"Do you need to keep it, miss?"

"No." She lifted her chin. "I'm not planning to cry another tear."

"Good. We've got about one minute to get back in the courtroom or that blustering windbag of a judge will make us pay. Ready, Miss McGovern?"

She pressed the folded handkerchief into his hand. "Yes."

"All right, then." He deposited it in his pocket and, taking her hand, walked her from the alley.

In between numerous recesses for fresh libations, always called for by the onlookers, they managed to select their six jurors. After the midday break, they presented opening statements. Judge Oakwell then heard and ruled on their motions—including Miss McGovern's well-thought-out request for a change of venue and her request to throw out the kidnapping and attempted murder charges based on Hattie Ingram's testimony of several days ago. He overruled every one. Miss McGovern asked pertinent questions and kept her composure firmly in check, despite Oakwell's attempts to bait her. Beside her, Braddock seethed as the judge needled the little gal, like it was personal. More personal than just her being his attorney. Was there something between Braddock and Miss McGovern?

What if there was? She'd never said she didn't have a beau.

There's a lot she's never said. Yet he'd rather enjoyed their alley conversation. If not for the short five-minute recess and the blasted judge threatening repercussions for tardiness, he'd have stood there quite a while longer.

"Miss McCoven."

Daniel bristled at the man's continued use of the wrong name. "Yes, sir?"

"You keep lookin' in those books on your table."

"Yes, sir."

"What are those? Bring 'em up here."

She collected the volumes and laid them out on his desk.

"These are English law. Not American. Says so plain on the covers." He looked at one after the other then swept them off the table.

"Hey!" Braddock moved to rise, his expression stormy, but Miss McGovern gave him a firm shake of her head.

"Sit!" she hissed, and the sheriff clapped a hand on his shoulder to keep him in his seat.

Facing Oakwell again, she scrambled to collect the books, tucking a piece of paper that came out of one into the pocket of her dress. "It's Blackstone, Judge. And Sir Edward Coke."

"Yeah, and both are old—*and English*. This is America, missy."

"I'm well aware, sir."

"Then why're you using books on English law? The English, as you ought to recall, oppressed our fathers and the law which they repudiated in the Declaration of Independence. You'll not impose such in my court!"

The crowd hooted, and someone ribbed one of the medicine show members—a man wearing spectacles with darkened lenses.

As Oakwell spoke, Miss McGovern slunk back toward her table, heavy books in hand, looking like a whipped pup.

"Begging your pardon, Your Honor, but these are all I have. What do you expect me to use?"

"Ain't my problem, missy—but I don't want to see those back here again." He stabbed a finger toward the books.

Daniel gripped the edge of his chair, incensed on her behalf.

The onlookers continued to chuckle as Oakwell sat in his smug self-righteousness. Miss McGovern looked lost.

"Understood, Your Honor."

"And with that, I'm callin' it a night. Court is—"

"I object!" Daniel belted the words, gripping the chair even harder.

"Oh, what now?" Oakwell lolled a look his way.

He stood. "I object."

"To adjourning for the day?"

"Yes, sir. At least until you address the fact that you've just undermined Miss McGovern's ability to argue this case—and hampered mine. Will you delay the start of the case to allow us time to rethink our strategies?"

"First she wants a change of venue, and now you want a delay. Are y'all ready to try this case or not?"

"Not after the monkey wrench you just threw in the works. I'll need a few days, and Miss McGovern probably needs more than that."

"Are you stupid? I'm handin' you the case."

Howls erupted again, and Miss McGovern stood cloaked in shame and embarrassment. Braddock seethed.

"Would you repeat that, please, Your Honor?"

Oakwell clammed up, seeming to recognize his mistake.

"Judge Oakwell, it's quite clear Mr. Braddock can't get a fair trial under you. I'm callin' for you to step down."

Judge Oakwell fouled the air with a string of curse words. "Denied! You're the one what called me to this trifling town. I ain't leavin' without hearin' this case."

Daniel shot Sheriff Downing an incredulous look, though the lawman pretended not to see him. Something wasn't right. Oakwell was obviously compromised. . .and the sheriff turned a blind eye.

"Then please. . .rethink your decision about books on English law—or I won't proceed as prosecutor."

Oakwell's eye twitched, and his nostrils flared. "You're a durn fool, Littrick. What do you need to stay on?"

Daniel leaned both hands on the desk and glared. "A fair and impartial trial, and enough time for the prosecution and defense to mount an appropriate case."

The judge spat on the floor and glared, tossed back the full glass of whiskey in front of him, and nodded. "Fine, Counselor. You got until Monday at nine, sharp—but neither of y'all are bringin' those English rules into my American court. We're dismissed." He slammed the gavel once, poured and drank another glass of whiskey, and seemed to slosh down the hall.

Daniel headed straight for Downing. "We need to talk!"

"Not now." The lawman shoved him aside. "I got a prisoner to escort." Downing beckoned the deputies over, then ordered Braddock to his feet and shoved him toward the door.

CHAPTER 9

Once Rion was out of the immediate area and headed toward the door, Andie bolted up and went to Mrs. Ingram's boarders. "Can you all help me? I need Kezia, Mr. Nesbitt, and Miss Peters to meet me at the jail as soon as possible."

The ladies nodded. "We'll find them and send them along."

She packed her books and papers then hurried on to Dutch's Café, heading to his private quarters where Seth and Lena Kealey were staying. She knocked, and a minute later, Seth answered.

"Howdy, Miss McGovern. Court's done for the day?" Behind him, Lena looked on, one hand on her belly, one on her back.

"Thank God, yes. It was awful. I need Rion's family at the jail so we can talk."

"Lena and me are welcome at this meetin'?" Seth asked.

"You're family, aren't you?"

"Near as."

Andie nodded. "Both of you are welcome—although, Lena, I realize you may want to rest, so please don't feel obligated."

"Thank you. I think I'll stay back."

As she waited for Seth to say goodbye to his wife and tell Dutch he was leaving Lena alone for a bit, Andie pulled her father's telegram from her pocket, where she'd stashed it after Judge Oakwell dumped her books on the floor. In that moment, after the happenings throughout the day, the words held little comfort. In fact, just like that morning, her midsection bucked and pitched. The day had been long, hard, embarrassing—and then the judge showed his obvious bias.

Thank God Mr. Littrick hadn't been any more welcoming of the judge's partiality than she. He'd fought for Rion getting a fair trial. For all the good it did. It earned them an extra few days. . .which meant nothing without her law books.

Once Seth was ready, he took her bag and they walked to the jail, arriving at the same time Callie, Joe, and Lu arrived.

"Where's Lena?" Callie asked.

"Restin', at Dutch's."

"No need to explain." Joe grinned.

Without further delay, Andie barged into the sheriff's office, and Downing looked up from his conversation with one of the deputies.

"I need to meet with my client. Alone."

"You ain't alone, Miss McGovern." He smirked at the group behind her.

"I mean without you and your deputies."

"We ain't goin' far." He jutted his chin in Rion's direction. "I don't trust that one."

"Fine—but leave so we can speak in private."

Downing and the other man walked out, and someone shut the door after them.

Closing her eyes, she settled a hand on her forehead. "We have an issue. Several. . . Rion can't get a fair—"

"Andromeda." Rion's deep voice snagged her ear. "Before you launch into all this, I know today was hard. Are you all right?"

For a moment, she could only stare and shake her head. "No. I'm sick to my stomach. I can't do this."

Joe grabbed Downing's desk chair and set it behind her, guiding her into it.

"Yes, you can!" Callie crouched next to her. "Rion needs you."

"I've never taken the lead on a case before. I've never argued anything in court. I've only helped prepare my father's cases. And now I can't use any of my law books."

"What?" They all stared.

This judge forbade me from using English law books. He's. . .tainted. He has his finger on the scales of justice, and I can't overcome that."

Lu stepped up. "We overcome it with the truth."

Andie's stomach churned. "But how? My thoughts are spinning so fast, I can't grasp them to put them in order. The courtroom, if you can call it that, lacked decorum. The onlookers from the gallery called for recesses just so they could get more whiskey, or they objected to points I brought up in the case. How was I to keep up, much less stay ahead of Mr. Littrick or that awful judge?"

Rion approached the bars. "You can't expect courtrooms 'round here to be solemn and respectful like back east. But this court, led by this judge, is the worst I've seen. You're right—I ain't gettin' a fair trial."

"I don't know what to do."

Joe folded his arms. "God'll provide a way."

"How? I have no other law books. Worse, if I can't find a way through this, they'll convict and hang Rion. In fact, as biased as Judge Oakwell is, I don't see any way around that outcome, and I can't live with myself if I tear my own family apart days after we reunited."

"That's not going to happen." Callie rubbed her shoulder as she continued to squat at her side. "God wouldn't allow us to find each other only to tear us apart, especially if it left the others feeling guilty."

"Andromeda, if I'm convicted, it'll be because of a corrupt judge." Rion gripped the cell bars so hard, his knuckles whitened. "Not because of anything you and Callie failed to do."

Arms folded, Seth leaned against Downing's desk. "We can't let it come to that."

"What d'ya mean?" Rion asked.

"You disappeared once. You can do it again."

"Downing's watchin' me a lot closer than the first time. And I don't want to be on the run the rest of my life."

Lord, what can we do?

⌒

DOWNING NEVER CONTACTED ABOUT COURT *STOP*
JUDGE VOST IN DENVER FOR NEXT TWO WEEKS *STOP*
DOCKET CLEAR *STOP* COMING YOUR WAY *STOP*

Daniel stared at the US Marshal's telegram that Heck had just handed him. Why had the sheriff *lied* about contacting the marshal for a court date? And why choose the worst judge to try Braddock's case? Things weren't adding up.

He scribbled out a response and handed it to Heck. "Send this back, please."

Once Heck had sent the response, Daniel paid him for the two telegrams he'd sent, thanked his friend, and walked out to mount Briar again. He needed to make Miss McGovern aware, though he wasn't sure where to look. Braddock might know—if Sheriff Downing or his deputies were in the office to let him speak with the man. Wouldn't hurt to check.

He rode across the town and stopped outside the sheriff's office. Daniel dismounted, tied Briar, and stepped onto the porch. At the door, familiar voices sounded from inside, and he paused, immediately recognizing Miss McGovern's voice.

"Worse, if I can't find a way through this, they'll convict and hang Rion. In fact, as biased as Judge Oakwell is, I don't see any way around that outcome, and I can't live with myself if I tear my own family apart days after we reunited."

Her own family? Did she mean Braddock?

"That's not going to happen." This time, Miss Jarrett spoke. "God wouldn't allow us to find each other only to tear us apart, especially if it left the others feeling guilty."

Wait. . . Kezia Jarrett, Rion Braddock, and Andromeda McGovern were related? And they'd just reunited? There was something much bigger goin' on here than he understood.

Daniel knocked and pushed the door open.

From the center cell, Braddock peered out. Miss McGovern faced him from a chair near the center of the room, Miss Jarrett crouched beside her. Nesbitt and Seth Kealey leaned against the sheriff's desk, and Lucinda Peters stood near the first cell, where the bars were warped out of alignment.

"What're you doin' here?" Braddock growled.

"Is the sheriff around?"

Pale, Andromeda McGovern stood. "I asked him to leave so we could have a private meeting. Last I saw, he walked around the side of the building."

"Actually, I was hopin' Downing wasn't here. I need to talk to you. Could we have a private word?"

She eyed him skeptically. "About?"

"I have news about the trial, and I was thinkin' it'd be better to tell you alone, although. . ."

Miss McGovern planted a hand on her hip. "What?"

"Are y'all related? I wasn't tryin' to eavesdrop, but as I came to the door, I did overhear you and Miss Jarrett say somethin' about y'all bein' family?"

Miss McGovern offered a sheepish look. "Guilty. Orion, Andromeda, and Calliope Braddock." She and Miss Jarrett linked arms. "Orphaned as children, put on an orphan train, and adopted to three different families in very different locales."

Miss Jarrett—or Calliope?—looked toward Nesbitt, who nodded, and she picked up the tale. "I was adopted by the Wilsons in Chicago and grew up to become a Pinkerton detective. Kezia Jarrett is an undercover name. With Mr. Pinkerton's blessing, I used my position to find Andie and Rion—reconnected with her by letter and came west to look for him. I finally found Rion as well, but Stephen—"

"My real name's Joe Trenamen."

"Yes, and he's also a Pinkerton. He and I were working the case of seven murdered women, and everything pointed straight to Rion."

"Too neatly, if you know what I mean," Trenamen offered.

"So. . .you three are brother and sisters." He pointed to the three Braddocks, then to Trenamen and Calliope. "You two are partners."

Trenamen nodded. "And. . .more. A recent development. . ."

"How're you related?" He pointed to Seth Kealey.

"Adopted brother. Rion, Dutch, and I are three out of five boys taken in by the same man."

"Garvin." He knew that name from his interviews and notes on the case.

"Right."

"And you, Miss Peters? How do you fit?"

Her cheeks flamed, and she looked shyly at Braddock.

Braddock grinned. "Reckon we belong with each other. And that's an even more recent event than those two." He waved toward Calliope and Joe.

Daniel nodded as he looked at the faces around the room. "Thanks for explaining the connections. Now things make sense." He stepped in and closed the door. "Like I said, I figured to tell you the news alone, but if you'd prefer your family here—"

"Right here's fine."

Miss Peters pulled a fabric-covered book from her skirt's waistband and poised to write.

"I didn't like what happened in the court today. Particularly Oakwell admitting he was handing me the case. So I sent a telegram to the US Marshal to ask when the territorial judge would be available." He glanced around him. "Sheriff Downing never requested to put this case on the district's docket. Judge Vost is in Denver now, and his schedule is free for the next two weeks. He, the marshal, and the court staff are coming this way. I promise, Vost will be impartial and by the book."

For a moment, they all stared.

Kealey cocked his head. "Correct me if I'm wrong. I'm no attorney, but since the one judge has already started the case, ain't we stuck?"

"Judge Vost is the territorial judge—appointed by the US president. Oakwell is a justice of the peace—appointed over a much lower court by local authorities. Vost is a rare breed in these parts. He won't like Downing havin' gone around him to ask Oakwell to preside, especially without askin' him for a court date. So I expect he'll pull rank on that point alone. But. . ." He shot them a sheepish grin of his own. "Vost also happens to be the brother-in-law of one of my favorite law school professors. I count him as a friend."

"Does Downing know that?" Nesbitt asked.

"Not to my knowledge. I don't make a lot of hullabaloo about it, but I do head to Denver from time to time to cultivate the friendship. You'll find him much more agreeable and easier to work with. And he won't be drunk in his own courtroom."

Miss McGovern grasped the back of the chair. "Wait just a minute. Oakwell seems to be in Downing's pocket. Now you're saying you're good friends with this territorial judge, Vost. How can I be sure that Rion's chances are any better with him, considering the connection you just admitted?"

"I swear to you before God, there'll be no bias shown from Judge Vost. We might be good friends, but one reason I like him is because he's fair and upright."

Braddock stared. "Why're you doin' this?"

"Like I said, I didn't like what happened today. Your rights were violated. You won't get a fair trial. And it grated somethin' fierce, seein' how that judge tried to roll over you." He caught Miss McGovern's eye. "I know how hard I worked to get through law school, and I reckon you worked as hard—or harder. You deserve a chance."

Relief lit Miss McGovern's pretty features. "Thank you."

Lu moved closer. "Will this Judge Vost accept a woman attorney?"

"He won't treat her near so harshly as Oakwell did." He turned in Miss McGovern's direction. "He'll expect you to have a solid case—and he'll want more modern arguments than what you'd find in Blackstone or Coke."

She sat heavily in the chair. "And if I was in St. Louis, I'd have access to my father's hefty library, but where am I to get that here?"

He nodded. "If you're willing to consider it, I might have a solution."

"What solution, Littrick?" Braddock's eyes narrowed.

"Understanding your difficult circumstances, I can grant you access to my law books."

"You would do that?" She looked befuddled. "Why? We're on opposing sides."

Daniel shook his head. "I might be the prosecutor, but I'm on the side of truth."

Trenamen straightened. "So you'd be willing to let Andie use your books, even if that loses you this case?"

"Believe it or not, yes."

And it didn't hurt matters that he'd get to spend time around her as she searched for the information she needed.

CHAPTER 10

Monday, July 21, 1873

"Good mornin', Miss McGovern."

As Daniel Littrick set his leather satchel on the prosecution's table, Andie's stomach fluttered, particularly at his sparkling blue eyes.

"Morning. I'll ask you again, please call me either—"

"Andromeda or Andie." His smile almost melted her. Her given name on his tongue sent a thrill through her. "But in this setting, I'd prefer to keep things a little more formal." He shot a discreet glance at some of the drunken men watching them. "If you follow my meanin'."

"I do. And I'll abide by your desire. Here. . ." Outwardly, anyway. Her stomach had been doing secret somersaults over the past several days as she'd spent several hours perusing his law books and debating him on points of the law. At moments, her sharp tongue had come out, and she'd breathed a little fire his way—but he'd heaped it back in her direction with equal vigor. And she'd enjoyed it.

As much as she'd relished debating Papa over some of the very same points, she'd never found so much delight as she had debating Daniel.

"Good luck today." He smiled, and she narrowed a glance at him.

"To you, as well. You're going to need it."

"Will I, now?" He shot her a spicy look. "We'll see."

When she returned to her own table, Rion was already seated. "What in the name of Juniper was that?" Her brother frowned.

She grinned. "A little verbal swordplay, I suppose."

He rolled his eyes. "Please tell me you're not growin' a romantic interest in that fella."

She wouldn't admit it—yet—but yes, the interest was strong on her end. She hoped it was matched on Daniel's, but until he made his feelings known, it wasn't her place to say.

"Don't you worry. I'm focused on your case."

Many of the same onlookers from their last court day came in, including the collection of odd folks from Dr. Chellingworth's medicine show.

She leaned toward her brother. "Did you hear you're an uncle?"

Rion swung a startled gaze her way. "Lena had her baby?" At her nod, he grinned. "When?"

"She labored through the night and delivered at about five this morning. She and her boy, Joshua Rion, are both well."

He slapped the table with a laugh, shackles rattling. "Oh, that's good."

A voice rose in the crowded room. "All rise for the Honorable Judge Ethan Vost."

The now-familiar sound of chair legs grating across the plank floor raked across Andie's senses. To Andie's relief, rather than the slovenly Judge Oakwell, stinking of whiskey and sweat, the suit-clad Judge Vost took the seat behind the front table. He smacked the gavel once.

"Court's in session. Be seated."

"Where's the other judge, Judge?" one onlooker slurred.

"If you'll be patient, I'll address that."

The man sat, and Judge Vost made sure he had the room's attention.

"As you just heard, my name is Judge Ethan Vost. *Territorial* Judge Ethan Vost. Justice of the Peace Oakwell was mistakenly appointed to sit on this case. It's a territorial matter that falls under the jurisdiction of my court, so I'll be taking the case from here on."

Several in the crowd groaned in displeasure, and the judge again banged his gavel.

"Order! I'll have order in my courtroom."

Once the din quieted, Vost looked around, pausing in the direction of the medicine show people before continuing. "I run my trials differently than Judge Oakwell. While court's in session, I'll not have anyone speak other than the prosecutor, Mr. Littrick, the defense attorney, Miss McGovern, a witness on the stand, or anyone else I might call upon. If you haven't been called on, keep your mouth shut. No asking for recesses to refill your whiskey. No calling out your questions, observations, or rude comments. You all are welcome to watch the proceedings, but do so quietly and respectfully. If you can't, there's the door." He stabbed a finger toward the main entrance. "If you won't abide by my rules, leave now."

He paused, and a couple of drunken men departed, grousing as they went.

"Anyone else?"

Everyone else stayed in their seats, although some looked less than enthused. Andie grinned at Rion, leaning nearer.

"This is already going better than last week."

He nodded, his handcuffs rattling against the table.

Judge Vost looked at Sheriff Downing.

"Sheriff, remove those shackles from the prisoner, please. I don't want to hear chains rattling throughout the day."

Downing stood. "Beggin' your pardon, Judge, but he's already made me look the fool once by escapin' my jail. I ain't takin' a second chance..."

The judge looked toward the hall behind him, then to the front door. "Am I correct in assuming the armed men at the back and front of this room are yours?"

"Yes, sir."

"And you're armed, sir?"

Downing patted his holstered pistol. "I am."

"So is Marshal Epps." Judge Vost nodded toward the stoic US Marshal standing nearby. Then, the judge himself stood and, unbuttoning his suit coat, produced a small revolver from some sort of leather sling contraption that hung under his left arm. He placed the gun on the table. "That makes five of us." He shifted his focus to Rion. "Mr. Braddock, do I have your word that if Sheriff Downing removes your chains, you'll make no attempt to escape this courtroom, under threat of death?"

"I been shot real recent, sir. It ain't to my likin'. You got my word, so long as we can get this case done—and done right."

"Oh, it'll be done right." He turned on Downing. "Unshackle that man."

The sheriff grudgingly removed Rion's chains and sat again. Rion eased into a more comfortable position and rubbed his wrists.

Hattie Ingram was correct. Her brother did have thick wrists. Thank the Lord she'd had the wherewithal to notice such a detail in the midst of her ordeal.

Judge Vost continued. "Miss McGovern, you have a motion?"

Her mouth suddenly cottony, she took a sip of water then rose. "Yes, Your Honor. Two. One is to drop the kidnapping and attempted murder charges against Mr. Braddock in the case of Hattie Ingram's disappearance. The other is to drop the murder charges for Mary Redmond and Sarah Jacobs, also known as Serafina."

"Let's deal with one at a time. On Miss Ingram's kidnapping and attempted murder, what grounds are you basing your motion on?"

"On the grounds that Hattie Ingram's testimony, heard by Mr. Littrick, Sheriff Downing, and me, that Rion Braddock was not the man who abducted her. I've written it up, Your Honor." She produced the several pages of documentation she'd painstakingly written out—both with her motion and Hattie Ingram's testimony, signed by Hattie, Daniel, Downing, and her.

Marshal Epps collected the papers and delivered them to the judge. She tried not to squirm as he read. When he finally looked up, he held the stack up and caught her eye.

"I appreciate the detail, Miss McGovern. I haven't seen many motions as well written as this since becoming a territorial judge."

She tried not to let her smile overtake her. "Thank you, Your Honor. I try to be thorough."

"It shows." He turned Daniel's way. "Mr. Littrick, you're aware of this motion?"

Daniel stood. "I am, sir."

"What objections do you have?"

"None. I heard the same testimony, and there was no question that Hattie Ingram believed Mr. Braddock was *not* her abductor."

Judge Vost nodded. "How is Miss Ingram doing after her ordeal?"

"Physically she's healing, Your Honor, but the episode took a toll. She's weak, she tires easily, and from what I understand, she's understandably fearful."

"Was it hard for her to talk about the events she endured?"

"Yes, Your Honor. Very."

He skimmed through the papers again then laid them aside. "All right, Miss McGovern. I grant your motion to drop the kidnapping and attempted murder charges."

Her breath whooshed out, and Rion slumped in his chair. She squeezed his fingers for an instant before she stood.

"Thank you, Your Honor."

"You're welcome. Now, your other motion?"

"Yes." She retrieved the second stack of papers and called her thoughts into order. "This motion is to drop the two murder charges against Mr. Braddock. Much of the evidence in those cases is the same as in Miss Hattie's abduction. A pair of boots with a similar mark in the heel. Similarities in physical appearance. Resemblances of horses. Mr. Braddock being near or with the deceased shortly before they went missing. These were all details linking Mr. Braddock to Hattie Ingram's disappearance, and some or all are present in the deaths of Mary Redmond and Sarah Jacobs. If they were untrue in one case, they are very likely untrue in all three cases."

Marshal Epps retrieved the motion and handed it to the judge, who perused it like before.

"Mr. Littrick, your thoughts?"

Daniel stood. "The previous motion was a simple matter, Your Honor. A believable witness gave compelling testimony that her attacker was not Mr. Braddock. Unfortunately, we have no such witnesses in Miss Redmond's and Miss Jacobs' cases, so I'd like to understand more of Miss McGovern's reasoning before I agree to dropping these charges."

The judge skimmed the motion. Pausing, he leaned back, seeming to read more thoroughly. Nodding, he finally looked up.

"I want to give this my full attention. Are there any other motions?"

Daniel held up a single sheet of paper. "One, your honor. Motion to seat a new jury, should the trial proceed."

A gasp rippled through the crowd, and she swung a startled look Daniel's way. Upon returning the look, he gave her a faint smile and a discreet wink.

"Order!" The judge banged his gavel, and the room settled. Judge Vost leaned his elbows on the table, shooting Daniel a quizzical look. "I'd expect such a motion from the defense, but it's rather surprising from the prosecution."

"I understand, Your Honor. But the six jurors may have picked up on Judge Oakwell's biases, sir. In the interest of justice, Mr. Braddock should have an impartial jury."

"What in the name of Juniper. . ." Rion breathed beside her.

Andie stared at Daniel as Epps collected the page and passed it to the judge. Then, craning to reach Rion's ear, she whispered, "He's doing exactly what he said—being fair."

Judge Vost gave the page a brief look.

"I'll rule on this once I've ruled on Miss McGovern's motion. Court's in recess until—" He studied his watch. "Eleven." He gave one strike of his gavel, and the room erupted in sound and motion.

⌒

Once court reconvened, Judge Vost heard arguments for and against Andie's motion to dismiss the two murder charges and, after deliberation, denied her request. "But, Miss McGovern, I would be willing to reconsider the matter at a later point, should the evidence warrant a second look."

"Thank you, Your Honor." She conferred with Braddock, seemingly reassuring her client she'd revisit the topic.

Judge Vost moved on to his motion to seat a new jury, and after questioning the existing six men, it was also denied.

"Let's get this trial underway. Mister Littrick, call your first witness."

He stood. "Thank you, Your Honor. I call Rion Braddock to the stand."

The big man made his way to the front where Marshal Epps swore him in.

Daniel smiled. "Howdy, Mr. Braddock. Thank you for being here."

The big man gave a sarcastic shake of his head. "Ain't got much of a choice, now do I?"

"I suppose not. Would you please inform the jury what your job is?"

"Of late, I work as a bounty hunter."

"And how long have you held this job?"

"Off and on since I was fourteen."

"That's a long time. I assume it's a dangerous job. Are you proficient with weapons, Mr. Braddock?"

He shrugged. "Most bounty hunters are."

"But are you?"

"Of course I am." Irritation marked his features. "All of 'em. Guns, knives, fists."

"Have you ever taken a life, sir?"

Braddock turned a hateful glare his way. "On a few occasions—in the line of duty."

"So you're obviously a dangerous man, capable of taking a human life at will."

"I didn't say that. Why don't you ask me *who* I killed or *why* I took their lives?"

"Objection, Your Honor." He shifted toward Judge Vost. "Please instruct the witness that I will ask the questions."

"Mr. Braddock, it's in your best interest to answer only the questions posed, nothing else."

Seething, Braddock stared in Andie's direction as she motioned for him to remain calm.

Daniel pulled a large pair of boots from under his table. "Are these your boots, Mr. Braddock?" He held them up so he and the rest of the room could see them.

"Looks to be. Can I see 'em?"

Daniel handed the boots over, and Braddock looked at the right one's sole.

"Yeah, they're mine."

"What did you see that tells you they're yours?"

He frowned. "The size, for one. And there's a mark in the right heel. A little quarter moon." He drew the shape in the air with his finger.

"Your feet *are* rather large. Would you mind putting them on so we can see they fit?"

"All of me is large, you flop-eared half-wit. I'm tellin' you they're my boots."

The room erupted in laughter, and Judge Vost banged his gavel.

"Order!"

"Oh, c'mon, Judge! That was funny!" someone hollered.

The judge searched the crowd and pointed. "Marshal Epps, remove that man, please."

Marshal Epps waded into the crowded room, hauling the drunken man up by the arm. After a momentary struggle, Epps shoved him out the doors with a warning not to return.

"Now, Mr. Braddock." Vost turned his way. "Save the insults and do as you're asked."

After fishing a pair of socks from inside, he slipped out of his worn moccasins and put the boots on.

"Thank you, Mr. Braddock." Daniel nodded. "They do seem to fit."

Braddock gave a contemptuous roll of his eyes.

"You may remove them now."

"I can't even wear my own boots?"

"Unfortunately, we'll need 'em back. They're evidence. That's all I have for this witness at this moment."

"Miss McGovern, cross-examine?"

As Braddock pulled off the boots, Andie rose.

"Mr. Braddock, you mentioned you've taken some lives. Would you care to elaborate on who you killed and why?"

"Yes, miss." He shoved the socks inside the boots and set both on the floor. "I've killed three men. All three were outlaws I was huntin', and all three got the drop on me. In each case, it was kill or be killed, so I did what I had to do."

"By what method did you take those lives?"

"Two of 'em, we were wrestlin' over a gun at close range, and they lost the match. The third, I snapped his neck."

"Have you ever stabbed anyone?"

"No, miss." He shook his head.

"Have you ever harmed a woman?"

His eyes turned fiery. "I wouldn't!"

"Why wouldn't you?"

"Ain't right, that's why."

"But there's a further reason, isn't there?"

Jaw clenched, he hung his head. "I was an orphan—taken in by an ornery ol' cuss when I was ten. Across the four years me and four other boys lived with him, he took in two orphan girls. Young pretty ones to cook and clean his house. But that wasn't all he kept 'em for, if you know what I mean. He had his way with 'em. Mistreated 'em bad—and, I think, killed 'em both." He looked at his sister then. "Not bein' able to save them has haunted me ever since. I was helpless then, but I ain't helpless now. I see a woman in danger these days, and I'll make sure she's not harmed."

"So it wouldn't cross your mind to use deadly force on a woman?"

"Like I said, I wouldn't."

"Thank you, Mr. Braddock. No further questions, Your Honor."

Judge Vost turned to him. "Mr. Littrick?"

"I may recall this witness, but I'm done with him for now, sir. Next, I call Pearl Johnson."

A woman in her thirties came to the door escorted by another US Marshal, and once Epps swore her in, she sat.

"Good afternoon, Miss Johnson."

"Afternoon."

"Would you please tell the court what you do?"

"Well, now, I run the brothel in Cambria Springs. The Mountain Rose."

"Did the soiled dove known as Sweet Serafina work in your establishment?"

"Yeah. For about two years."

"And on the night that Serafina went missing, do you recall seeing the defendant, Rion Braddock, in your establishment?"

She turned a hard look on Braddock and nodded. "Yep, he was there. Right in the middle of our busiest time."

"And who did he see that night?"

"He asked to see Serafina, though I've trained all my girls to offer their services if a gentleman caller waits too long."

A murmur rippled through the room, particularly from the women in attendance, and Judge Vost reminded them to be quiet with a rap of his gavel.

"Did he see any other dove in your establishment?"

"To my recollection, no. He was intent on seein' her."

"Did you happen to see him leave?"

"No."

"So you can't say whether he left alone?"

"No, sir. I don't recall."

"Thank you, miss." He smiled as he turned to Andie. "Your witness."

"No questions."

Daniel proceeded to call two other soiled doves from the Mountain Rose, asking similar questions, with similar information learned. In each case, Andie strangely declined to clarify any details through cross-examination.

"Next, I call Dutch Uttley."

Dutch entered, was sworn in, and took the witness stand.

"Afternoon, Mr. Uttley. Sorry to pull you away from your café. When was the last time you saw your waitress, Mary Redmond?"

"The Saturday of the Founders Day Weekend."

"What do you recall from that day?"

"We were busy. Mary worked from open to close, and about midday, Rion Braddock came in and ate, then showed up again after we closed." He rubbed his forehead as if it pained him. "They left together, headed toward her place. That's the last I saw of her. We're closed on Sundays, and she never showed Monday."

"So it's possible—even probable—that Mr. Braddock was the last one to see Miss Redmond alive?"

"I have no way of knowin' that." The man glared.

"But he's the last one you saw her with, correct?"

"That's right."

"Thank you, Mr. Uttley." He turned. "Miss McGovern, your witness."

She jotted something on a paper, then looked toward Vost. "No questions, Your Honor."

Beside her, Braddock whispered something, looking peevish that she wasn't taking the opportunity to cross-examine witnesses. Daniel couldn't blame Braddock. If he were defending the man, he'd have cross-examined several she'd dismissed.

For a moment, a heated—but whispered—discussion ensued, ending when Andie laid her hand on his, and Braddock jerked back and folded his arms.

"Are you and your client ready to proceed, Miss McGovern?" the judge called.

"Yes, Your Honor. Forgive the interruption."

Vost nodded. "Proceed with your next witness, Counselor."

"I call Miss Kezia Jarrett to the stand."

Calliope entered, and once Epps swore her in, she sat.

"Good afternoon, Miss Jarrett. Please tell the court your real name and how you're employed."

She cleared her throat. "Calliope Wilson, and I'm a Pinkerton Detective."

Gasps and murmurs ripped through the room, causing Judge Vost to bang his gavel.

"Order!"

Once the silence returned, he continued. "Why did you come to Cambria Springs?"

"For five years, the Pinkertons have been investigating a series of murders in various locations, from Chicago to Wyoming Territory. All were women, stabbed, with their hair shorn. When we learned of Mary Redmond's death, it was the natural next place for the Pinkertons to investigate, though I came to the case when Serafina was found."

Daniel eyed her for a moment. "You have an unusual skill, don't you?"

"I'm an artist. I sketch faces, scenes, details of a crime."

"Is this one of your sketches?" From his table, he produced the sketch of the boot track with the crescent in the right heel.

"It is." Her tone held a note of reluctance.

"And where did you see and draw this?"

"In the cabin where Serafina's body was found."

"There must have been many tracks in that cabin, considering the boys who found her, the sheriff and his men who removed the corpse, and yourself. Can you recall anything distinctive about the placement of this particular track, Miss Wilson?"

She heaved a breath. "Other tracks—both human and animal—were laid down over it. This was one of the earliest tracks to be left in the cabin, which led me to believe it was the killer's, or perhaps an accomplice's."

"Thank you, Miss Wilson." He sat.

Vost turned to Andie. "Miss McGovern?"

Again, she looked up from jotting a note. "No questions, Your Honor."

Heaviness settled in Daniel's stomach. Why wasn't she asking anything? He prayed, asking God that she would put up some kind of a fight. He didn't want to roll over her with no opposition.

"Mr. Littrick?"

"I call Josiah Tunstall."

A wide-eyed nine-year-old boy entered and was sworn in.

"Howdy, Josiah. How are you today?"

He looked around, posture stiff. "I'd rather be fishin', sir."

Daniel laughed. "I think there's probably a few of us who feel that way." He leaned in and whispered from behind his hand. "Don't tell, but I'm one of 'em."

The boy eased a little and also whispered from behind his hand. "I won't, sir."

He winked at the boy. "I need to ask you a few questions about—"

"Miss Hattie goin' missin'?"

Daniel nodded. "Yes."

"Objection, Your Honor!" Andie bolted to her feet. "My

client is not charged with Hattie Ingram's kidnapping."

"You're correct, Miss McGovern." The judge nodded. "Mr. Littrick, why're you bringing this up?"

"It'll show a pattern—that Mr. Braddock was around each of the women. Perhaps in Miss Hattie's case he wasn't directly responsible, but there's still a connection."

Judge Vost looked first at him, then Andie. "I'm going to allow this for now, but mind yourself, Mr. Littrick." He faced the jury. "Jurors, keep in mind that Mr. Braddock is not charged with the kidnapping of Hattie Ingram."

Daniel focused on Josiah. "Let's see if we can't get you out to do some fishin' before dark, all right?"

"Sure. What d'ya want to know?"

"Miss Hattie came to stay with your ma, right?"

"Yeah. Pa had to take a trip, and Ma was expectin' her baby real soon. So Miss Hattie came to look after us."

"What did you see when she went out to take care of the barn animals after dark?"

Josiah nodded. "A big man with two horses came out of the shadows and grabbed her."

"Can you identify the man, Josiah?"

"It was pretty dark, but the lantern was lit, so I could see a little. The fella had a hat and a beard. The beard looked dark. I didn't see the horses real good, but both was darker colors, and one of 'em had some white socks."

"You're sure."

He nodded. "I saw the white in the lantern's glow."

"Very good, young man. Is there anyone in the room who might be that fella?"

"First one I wondered about was him." He pointed in Rion Braddock's direction.

"All right. Thank you, Josiah." He turned in Andie's direction. "Your witness."

For once, she rose. "Hello, Josiah, I'm Miss McGovern."

"Howdy, miss."

"You're very brave to come speak with us."

"Thank you."

"You said, as far as the man who might fit the description you saw, the first fella you wondered about was Mr. Braddock."

"Yeah. He's big, and he's got a dark beard, kinda scruffy."

"Do you see any others in the room who are big with dark, scruffy beards?"

"Sure, miss. Sheriff Downing, Bobby Hawkins' pa, there." He pointed to each man, then swung his pointer toward the jury box. "Mr. Sanderson." Craning his neck, he peered over the heads of others seated toward the back. "And that fella there in the corner."

Daniel looked where Josiah pointed. The man in question—a fella with a tall frame and wide shoulders, but no beard—seemed to come out of a stupor as attention shifted his way. Wide-eyed, he darted a panicked look around the room.

Miss McGovern looked in the man's direction. "But Josiah, that gentleman doesn't have a beard."

"Not right now. But you know how men's faces are, miss. Lots of 'em can grow a beard quick, then shave it and look different. That fella and the one sitting with you are both big like I saw."

She smiled. "Thank you, Josiah. That's very astute."

Confusion marred his features. "What's *astute*?"

"It means you made a very smart point. Thank you."

He grinned. "Sure, miss. Glad I could help you."

"You did." She turned toward Daniel, a challenge in her eye. "I'm done with this witness."

Daniel approached the young man again. "Josiah, just to

clarify, have you ever seen that gentleman with a beard?" He motioned to the corner.

"No sir. Only time I ever seen him was at the medicine show a while back. He got picked outta the crowd to help the sharp-shooter lady by throwin' the balls up in the air." He mimicked the motion. "He didn't have a beard then, either."

"Thank you. You did very well, Josiah. Now, go see your parents. Maybe they'll let you go fishin' after all."

The boy hurried off to meet his pa, waiting at the back of the room.

"I call Stephen Nesbitt to the stand."

Once he was sworn in, Daniel began.

"Mr. Nesbitt, please state your real name and occupation."

"Joseph Trenamen, operative for the Pinkerton Detective Agency."

Another disturbance rippled through the crowd but quieted before the judge picked up his gavel.

"Did you investigate at the Tunstall property after Hattie Ingram disappeared?"

"I did."

"What did you find?"

An irritated look in his eyes, he glanced away, then back. "Boot tracks."

Daniel nodded. "Anything distinguishing about those tracks, sir?"

"They had a crescent-shaped indentation in the right heel."

"Same as Miss Wilson drew." He picked up the drawing and showed it in the direction of the jury. "The one she surmised was left by the killer at Serafina's murder scene?"

"Yes."

"And the same identifying mark on Rion Braddock's boot?" He showed the boot to the jury.

"Yes."

"As a trained investigator, what conclusion do you draw?"

He inhaled deeply. "Appears like Rion Braddock was somehow involved in both Serafina's death and Hattie Ingram's disappearance."

"Thank you, sir. You've been working this case since the first murder five years ago, correct?"

"Yes."

"And who is your prime suspect in Mary Redmond's murder?"

"Rion Braddock was the last person we know who saw her alive."

"Have these boot tracks shown up at any of the previous murder scenes, Mr. Trenamen?"

"Several."

"Thank you. No further questions."

Andie rose and shook her head. "No questions for this witness at this time, Your Honor."

When Vost's attention swung back in his direction, Daniel drew a deep breath. "Members of the jury, I believe I've given ample evidence to show that Rion Braddock was in the vicinity of all three crimes that were committed here in Cambria Springs. I rest my case, Your Honor."

He took his seat, his heart heavy. If Andie couldn't answer the points he'd made, Rion would probably be convicted, and after getting to know Andie and her brother and sister a little, that idea left a gaping pit in his belly.

Lord, please let her have something good.

CHAPTER 11

Tuesday, July 22, 1873

Once Judge Vost called the court to order, he turned Andie's way. "Miss McGovern, the defense may proceed."

Breathing deep, she prayed for favor and clarity, then rose. Just as when Judge Oakwell still presided, her stomach pitched, though not as forcefully. "Thank you, Your Honor. I call Rion Braddock to the stand."

Her brother came forward and was sworn in.

"Mr. Braddock, please remind the court what you do for a living."

"I'm a bounty hunter—have been for my whole adult life and then some."

"Are you on friendly terms with a lot of the people you meet?"

Rion chuckled. "I tend to be hated among some parts of the world. Folks don't look kindly on my sort gettin' paid for turnin''em in."

"How many would you guess feel that way?"

"More than a few." He shrugged.

"Thank you. When you escaped from the Cambria Springs jail, what was your intention? Did you plan to run away, or was there another thought?"

"I needed to clear my name."

"So your intention wasn't to run as far as possible."

"My intention was to find out who's framin' me and bring 'em to justice."

"How were you recaptured?"

"I wasn't captured either time." Rion straightened. "I willingly turned myself in, first when Calliope Wilson said all the evidence pointed to me for the murders, and again after I broke out."

"Hardly the actions of a guilty man, Mr. Braddock."

"I ain't guilty."

"Have you ever been in the brothel where the soiled dove known as Sweet Serafina worked?"

"Yes."

"Why?"

"I was hunting the man who'd roughed her up some time earlier, and I needed to ask her some questions."

"How long were you there?"

His cheeks reddened. "Longer than intended. She was, uh. . .busy. . .at the time I showed up. I had to wait for her to"—he cleared his throat—"unbusy herself."

Laughter erupted, and some of the women in attendance looked mortified.

"Order!" Judge Vost banged his gavel.

Once silence returned, Rion continued. "I waited maybe an hour, and once I got in to talk to her, it was—I don't know—ten minutes more."

"Did you see or speak to anyone as you left?"

"Can't say as I spoke to anyone the whole time I was there, other than to rebuff the offers from the other doves. I waited, I spoke to Serafina, and I left. I dunno who mighta saw me leavin'."

"Was she alive when you departed?"

"Very much, miss. She threw a metal candlestick at my head

for wastin' her time. I ducked, and it hit the wall."

More laughter rippled through the room, and the judge called the room to order. Daniel shifted sideways, probably to allow himself to see the crowd, as well as her.

"What about the night Mary Redmond disappeared? Did you return to walk her home at the end of business?"

"I did."

"Was this a normal occurrence?"

"No. It was the Founders Day weekend, and the town was busy. When I saw her earlier in the day, she was concerned about gettin' home that night with all the extra folks around. So I offered to come back and walk her home."

"And she was alive when you left her?"

"Standin' in her doorway, very much alive."

"Did anyone see you?"

He shrugged. "Durn if I know. The streets weren't empty, but I didn't talk to no one. Just mounted up and rode off."

"The night of Hattie Ingram's disappearance, were you in Cambria Springs?"

"Yes."

"Doing what?"

"I shot and field dressed a deer and accompanied Calliope Wilson back to the boardinghouse, gave Mrs. Ingram the meat, shared a meal with 'em, then headed back to the cave where I intended to sleep that night."

"Was Miss Hattie there that evening?"

"No, miss."

"Did you know where she was?"

Braddock shook his head. "I knew she was stayin' elsewhere, but no one said where, and I didn't ask. Wasn't my business."

"So in all three cases, you had legitimate reasons to be in Cambria Springs, even in the direct vicinity of the victims, that had nothing to do with any murderous intent."

"That's right. Like I said yesterday, I got no desire to harm a woman. Ever."

"Thank you. The boots that you wear"—she scooped them up from the table where they sat—"do you wear them everywhere?"

"No, miss."

Her stomach eased as she settled into her line of questioning. "When do you not wear them?"

"If I'm trackin' someone or have need to be real quiet, if I don't want to leave an easy trail to follow, then I switch to moccasins."

"Like what you're wearing now." She motioned to his feet.

"Exactly what I'm wearin' now—except this pair's pert near wore out, since I been wearin' 'em constant for weeks. Need to make a new pair."

"Thank you, Mr. Braddock." She marched back toward her seat. "Your witness, Mr. Littrick."

Daniel approached. "Good morning, Mr. Braddock. What portion of the time do you wear moccasins instead of boots?"

"If I'm on a man's trail out in the mountains or open country, I'll live in moccasins. About town, I'll be in my boots."

"And if you're not on a man's trail?"

"I wear those boots most often, unless maybe I'm huntin' for supper."

"Thank you, sir." Daniel nodded at her. "Your witness."

She rose. "Mr. Braddock, you may return to your seat. Your Honor, I reserve the right to recall this witness."

"Noted."

She addressed her notes. "I call Dutch Uttley to the stand."

After his entrance and swearing in, she approached. "Good morning, Mr. Uttley. Forgive me for interrupting a second day of your business."

"I don't mind it so much today."

She grinned. "Thank you. What's the nature of your relationship with Mr. Braddock?"

"Kin—by adoption. Or close enough."

"Would you explain that, please?"

"Rion Braddock, Seth Kealey, and I were three orphan boys taken in by Ellwood Garvin. We spent four years at his place. We were just fostered, not adopted, but we learned to rely on each other like kin. It carried over. We ain't blood, but we're brothers."

"Would your brother ever harm a woman?"

He shook his head vehemently. "No, miss. None of us would."

"And why not?"

He was silent for a time, his jaw popping. "Garvin took in two orphan girls, and it didn't take long to figure out he was mishandling them. We were young and scared. Wasn't much we could do to help 'em, but we all vowed we'd never let such things happen to a woman around us again."

"Thank you, Mr. Uttley. Your witness, Mr. Littrick."

He rose. "I have no questions."

She motioned for him to be dismissed. "I call Lucinda Peters to the stand."

Once she was sworn in, Andie grinned to put Lu at ease. "I understand, Miss Peters, that you were present when Mr. Braddock escaped from jail."

"I was."

"Why were you there?"

"I'm a dime novelist and an aspiring reporter. I'd come to get Mr. Braddock's story, and when Sheriff Downing threatened to remove me from his office, I made a calculated move and locked myself in one of the empty cells."

Chuckles rose, bringing Judge Vost's gavel into play.

"Order!"

As the din quieted, Lu continued. "To spite me, the sheriff chained me to the tree outside and didn't return for most of that day—the same day of the terrible thunderstorm."

The crowd's levity quickly rolled into scowls and grumbling, and Sheriff Downing squirmed in his chair.

"I said order!" The judge rapped his gavel. "Next time I say it, I'll start removing people."

Quiet fell, and Andie prodded Lu to continue.

"Mr. Nesbitt, or Joe Trenamen—who was deputized at the time—rescued me from the storm, but he didn't know whether I was under arrest. So, until he could find Downing, he locked me in the jail."

"At the time of his escape, was Mr. Braddock wearing boots or moccasins?"

She scowled. "As I recall, boots."

"How did you get out of the jail?"

"Once Mr. Braddock overcame his cell door, he found the keys, unlocked my cell, and told me to leave. He knew I was just there to talk to him."

"What did you do?"

She gave a sheepish shrug. "I followed him. I still wanted his story."

"Followed him?"

"He'd gone to the livery and saddled his two horses. I found him near there, stopped between buildings. His second horse was saddled, and during a loud peal of thunder, I mounted the horse and let him lead me away in the dark."

Daniel and others covered their mouths and chuckled silently.

Andie shot Lu an amused look. "That was bold. How long were you with Mr. Braddock?"

"I don't remember exactly."

"Minutes? Hours? A day?"

"Days. . .about a week, I think."

Andie's eyebrows shot up. "That long?"

"Yes."

"And during that time, how often did he wear his boots?"

"He didn't. From the time we rode away from those buildings until the sun came up, we almost didn't stop moving. There was no time for him to change to his moccasins. And as the sun rose, he already had them on, so I assume he changed into them after he left the jail and before I mounted his horse. The remainder of the time I was with him, he was either in moccasins or barefoot."

"During that time, a posse was searching for Mr. Braddock?"

"Yes."

"And where were the two of you?"

"Either on the run, or—most of the time—at Seth and Lena Kealey's house."

"Why did you go there?"

"We went down the mountain after leaving Cambria Springs, but Mr. Braddock turned around. On the night after his escape, he was spotted passing through town and was shot in the shoulder. We went to Seth and Lena's for help. Neither of us left the house for several days while he recuperated."

"You're certain?"

"I'm well-versed in wound care. Other than a very brief span, I stayed with him the entire time, tending to the infection from the gunshot."

"At what point did you and Mr. Braddock separate?"

"The day the posse returned to the Kealey's and discovered Hattie Ingram had been found. I accompanied her home to help with her wounds."

"Thank you, Miss Peters." She paused, thinking through

her next questions. "Did it frighten you at all to think the man who escaped from jail—whom you'd attached yourself to—was accused of killing two women...or that he might have kidnapped a third?"

"No. Sometimes, you just get a sense about people. I saw his concern and relief when I was rescued from being chained to that tree while lightning struck so close. He seemed truly worried for me. And the fact that he didn't leave me locked up, nor did he force me to come along with him, showed he was concerned but without ill intentions."

"You were with him for days. How did he treat you during that time?"

She turned a gentle smile Rion's way, locking eyes with him as she answered. "Like a complete gentleman. He risked capture to get food for the both of us, among other things. Even after he was shot, he made sure I was safe." Lu returned her focus to her. "Frankly, Miss McGovern, I've never felt more secure than when I was with him."

"You mentioned leaving Mr. Braddock and the Kealey house for a short while. Why did you leave?"

Lu looked around the room. "I overheard a conversation while the posse was at the Kealey house. Rion and I were hiding, so I couldn't see who was speaking, but it seemed to be between a posse member and someone else. One whispery voice asked how the other person lost *a crippled woman*—an injured, *crippled woman*—and I realized they were talking about Hattie."

Gasps punctuated the air, and Andie looked around. Most wore shocked expressions as the judge banged his gavel and called the room to order.

Returning her focus to the witness, she continued. "And where was Mr. Braddock at the time?"

"Hiding in the same spot, very likely passed out."

"You're not sure whether he was awake?"

"We were in a narrow tunnel. I had crawled toward one end. He was at the other, but his moccasin-clad feet were within my view."

"I'm sorry. I interrupted you on why you left Mr. Braddock for a little while."

"Yes. After overhearing that conversation, I asked the Kealeys about who else lived in the area. They told me about Ollie Sapey, so after deliberation, we decided I would ask her if she knew about Hattie. I left to contact her."

"Did she know anything about Miss Ingram?"

"At first, she didn't let on that she did. In fact, she fired a shotgun over my head and told me to leave and not return."

"At first. But she changed her story?"

"The next night, after dark, she came to Seth and Lena's door and told us she had Hattie. That she'd rescued her the day of that awful thunderstorm, and she wanted us to take her back to her family."

"Thank you, Miss Peters." She waved toward Daniel. "Your witness."

⌒

Daniel shook his head in appreciation. As Andie passed him, her brown eyes held a victorious glint. His case was unraveling, and she knew it. Whatever fears he had that she couldn't rebut his case were ill-informed.

"Miss Peters, am I understanding correctly that you met Mr. Braddock the day of your calculated move at the jail?"

"That's correct."

"And you've known him for less than a month now."

Redness stained her cheeks. "Yes."

"You were together for roughly a week of that time."

"Before we separated." She sat taller. "I've spent time with him each day since he turned himself in."

"But you didn't know him at the time of Mary Redmond's or Serafina's deaths."

"No."

"So you took a gamble that he would be safe."

Her cheeks grew even redder, though her tone was mildly defiant. "As I said, sometimes you just have a feeling about people."

"That was a mighty big risk." He turned toward Andie. "I'm finished with this witness."

"Thank you, Miss Peters. You may step down."

Daniel leaned an elbow on the table. Would she make her motion again now?

"I call Joe Trenamen to the stand."

Not yet. . .

Joe replaced Lu, and Epps swore him in. Andie approached. "Mr. Trenamen, were you in the posse searching for Mr. Braddock?"

"Yes, the one that went up the mountain."

"Why did you choose that one, sir?"

Trenamen rubbed his eyebrow. "One, I knew Braddock had a friend up that way, and two, I've tracked in mountainous terrain before."

"Miss Wilson went with you, correct?"

"She did."

Daniel frowned. Where was she going with this?

"Why would you take a woman along on a posse?"

"If we found either Hattie Ingram or Lu Peters alive and in a bad way, we wanted a woman along to provide care that us menfolk can't offer. Miss Wilson was willing to endure the harsh conditions, and she's a Pinkerton." A hint of pride shone in his eyes. "She wouldn't be denied."

"But at some point, you and Miss Wilson left the posse to watch the Kealey house, correct?"

"Right. Knowing Braddock and Kealey are friends, we figured he might show up there."

"What did you find around Seth Kealey's house?"

"Lots of boot tracks. Large ones, with a crescent-shaped notch cut out of the right heel."

"Did you confirm they were Mr. Braddock's?"

"No. Mr. Braddock and Miss Peters were there, so we took his boot and compared it to the tracks. The tracks were shorter and narrower than his actual boots."

"You must be joshing, Mr. Trenamen. Are you suggesting someone else might have a pair of boots with a crescent-moon-shaped mark in exactly the same spot of the right heel?"

"Seems so, miss."

"You said there was one place very close to the Kealey house where you found these tracks. Where was that, sir?"

"Yes. At the end of the tunnel Lu Peters and Rion Braddock were hiding in when she overheard the conversation about losing Miss Hattie."

"So one of the people she overheard could have been wearing boots like Mr. Braddock's."

He gave an emphatic nod. "That's what I thought."

"What condition was Mr. Braddock in when you found him at the Kealey place?"

"Weak and ill from a gunshot wound in his shoulder. He was in no shape to travel."

"Was he wearing these boots when you found him?" She motioned to them.

"He wore moccasins the whole time we were there."

Daniel grinned. She was casting doubt on whether the boot tracks were Braddock's, and she knew it. In fact, she seemed to be having fun putting him in his place.

He shouldn't be surprised. From those first moments on the train, she'd proven that. This was just a different method to the same end.

"Thank you, Mr. Trenamen." She turned toward her seat. "Your witness."

Daniel rose. "Did you see anyone else with similar boots in the area? And when I say similar, I mean shape and size. . ."

"Well, now, lots of men wear similar boots, but I didn't make a specific study of anyone's footwear up until we realized Braddock couldn't have been making all those tracks."

"You said it *seems* someone has boots with that crescent mark, but are you certain?"

"I suppose I'm not."

"Thank you." It was a weak rebuttal—but it was all he could think of.

Andie faced Mr. Trenamen. "As a trained investigator, what conclusion do you come to in a situation like this, where Mr. Braddock's boots *nearly* match, but the tracks are a little different?"

"Leads me to believe that there's a second set of boots, and I wonder if someone is making it look like the owner of the real boot did something he didn't do."

"Thank you, Mr. Trenamen. You're dismissed. I call Seth Kealey."

He entered, looking tired. Epps swore him in.

"Thanks for being here, Mr. Kealey. I'll keep this brief so you can return to your wife and newborn son." Andie smiled. "I understand you and Mr. Braddock have a long history."

"Yes, miss. We were both taken in by Ellwood Garvin as kids, both ran from him at the same time, and worked together as bounty hunters for years before I gave it up. We're brothers, through and through."

"Would your brother ever harm a woman?"

"No." A derisive snort punctuated the statement. "We each vowed not to after our time at Garvin's. He's always been real kind to any woman I've seen him with, includin' my wife Lena."

"Thank you. On another topic...while Rion Braddock and Lu Peters were at your house, you found a man watching your property around dusk. Did you see who he was?"

"Wish I had, but night was fallin', and he was under the cover of trees. I knocked him unconscious, tied him over his saddle, and led his horse away."

"The following day, you took Mr. Trenamen to the spot where you found this man. What did you see?"

"Boot tracks, like Rion's, but Trenamen put Rion's boot over the tracks, and they were too small to be his."

"So it's likely the man you knocked unconscious and tied over the saddle has a very similar pair of boots to Mr. Braddock's."

"Yes. That's why I wish I'd seen his face."

"Although you didn't see his features, you did struggle to get his unconscious frame over his saddle. Is there anything that stands out about his size, his build...?"

Mr. Kealey nodded. "He was about Rion's height but not as heavy. Rion passed out from his wound, and I had to wrestle him up on a horse, same as I did with the fella. The peepin' tom was easier to get over a saddle than Rion, by far."

"Anything else that stood out, Mr. Kealey?"

"I pulled the fella up by his arms." He mimicked the action. "He had small wrists. Twiglike, almost."

"Thank you, Mr. Kealey." Andie grinned. "Your witness, Mr. Littrick."

Daniel scanned the courtroom. Most sat in rapt attention—even the drunken contingent. Judge Vost's rules had quelled the raucousness in the room, though a few—like the fella in the corner—still poured and tossed back plenty of whiskey. It seemed most everyone was enjoying Andromeda McGovern's performance today.

He surely was.

Clearing his throat, he faced Seth Kealey. "I understand congratulations are in order."

He nodded. "Yes, sir."

"Son or a daughter?"

"A son."

"Congratulations." He paused. "Did you ask the posse whether they'd sent anyone to watch your house?"

"I asked Trenamen and Miss Wilson if anyone else came to watch us. They were the only ones."

"But you didn't ask Sheriff Downing?"

The man closed his eyes. "As I'm thinkin' about it, I did. When the posse returned, I asked the sheriff. He sent Trenamen and Miss Wilson. No one else."

"Thank you." He sat again.

"Yes, thank you, Mr. Kealey." Andie smiled. "You've been a great help."

Judge Vost shifted in her direction as Kealey left the stand.

"Miss McGovern, I'm trying to judge the time with your remaining witnesses and when I should call a recess."

"I have one more witness, Your Honor, and then I'd like to recall Mr. Braddock for just a moment. I can be done in fifteen minutes, unless Mr. Littrick has lots of questions."

Vost nodded. "Then by all means, proceed."

"Thank you. I call Hattie Ingram to the stand."

She shuffled in, looking as pale and thin as when they'd interviewed her days earlier. Marshal Epps swore her in.

"Thank you for coming today, Miss Ingram. I know this has been a very trying time. It can't be easy to talk about."

"No."

"I won't ask you to describe the events of that night. What I'd like to know is whether you saw the man who took you."

"He grabbed me from behind, so I never saw him when I was first taken. He drugged me and tied me over a saddle because, later, I saw him mounted on another horse ahead of me."

"Can you say whether or not it was Rion Braddock?"

She swallowed hard. "I know for sure it was *not*."

"How can you be sure?"

"The man on the horse had a leaner build. Mr. Braddock is thicker. And—" Her chin quivered. "When the man grabbed me in the barn, I latched onto his arm. His wrist was too dainty to be Mr. Braddock's."

"And you knew Mr. Braddock had larger wrists because. . .?"

"He let me hold his arm as he walked me to our wagon the day of the medicine show. I couldn't help but notice how big he was."

"Do you recall anything about the horses—either the one he rode or your own?"

"Not much. Like I said, he kept me drugged. But I did notice one time that his horse was a pretty black with white stockings. Only the stockings looked strange."

"Strange, how?"

"They weren't solid. Any stockings I've seen on a horse are just white. These looked. . .cracked, maybe?"

"Cracked?"

"There was black showing through from under the white."

"Miss Hattie, are you able to walk to the door and look out?"

"Yes, miss."

After attaining Judge Vost's approval, Andie led her witness to the door and, with the help of Marshal Epps, led Braddock's horse to the front of the saloon.

"Is this the horse you saw?"

"Similar, but those aren't the stockings I saw."

"Thank you, Miss Hattie. Mr. Littrick, do you have any questions?"

For Hattie's sake, he shook his head. "No."

"Then you can go on, miss. Thank you again for coming down."

It took a moment for Epps to retie Braddock's horse and get the room settled again. Then Andie called Rion Braddock back to the stand. The judge instructed him that his former swearing in was still in effect.

"Your boots, Mr. Braddock. Where did you purchase them?"

He shook his head. "I didn't. They were given to me."

"A new pair of boots, given to you? That's a generous gift."

"Not new. Used."

"Used?"

She looked surprised, although by now, Daniel knew she was playing to the crowd. She was rather good at it.

"What nice person gifted you a pair of used boots."

"A woman I used to be romantically involved with. Maya Fellows."

The name clanged in Daniel's mind. As he recalled the wild woman in the cemetery, a murmur rattled through a part of the audience. Before he could turn to look, Judge Vost employed his gavel.

"Order, or I'll clear the courtroom!"

The whispers died, although Daniel glanced toward the din, noting the faces. Several—mostly those associated with Dr. Chellingworth's medicine show—wore shocked looks. Why?

"How did Miss Fellows come to possess those boots?"

He faced front.

"Her brother died, and she had some of his possessions, including his boots. They weren't doin' no good just sittin' there, so she gave 'em to me."

"Did you place this mark in the heel?" Andie indicated the marked boot.

Braddock shook his head. "That was there from the time Maya gave 'em to me."

"So would you say, then, that someone else could've known of that mark?"

"I reckon so."

"Thank you, Mr. Braddock." She nodded to him. "Your witness."

He stood.

"Who do you think knew of that mark, Mr. Braddock?"

Braddock shrugged. "Probably Maya. I don't know beyond that. She's got plenty of friends and often sees 'em."

Behind Daniel, chairs scraped, and he turned to see the bearded woman and the man with the darkened spectacles walk out while the others in the medicine show group looked on, flummoxed.

"I appreciate it, Mr. Braddock."

Once he sat, Andie rose again. "Your Honor, at this time, I would like to revisit my motion to drop the two murder charges against my client. There's ample evidence to show others kidnapped Hattie Ingram, and all the same evidence of boot tracks and matching horses was used in Mary Redmond's and Serafina's murders. If it wasn't true in Hattie's case, it strongly calls into question whether it is true in the other women's cases."

Judge Vost nodded. "I guessed you might call for that, Miss McGovern. We could all use a recess. I'll consider it during the break." Again, he checked his watch. "Court is in recess until one this afternoon." He banged his gavel, and the room came alive.

CHAPTER 12

People stood. Conversation started. Men called out to the bartender for drinks, and folks milled.

Andie grabbed Rion's hand, keeping her voice low. "This is going in the right direction."

"I trust you—but I gotta say, you had me sweatin' some yesterday when you weren't askin' many questions."

"I know, but I think that tactic worked beautifully today."

"Hope so."

Sheriff Downing came to handcuff Rion and take him back to the jail for the two-hour break. As he locked the handcuffs in place, someone tapped her on the shoulder.

"Miss McGovern?"

It was one of the women from the medicine show, a buxom woman with dark hair. Behind her, several others—including the tall, muscular man and the especially small fellow—crowded around.

"This was real entertaining, hon." The woman reached to shake her hand. "We've never seen a woman lawyer before."

Several others pumped her hand as well. A giggle rose in her throat at the strangeness of it all. "Thank you, but I'm not sure I've seen a collection of people quite like you, either."

They laughed and pressed in close to the table, several

offering kind words or congratulations until, from the door, a lone voice rang out.

"Is there an Andromeda McGovern in the room?"

"Here!" she shouted, and the crowd parted to allow the man from Wells Fargo to approach.

"Telegram for you, Miss McGovern."

"Thank you." She tucked the paper into her pocket. With the crowd pressing in, it wasn't time to read the response. Hopefully, it was news about her final witness. She'd sent word she would need help clearing Rion, and she'd not heard back yet. With the way today had gone, hopefully they wouldn't need another witness.

The man stopped to talk with Daniel a moment before he left. She faced the medicine show troupe. "Thank you for your kind words. Now, please excuse me, there are some things I need to attend to before court reconvenes."

Graciously, they bid her farewell and filtered away.

Sheriff Downing had managed to shackle Rion's hands, though since Judge Vost had demanded he be unchained in court, the lawman hadn't bothered with his feet. Rion looked back at her.

"See you in a couple hours."

She looked Downing's way. "Have you made arrangements for Rion's noon meal, Sheriff?"

"I got to get that worked out yet."

"Then I'll stop by Dutch's Café and bring something to him shortly."

"Make sure Dutch don't slip no files or weapons in the basket, miss."

Rion laughed without humor. "Funny, Downing. But I already proved I can overcome your jail anytime I want."

Glowering, Downing jerked Rion up by the arm and herded him toward the door. The two deputies fell in behind them and, moments later, led Rion away on horseback.

"Miss McGovern." Daniel's warm voice snagged her ear. His smile was warm and approving. "Well done today."

"Thank you."

"Do you have plans for your noon meal? Maybe we could go to Dutch's together if you don't."

"Are you saying you'd be willing to be seen in public with a sharp-tongued, fire-breathing woman like me, Counselor?"

A sheepish grin overtook him. "After your presentation in court today, I'm already a little scorched. What's a little more?"

She laughed. "I'd like that very much, but I promised Sheriff Downing I'd bring food to the jail for Rion."

Disappointment clouded his blue eyes. "I understand. Maybe another time."

"You could walk me to the café if you're heading that way. I might be able to muster a few more flames between here and there." She bit her lip.

His blue eyes twinkled. "Only if you promise to walk on my left side."

"Your left side. Why?"

"You been on my right all day. I need to even out the char."

She belly laughed. "Your left side it is." She nodded toward her table. "Let me gather my things."

"I'll get packed too."

Andie arranged her files and notes into a neat stack. As she reached for her carpetbag stashed under the table, she noticed a small, folded paper with her name scrawled in block letters tucked under her water glass. She slid it toward herself. Before she opened it, she checked her pocket and withdrew the telegram. They weren't the same.

She unfolded the paper and read the words once, then

again, trying to understand, then perused the telegram. Her stomach dropped.

Daniel approached. "Are you ready?"

She continued to stare at the two papers, processing their meaning.

"Andromeda?" He knelt in front of her. "Are you all right?"

Pocketing the papers, she scribbled a message on her pad and tore the paper off. "I'm sorry, Daniel. I can't walk to the café with you after all. There's something important I need to look into before we reconvene. Would you please give this to Dutch?"

He read the note asking Dutch to send food to the jail for Rion and saying that she'd pay for it that afternoon once court was finished.

"Don't worry about this. I'll see to it. But is everything all right?"

"If I can tie up the loose ends, I think it will be."

⌒

Daniel delivered the food to the sheriff's office—to the surprise of Downing and Braddock.

"What're you doin' here?" Braddock approached the cell bars. "Where's Andromeda?"

"Looking into something. She was fine when we parted ways thirty minutes ago." Fine, although something was weighing on her. He swung toward Downing. "Would you mind giving me and Braddock a couple of minutes, Sheriff?"

"For what?"

He turned a steely look at the lawman. "A private conversation."

"Let me look at that basket of food, and once I know it's safe, I will."

Braddock rattled his cell door. "Are you plumb weak north of your ears, Downing? I'm not lookin' to escape, especially when my attorney's about to get my charges dropped."

"*If* she gets 'em dropped, it don't mean you're acquitted. It just means they can't prove you killed Sar—"

"Ain't you been listenin', you dim-witted polecat? Somebody's been settin' me up, Andromeda pert near proved it. I'm as much a victim in all this as anyone."

"But you're still alive."

Daniel set the basket down on the desk. "Do what you need to do and get out."

Downing glared. "Don't you come in my office and order me around."

"You said if you checked the food, you'd give us time to talk." He tipped the basket so the sheriff could see inside. "Get on with it."

Sullen, the sheriff pawed through two paper-wrapped sandwiches and two slabs of apple pie. Once he'd checked them, he removed the keys from his desk drawer, shoved his hands in his pockets, and walked out—warning them he'd be nearby.

"That man really doesn't like you." Daniel grabbed one of the sandwiches, unwrapped thanks to Downing, along with a plate of pie and carried both to Braddock.

"The feeling's mutual." He took the food and paced back to his cot.

"Do you know why?"

"Not rightly, no. I've dealt with him some since he's been sheriff, and we tolerated each other. But of late, he's been different."

So what had changed...?

"What do you want, Littrick? Why'd you come to see me?"

Daniel grabbed Downing's chair and set it in front of Braddock's cell. Retrieving the other sandwich, he sat. "Andromeda's done a fine job of castin' doubt on my case today, so the judge will likely dismiss your charges."

"She's sharp." Braddock bit into his sandwich.

He'd noticed. She'd outwitted him but good in the courtroom, and he'd never enjoyed trying a case so much. "I want you to know, anything I said in the courtroom. . .it wasn't personal. I didn't *like* having to prosecute you." He also took a bite.

Braddock stalled, rolled the food to one cheek, and shook his head. "Why do you think that matters to me?"

Daniel chewed and swallowed. "Do you know what Andromeda's plans are after this case?"

With the sandwich halfway to his mouth, he paused. "Don't rightly know what either of my sisters plan once this is done. I don't even know what I'm gonna do. Why?"

"I'm kinda interested in her, and if she's plannin' to stay, I'd like your permission to come callin'."

Braddock's eyes grew wide, and he almost looked scared. "My permission?"

"You are her brother, aren't you?"

He stared a minute then shook his head. "Well, yeah. But. . ."

Daniel waited.

"Durn. . ." The man almost exhaled the word, a mix of wonder and fear in his tone.

Daniel laughed. "What?"

Braddock finally met his eyes. "The last time I was in any position to speak for Andromeda or Calliope, I was ten. It about broke me, losin' them. Felt like I failed 'em both, and I never really believed I'd see 'em again. Now that they're here and I'm almost free. . .life's lookin' a lot different." He set the sandwich aside, settled his elbows on his knees, and cradled his forehead in his hands.

"I didn't mean to stir up a hornet's nest."

Braddock's cheeks puffed as he blew out a breath. "I don't

want 'em to go. I want 'em to stay so's we can get to know each other again, but. . .I'm gonna need to make some changes too. Bounty huntin' ain't advantageous to life with close kin—or havin' a woman you're sweet on."

Daniel let him ramble.

He lifted his gaze. "As far as speakin' for Andromeda, she's real fond of her adopted pa."

"She's fond of you too, Braddock, and you're here." With Andie's father being territories away and Braddock's imposing figure being within arm's reach, Daniel would lend more weight to Braddock's say-so than Mr. McGovern's. Not that he wouldn't ask Andromeda's father's permission—but out of proximity, he wanted Braddock's blessing first.

"Well, if it counts for anything, you been decent, Littrick. You called for a new judge when Oakwell coulda handed you an easy conviction. You been fair in your dealings in the courtroom, and it was an unexpected kindness that you'd let Andie use your law books. If that's how you are outside of court, I'd give you my blessin'."

He crossed toward the cell bars, stretching a hand between them. "Thank you."

As Braddock reached to shake his hand, the office door opened and Andie stepped in, looking pale.

"Oh, good. Daniel."

He released Braddock's hand and crossed to her. "Are you all right?"

"I think I know who's framing Rion, but I need help proving it."

"What kind of help?"

She drew him toward Braddock's cell and pulled out the papers she'd pocketed earlier.

"I sent a telegram days ago to the people Maya was

supposedly staying with in Denver, requesting that she come and testify about giving you the boots. I wanted to ask her if she knew about the mark in the heel."

"Your case is plenty strong without that."

"Yes. But I'd already sent the telegram, and Wells Fargo delivered this just after Judge Vost called the recess."

He read Heck's handwritten message aloud.

Maya Fellows not in Denver *STOP*
Haven't seen her since her father brother
and her started medicine show *STOP*

"That's how she got here!" Rion almost howled the words. "She showed up the day I was arrested, sayin' she'd come to see the medicine show. Acted like she was disappointed she missed it!"

"There's more! Someone left this note on my table." She showed the other paper first to Braddock, then him. Daniel read it aloud.

Hunneys at medicine
show.
July 4, 1867

He shook his head. "I don't understand. The honey's at the medicine show? And a six-year-old date?"

"Not *the honey*. Hunneys." She produced a wanted poster for Edward Hunney.

Why was that name familiar?

"See these dates?" Andromeda pointed to two dates scrawled in the upper right corner. "The first is the date Rion arrested him."

"And the second is the date he was hung." Rion flicked the corner of the paper with his finger. "July 4, 1867. The last thing that one said before the trapdoor opened under him was

'God have mercy on your soul, Braddock, 'cause my kin won't rest until you pay.'"

Daniel resisted a full-body shiver. "All right. What do you need to prove the Hunneys are framing Rion?"

"The day that we arrived on the train in Denver, we both ended up at that cemetery. Maya was visiting her brother's grave. Did you happen to see the name on the marker as you rode past? Because I recall the date—July 4, 1867."

He searched his memory for that detail. "Oh my word." Daniel nodded. "It was Edward Hunney."

CHAPTER 13

"Court's in session." Judge Vost punctuated the statement with his gavel.

"After hearing both the prosecution's and defense's cases, I've given Miss McGovern's motion another thought. Mr. Littrick, do you have any objections or concerns about dismissing the two murder charges?"

"No, Your Honor. In fact, some further information came to light during the recess that cements Miss McGovern's case."

"And that would be. . . ?"

"May we approach, Your Honor?"

Judge Vost motioned, and they walked to his table.

"What's goin' on?" Vost spoke in a whisper.

"New evidence has come to light that indicates the family members of one of the men Braddock caught six years ago, and who was subsequently hung, are to blame for all the murders. Just before hanging, the man threatened that his family would make Braddock pay. Seems they've made good on that threat."

Vost held up a hand. "All right. With everything else you've presented, there's ample evidence to make a ruling. Return to your seats."

As they walked back, Judge Vost called for Rion to stand.

"Mr. Braddock, I am dismissing the charges against you for

the murders of Mary Redmond and Sarah Jacobs."

The room exploded as onlookers jumped out of their chairs, some cheering, others angry, many passing money back and forth as they settled bets on the trial's outcome. Vost banged his gavel repeatedly.

"Order! Order! I want silence."

When decorum finally prevailed, the judge shot Rion a stern look. "Two final points, Mr. Braddock."

"Yes, sir."

"First, regarding your escape, I'm charging you a fine equal to the cost of the cell door's repair or replacement, due by the end of this month."

"I'll pay it, sir."

"And second, Sheriff, you're to release Mr. Braddock immediately."

"You don't have to tell me twice."

"Case dismissed!" He gaveled out, and Andie launched into Rion's arms, eyes stinging.

"Thank you!" he whispered as he lifted her off the ground in a hug.

She squeezed him back, too overcome to speak. After a moment, he released her and bent to look her in the eye.

"I knew you could do it."

Something between a laugh and a sob boiled up from her depths. "No, God did. I simply got to be a part of it." She sat, her legs suddenly weak.

Marshal Epps approached. "What're your plans, Braddock?"

"In the short term, I'm goin' after the people who did this to me. Anything beyond that, I haven't thought that far."

"Want company?"

"Don't need it."

The man lifted a brow. "Without wanted posters on those folks, you got no jurisdiction."

Rion nodded. "You're right. I'll take the company."

"Got room for one more?" Daniel came alongside Andie but looked toward Rion.

Her brother looked skeptical. "Know your way around a horse, Counselor?"

"And guns, if need be."

Andie grinned. "He almost drew his pistol on me when we first met."

Rion's brown eyes rounded. "You didn't tell me that when you asked your question, Littrick."

"It's not as bad as it sounds." Rion's full statement registered then, and she furrowed her brow. "What did he ask you?"

Daniel shook his head. "Nothin' important."

"I beg to differ. If you failed to tell him how we met, you were talking about me. I want to know—"

"You can come." Rion then turned to Downing. "I need my weapons."

The lawman only nodded.

"You ready, Littrick, or. . ."

"I need to saddle my horse and get my gun belt."

"Meet me at the sheriff's office in twenty minutes."

"I'll be there."

Andie caught Daniel's arm. "Answer my question!"

Daniel swept the couple of papers she had on the table into her carpetbag and walked her outside, both their bags in his hand. Leading her away, he pulled her into the shadows of the nearest alley.

"This isn't where I intended to make my feelings known— but I was askin' your brother for permission to come callin'. If you're plannin' to stay, that is."

Startled and smitten, she grinned. "The reasons are growing more compelling."

After changing into more comfortable clothes, Daniel rode up to the sheriff's office as Braddock exited, gun belt around his hips and rifle in the crook of his right elbow. Epps was already waiting outside, and once Braddock checked both guns' loads and slid the rifle into the scabbard, he mounted up.

"I been locked up long enough, I don't know what's goin' on in the outside world. Either of you have an idea where that medicine show crew's been hidin' out?"

Sheriff Downing exited his office, rifle in hand, and locked the door. "After your escape, they'd moved up to the abandoned cabin where Serafina's body was found." He crossed to his horse and slid the rifle into his own scabbard.

"Where do you think you're goin'?" Rion watched him closely.

The lawman met his gaze "With you."

"I don't think so. You been nothin' but hateful since I was arrested."

"You escaped my jail, made me look like a fool before the town."

"And since I turned myself in, I've been a model prisoner. But even a couple hours ago, you were givin' me grief." Braddock shook his head.

"You need me. There's no warrants on Maya Fellows or her kin, so you got no authority."

Epps stepped up. "Lest you forget, Downing. You're a *town* sheriff. I'm a *federal* marshal. I've got the authority outside the town limits."

Daniel rode up alongside Braddock and dropped his voice. "Let him come along. At least then you can keep an eye on him. Otherwise, you don't know what he's up to."

The man pondered. "Downing, come if you want, but you

give me a reason, and we'll have it out. It won't go well for you."

As they rode toward the trail up to the cabin, Joe Trenamen, Calliope Wilson, and Lu Peters rode their way.

"Leaving without us?" Miss Wilson called.

Rion glared. "Calliope, I don't want you along. You either, Lu. It's too dangerous."

"I'm a Pinkerton." Miss Wilson shook her head. "It's my case."

"She won't be persuaded, Braddock." Trenamen shrugged. "I've tried."

"And there'll be a story to tell here..." Lu held up her journal.

Rion seethed. "Is Andromeda comin' too?"

Daniel held up his hands. "I dropped her at Dutch's. She wanted to see Lena's baby."

"Good."

Epps urged his horse forward, the others falling into line after him. Daniel stationed himself behind Downing to keep an eye on the man. Something had felt off since Daniel had returned to town.

As they neared the clearing where the dilapidated cabin sat, many heated voices rose, and Epps signaled for caution. Daniel removed the leather loop from his pistol's hammer, and the others did the same. At Braddock's signal, they dismounted and fanned out through the trees.

The medicine show wagons sat in a large circle, and the many horses used to pull those wagons grazed in a rope corral farther down the meadow. The show members gathered inside the circle.

On foot, they all closed in, guns in hand, and stepped into the inner circle.

"I'm tellin' you, I can lead this show!" one blustered.

"But without their money, how're we gonna pay for—"

Braddock released an earsplitting whistle, and the whole bunch turned and raised their hands in surrender.

"Where's Maya Fellows and her kin?" Marshal Epps called.

The same plump, dark-haired woman who'd congratulated Andie at the last recess stepped forward. "They aren't here."

"We had nothin' to do with any of the murders." The tall, muscular fella shook his head. "We were duped like you."

Daniel watched the sheriff, who eyed the crowd.

"Where'd they go?"

"We don't know. You might remember them leavin' the trial before the rest of us."

Braddock looked stunned. "Maya was there?"

Humorless chuckles rippled through the crowd, and Daniel studied those around him. None resembled the pretty blond wild woman he'd met in the cemetery.

"Through the entire trial," someone called.

"None of us understood why she chose to dress as Annalee until you said Maya gave you the boots." This came from the muscled man.

"The bearded lady?" Calliope's voice dripped shock.

"Maya's a master of stage makeup and costuming." The plump woman beckoned. "She's sewn all our costumes. Even weaves wigs."

"Wigs?" Calliope looked suddenly ill.

"Come see." She beckoned.

The crowd parted, making a path. Calliope and Trenamen followed, though Braddock hung back. Daniel edged around the crowd, preparing in case something happened.

Trenamen entered the wagon first, gun drawn, and at his call, Callie hurried inside.

"Honestly, Mr. Braddock, we had no idea what they were involved in." The muscular man looked repentant. "Those three were always odd, but we all thought it was their personalities.

After hearing the evidence at your trial, their behaviors make much more sense."

Calliope wailed, and Daniel ran to the wagon door, Braddock crowding in behind him.

Calliope sat on a padded bench as she stared at a cabinet built into the wall. In it were a variety of wigs in all manner of colors.

"I think we know what happened to the victims' hair. . ." She covered her mouth.

Joe touched one of the wigs but shook his head. "I understand the wigs, but how did she become the bearded lady?"

"Spirit gum." The plump woman picked up a small vial of something and handed it to him. "You apply it with a small brush, let it set for a moment, and tap the hair into it." She opened a cubby in the cabinet and removed a cloth bag. Inside was more hair, of a coarser nature.

"Holy Moses." Joe touched it, then brushed his fingers against his trouser leg. "How many parts did she play in the show?"

"Her big parts were Elisabeth Gates and—"

Calliope jerked her gaze up. "The sharpshooter and trick rider?"

The woman nodded. "And Annalee Ralston, though she does other parts as needed."

"Was this just Maya's wagon?" Braddock stabbed a finger at the doorway, then looked around at the group.

"Yes. Chellingworth's is over here." The woman pointed. "Sometimes Charlie stayed with him, but he's"—she tapped her temple—"a little teched. It's not clear whether Chellingworth actually liked his son. Mostly, Charlie did his own thing, except when we'd do our shows. Then, he and our other family members would be in the crowd. They're the lucky ones we picked out of the crowd for parts of the act."

When Braddock stomped toward the next wagon, Daniel

followed. Gun at the ready, the bounty hunter checked for danger, then climbed into the wagon, pawing through clothes and props. Daniel searched another, finding several pairs of shoes and boots on the floor. He grabbed the only pair similar to those Braddock wore and looked at their bottoms.

"Rion!" He held the sole of the boots so Braddock could see. A crescent-shaped impression marred the heel.

Braddock snatched the boots from Daniel's hand.

"Marshal?" He charged out the wagon, but as Daniel emerged, something smacked the edge of the flat roof. A gunshot sounded, and wood splinters showered him.

Daniel hit the dirt, and pandemonium ensued. Someone screamed, and people ducked for cover. Gun in hand, Daniel crawled behind Maya's wagon, heart racing. He peeked out, ready to return fire—but his gaze snagged.

On Downing.

Wrestling the tall, beardless man Josiah Tunstall had pointed out from the corner table that morning from between the trees.

"Drop it!" Downing leveled his rifle at the man's head.

The fella dropped his own gun and lifted his hands, and Downing kicked the weapon away.

"Who are you?"

"That's Maya's brother!" someone hollered. "Charlie Hunney."

Gaze stony, Downing slammed the butt of the rifle hard against Charlie's skull with a sickening thud. Charlie dropped.

His limbs still shaking from the near miss, Daniel moved forward as the lawman knelt and rolled Charlie's half-conscious form onto his back and removed a knife from the downed man's belt.

"Thank you, Sheriff," he called as he neared.

Rather than lay the knife aside, Downing trapped Charlie's nearest arm under his knee, then traced the blade along Charlie's cheek until it lodged just beneath his jawbone. "You stupid fool! You and your kin killed my Sarah."

Alarm bells clanged in Daniel's mind. "Downing!"

The sheriff flicked one glance his way, then back to the man. "Don't do this!"

"He killed my daughter! Him and his kin. They killed Serafina."

"Put the knife down, Sheriff!"

Charlie seemed to come around some then, and with his free hand, he grasped Downing's wrist. The sheriff shoved Charlie's face into the grass, wrestling to keep the blade in place.

Braddock, Trenamen, and Epps all rushed up, guns drawn.

"Downing," Epps called. "You don't want to do this."

"Yeah, I do. Been thinkin' about it since the day Sarah disappeared."

Epps shook his head. "You kill him, you'll hang. Put that knife down, and you can watch *him* hang. Him, his sister, and their father."

"We don't have them. Not Maya and Chellingworth."

"We'll find 'em, Sheriff," Braddock called. "Just put the knife down."

"I'll tell ya where they are." Charlie's voice shook. "Or where they're goin' anyway."

"Hear that, Downing? We can get 'em all, and you'll see 'em hang for Serafina's death. Between these witnesses and what we've got in these wagons, there's more than enough to convict."

For several seconds, Downing only shook but finally removed the blade from Charlie's neck and rolled free. Braddock ushered him away while Epps and Trenamen tied Charlie's hands.

"Counselor? If you have a minute, I need to show you some things." Calliope waved a man's shirt and a book not unlike Lu Peters' journal.

"What's this?"

"I found a scrap of fabric at Serafina's murder scene, and it appears to have come from this shirt—found in Chellingworth's wagon. And a diary—of all their plans and how they carried them out—from Maya's."

EPILOGUE

Cambria Springs, Colorado Territory
Monday, September 1, 1873

Andromeda stared around the large round table in the corner of Dutch's Café. Joe slung his arm across the back of Calliope's chair. Beside them, Rion leaned back, long legs stretched out before him, hands clasped over his stomach.

"They painted the white stockings on the horse." From between herself and Rion, Lu Peters scribbled the detail into her journal.

"It's why, the day Charlie scattered our horses, I ruined my dress with those strange white marks." Callie brushed at her skirt as if she wore the ruined attire. "I thought it was the leavings from a large bird, but it was wet paint on the underbrush from Charlie riding through."

"I'm going to have to use that in a story or article somewhere." Lu continued to scribble.

Joe cleared his throat. "Also explains why Hattie said the stockings looked strange. They weren't real."

"I feel like a fool." Rion shook his head. "They followed me around the country, and I didn't catch on."

Daniel sat forward to look at her brother. "They had about

twelve wigs for Maya, with multiple costumes and props she could choose from—and quite a few disguises for her father and brother. They could take on all sorts of looks. If you weren't expecting 'em, you wouldn't know."

"They set me up in Chicago, St. Louis, Omaha, Cheyenne, Denver, and here. You'd think, with that birthmark on Maya's wrist, I'd have recognized her."

Lu raked her gaze up. "She covered it. As the sharpshooter and trick rider, she wore a leather cuff over her wrist. Or she did while riding with the posse. And during her shows, she wore long gloves that covered half her forearms." She indicated where the gloves stopped.

Callie nodded. "And anytime I saw the bearded lady, she had a flesh-colored stain on her sleeve. She must've used stage makeup to cover it."

Rion shook his head. "I dunno. You'd still think I'd have recognized her height, build. . ."

"Go easy on yourself. She had shoes with over-tall soles so she could make herself taller." Joe cocked his head. "She even had dresses with some kind of padding sewn into the lining to make her look plump."

Rion looked around. "Is that true?"

"Very." Andie nodded. "Marshal Epps has all that evidence from their wagons under lock and key, but I saw it with my own eyes."

"Wicked woman." Rion glowered.

"Wicked family," Callie corrected. "Oldest brother Edward murdered two, and when you brought him in and he was hung, the others took revenge—by killing seven and attempting an eighth."

Rion scrubbed his beard. "What a legacy."

"A dark one," Andie whispered.

The bell on the café door jangled, and one of the judge's men waved. "Jury's done deliberatin'."

Her heart leaped into an anxious pace.

Daniel grasped her hand. "Ready, Counselor?"

Her stomach flip-flopped. "I'd better be."

They headed back toward the Rocking J, Daniel carrying her carpetbag and his leather satchel. Once inside the packed saloon, she and Daniel proceeded to the prosecution table. Marshal Epps, Sheriff Downing, and several deputies walked the defendants to the other table, and a moment later, Judge Vost called the court back into session.

Andie's heart pounded as the jury took their seats. To her amazement, the crowd was silent.

Judge Vost looked at the six men. "Has the jury reached a verdict?"

One man stood. "Yes, Your Honor."

"Would the defendants please rise?"

Chairs raked across the plank floor and feet shuffled as Earl Hunney, better known as Dr. Darby Chellingworth, Emmaline Hunney—or Maya Fellows—and Charlie Hunney all stood.

"How does the jury find in the case of Earl Hunney?"

"We find him guilty on all counts, Your Honor."

Gavel already in his hand, Judge Vost waited for the eruption, but none came. "In the case of Emmaline Hunney, how do you find?"

"Guilty on all counts."

Still no sound came, but it felt as if the room held its collective breath.

"And in the case of Charles Hunney, how do you find?"

"Guilty on all—"

The room erupted as men celebrated or mourned the outcomes, passing money like they had at the dismissal of Rion's charges.

Would Andie ever get used to such a thing? St. Louis certainly wasn't the height of civilization and Eastern sensibilities, but it undoubtedly had more decorum than this.

But now that she'd seen it, she found a certain humor and charm to it, in its own odd way.

As the judge banged his gavel, Daniel gave her hand a hearty squeeze.

The commotion ceased after a third bang of Judge Vost's gavel.

"Earl, Emmaline, and Charles Hunney, considering you've been found guilty of six murders, kidnapping, and attempted murder—I sentence you all to hang by the neck, one week from today at ten in the morning. Any questions?"

"Don't we get an appeal, Your Honor?" the man once known as Darby Chellingworth called, his proper English lilt gone.

"Let's see." Vost tapped his finger against his cheek. "Considering I'm the territorial judge, that means I'm also one of the three Supreme Court justices for Colorado Territory, so I'd be hearing your appeal." He shrugged. "I've heard the evidence of this case twice already—once during Mr. Braddock's trial, and again in yours. I'm not inclined to hear it a third. No appeal. My sentence stands." He turned to Downing. "Keep these three safe, Sheriff. They've got an important appointment in a week."

"Yes, sir, Your Honor."

"And. . .Marshal Epps."

The marshal stood. "Yes, Your Honor?"

"You, Mr. Trenamen, and Miss Wilson notify the other jurisdictions that the culprits of the murders in their locales have been found and executed. I don't want Mr. Braddock to have any further trouble because of this scheme."

The marshal made eye contact with Joe and Callie, then nodded. "We'll get that word out, sir."

"Thank you. This case is closed, and court is dismissed." Judge Vost gaveled out, and like before, everyone moved, milling and chattering about the verdict.

Daniel turned a wide smile on Andie. "Congratulations, Counselor. That's two wins in six weeks."

"You helped."

He shook his head. "This was all you. You led an amazing prosecution."

She wobbled a smile at him. "I still have so much to learn."

Daniel pulled her to her feet. "I have a bit of a proposition about that." He took her hands. "I never wanted to be an attorney. . .and I haven't enjoyed it."

She dipped her chin, her happiness dampening. "You said that before."

"Then you came along."

She dragged her gaze up. "Me?"

"Yeah. . .you, Counselor."

Heat filled her cheeks.

"I was wonderin' if you'd be interested in stayin' in Cambria Springs. Maybe partnerin' up with me?"

"As attorneys, or. . .something different?"

A slow smile spread across his face. "Attorneys to start, but. . ." He whispered in her ear. "I'm hopin' for a lot more."

Heart racing, she stole a chaste little kiss. "Yes."

Daniel pulled back, eyes wide and brows arched. "You don't want to think about it?"

She shrugged. "Let's just say I had a feeling about you from the first moment we met."

"Even though I smelled a little ungodly?"

Andie stood a little taller, looking into his intense blue eyes, then leaned in and sniffed the woodsy scent of his cologne. "You seem to have redeemed your ways."

He laughed and kissed her palm. "This partnership's gonna be fun."

"I certainly hope so."

⌒

Callie waited to congratulate Andie and Daniel as the pair shared a teasing exchange. The compliments could wait. However, when she turned to point out the charming interaction to Joe, he'd gone. She looked around the packed room.

"He went that way." Lu motioned and went back to scribbling her thoughts in her journal.

There. Talking to Marshal Epps and Rion. Probably working out the details of informing the other jurisdictions of the Hunneys' convictions. It would require traveling to the various locales, hauling evidence, and making the case.

She headed that way, but as she neared, Marshal Epps coughed, and the conversation stalled.

"Am I interrupting?" She glanced at them.

"No." Joe shook his head. "Talking about logistics. The case, y'know?"

She stood a little taller. "Shouldn't I be involved in that?"

"I didn't want Marshal Epps to get away."

All three men shuffled their feet or avoided eye contact. "All right."

Epps clapped Joe on the shoulder. "I need to help Downing with the prisoners. Come find me at the hotel this evening, and we'll work out the details."

The man slipped away, hurrying to where Sheriff Downing and his deputies shackled Maya and her kin.

"Are y'all ready to go?" Rion nodded toward the door.

"I am, and Andie and Daniel should be too."

"Let's get Lu and go." Rion approached the table where

Lu still wrote, and the six of them walked out, mounted their horses, and departed.

As they reached a more respectable part of the town, Joe nodded for her to turn the opposite direction from Mrs. Ingram's boardinghouse, where the others seemed to be headed.

She drew Lady to a halt. "What are you doing?"

"May I have a private moment?"

"For. . . ?"

After a second, he waved in the direction of the meadow where the medicine show had performed. "If you'll give me that moment, I'll tell you."

The others had ridden ahead, and she turned aside with Joe. At the center of the meadow he dismounted and helped her down.

"What's wrong?"

"We're at the end of our case."

"No. We've got to get the evidence to all the other towns where these poor women were murdered, and—"

"Let me finish. Please."

Cheeks warming, she shut her mouth.

"We're at the end of our case. Once we deliver the news of this conviction, we'll be assigned new cases, and we may not be working together anymore."

Reality crashed over her. With all the turmoil—of finding both her brother and her sister, arresting Rion, his escape, the first trial, and the hunt for Maya and her kin—she'd barely thought about how today's verdict would impact things.

She swallowed. "I don't know how I feel about that." Her voice quavered.

"I, for one, don't like it."

"But what can we do?" They were at the mercy of what the agency needed.

"We could. . ." He hesitated then dropped to a knee. "Calliope

Ann Braddock Wilson, I've fallen in love with you. Will you marry me?"

Stunned, she was almost unable to breathe.

When she didn't answer immediately, he turned a pleading glance her way. "Please?"

She blinked twice, seeming to come back to herself, and laughed. "Yes, I'll marry you."

Joe launched to his feet, grabbed her, and twirled her in a circle. From some distance off, applause and a sharp whistle filled the quiet meadow, and when Joe set her down, she noticed that Andie, Daniel, Rion, and Lu stood at the meadow's edge, watching.

"Just so you know—I asked Rion and Andie both, and I wrote your Ma and Pa a letter and sent it to them in Chicago. They all gave their blessing."

She grinned. "Good. Now, are you going to kiss me or not?"

Grinning like a schoolboy, he gave a laugh. "You don't have to ask me twice."

He bent and claimed her lips, tenderly, then with more passion. Her heart pounded and she slipped her arms around his neck, twining her fingers. His arms circled her waist, and for a second time, he picked her up so her feet dangled above the ground. Their kiss ended as she began to giggle, and she laid her head against his shoulder.

"Yes, I'll gladly marry you. When?"

"Sooner rather than later, but I promised your pa we'd get married in Chicago. He and your ma don't want to miss the nuptials."

"Then it needs to be far enough out we can get Andie, Daniel, Rion, and Lu there."

"I figured." His voice tinged with disappointment, and she lifted her head and brushed his lips again.

"It'll go by fast."

Another earsplitting whistle shattered their silence, and Rion beckoned. "C'mon, you two. We got some celebratin' to do!"

Joe set her down, and hand in hand, they started back toward the others.

⌒

As Joe and Callie rejoined the group, the pair nearly glowed.

"Congratulations." Rion grinned as the others added their well wishes.

For once, Callie looked a little shy.

Lu grinned. "Maya and her kin were convicted. Andie says she's staying in Cambria Springs to partner up with Daniel. And now you two are getting married. This is turning out to be quite the day."

"So you are stayin'?" Rion turned toward Andie.

"I am." She turned Daniel's way. "It's only right. This one needs my help."

They all laughed.

Joe and Callie mounted up, and the group turned toward town.

"Everyone come to my place," Lu called, leading the way toward her rented house. "My dime novel, *Rion Braddock, Bounty Hunter*, is published."

The group congratulated her, but as they rode past the livery, the young hostler stepped out. "Mr. Braddock?"

He slowed. "Yeah?"

"Sheriff Downing's lookin' for you."

His shoulders slumped. "Sorry, Lu. I ought to see what he needs."

"We'll all go." She smiled.

Outside the log building, he dismounted, leaving Trouble's reins to dangle as he strode into the office. One glance at the two functioning cells—one with Maya and one with her pa and brother—reminded him that he still needed to pay for the door.

He walked up to Downing's desk. "Reckon you're looking for the money to fix that door, aren't ya?"

"Well, there's that, but I asked to see you on a personal matter."

He shot another glance toward Maya and her kin. "You got somethin' to say, let's go outside."

Downing nodded to the two deputies as he rose. "Watch them." He motioned to the prisoners.

They stepped out onto the porch and shut the door, but seeing the others waiting, Downing beckoned him around the corner of the building.

It took a moment for the lawman to find his voice. "There's a couple things I need to say to you, Braddock. One is, I'm sorry. I—I took my distress at losin' my daughter out on you. All the evidence pointed at you, so I made my assumptions, and. . ." He shrugged. "It wasn't right, how I treated ya."

"I appreciate that. It all worked out, so. . .no hard feelings."

Downing cleared his throat. "And. . .I wanted to say thank you."

"For?"

"Not lettin' me gut that kid in there." He pushed a pebble with the toe of his boot. "I'd've done it had you and the others not stopped me."

"I'm hopin' you'd've done the same for me if the tables were turned."

He nodded.

"I didn't realize Sarah Jacobs was kin. I'm sorry about your daughter."

The man shrugged. "She didn't know, and her ma didn't want me tellin' her. But she's the reason I came to this town. To keep an eye on her." His expression twisted into a mask of pain. "I failed her. I didn't protect her from them." He flung a hand toward the office, seeming to indicate the prisoners inside.

"I know it won't bring her back, but at least now, they'll pay the price."

"Yeah." He nodded. "And I can retire in peace."

"Retire?" Rion turned a quizzical glance on him. "You're hangin' up your badge?"

"It's too painful stayin' around here."

After a moment, Rion nodded. "I understand."

"I'm stayin' until the hangin', but the town's gonna need a good man as Sheriff. What d'ya think about takin' my job?"

"Me?"

"Folks 'round here know you because of the trials, and they respect ya after hearin' all Maya and them did to get you. I'll put in a good word if you want the job."

Rion stared. "You joshin' me?"

"No, sir. I figure you're the right man—especially considerin' you got kin about these parts."

"You heard about Andromeda."

"I meant Dutch and the Kealeys. She's stayin' too?"

"Just found out."

"What about the other sister?"

"They'll still be workin' for Pinkerton, but maybe he'll assign 'em out this way so we can keep a connection."

Downing grinned, the expression tinged with sadness. "Betcha he will."

"I—" Rion extended a hand. "I been thinkin' about settlin' down. It'll make it easier to get to know my kin—and Lu. If you think Cambria Springs'll accept me as Sheriff, I'll take the job."

"They will." He shook Rion's hand. "The town council liked the idea."

"Town council. That's movin' kinda fast."

"Time's short. I got a week until those three hang. Then I'm out."

Rion shook his head. "I guess you're right."

"Least I can do after the hard time I gave you."

They spoke a moment more; Rion paid him for the cell door he'd mangled and then returned to the others out front.

"Everything okay?" Lu met him as he approached.

"I just got offered a job."

"A job?"

"Sheriff of Cambria Springs." A smile overtook him. "I took it, effective after the hanging."

"You're not going back to bounty hunting?"

He pulled her close. "When Seth met Lena, he had to give up bounty huntin' so he could court her proper. Now that I got you and Calliope and Andromeda, that job ain't the right fit anymore. I need to be more settled. Unless y'all don't want me around."

Lu laughed. "What do you say, ladies?"

Calliope and Andromeda slipped from their saddles and came to throw their arms around him. "It's the best news we've heard in fifteen years."

AUTHOR'S NOTE

Dear Readers,

Thank you for coming along on this journey with me. I hope you enjoyed Calliope, Andromeda, and Orion Braddock and their respective love interests. This story has been percolating in my mind for nearly a decade. The idea came about while brainstorming novella collection ideas with several other historical authors. I tossed out the idea of each of us writing one novella in this interconnected storyline, but they all agreed it should be my story alone rather than a shared endeavor. And so, the idea sat...and sat...waiting for the right time to be told.

In my mind, I kept going back to it, intending to make it my next project, right after I finished whichever contract I happened to be working on at the time—but I would always get sidetracked with another project. But God knew the right time for this story to come about. As I was nearing the end of writing another (yet unpublished) novel at the end of 2023, I made up my mind that I was finally going to focus on writing *Love and Order*. To my surprise, about two weeks after making that decision, my editor at Barbour asked if this project was still available. I had pitched the idea to her two years earlier at a writing conference, and she'd been going back through her files and discovered it again. So I happily answered that it was available—and within a short time, I had a contract in hand and a deadline to meet.

I wanted to share with you some of the research details that went into writing this story. First—this story is purely a work of fiction. Other than mentions of the historical figures of Allan Pinkerton, Kate Warne, and Ulysses S. Grant, all characters and events are fictional. That said, plenty of real history went into making this story feel authentic. I found myself researching everything from orphan trains to the Pinkerton National Detective Agency, medicine shows, stage makeup, bounty hunters, jailbreaks, court trials, and more. I won't go into every detail of my research. I've written on several of those topics at the Heroes, Heroines, and History blog (www.hhhistory.com), so if you are interested, please look for the broad topics of the orphan train movement, Allan Pinkerton, Kate Warne, the Pinkertons, Old West courts, methods of becoming an attorney in the Old West, and medicine shows there.

I did want to touch on some of the more specific topics that didn't make it into the above-mentioned blog posts. One of those topics is the jailbreak in Part 2. If you've read some of my author notes from past books (specifically *The Scarlet Pen*), you may know that my husband spent twenty-six years working for our county sheriff's office, the entire time in the county jails. He saw many things in those two and a half decades, from real-life serial killers to attempted and successful escapes. When it came time to write the actual jailbreak scene, I had no idea how I would have my character successfully escape—though in the Old West, that wasn't a hard thing to achieve. Jail cells back then tended to be easily overcome. But I wanted the escape to ring true and show the resourcefulness of my characters.

Thankfully, my husband's career proved to add the detail and dimension I needed. In the jails, he saw plenty of ropes made from torn-up bedsheets, and more than one inmate did attempt to overcome his cell door with a come-along. What I depicted in Part Two's escape attempt wasn't an exact replication of how my husband saw it happen in real life (the method of making/tightening the come-along was performed differently in the two instances), but in my husband's experience, at least one of these attempts was a nearly successful escape. He and his fellow deputies caught the inmate before he fully succeeded in overcoming his cell bars, but the come-along made from a makeshift rope was powerful enough to permanently bend the door out of shape, almost allowing this man to get away. So I felt confident in using this method as the means to accomplish the jailbreak in *Love and Order*. In real life, the inmate twisted his come-along with a mop handle, cinching the rope tighter and tighter until it grew taut enough to bend steel. In my fictional version, nothing other than a rope looped through a slipknot and tightened by brute strength was used. I hope it rang true to you, the readers, and proved to entertain you as well.

Another interesting detail of my research was the court system in the territories of the Old West. Based on the western novel-reading and movie-watching habits of my youth, actual trials didn't happen much in the Old West, based on how rarely such things were depicted in the westerns I grew up with. However, attorneys were quite prevalent in the Old West, based on what I learned in researching this story. In fact, they were so prevalent that most attorneys couldn't support themselves by that job alone. They had to have a side hustle. So, many of them became land surveyors, ranchers, and miners, among other things.

The territorial court system was set up with three Supreme Court justices per territory, each appointed by the president of the United States. The territories were broken into three zones, and those justices would become the traveling judges who oversaw cases in one of the zones. They had a whole company of people who traveled with them, from attorneys (both prosecutors and defense) to US marshals who served as court schedulers, bailiffs, or any other position that was needed to run the territorial court. Because of the traveling nature of these courts, trials were scheduled months out, and wouldn't happen until the court made its circuit back to the area where that crime happened.

Many of the judges felt that being appointed as a Supreme Court justice in a western territory was a punishment. This led to these judges taking a very apathetic approach to the trials they heard, and many allowed all sorts of shenanigans in their courtrooms. As I depicted in the trial scenes with Judge Oakwell, drunkenness on the part of the judge, attorneys, and spectators was common. Judges were also known to be very lax in their decorum. They'd put their feet up on the desk, allow the spectators to call for recesses so they could refresh their drinks, and other such oddities. One fun fact from my research is that one court crier actually introduced the judge in the manner I had Oakwell introduced: "Hear ye! Hear ye! Court's in session. All you mulligrubs in the back of the courtroom keep your traps shut and give these fellers up front a chance to talk." As soon as I read that, I knew I had to use it.

Trials could be wild events full of drama, including gunplay. More than one judge was known to pack heat, as were the attorneys. I even read of a widow pulling a gun on the defendant in one trial as he was accused of having killed her husband. So I made sure to show that guns were in the western courtroom when I depicted Judge Vost, Marshal Epps, Sheriff Downing, and others carrying guns during the trial. And another interesting tidbit: Judge Vost's gun was in a shoulder holster.

Many may have the impression that the shoulder holster was an invention from the Prohibition Era of the 1920s, but the earliest commercially produced shoulder holsters were from the 1870s. So it is possible that he could have had an early version of such a holster. And even if I was off by a few years (some of my resources said that such holsters didn't become available until the *late* 1870s), men and women of the Old West tended to be very inventive people. They made what they needed, so it is possible Judge Vost's rig was his own invention.

As always, it is my goal to put as much realistic detail into this fictional story as possible, even if the story itself is purely about fictional events. I am grateful to each of you for taking the time to read it. I couldn't do what I do without you! Hopefully, you've enjoyed the effort.

Many blessings to you all,
Jennifer

ACKNOWLEDGMENTS

First and foremost, thank you to my Lord and Savior, Jesus Christ, who stretched me greatly in writing this story! It was an act of faith and trust, keeping my eyes focused on You to get the story completed on time. I wanted to panic, but You kept whispering to my heart that we would get it done in time—and we did. You are my Ephesians 3:20 God!

Thank you to my amazing husband, Dave, who supports this crazy writing life of frantic deadlines and having to pick up the slack when I can't be the full-time wife. You are awesome, and I couldn't do this without you.

Donna, I couldn't have gotten this one done without you! Thank you so very much for always being willing to read chapters and offer feedback. You were amazing and so generous with your time and helpful suggestions. I owe you big, my friend.

As always, thank you to Becky Germany for another opportunity to tell my stories! I am always honored to work with you. Thank you for believing in me and my crazy tales.

And thank you to JoAnne Simmons for making this story shine. It's been a pleasure working with you.

Jennifer Uhlarik discovered the western genre as a preteen, when she swiped the only "horse" book she found on her older brother's bookshelf. A new love was born. Across the next ten years, she devoured Louis L'Amour westerns and fell in love with the genre. In college at the University of Tampa, she began penning her own story of the Old West. Armed with a BA in writing, she has finaled and won in numerous writing competitions and been on the ECPA bestseller list several times. In addition to writing, she has held jobs as a private business owner, a schoolteacher, a historical research consultant, a marketing director, and her favorite—a full-time homemaker. Jennifer is active in American Christian Fiction Writers and is a lifetime member of the Florida Writers Association. She lives near Tampa, Florida, with her husband, teenage son, and three fur children.